Night Predator

"Do you need help finding a candle?" he asked as they mounted the steps.

Sam hesitated, tempted to say yes, invite him inside, and see if he might try to kiss her, or . . .

She caught herself. She wasn't ready for that.

"No, that's okay. We keep the flashlights on a shelf just inside the door. But thank you," she added, pausing by the door.

Turning back, she opened her mouth to say something.

What it would have been she didn't know, because it slipped from her mind the moment she saw the way his eyes were shining in the darkness.

It was as if they were soaking up the moonlight and reflecting it back at her.

Like a night predator, she thought, and felt a shiver run up her back under her T-shirt . . .

LYNSAY SANDS

The Rogue Hunter

AVON

An Imprint of HarperCollins*Publishers*

This is a work of fiction. Names, characters, places, and incidents are products of the author's imagination or are used fictitiously and are not to be construed as real. Any resemblance to actual events, locales, organizations, or persons, living or dead, is entirely coincidental.

AVON BOOKS
An Imprint of HarperCollins*Publishers*
10 East 53rd Street
New York, New York 10022-5299

For Dave

Prologue

*W*arm summer air swam over Tanya as she stepped out into the night. It was cooler than it had been earlier in the day, but still hot compared to the air-conditioned coffee shop. She sucked in the humid air as she started across the pavement, her eyes moving around the nearly empty parking lot, noting the van now parked beside her eighteen-wheeler. Hers had been the only vehicle when she'd stopped here for a coffee break after her long haul. She'd also been the only patron in the coffee shop until a few minutes ago when the owner of that van had entered. His arrival was why she'd left. The man was tall, lean, and dark-haired, but something about his pale features and the hungry way he'd watched her had made her decide she'd taken a long enough break.

She'd nearly reached the driver's side of her truck when the sound of a skittering pebble drew Tanya's head around. Her gaze turned wary as she recognized the man from the coffee shop. His dark hair and clothes blended with the night around them, but his pale face and silver eyes couldn't be missed.

"I wanted to show you something in my van," he announced as he crossed the short distance separating them.

Tanya's upper lip curled in a sneer. She'd just bet he had something he wanted to show her. Men! Find out she was a trucker and they seemed to immediately think that was slang for slut.

"I don't—" The words died in her throat, the *want to see anything you've got* seeming to evaporate from her head.

"It's all right. You'll like this." His tone was soothing, almost crooning, and Tanya felt herself relax, the warning bell in her head fading to a distant chime.

"I'll like this," she echoed in a whisper.

"Yes, you will," he assured her, and gestured for her to move forward as he opened the back door of the van.

Tanya found herself climbing in. She watched him close the door, shutting out the world. When he turned toward her, the silver of his eyes was afire, almost seeming to bubble in his irises as he caught her arms and drew her closer. Her gaze dropped to his mouth as his lips parted, and she saw the fangs slipping out.

Tanya stared at those fangs as he lowered his head toward her. She followed them right up until his face moved to her throat and she could no longer see them anymore. She felt a quick pinch as they sank into her neck, and then a wave of pleasure rolled over her, drowning any other emotion.

I told you you'd like this, Tanya heard him say, though the words were in her head not her ears.

"Yes. Oh yes," she moaned with ecstasy, her arms rising to clutch at his shoulders as he drained her life-blood away.

Chapter 1

"Sorry about leaving so late."

Samantha Willan tore her gaze away from the star-littered sky overhead and turned a surprised glance to her younger sister. They were reclining on the wooden dock in front of the family cottage, enjoying the evening air and the beautiful view. Or they had been until Jo's apology. Seeing her guilt-ridden expression, Samantha frowned and leaned to the side, bumping the younger woman affectionately with her shoulder as she teased, "You should be. We missed all the crazy traffic, didn't have any of the usual stop-and-go nonsense, and made great time here. All in all it was a horribly pleasant ride for a change. Shame on you for forcing that on us."

Jo grinned, but shook her head. "It's also now after two A.M., we've just finished unloading the car, and we still have to let the cottage air out before we can sleep." She raised her eyebrows in challenge. "It's going to be a late night for all of us thanks to my stupid job."

Sam wrinkled her nose. It was summer. The sun had

baked down on the closed-up cottage all day, heating it like an oven. Despite the fact that the night had cooled with the setting sun, the small, well-insulated building had still retained that heat when they'd arrived. The first thing they'd done—even before unloading the car—had been to open all the windows. They would have turned on the ceiling fans too, but there'd been a storm that afternoon and the power had been knocked out. No power meant no ceiling fans to help bring down the temperature. They'd have to wait for the night air to slowly seep in and displace the hotter air. That could take a while.

"So?" Sam said lightly. "We've unpacked, the beds are made, and we don't have to get up early. We're on vacation; we can go to bed as late as we want. In the meantime, we get to relax here on the dock and enjoy this lovely view . . . so stop fretting. Besides," she added solemnly, "your job isn't stupid."

"Yeah, right," Jo said on a laugh. "You're a lawyer, Alex is a gourmet chef with her own restaurant, and I work in a bar."

"You are now *night manager* in that bar, thank you very much," Sam pointed out firmly. "And stop comparing yourself to us. Alex and I are both very proud of you for getting that promotion," she said firmly. "Besides, it's paying your way through university, isn't it? That makes it far from stupid in my book."

Jo relaxed, a small smile claiming her lips. "I guess."

"You can guess if you like, but I *know*," Sam assured her with another affectionate bump. They fell silent then, and both turned their gazes skyward, taking in the sparkling, star-strewn black above. It was hard to believe they were only two hours north of Toronto; the sky here made it seem like a whole other world. It was awe-inspiring.

"We should have brought sleeping bags," Jo said on a little sigh. "We could have slept out here under the stars."

"On the dock?" Sam asked with a disbelieving laugh. "No way. All three of us would probably end up in the lake somehow . . . Or we'd wake up to find chipmunks curled up in the sleeping bags with us and seagulls circling overhead, relieving themselves on our sleeping faces."

"Eww!" Laughing, Jo gave her shoulder a push and shook her head. "You are such a pessimist. I swear I've never met anyone who could be such a downer."

"Not a downer, sensible," Sam corrected.

"Ha! You always see the glass as half empty. Honestly, you find the flaw in everything."

"In other words, she acts like the lawyer she is."

Sam and Jo sat up and turned to glance toward shore where that amused voice had come from. At first all they could see were shadows in the darkness, but then Jo turned on the flashlight they'd brought with them and raised it. The beam of light splashed over and then settled on their eldest sister, Alex, as she made her way down the sloping yard to the dock.

"Get that light out of my eyes," Alex complained with a laugh, raising a hand to stave off the glare, and Jo lowered the beam to the ground so that she could negotiate the last few feet without incident.

"Thanks," Alex said as she stepped onto the dock to join them.

"No problem." Jo said. The beam then bounced away from Alex, flashing over Sam's face and briefly blinding her before it blinked out.

Sam was left with white spots burned in her eyes and was trying to get her normal vision back when the light suddenly blinked on again, once more aimed straight at her face.

"Hey!" She raised her own hand to shield her eyes and scowled into the glare of light moving over her. "Turn that out!"

"Sorry. I thought I saw—I did!" Jo exclaimed triumphantly as the beam reached her neck. "You're bleeding."

"Damn blackflies," Sam muttered. It was the season for it. Grimacing, she wiped blindly at her neck.

"The other side," Jo said helpfully. "There are two of them."

"Hmm." Alex dropped to her haunches to get a look. Whatever she saw brought a grin to her face. "There *are* two . . . side by side. It looks like a vampire bite."

"Yes," Jo agreed, and then teased, "If I hadn't been here the whole time I'd have said Dracula got you and didn't clean up after himself."

"Ugh. Don't even joke about that," Sam said with a shudder.

Jo laughed at her disgust. "Most women would love to have that happen. They fantasize about things like that happening to them."

"Most women don't have phobias about bats," Sam responded dryly. "Besides, I hardly think most women fantasize about being bitten by flying rodents."

"Not flying rodents," Jo said with exasperation. "A *vampire*."

"Same thing," Sam muttered with disgust. "They turn into bats and rats and wolves and Lord knows what else. I'm not into bestiality, thanks."

"Gawddddd. You are such a . . . a . . ."

"Lawyer?" Alex suggested with amusement.

"Yes," Jo snapped.

"Stop saying that like it's a bad thing." Sam scowled at them both. "I worked long and hard to become a lawyer."

"Yes, you did," Alex agreed soothingly, and then informed her, "You're still bleeding. Maybe you should try some of that After Bite stuff on it."

"Yeah. I need a refill on my drink anyway," Sam murmured. Giving up on her neck, she got to her feet, asking, "Can I get something for anyone else while I'm up?"

"Nothing for me, thanks," Jo said.

"I could use another beer. I meant to grab one while I was up going to the bathroom, but forgot," Alex said and then grabbed at Sam's elbow to steady her as she swayed unsteadily. Amusement clear in her voice, she commented, "Maybe you should switch to soda."

"She already *is* on soda," Jo announced. "She isn't drinking."

Alex's head swiveled sharply to Sam. "Not another ear infection?"

Sam nodded reluctantly, not surprised when Alex began to curse. Knowing it was just a result of her worry and that it would be followed by a rant about rotten doctors, the useless health care system, and the length of the wait to see a specialist, Sam didn't stick around to listen. She moved cautiously off the dock and up the lawn, but wasn't halfway to the cottage before she began to regret not having grabbed the flashlight from Jo. This was not the city with streetlights to brighten the situation. Here in cottage country, night was black velvet, dark and heavy. While it had seemed lighter on the dock with the starlit sky overhead, here the trees blocked out the starlight. It was much darker, and Sam found herself stumbling over exposed roots and rocks in her path. Between that and the lack of balance her ear infection was causing, she was having a bit of a struggle.

Grabbing at the thigh-sized trunk of the young maple tree between the cottage and the dock, Sam paused briefly to get her bearings. She was about to continue again when the sound of a door closing drew her eyes to the cottage next door. It was in darkness, as it had been when they'd arrived.

As it always was, in fact, she thought with a grimace. The cottage had been sold two years ago, but they still hadn't yet met the new neighbors. The new owner never seemed to be up here, at least not when Sam or her sisters were at their cottage. They checked every time they came up, hoping to finally get to meet them. It wasn't that they were overly sociable. The fact was, life here wasn't like life in the city. Neighbors depended on neighbors up here. They didn't bother each other, but did like to know who they were and tended to look out for each other. It was a necessity in an area where the power was frequently knocked out and amenities could be so far away in an emergency.

There had been a lot of speculation on the lake last summer about the new owners. Grant, their neighbor on the other side and a year-round resident, had said that the cottage had been in use at a couple of points during the winter. He'd seen the lights on at night, and a man walking around the building to the shed a couple of times, but the man had kept to himself. Sam doubted Grant had encouraged him to do otherwise, however. He pretty much kept to himself too and only talked to those on the lake for whom he did handyman work, and then only when—and as much as—absolutely necessary. He probably wouldn't even have mentioned it if she hadn't asked if he'd met the new neighbors yet.

That thought made her glance toward Grant's dark cottage on the other side of theirs as she briefly wondered if the noise she'd heard hadn't come from his place. Sound carried oddly on the lake, and it could have come from just about anywhere, even from one of the cottages across the lake.

Shrugging the worry away, she released her hold on the tree trunk and continued up toward the cottage.

"Cottage country."

Garrett Mortimer chuckled at the disgust in his partner's voice. "I can tell you're thrilled by this assignment."

Justin Bricker grimaced. "It's cottage country, Mortimer. Cottages are all about sun and sand and fun. We're vampires. We avoid sunlight like the plague. What are we *doing* here?"

"Looking for a rogue immortal," Mortimer said calmly, managing not to wince at his younger partner's use of the term *vampire*. He couldn't help it, he—like many of the older ones of their kind—had a terrible abhorrence for the word. It brought back memories of marauding villagers with torches and stakes.

"Right," Bricker said dryly. "But what would any self-respecting vampire—rogue or not—be doing here? We haven't seen a streetlight in hours. It's black as pitch out here and has been forever. If there's anything at all beyond the headlights of our car, I'd be surprised."

Mortimer chuckled. "There's a lot more than you think beyond the headlights."

"Bears, raccoons, deer, and bunnies," Bricker said, obviously unimpressed.

Mortimer shook his head, but waited to negotiate a rather sharp curve in the road before saying, "We've probably passed a couple hundred cottages and houses since getting off the main highway. Believe me, hidden in the darkness are loads of people."

"Maybe," Bricker allowed with some disgruntlement. "But I guarantee you there won't be a single immortal among them."

"No?" Mortimer arched an eyebrow even as his lips twitched again.

"No," Bricker assured him. "No self-respecting immortal would stick himself out here. It's just not our scene."

"Right. So . . . What?" he asked dryly. "You're saying that all self-respecting immortals are presently hanging out on the other side of the globe where it's winter and the days are shorter?"

"No, of course not," Bricker growled with irritation. "But they aren't likely to be at a *cottage*. They'll be in cities like Toronto and Montreal where they have underground concourses and don't have to expose themselves to the sun to go places and do things."

Mortimer nodded, but didn't agree or disagree. The

truth was, he knew a lot of their people would indeed be spending the summer in such places. While mortals enjoyed the underground cities in the winter because it allowed them to avoid the bitter cold outside, and some sought it out in the summer to avoid the harsh heat, immortals simply enjoyed the underground concourses during daylight in both summer and winter. It gave them a freedom they had never imagined they might enjoy before the advent of such things. They could walk around during daylight without worrying about the damage it was doing to them.

Mortimer peered at his partner, noting the dissatisfaction on his handsome, angular face and the frustrated way he ran one hand through his dark curls. Glancing back to the road ahead, he pointed out mildly, "The intelligence we have says that half a dozen mortals have been spotted with bite marks."

"I know, but it makes no sense that a vampire would hang out up here."

"And maybe that's why he or she is," Mortimer said. "After all, as you say, it's the last place anyone would expect to find an immortal . . . and because it *is* cottage country, it's full of mortals who come and go, concentrate on sun and fun, and don't bother neighboring cottagers."

Bricker looked startled at the suggestion. It obviously wasn't something he'd considered.

"You have to admit it's a pretty good place to hide out," Mortimer continued. "Almost every cottage we've passed is surrounded by trees, and the people up here feel safe so they won't be as aware or cautious . . . A rogue immortal would be a wolf among sheep."

"I suppose you're right," Bricker murmured, his expression thoughtful. "It's dark as death out here. He could creep up on people around a campfire, lure someone into the trees for a bite, and be gone without ever being seen."

Mortimer grunted in agreement, his attention on the small, green, numbered markers among the foliage on the side of the road. Each glowed brightly in the headlight's beam and each marked a driveway that disappeared into the trees, leading to cottages that they couldn't see from the road. Their cottage turned out to be the last one leading off the gravel road. Mortimer steered them down the dirt lane, wincing as they bumped over ruts and rocks. They traveled through trees for at least a full minute before the headlights flashed on a brown building ahead.

"Welcome to the boonies," Bricker said with a sneer. Holding on to the strap above the passenger door to steady himself during the bumpy ride, he added almost under his breath, "This *so* isn't my bag."

Mortimer smiled faintly and admitted, "It isn't really my bag either, but it's someone's or we wouldn't be up here."

"Right. Our rogue," Bricker muttered unhappily.

"And Decker," he pointed out. "It's his cottage we're using as a base while we're up here."

"Yeah, but he always was a strange bird," Bricker said. "Only he would enjoy living at the end of the world."

Mortimer smiled faintly at the insult to their comrade Decker Argeneau Pimms. As hunters for the Council, they often worked in concert with other teams, and more often than not, they seemed to be put together with Decker and his partner Anders. The four of them got along well and liked one another, but you wouldn't know that from the way they insulted one another.

"Well, I can't argue with Decker being strange," Mortimer said with amusement, and then pointed out, "But cottage country is apparently attractive to at least one other immortal too. It had to have been an immortal who spotted the bite marks and reported them to the Council."

That report was the reason they were here. Biting mortals was forbidden, and the Council had sent them up here to cottage country to look into it. They were to find the culprit and bring him—or her—back for the Council to deal with.

"Do we know who made the report?" Bricker asked curiously.

"I'm sure Lucian knows, but he didn't tell me who," Mortimer said, and then added, "I guess it really isn't important anyway."

"No," Bricker agreed, and then breathed, "Jesus," as Mortimer killed the car engine and the headlights blinked out at once, leaving them in a black and silent world.

The darkness was so absolute, Mortimer could almost believe they *had* reached the end of the earth and were now staring off into the emptiness of space. He didn't comment, however, but merely sat, waiting for his eyes to adjust. After a moment or so, the solid black around them gave way to differing shades of gray as well.

"Do you hear that?" Bricker asked in hushed tones.

"What?" Mortimer asked with a frown. He didn't hear anything.

"Nothing," Bricker said dryly. "Absolutely frigging nothing."

Releasing his breath on a soundless laugh, Mortimer grabbed his knapsack from the backseat, opened his door, and unfolded himself from the car. He then began to stretch and bend beside the vehicle to get his circulation going again. While they'd stopped several times along the way, this last bit of driving had been the longest, and he was stiff from the journey.

"Jesus."

The repeated exclamation, this time breathed with awe, made Mortimer glance sharply around to find Bricker standing in the frame of his open door, staring wide-eyed up at the sky. Eyebrows rising, Mortimer glanced up and found himself staring at a canopy of stars spread overhead like diamonds on a blue-black canvas. It wasn't a new sight to Mortimer. Before the world had become so crowded and electricity had been invented, every night had offered such a view. But of course Bricker wasn't old enough to recall that time, he realized, and glanced toward the awestruck man. "Nice, huh?"

"I've never seen so many stars in my life," Bricker murmured, eyes hungrily eating every inch of sky. "I didn't even realize there were this many."

Mortimer cast one more glance upward, but then started slowly forward across the uneven ground to the cottage. It was much larger than the tiny three-room building he'd expected. This was a proper house at the very least, and larger than even the average house. It was framed with dark wood, and most of the walls appeared to be made up of windows. The sight made

Mortimer's eyebrows rise. It was the last thing he would
have expected from the home of an immortal.

"Wait for me," Bricker hissed, hurrying after him as
Mortimer started up the stairs that led onto the deck
surrounding the second level of the house.

Mortimer slowed a bit but continued up and along
the deck to the door of the cottage. There were no lights
on and the building was obviously empty, but he still
frowned when he found the door locked. Decker was
supposed to be here. After a slight hesitation, Mortimer
reached above the door frame and felt along the ledge
until his fingers closed over a key.

Relaxing a little, he unlocked the door, and then
stepped inside the stuffy interior. A quick feel along the
wall was all that was needed to find the light switch, but
when he flipped it, nothing happened.

"The breaker probably has to be turned on," Bricker
said when Mortimer flipped it again to no avail. "I'll
find it and get the lights going."

Mortimer merely nodded and moved farther into the
cottage to make way for the other man to enter. He set
his bag on the table and then turned back to see Bricker
setting his own on the floor by the door. "I'll get the
cooler while you see to that."

He heard Bricker grunt an acknowledgment as he
stepped back out onto the deck. Mortimer paused on
the top step when a burst of feminine laughter filled the
air. He glanced across the surrounding darkness, not
sure from which direction the sound had come. It had
seemed quite close, but they were on the lake, and he
knew sound carried on water.

After another moment, Mortimer descended the

stairs, but rather than move toward the car, he went around to the lakeside instead. There was nothing to see. The lawn lay before him, running about fifty feet down to the shoreline and stretching out about twice that width before reaching the thick line of trees that bordered each side.

A good-sized boathouse sat at the water's edge, but the rest was open beach and left a lovely view of the calm surface of the small lake. The opposite shore was a strip of black bordering the lake itself, which was a lighter shade of dark, and the sight made him frown. There wasn't a light in evidence on the opposite shore, no sign at all of the occupants he knew must be there. Of course, it was after two A.M. and everyone was likely asleep. Still, had he not passed all those markers at the ends of driveways, he could almost believe he and Bricker were alone up here.

Another burst of sound, this time giggling, brought an end to that thought, and Mortimer jerked his head to the left, eyes narrowing as he peered through the trees. He made out the large dark shape of the neighboring cottage, an upside-down canoe, a dock with two boats moored to it, and two figures sitting side by side on the planks of the small dock. They were in a relaxed pose, legs stretched out and crossed at the ankles as they leaned back on their arms and stared up at the sky while chuckling over something.

Women, he realized, noting their very feminine shapes. One had shorter hair that barely reached her shoulders in a smooth bob. The other had longer hair, but had it scraped up into a ponytail at the back of her head.

The sound of a screen door clanging drew his gaze back to the neighboring cottage as a light beam came bobbing down its steps. A third woman, Mortimer realized, and his eyebrows rose slightly as he watched her stumble clumsily down the lawn, muttering to herself. It hadn't occurred to him that the two mortal women on the dock might be drunk, but this one definitely was, he thought dryly as she staggered sideways slightly and then fell. He wasn't the only one to notice, Mortimer realized, as both women on the dock turned and a flashlight beam shot from the hand of the one with the ponytail, bathing the fallen woman in light as she got to her feet.

"Sam? Are you all right?"

Caught in the beam as she was, Mortimer got a good look at the third woman. Her features suggested she was related to the other two, but she very definitely had a different body shape. While the other two were shapely and voluptuous, this one was tall, lean, and flat-chested. Her hair was as black as the night and fell in a straight curtain, framing a face filled by huge, dark eyes; a slightly crooked nose; and a large mouth that was presently twisted in an embarrassed grimace.

"Yes, yes," the woman named Sam answered on a laugh as she brushed at a large dark spot on her T-shirt. Not only had she stumbled over her own feet, she'd spilled her drink over herself.

Tsking with irritation, the woman turned back toward the cottage. "I'll be right back."

"Oh, don't bother changing, Sam," one of the women, the one with the bob, said. "There's no one here to impress."

"Yeah, but it's sticky, Alex," the woman named Sam complained.

"So. We have yet to take our first night swim. That will wash it away."

"True." A slow grin claimed Sam's lips, and she continued down toward the dock.

A low whistle drew Mortimer's attention to the side to see that Bricker had joined him and was ogling their neighbors with a wholly male appreciation.

"Maybe cottage country won't be so bad," Bricker whispered, and then tore his gaze away from the women to ask in hushed tones, "Sidetracked, were you?"

Mortimer shrugged. "I heard laughing and came to investigate."

The younger immortal nodded, his eyes shifting back to the women. "Yeah. Girls tend to do that a lot when they get together. At least my sisters do. They get together and laugh and giggle and . . ." He paused and peered back toward the next yard as another burst of laughter sounded from the women.

Mortimer followed his glance. Sam had reached the dock, her flashlight beam bobbing over the other two women as they got to their feet. Mortimer chuckled as it caught them rising with their backs to each other just as they bumped butts and nearly sent each other flying off the dock in opposite directions. A burst of laughter exploded from the women as they steadied themselves.

"And you say *I'm* clumsy?" Sam asked with dry amusement as she turned away, only to ruin the effect by nearly overbalancing and tipping off the dock herself, without bumping anything as an excuse for her own clumsiness.

Mortimer shook his head at their antics as another round of laughter erupted. The trio had obviously had quite a bit to drink. He'd barely had the thought when Sam said with disgust, "Dear God, anyone would think I was drunk, stumbling around like this."

"Not if they knew you and knew how clumsy you are," the one with the ponytail teased.

"Oh, who cares?" the one with the bob, whom Sam had called Alex, said. "We're on vacation. People can think what they want."

"Eww! Ew, ew, ew!"

The trio halted abruptly, and Sam swung the flashlight beam around toward the girl with the ponytail. "What is it, Jo?"

"I think I stepped on a baby frog," came the disgusted moan.

The beam of light immediately dropped to illuminate the feet of the woman with the ponytail—Jo—as she raised one foot for examination.

"It looks like mud," Sam said reassuringly.

"It was cold and squishy," Jo said uncertainly. Teetering about in her stork-like position, she bent to better examine the bottom of the foot in question and would have lost her balance and tumbled to the grass had Alex not stepped into the beam of light to catch her arm and steady her.

"Mud is cold and squishy," Alex said reasonably. "Besides, if you'd stepped on a baby frog it would be a pancake on the ground here, and there's no sign of frog pancake that I can see."

Sam moved the beam of her flashlight over the ground.

"No frog pancake," she pointed out with a shrug.

The beam of light then whirled away as she turned and moved forward once more, this time at a fast clip. She called out, "Last one in has to cook breakfast in the morning."

That set off a round of squeals, and Mortimer watched the moonlight silvering off pale skin as the two women rushed after Sam toward a small stretch of beach at the end of the lot nearest where he and Bricker stood. While the women did squeal, the very description was somewhat misleading. They were making an obvious effort to keep their voices down to avoid disturbing anyone. Understandable considering the hour and the way sound carried across water, Mortimer supposed, and frowned as the women moved down a small incline to the shore's edge. They hadn't gone inside to change into bathing suits. Surely they weren't going to—

"Are they stripping?" Bricker asked in a hopeful whisper.

Rather than answer, Mortimer moved closer to shore until they were almost parallel to the women again. *Almost* because the three women had thrown off their clothes in a rush and charged into the water with stifled squeals by the time he stopped.

"Damn," Bricker breathed, pausing at his side to watch the women jumping about and gasping in the water. "I think I'm going to like it here."

Mortimer barely caught back the bark of laughter that tried to escape at those words. Sometimes he forgot how young his partner was, but then something like this happened, and he was reminded that Bricker was still under one hundred and still suffered all kinds of hungers and appetites that older immortals were free of.

The man was ravenous in most of his appetites, whether it was food, drink, or sex.

That would change with time, he thought almost regretfully. Food and drink would all start to taste the same and hold less and less interest until it was something Bricker wouldn't bother with. As for sex . . . after a couple hundred years even sex became a time-consuming and troublesome bore, and when that happened, it was soon dropped as an activity. There were only so many positions, so many exciting places to perform it, and really, women—when you could read their every thought and desire, could be quite tedious. Having read thousands of mortals, hundreds of thousands even, Mortimer had come to the conclusion that women were the worriers of the species. Their minds seemed consumed with worry about everything from the weather to what to serve for the next meal. They worried about the health of each and every loved one around them, worried about finances, about time constraints, about whether they were meeting everyone's needs. They worried about rising crime, the threat of terrorism, aging . . . The list of worries was endless and exhausting just to have to read from their thoughts. Mortimer couldn't imagine having to live with such constant high levels of anxiety.

In contrast, mortal males didn't seem to suffer the same degree of anxiety. From what he'd read of mortal male minds there were only two areas where they suffered any sort of worry: at work and in bed. Work worry—which usually translated to financial worry— depended on the job they held. The other worry . . . well, size and performance were the key factors there, but that wasn't true with all men. Some men thought they were "hung" or that they were super skilled in the bedroom. However, a quick read of the mind of his wife or girlfriend often proved that to be delusional thinking on the part of the man.

A sharp gasp and splashing drew his attention back to the women in the lake. Moonlight was reflecting off the water and glinting on their wet skin, making it easier for him to see them. Their skin was exceptionally pale, or appeared to be under the moonlight.

"They're sisters." Bricker whispered the words to prevent the women from hearing him. "This is the family cottage. They arrived about an hour ago, unloaded their vehicle, unpacked everything, and this is their traditional first-night skinny-dip."

He merely nodded. Bricker was obviously reading from the mind of one—or all—of the women. Mortimer hadn't bothered to do so himself, and didn't now. Instead he pointed out, "We still need to unpack ourselves."

"Yeah, but we should wait until the girls are done swimming. They might run into trouble and need rescuing or something and . . ." Bricker's voice faded when he saw the expression on Mortimer's face. "Yeah, all right. We unpack."

Mortimer turned quickly to hide the smile tugging at his lips.

Chapter 2

"*I* take it you couldn't find the breaker panel?" Mortimer asked as they passed the still-dark cottage.

"I did," Bricker countered. "I flipped every single switch, but nothing happened. That storm this afternoon must have knocked out the power."

"Storm?" Mortimer asked as they continued on to the SUV.

"Yeah. I checked the Weather Channel this morning before lying down for the day and they were predicting a storm up this way," the younger immortal explained. "It must have taken out the power."

Mortimer grunted an agreement as they opened the back of the SUV and peered at the supplies inside. It was an Argeneau vehicle. Sometimes they had to make do with rentals, but usually when they were on an assignment they had special vehicles supplied by Argeneau Enterprises or one of its subsidiaries . . . like this SUV. It was all tricked out with special features, a state-of-the-art GPS system, specially treated glass to block the sun's UV rays, souped-up engines to give them more power, special racks and storage compartments built in all over the vehicle to hold weapons they would need, and a unique resting spot and hookup in the back for a specially designed cooler to store blood.

That was something new, actually. The SUV's cooler was the same size and shape as a large picnic cooler, but it was really a refrigerator that could be plugged into a special power source installed in the SUV or a normal plug inside a building. When without power, it ran on a battery that recharged every time it was plugged into a power source. One of the Argeneau scientists had come up with the design and this was a prototype, the first time they'd used it in the field. Mortimer thought it would definitely come in handy.

Bricker leaned in and grabbed two long rectangular leather cases by their handles. They were full of weapons and were heavy. A mortal would have been struggling under the weight of one, but Bricker lifted out the pair as if they were feather-light.

Once he was out of the way, Mortimer snagged the cooler and tugged it closer to the edge of the vehicle.

"Will the blood be okay in the cooler until the power's back on?"

Mortimer nodded as he lifted it out. "It should be fine for tonight, but come morning we might need to hit a store for ice."

"When is Decker going to show up?"

"Actually, he was supposed to be up here already," Mortimer admitted with a slight frown as he started toward the steps to the cottage.

"He was?" Bricker asked with surprise. "Well, I've been through the whole cottage, and he isn't here."

Mortimer shrugged. "Perhaps he had to go out for something."

Where a mortal would have been shocked at the idea of the man's needing to go out for anything at this hour, Bricker merely nodded. This was their daytime, when they usually performed their chores and what daily tasks could be done. All he said was a disgruntled "You'd think he'd have stuck around and waited for us. He knew we were coming."

"True," Mortimer agreed and then added heavily, "But then we were expected to arrive here by midnight and it's now after two A.M."

Bricker grinned and said innocently, "You make it sound like that's my fault."

Mortimer laughed at his feigned innocence and said, "Oh please. I waited an hour and a half for you to finish your packing, and *then* you insisted on stopping at absolutely every damned roadside stop there was, whether it was McDonald's or a greasy spoon diner. Honestly, if you weren't an immortal, I wouldn't bet on you living more than another five years with all the grease you consume. I swear you're starting to smell like a French fry."

"I am not!" Bricker protested, and then frowned and asked, "Am I?"

Mortimer just shook his head and moved in front of the other man to mount the steps. At the door to the cottage, he shifted the cooler to his hip again and opened the door for Bricker to precede him inside.

"I don't know why Lucian insisted on us bringing so much in the way of weapons," Bricker commented as he led the way inside. "For that matter, I don't know why he thinks we need three hunters up here. From the sounds of it we're only chasing after a lone rogue vamp, and all he's doing is biting the occasional mortal. It's not like he's a dangerous character or anything."

"Yeah," Mortimer said as he followed and set the cooler on the table. "But Decker is kind of an add-on. He's really supposed to be on vacation but his cottage was handy. Besides, while it may look like a lone neck biter, for all we know that may just be the tip of the iceberg, and it's better to be safe than sorry. That's Lucian's motto."

Bricker didn't comment as he set down what he'd brought in.

"I'm going to go lock up the SUV," Mortimer said, turning back toward the door. "I'll just be a minute."

Mortimer had closed the back of the SUV and was headed to the stairs when a startled shriek made him freeze. His head immediately jerked toward the trees between the cottages. After a hesitation, he turned in that direction, walking quickly down to the shore to make sure all was well.

"What is it?" one of the women asked in anxious tones as he neared the shoreline.

"Something bumped up against me in the water," came the answer, and Mortimer thought it was the girl with the ponytail who spoke. Jo.

"It's probably just a fish," Sam's reassuring voice said.

That reassurance was ruined when the one with the bob, Alex, said, "Of course, we do have snapping turtles here."

There was a moment of silence as the three women

stared at one another, and then they suddenly turned as one and made a swift exodus from the water. Mortimer stood completely still and watched, finding his gaze repeatedly drawn to the clumsy Sam. For some reason he found himself fascinated by the sight of her pale skin painted with water and moonlight.

"Nice view."

Mortimer turned his head sharply at that whisper to find Bricker standing at his side again. Shrugging, he explained, "I heard one of the girls scream and thought I'd make sure everything was all right."

Bricker nodded. "I heard it from inside the cottage. The girl has a healthy set of lungs."

Mortimer nodded, his glance returning to the women as they slipped inside the cottage next door. He saw the flashlight beam bounce around, sliding past the windows and moving over the room as candles were lit to ward off the darkness. Then the flashlight was shut off and the candles moved out of sight of the windows at the front of the cottage. The women were going to bed, each taking a candle with her to her room.

"I'll go see if we have candles." Bricker turned away to head back toward their cottage.

"I'll help," Mortimer murmured, but didn't follow right away. A faint glow had appeared inside the very last window on this side of the neighboring cottage, and Mortimer found himself watching as light and shadow danced behind the glass. For some reason he was absolutely positive it was the window to Sam's bedroom, and he found himself standing there, silently watching until the candlelight went out.

It was only then he noted the flicker of light to his

side. Turning, he saw that Bricker had found a candle and it now shone from the window.

Mortimer glanced one last time toward the cottage next door, wondering if the girls would be a problem. He didn't think so or Decker would have said so to Lucian, but it was something to consider. He turned and made his way back across the yard.

"Only an Argeneau would think this was a cottage," Bricker said dryly as Mortimer entered.

Pausing inside the door, Mortimer let his gaze slide over the large open kitchen/dining/living area with its high, cathedral ceiling and huge, old-fashioned fan hanging in the center. The kitchen was on his right, sectioned off by a large, L-shaped, marble-topped counter. The floors and cupboards were pine, the appliances stainless steel, and included a microwave and dishwasher along with the standard stove and refrigerator. A large island filled the center of the kitchen, with glasses and copper pots and pans hanging overhead.

The dining area on his left ran along the glass wall overlooking the lake. The hardwood continued there, and a large, long table and twelve chairs of light wood filled the space.

The living room took up the other half of the open space and held white leather furniture and stone-topped tables, as well as a huge sixty-two-inch television.

All the comforts of home, Mortimer thought with amusement. This was a rich man's idea of a cottage, but then Decker was a rich man.

"It doesn't belong to an Argeneau," Mortimer reminded Bricker as he finally turned back to push the door closed. "It's Decker's cottage, remember."

"Yeah, but he's Martine's son and she's an Argeneau by birth," Bricker pointed out.

Mortimer didn't argue the point. Martine *had* been born an Argeneau. In fact, she was the eldest Argeneau daughter, and while she'd taken on her husband's last name when she married Aloysius Pimms, they switched off between Argeneau and Pimms each century in an effort to avoid their failure to age from being detected. This century, Decker was a Pimms, but an Argeneau by any other name was still an Argeneau.

"I never would have taken Decker for a cottage-country-type guy," Bricker commented, interrupting Mortimer's thoughts. "He always seemed to have too much class."

"Yes, well, as you said, this place isn't exactly your average cottage," Mortimer said dryly as he turned from closing the door and glanced around again. The windows were all open now, when he was sure they hadn't been the first time he'd entered. Bricker, he assumed, had opened them to let the night air circulate.

"There are three bedrooms up here and another two downstairs, as well as a rec room and laundry room," Bricker announced, waving back toward the door they'd entered through.

Mortimer followed the gesture, surprised to realize that there were stairs right next to the entrance.

"Every outer wall on this level of the cottage seems to be full of windows," Bricker said. "There's no way of knowing how good the window coverings in the upstairs rooms are, but the bedrooms downstairs have no windows so I took our stuff down there. I put my stuff in the room closest to the stairs and yours in the far room."

"Thanks," Mortimer murmured, walking past the table into the unlit living room. While he was surprised one of their kind would own a home with so many windows to allow damaging sunlight in, it did come in handy at that moment. The windows allowed what little light the stars were shedding to seep inside. Like any good night predator, Mortimer had incredible night vision, and even without electricity, that bit of light was enough for him to see by as he moved toward the door leading into a hall.

"There's a bathroom up here and one downstairs," Bricker announced as Mortimer crossed the hall to peer through an open door into a three-piece bathroom.

Mortimer noted the standard services and then wandered up the hall to the right, glancing in one bedroom before continuing on to a second at the end of the hall. He walked back to find the last bedroom at the opposite end of the hall before turning back into the living room.

"So," Bricker said as Mortimer joined him by the sliding glass doors overlooking the deck. "What do we do until Decker gets back?"

Mortimer grimaced at the question. They should be unpacking; unloading the blood bags in the cooler and shifting them into the refrigerator, and then unpacking their bags, as well as unpacking and prepping their weapons. Once that was done, he would have pulled out the maps of the area and the information they had about where bitten mortals had been seen. The two of them would have pored over those while making up some sort of plan to hunt down and find the rogue that was biting mortals in the area.

However, not having power rather buggered up all of that.

"There's nothing much we can do at the moment," he admitted finally.

"Are you hungry?" Bricker asked suddenly.

Mortimer glanced at the younger immortal with amusement. He hadn't been hungry for a couple hundred years. The younger man couldn't know that, though, since Mortimer ate on the odd occasion just to keep him company. Mind you, eating was an ambitious description, since he really mostly picked at the food and pushed it around his plate to be polite.

"We don't have anything besides blood in that cooler, do we?" Bricker asked when Mortimer didn't respond at once and then complained, "I'm hungry."

"You're always hungry," Mortimer said dryly, and then turned away from the window saying, "Come on then, we'll go find an all-night diner or coffee shop with food and lights and look over the information and maps Lucian gave us."

Chapter 3

"Poor Alex."

Sam glanced over at Jo, who sat at the dining room table. She was supposed to be shucking corn, but now held a half-shucked cob forgotten, her attention directed out the front window of the cottage. Her mouth was pinched with worry, Sam noted. "What's wrong with Alex? Has she hurt herself?"

"No," Jo assured her. "She just looks so miserable out there."

Sam set down the half-peeled potato she'd been working on, snatched a piece of paper towel off the roll, and dried her hands as she crossed the room to look out the window too. They were both silent for a moment, eyes following their older sister as she pushed a lawn mower across the grass in front of the cottage. She was obviously struggling to move the old mower up the slanted lawn. Beads of sweat were rolling down her forehead as she worked under the blistering late afternoon sun. And she did indeed look miserable. Alex's face was red and fixed in a scowl so fierce Sam feared it might become permanent.

"I did offer to do it for her, but she insisted," Sam said with exasperation. "She'd rather do that than food prep any day."

"I suppose when you cook all week for a living, doing it on vacation would be a drag," Jo commented sympathetically.

Sam snorted. "More like she has little lackeys to do this stuff at work and she thought she'd rather mow than play lackey herself . . . but she forgot about the deerflies."

"Is that what that gray fog is around her head?" Jo asked with alarm. "Why didn't she put on some bug spray?"

"She did," Samantha assured her. "She used the heavy-duty stuff too. Twice. But it's hot out there, and she sweats it off after ten steps."

They watched silently as Alex and her swarm crossed the yard again. She wasn't even halfway done. She'd be eaten alive by the time she was.

Mouth tightening, Sam headed for the door. "I'm going out there and try to help keep the bugs off her."

"How are you going to do that?" Jo asked with amazement.

The question made Sam pause and turn back. She'd need weapons to defend Alex.

"What on earth is that woman doing?"

Mortimer gave a slight start at Decker Pimms's words and turned from the window to glance at him with surprise. He'd been concentrating so hard on what was taking place next door that he hadn't even heard the man approach. "You *are* here. Lucian said you were, but the cottage was empty, and I began to think I'd misunderstood."

"No, you didn't misunderstand," Decker said with a shrug. "I was up here on vacation when Mother called saying Uncle Lucian was trying to reach me about this biting business."

Mortimer nodded, but kept back any sympathetic comments about his vacation being wrecked. Decker wasn't the sort to appreciate sympathy.

"I was told to expect you two around midnight."

Mortimer grimaced at the pointed comment, but merely said, "The journey took longer than expected."

"Bricker made you stop at every restaurant you passed along the way?" Decker guessed with amusement.

"Yeah," Mortimer admitted wryly. Anyone who had worked with them was familiar with Bricker's voracious appetite.

Smile widening at his expression, Decker explained, "I waited until two A.M., but when you guys hadn't shown up by then I ran out to run some errands. I checked back after dropping some mail in the box in town and hitting the garbage dump, but you still weren't here, so I went out to reconnoiter on my own."

"Garbage?" Mortimer asked doubtfully. "Don't they pick up here?"

Decker shook his head. "And you can't leave containers of empty blood bags in the shed; it attracts bears. I pay extra to the local guy who takes care of the dump to let me in late."

"Ah," Mortimer said with a small smile.

Decker shrugged. "Anyway, it was a little after dawn when I got back."

"It sounds like you missed us both ways," Mortimer announced. "We arrived just after two, then went in search of an all-night coffee shop for Bricker to eat."

"I take it that means you didn't have any trouble finding the key over the door?"

"No problem at all," Mortimer assured him.

Decker nodded. "Most people don't bother to lock their doors up here, and I wouldn't either, but I worry about kids, or the curious, or even ne'er-do-wells wandering in and happening on the blood . . ."

Mortimer merely nodded in understanding. Their kind were trained from birth to hide what they were, as well as any evidence that might give them away.

"I gather you took the spare room down here?" Decker asked.

"Yeah. Bricker put my stuff in there when we arrived," he admitted, and then raised an eyebrow. "Is it a problem?"

"No, not at all," Decker assured him, and then smiled wryly and added, "His being in my room was, though. When I found him there, I invited him to choose one of the empty rooms upstairs and then I crashed."

Mortimer grinned, knowing Decker well enough to be able to say with some certainty that the invitation had probably been offered via rousting Bricker from the bed. He didn't feel much sympathy for the younger man. When he'd seen the large, opulent room Bricker had chosen for himself, Mortimer had suspected it was the master bedroom. But when he'd suggested as much that morning, Bricker had just shrugged and said that if Decker wanted the room, he'd move. He probably hadn't expected that to be in the middle of the day, though.

Mortimer was surprised the noise hadn't woken him up. He was usually a light sleeper, but that morning he'd dropped off the moment his head hit the pillow and— despite being in a strange bed—he'd slept right through . . . until about twenty minutes ago, when he'd woken to the raucous growl of their neighbor's lawn mower. Mortimer had tried to filter out the sound at first, but it was hard to ignore. This lawn mower's muffler appeared to be broken . . . if lawn mowers had mufflers, he thought with a scowl.

"Jesus," Decker said, his attention again shifting to their neighbor's yard. "What *is* that woman doing?"

Reminded of what he'd been watching, Mortimer turned to glance out the window again. Decker's cottage had been built on a hill. The upper floor was completely above ground and had a deck surrounding it, but only this large rec room was above ground on the second floor. All the rooms at the back of the cabin, or facing toward the road rather than the lake, were built into the hill itself, hence the reason there were no windows in the downstairs bedrooms. But the front of this room—like the one above—was a wall of windows, and every one of them was shaded by the deck outside. It left a lovely shady spot to stand and peer through the trees at the lawn next door and the two women mowing it.

Well, only one was mowing the lawn, he supposed. The sister named Alex. The other, the woman he recognized as being the clumsy Sam, was following along beside her, madly waving a dish towel and fly swatter about her sister's head.

When he'd first spotted the pair, Mortimer thought Sam was attacking Alex, but the mad waving continued while the two women walked in sync. Mortimer had watched perplexed as the clumsy Sam staggered along, stumbling over her own feet as she madly flailed her items. She was mostly wielding them about Alex's head, but stopped every few minutes to flail them around her own before chasing after the mower to wave them around Alex again.

As he watched, Mortimer's irritation slowly turned to concern. He was quite positive that one of these times, in her mad dash after the lawn mower, Sam would stumble and fall right into it. She really was the clumsiest creature he'd ever seen. As unsteady on her feet as a new foal . . . or a drunk, he supposed, and frowned. Surely it was too early in the day to be drinking.

He glanced to his wrist, but had taken off his watch before crawling into bed and hadn't thought to retrieve it when the lawn mower noise had woken him.

"What the *hell* is she doing?" Decker breathed with dismay.

Mortimer glanced back out to see that Sam had once again paused to wave the dish towel and fly swatter about her own head. He wasn't surprised at Decker's shock. The woman looked spastic . . . The first time she'd done that he'd thought she was having some sort of seizure. "I think she's trying to chase off mosquitoes or something."

"Ah." Decker nodded, but said, "Probably deerflies."

"What about deerflies?"

Both men turned to see Bricker as he stepped off the stairs and crossed the carpet toward them.

"They tend to be pests up here for the mortals," Decker explained. Insects generally left immortals alone. It had been hypothesized that immortals secreted some hormone that either confused or was unattractive to them. "I guess they're bothering our neighbor while she's mowing the lawn."

Bricker nodded at the explanation and paused next to them to peer out the window too. He watched Sam's antics for a moment, his expression becoming increasingly perplexed, but merely asked, "Do you know them?"

"No," Decker said. "The Realtor gave me a short rundown of the neighbors when I bought this place, but I've avoided the whole getting-to-know-the-neighbors thing."

Mortimer wasn't surprised to hear this. Getting to know the neighbors would limit how long Decker could keep the cottage. The best possible scenario was that he didn't see them at all.

"So what did the Realtor say about them?" Bricker asked curiously.

Decker's expression turned thoughtful as he tried to recall the information. "They're three sisters. I think the family name is Willan, but I don't remember their given names. The Realtor told me, but . . ." He shrugged with indifference. "Their parents bought or built the cottage when the girls were just kids and the family spent a lot of summers up here. The parents died a couple of years ago—some kind of accident—and they left the cottage to the three sisters."

Mortimer saw his gaze narrow on the women on the lawn, and then Decker admitted, "In the two years since I bought the cottage, this is the first time I've been here during high season. I usually only come up in fall, winter, and spring. It's pretty quiet then, with just a handful of year-round residents, who are generally easy to avoid. On the rare occasions I haven't been able to avoid them, I simply took control of their minds and sent them on their way."

A moment of silence passed, and then Decker glanced at Bricker and asked, "Did the lawn mower wake you up as well?"

"Yeah," the younger immortal admitted, irritation wreathing his face. "These walls are paper-thin, Decker. What did they build them out of? Toilet tissue?"

"I don't think that would be up to code," Decker said with amusement and then added, "I plan to tear it down eventually and build new. I'm just waiting for my neighbors to decide to sell so I can buy their land and spread out a bit."

Mortimer raised his eyebrows at the ambitious plan. "Do you intend to help your neighbors decide to sell? If not, it could take a while."

"I have time," Decker pointed out dryly.

He couldn't argue that point, Mortimer supposed. Barring murder or an incredibly rare accident, time was the one thing they all had a lot of.

"The heat up there didn't help me sleep either," Bricker commented, and then added enviously, "It's much cooler down here."

"The air conditioner must not have kicked in," Decker said with a frown. "I'll have a look at it."

"It can't kick in; there's no power," Mortimer announced, forestalling him.

"No power?" Decker asked with surprise. "It was on when I left last night."

"It wasn't when we arrived," Bricker informed him.

"Christ." Decker turned to stride away across the room to a refrigerator. He pulled the door open and groaned when the light didn't come on. Even without the light, it was bright enough in the rec room to see the neat rows of bagged blood inside. Blood that would now be useless.

"It'll be tainted," Decker said with disgust. He bent to feel the bags anyway, but apparently wasn't pleased with their temperature. Straightening, he closed the door with a slam. "The storm must have knocked it out. I should have checked when I came back. The tiniest rainstorm can knock out the power up here."

"Don't worry, we brought plenty of blood. You can share ours," Mortimer told him.

"Well, it won't be any good either if you put it in the refrigerator upstairs," Decker pointed out.

"We didn't," Bricker assured him, and quickly explained the special cooler they'd brought.

"How long will it run on battery?" Decker asked.

Mortimer frowned. "I think they said twenty-four hours."

"Well, there's no need to run it down. I have a generator. I'll go turn it on and we can trade the bad blood in the refrigerator for your good blood." He started for the stairs, muttering, "This means another trip to the dump tonight."

"I didn't see a generator when I looked around last night," Bricker commented.

"It's out behind the cottage in a shed," Decker explained, disappearing up the stairs.

The sudden silence as the growl of the lawn mower next door died reminded Mortimer of the women. He was swinging toward the window to peer out again when the racket that had woken him was replaced with the blare of music.

It seemed they were done mowing the lawn. Alex was pushing the mower back toward the garage and Sam was moving toward the deck stairs. She paused abruptly, however, when the third sister, Jo, rushed out of the cottage with three clear bottles with golden liquid and lime slices floating in them. Despite the distance, he could make out the name Corona on one of the bottles. Mexican beers then.

"It's starting to look like the neighbors are party animals," Bricker commented, moving up beside him to peer outside. "I hope they don't keep us up every day with loud music."

A burst of laughter slipped from Mortimer's lips. "Three women do not constitute a party, and having a beer at . . ." He paused to glance around until he found a clock on the wall. The fact that the second hand was still moving told him it was battery operated and—hopefully—correct. It wasn't as early as he'd supposed. "A beer at four P.M. after mowing the lawn in this heat hardly makes them party animals."

"If the power's out, how are they playing music?" Bricker asked.

Mortimer didn't comment, but glanced toward their neighbors. Alex was back from the garage sans the lawn mower, and she and Sam had each taken one of the bottles of golden liquid. Jo was now only holding one bottle. She was also doing something of a dance and trying to get the other two to join her.

"It must be a battery-operated CD player or something," Bricker said after moving to the light switch next to the sliding glass doors and flicking it on and off with no effect.

"Or maybe they have a generator too," Mortimer suggested.

He'd barely spoken the suggestion when the air was filled with the very loud sound of an engine roaring to life. The generator, Mortimer realized, and glanced toward Bricker. He immediately flicked the light switch again, grinning when this time it turned on.

They were both silent for a moment, and then Bricker asked hopefully, "Do you think it's got enough current to run the air conditioner as well as the lights?"

"No," Decker answered as he stepped off the stairs and moved to rejoin them. "This generator came with the cottage when I bought it. It's old and not very powerful despite how noisy it is. I've been meaning to replace it, but haven't got around to it. I'll have to look into it, I guess. In the meantime, this one will run the refrigerator and some lights, but I wouldn't tax it more than that."

Bricker looked truly disappointed at this news, which made Mortimer wonder just how hot it was upstairs.

"Look," Bricker said suddenly. "It would seem the noise has caught the attention of your neighbors."

Mortimer and Decker followed his gaze out the window. Sure enough, all three women stood stockstill, their gazes focused on this cottage.

"How the hell did they hear the generator over the sound of their music?" Decker muttered.

"The generator is pretty loud," Mortimer pointed out, and then fell silent as the women began to move as one, crossing their yard toward the border of trees that separated the properties.

"Damn," Decker muttered.

"This is easily resolved," Mortimer said calmly. "We'll just convince them that they don't want to come over here. I'll take the clumsy one."

"Which one's that?" Bricker asked with confusion.

"The one with long hair."

"Right." He nodded. "I'll take the one with the pony-tail."

"I guess I'll take the other one then," Decker said dryly.

Mortimer smiled faintly and then concentrated on Sam, sending his thoughts out to find hers and take control of them. He was vaguely aware of first one sister stopping and then the other as he worked, but Sam continued happily forward, oblivious of his struggles to get into her thoughts and take control. Something he seemed to be having difficulty with. Frowning, he redoubled his efforts.

"Um, Mortimer," Decker said with concern as Sam continued along the trail. Leading the way, she hadn't yet noticed that her sisters had both stopped and were no longer following. "What's happening?"

"Nothing, just give me a minute," he muttered unhappily and redoubled his efforts. Another moment of silence passed, but he still couldn't seem to get into her thoughts.

"Are you going to stop her or not?" Decker asked with exasperation. The two other sisters stood like frozen dolls, waiting for the men to put a thought in their heads and release the control they had over them. But the men were waiting for Mortimer to get control of Sam. Only he didn't appear to be able to do that.

"Mortimer?"

"I'm trying," he snapped with frustration.

"*Trying?*" Bricker asked.

Something about the tone of his voice made Mortimer give up on the woman and turn a reluctant gaze to the other men.

They were both staring at him wide-eyed.

"Can't you get into her thoughts?" Bricker asked

"Of course I can," he said quickly, irritation making his voice short.

"Then what's the problem. Stop her," Decker insisted.

Mortimer turned back and tried once more.

"You can't, can you? You can't get into her thoughts," Bricker said with what sounded like mounting excitement.

It wasn't shared by Mortimer. He scowled, but finally admitted, "No, I can't."

"I'll handle it," Decker murmured.

The moment she was under control and still like the others, Bricker slapped Mortimer on the shoulder. "Woowoo! Congratulations, Mort, my man!! You've found your life mate."

"Shut up, Bricker," he growled furiously.

"You're not looking happy," Decker said slowly, and then pointed out, "Most immortals would be jumping for joy at the prospect of finally meeting their life mate."

Mortimer opened his mouth to snap again, but then let his breath out on a sigh and said more calmly, "And I would be too if she truly were my life mate. But she isn't. She can't be."

"She can't?" Decker asked with surprise, and when Mortimer shook his head firmly, asked, "Why not?"

"Well, just look at her, Decker," he said, amazed that he would even ask. "She's clumsy and awkward and flat and—That woman in no way resembles the mate I—" Mortimer snapped his mouth shut before he could blurt the words *have fantasized about for well over seven hundred years.*

And he had. In his eight hundred years of life, Mortimer had lain awake many a night imagining what his life mate would be like. In his dreams she'd been blond, and cool, and intelligent in a sexy Jessica Rabbit kind of way. He smiled just thinking about the glamorous cartoon character, and then his eyes settled on the woman named Sam, and his smile died. This woman was nothing like the fantasy character. Tall, skinny, awkward, and clumsy, she was more like Olive Oyl. She even had the dark hair, though hers was long.

Mortimer's seething thoughts were distracted when Decker patted his shoulder sympathetically.

"I have a certain vision in my mind of what my life mate will be like too," the other immortal admitted. "Mine's Angelina Jolie in *Mr. and Mrs. Smith* . . . or *Tomb Raider* . . . hell, pretty much in any role she's played. But I'll probably end up with a short Betty Boop."

Mortimer closed his eyes on a sigh as he realized that Decker had read his thoughts, something he normally wouldn't be able to do. It was starting already the<u>..</u>, he thought unhappily, the lack of control over his own mind, leaving his thoughts vulnerable to every immortal who wished to read it. Like not being able to read the life mate's mind, this too was a symptom of meeting the life mate. He supposed he'd start eating soon too, and not that fake push-food-around-your-plate business he normally indulged in to keep Bricker company. No. He'd really start eating; scarfing down food, enjoying it, and hungering for more.

Damn. This was the last thing he'd expected from this trip.

"Jessica Rabbit?" Bricker said suddenly with disbelief. "Olive Oyl? Jeez, Mort. I mean, I've heard of sexism, but . . . seeing women as cartoon characters? You've got a major problem there, my friend." He shook his head. "Maybe it wasn't such a good thing we watched that animation marathon on television last week. It was my fault. You didn't want to watch it, but I—"

"Bricker," Mortimer said wearily, running a hand through his hair. "This isn't your fault and it isn't about cartoons. She just isn't to my taste."

A moment of silence passed as the men all turned to peer at Sam. Decker had taken control just as she'd stumbled and landed on her butt on the muddy path under the trees between the two properties. She still sat there, living proof of her own clumsiness.

Mortimer noted the exchange of glances between the other two men, and then Decker asked, "So, how old are you, Mortimer? Eight hundred and something, isn't it?"

"Yes," he agreed warily, knowing it wasn't just mild interest.

Decker nodded. "And how many women have you met in that time that you can't read?"

His mouth tightened at the question. Sam was the first. And it had been a long eight hundred years too. Lonely. Was he being a fool?

No, Mortimer decided grimly. If he was judging the woman on her looks, that would have been one thing, but it wasn't just that. It was her complete lack of grace and— What if she really was an alcoholic? Maybe that was why he couldn't read her, he thought suddenly. Maybe she was drunk right now and—

"Alcohol usually makes it easier to read them," Decker pointed out quietly, revealing that he was still reading Mortimer's thoughts. "A drunk's thoughts might be sloppy and disorganized, but they have no barriers at all when drunk."

Mortimer peered at Sam again, knowing he was being a fool to even hesitate.

"Do you really want to wait another eight hundred years for another possible life mate to come along?" Bricker asked quietly.

Mortimer grimaced at the idea, but argued, "We're up here to do a job, not chase women around."

Bricker arched one eyebrow and then turned to Decker and asked, "Am I right in guessing that you don't know much about the social scene up here?"

"Yes. How did you know?"

"You don't even know your neighbors," he pointed out dryly, and then suggested quietly, "So, these gals may come in useful. We could perhaps learn the social hot spots and where most people go . . . which will be where the rogue is."

Decker nodded slowly and then followed his thought to the obvious point. "And it will give Mortimer a chance to get to know this girl and better decide if she wouldn't make a fine life mate after all."

"Exactly." Bricker beamed.

Mortimer grimaced, but nodded in reluctant agreement. He'd give Olive Oyl a go, but really, he couldn't see them suiting. She just wasn't his sort at all.

"Hello?"

Mortimer turned sharply to see the woman in question now standing on the other side of the door. Tall, slender, lips curved in a wide smile, Sam peered at them through the screen.

When he turned to glare at Decker, the other immortal shrugged and said, "I was controlling two. I lost my concentration."

Mortimer snorted, not believing it for a minute.

"We heard your generator start up and decided to come over and introduce ourselves," Sam said cheerfully, recapturing his attention. "We'd have done it sooner but you're never here when we are."

When the men simply stared, she tilted her head and added with a grin, "If you actually *are* here now. You *are* the owners and not just renters taking the cottage for the week or something, aren't you?"

"I'm the owner," Decker announced, sliding the screen door open and stepping out into the shade of the deck to take her hand in greeting. "Decker Pimms."

"Hello, I'm Samantha Willan," she said, accepting his hand. "And these are my sisters Jo and— Oh."

Sam blinked in confusion as she turned to gesture to her sisters, only to find them absent. A frown claiming her lips, she stepped back the way she'd come and squinted toward the yard where the other two women still stood. Mortimer followed her gaze, grimacing when he saw that they were both frozen in their own yard, their expressions blank.

"I believe the one with the ponytail stepped on something," Decker said smoothly, his expression becoming concentrated on Samantha Willan's face. When her expression smoothed out, losing its confused look, Mortimer knew he was slipping into her thoughts and soothing her worries about her sisters' odd behavior. For some reason, that bothered him. He didn't particularly want her for his life mate, but didn't want anyone messing with her thoughts either.

"They're coming now though, see." Decker's words made Mortimer glance toward the trees to see that the other two women were indeed moving forward now. He and Bricker were obviously bringing them along and probably giving them the thoughts that the ponytailed sister had stepped on something that held them up. Oddly enough, Mortimer didn't care that the men were controlling the other two women. It wasn't that he liked Sam better, but if she did turn out to be his life mate, he didn't want anyone playing with her head.

"Are you all right?" Sam asked the girl with the ponytail as the pair reached them.

"Yes, fine. I just stepped on something," Jo assured her vaguely, and then offered a smile to the men. "Hi, I'm Josephine Willan."

"And I'm Alexandra," the last sister announced.

"It's nice to finally meet my neighbors," Decker said

calmly, and Mortimer just managed not to snort at the lie.

"Things change," Decker muttered, letting Mortimer know he was still reading his thoughts.

The knowledge just made him scowl. He thought it incredibly rude of the man to take advantage and read him when he was vulnerable.

"I'm Decker Pimms," Decker said, doing the honors and introducing them. "And this is Justin Bricker and Garrett Mortimer."

Mortimer forced himself to stop scowling and nodded a grim greeting to the women.

Hellos were offered back and forth, and then Alex commented, "We heard your generator start up and thought we'd come ask you about it. We've been thinking of getting one for our cottage too, but . . ." She shrugged and then said, "They're very loud, aren't they?"

"This generator came with the cottage. I don't think the newer models are as loud," Decker said quietly. "I'm sorry if it disturbed you."

"Oh, not at all," Jo assured them. "It's no louder than the lawn mower, really. It just got our attention, and we thought we'd come say hello and share information."

"What information?" Bricker asked curiously.

"You know, about the power outage." Jo smiled, her eyes moving over the younger immortal with interest. "The official word is that the power should be back up again by eight o'clock tonight."

"Mind you," Sam said wryly, "the official word when we first got up this morning was that it would be up by four P.M., so I wouldn't count on having power before tomorrow morning."

"Is it always so unreliable up here?" Bricker asked with surprise.

There was an exchange of glances and wry expressions among the three women, and then they all turned back and said as one, "Yes."

"Hmm," Bricker muttered, and then asked, "You couldn't direct us to the local grocery store, could you? We thought we could pick up groceries here and didn't bring any."

"Oh." Sam frowned and glanced at her sisters before saying, "I'm not sure it would still be open. Our grocery store back home is only open until four on Sundays and it's past that now."

"They might stay open later because it's cottage country," Alex pointed out.

"True, but I doubt they opened at all today if their power is out too," Sam countered.

"Oh, they have to have generators in the grocery store," Jo protested. "Otherwise the food would go bad every time the power went down."

"Yes," Sam agreed. "But they may only have generators hooked up to the refrigerators and freezers and not for the lights and cash registers. I'd think it would be terribly expensive to run the whole store on gas-powered generators."

Jo clucked her tongue and muttered what sounded like "Gawd, you're such a lawyer."

Sam rolled her eyes as if this was an oft-heard comment. She then forced a smile, grabbed her sisters by an arm each, and backed away saying, "Excuse us just one moment."

Mortimer and the others exchanged glances as the women huddled together a few feet away and began to whisper frantically. It was a short powwow. Within seconds they were back to stand before the men.

It was Jo who offered a wide smile and said, "We'd like to invite you to a power outage party."

When the men stared back blankly, Sam explained, "We brought food with us. We always do and usually it's fine. The power rarely stays off for this long, but this time . . ." She shrugged. "It's probably better to eat it all than hope it lasts in the cooler until they manage to get the power back on. There's a lot of food. You're welcome to join us."

"A lot?" Alex echoed with a snort, and then told them, "A week's worth. We have sausages, hot dogs, hamburgers, steaks, pork tenderloin . . . We have *a lot* of food."

"I'm sure we won't eat a week's worth of food," Decker said with amusement.

"But we'd be happy to join you in a power outage party," Bricker said quickly, obviously worried the man was about to do him out of a meal. "And you're welcome to store your meats and such in our refrigerator. After all, we didn't bring provisions up with us so there's plenty of room."

"Oh. That's so sweet," Jo said, wide-eyed.

"Yes, sweet," Mortimer said dryly, scowling at the younger man. He fully expected Decker to stomp on the offer, but he didn't.

"Yes, it is sweet," Alex agreed, and turned to her sisters to say, "We could throw the milk and cheeses and tenderloin in their fridge and then cook up the sausages, hamburgers, hot dogs, and such tonight."

"We have the three steaks too," Jo suggested. "We could cook those up and split them in halves or something so everyone gets a bit."

"I'll double the amount of potato salad I was making," Sam decided.

In their excitement the trio had started walking back toward their own cottage as they planned. They were nearly to the trees when Sam apparently realized how rude they were being and paused to glance back. "Sorry. We'll be right back. We just have to get stuff."

The other two women nodded in agreement, and then the trio rushed off through the trees.

"A power outage party," Bricker said with a grin. "Potato salad, hamburgers, sausages, and steak. It could be fun."

"And their food right alongside our bags of blood in the refrigerator," Mortimer said dryly, mildly satisfied by the way the reminder wiped the smile off the younger immortal's face.

Decker, however, didn't look upset at all. "I have two refrigerators here. One is upstairs and one down. Both are set to two degrees right now like ABB recommends for bagged blood, but we can bring up the temperature on the one upstairs and let them store their food there."

"See," Bricker chided Mortimer. "It's fine. We have the two refrigerators. We can help the girls out."

Grinding his teeth, Mortimer nodded. "There are

two spare rooms upstairs, one with bunk beds. Shall we offer them those as well so they don't have to sleep in a cottage without power?"

Bricker merely grinned. "You've obviously spent too much time with Lucian. His grumpiness is wearing off on you. Come on, Mortimer," he chided. "This could be fun."

Mortimer narrowed his eyes on the man and then turned away to head back into the cottage with an irritated "hrrumph."

Chapter 4

"*H*urry up, Mortimer. It's nearly seven and we still have to feed."

Mortimer finished tugging his T-shirt into place, and then reached for the door handle, jerking the bathroom door open just as Bricker would have knocked again.

"Oh. You're ready," the younger immortal said, letting his hand drop back to his side.

"Yes," he said dryly. "And stop chivvying me. You are the one who spent more than an hour in here. I haven't been in the bathroom ten minutes."

"I like to soak in the tub," Bricker said with an unapologetic shrug. "Come on, we can feed while Decker takes his turn at the shower."

Mortimer just grunted with irritation. It seemed the shower downstairs had a leak or something, so they'd had to take turns with the upper washroom.

Muttering under his breath, Mortimer followed the younger man downstairs to the rec room and to the refrigerator where the blood was stored. His eyes slid over the sky outside as he went, noting that while it was still light out, the sun at least was no longer in view. It would be safe enough for them to go out, but he still thought he might have an extra bag of blood just the same.

Mortimer accepted the bag Bricker handed him, waited for his fangs to descend, and then slapped the cold bag to them even as the younger immortal did the same with his own. The need to feed prevented speaking, and that was fine with him. He didn't wish for another lengthy discussion about how life mates were rare and to be cherished and he shouldn't be so resistant about accepting Samantha Willan as his. Both Decker and Bricker had had a go at him one after the other after the women left. He was heartily sick of the topic, mostly because he was torn on the subject himself. Mortimer was very aware of how rare not being able to read a mortal was.

"Here." Bricker handed Mortimer a second bag as he removed the now-empty first.

They stood in continued silence through three bags each, debated, and then had a fourth before deciding it was enough to counter any ill effects the remaining light of day might cause.

"I'll just go check on Decker and see if he's ready," Bricker said, taking the empty blood bags with him to throw away in the kitchen.

Mortimer nodded in acknowledgment and then moved to the windows and peered outside. The clack of a screen door drew his attention to the neighboring lawn. Mortimer slid the screen open and stepped out to see Alex and Sam huddled over a pot on the barbecue. Mortimer didn't know what was in it, but he'd seen them put it on the barbecue to boil when Bricker had first gone into the bathroom to take his bath.

Mortimer had found himself repeatedly drawn to the screen doors to watch the activity next door. Even as the men had lectured him, he'd stood grumbling suitable responses as he watched the women hustle about, preparing for their "power outage party."

Unfortunately, doing so had only made him more certain than ever that Samantha Willan was not for him. The woman was unbearably clumsy. She'd lost her balance countless times, dropping two drinks, a plate, silverware, and Lord knew what else as they'd rushed about setting the table and working at the barbecue. She couldn't possibly be meant for him.

The clatter of Bricker's feet on the stairs made him sigh heavily and turn back to move inside. He was pulling the door closed when the younger immortal stepped off the bottom stair and announced, "Decker is just getting out of the shower. He said to go ahead without him; he'll finish up and bite a quick bag or two and then follow."

"Why don't we just wait for him and go together?" Mortimer suggested.

"Because it's seven o'clock and that's when the girls said to be there when they brought their food over to put in the refrigerator. We'll just go over and tell them Decker will be right along." Bricker moved past him as he spoke and slid through the still-open screen door. "Come on, buck up. Parties are supposed to be fun."

"Right," Mortimer said on a small sigh, and followed reluctantly.

Sam was gone from the deck when they reached the

Willan cottage, as was the pot that had been on the barbecue for the last hour or so. Alex was still there, however, hovering over an assortment of burgers, sausages, and strips of steaks grilling on the barbecue.

"Welcome." She greeted them with a bright smile as they stepped onto the deck and then frowned slightly as she saw there were only the two of them. "Isn't your friend coming?"

"Decker will be right along," Bricker assured her. "We had to take turns at the showers and he's still getting ready."

"Oh." A crooked smile curved her lips, and then she shrugged. "I hope he doesn't take too long. This stuff is almost done."

"He'll be quick," Mortimer assured her, and then added, "Bricker is the only beauty queen in the bunch. He takes forever about his toilette."

"I do," Bricker admitted with a shameless grin. "I like to soak until my skin is nearly falling off."

"So does our Jo," Alex said with amusement, and then offered, "Would the two of you like a beer?"

Mortimer hesitated, his glance slipping to Bricker. Alcohol didn't have the same effect on them that it would on a mortal. While it gave them a very short-term buzz, it also forced their blood to work harder to remove the chemicals that caused that effect, which made them thirsty for something else entirely. Still, he knew it was a social drink and expected at barbecues. It might seem odd if they declined. And they *had* consumed extra blood.

"They're cold," Alex added temptingly, and when they both glanced at her in surprise, added, "We've been using Mother Nature's cooler. The lake," she added when that didn't clear their confusion. "It was Sam's idea. We put some pops and beer and such in fish baskets and sank them in the lake off the dock."

"That's clever," Bricker said with admiration. "Isn't that clever, Mortimer?"

"Yes, it's clever," Mortimer agreed, just managing not to roll his eyes at the man's obvious ploy to point out the woman's good points. It was going to be a long night.

"We'd love a couple beers," Bricker decided for them, moving toward the steps. "Which side of the dock did you sink the fish basket?"

"I'll get them," Alex offered, closing the lid on the barbecue.

"Where is Sam?" Bricker asked as she started down the steps.

Alex glanced back, a slightly surprised expression on her face, but she answered, "Inside draining the potatoes for potato salad. Jo's in there too. She's cutting veggies to go with the dip."

"Thanks." Bricker smiled, and when Alex nodded and turned to continue off the deck, he immediately turned to Mortimer. "Sam's inside making potato salad."

"So I heard."

"Well . . . ?" the younger immortal said grimly.

"Well what?" Mortimer snapped with exasperation.

"Well, you should go offer her a hand."

Mortimer peered at the younger man as if he were mad. "What on God's green earth makes you think I know anything about cooking?"

"I don't," Bricker snapped. "I just thought you might

know at least a little about women and that wooing them means you have to be in the same general proximity."

"Wooing?" Mortimer almost choked on the word.

"Getting to know her then," Bricker said dryly. "Go on, go see if she needs a hand or wants company while she's chopping and stuff." When Mortimer hesitated, he added, "You can ask her where everyone around here goes to party while you're at it."

"Right." Mortimer sighed and headed into the cottage.

Jo had just gone into the bathroom when Sam heard the screen door squeak open and then slap closed. Standing at the sink, draining the boiled potatoes into a strainer, she assumed it was Alex. "How are the steaks doing? I just have to finish draining these and run them under cold water then mix everything up and the potato salad will be done."

"The steaks looked nearly done to me, but then I like mine rare."

Startled by the deep male voice, Sam jerked her head around to see their tall, good-looking neighbor, Garrett Mortimer. Unfortunately, it was not a good move with her ear infection. The world immediately tipped, and she instinctively dropped the pot to grab for the counter and keep her balance. The pot hit the bottom of the sink with a thud and boiling water splashed upward, creating a mini tsunami of scalding liquid that hit her arm. Crying out in startled pain, Sam instinctively jerked backward, then immediately slipped on the hot water on the floor and lost her footing, ending on her bottom on the kitchen's linoleum tiles.

Sam was vaguely aware of Mortimer shouting out and rushing toward her, but stunned as she was by the fall and the pain now shooting through her bottom and throbbing arm, she simply sat where she'd landed, cradling her pained arm and gasping for breath.

"Are you all right?" Mortimer asked, dropping to his haunches beside her. "Let me see your arm."

"Sam? What happened?" Jo cried, rushing back up the hall into the kitchen.

"I'm fine, I fell," she answered her sister shakily, but her gaze was on Garrett Mortimer's face. While Jo looked alarmed and concerned, their neighbor actually looked angry. What the devil did he have to be angry about? Sam wondered with bewilderment. She hadn't burned *him*, she thought, and then gasped as he grasped her arm to examine her burn.

A second slap of the screen door had her glancing toward it to see who else had come to witness the latest humiliation caused by her stupid ear infection. She didn't mind so much when she saw Alex rushing in, but could have done without Justin Bricker, who was on her heels. The man paused just inside the door, his gaze sliding around the cottage, and Sam looked around herself.

Her parents had built this cottage when she and her sisters were just children, and it wasn't nearly as big or fancy as the cottage the men were staying in. While the front was one mid-sized room making up a small living room/kitchen area combo, the back consisted of three very small bedrooms, a tiny bathroom, and an equally tiny storage room holding the water heater and so forth. There was no second level as in the house next door, and the one floor was only half the size of that of the building next door. It was a real cottage, not a luxurious retreat for a rich man . . . and Sam wouldn't have traded it for the world. There were too many lovely memories tied up in this smaller, cozier cottage.

"The ear infection strikes again," Alex said with disgust, drawing Sam's gaze her way as she reached them. "Are you all right?"

"She's burned herself," Mortimer muttered, and there was no mistaking his tone for anything but being put out.

"Ear infection?" Bricker asked, pausing behind Alex and peering curiously over her shoulder at Sam.

"She has this recurring inner ear infection that puts her off balance," Jo explained, her worried gaze on Sam's arm as Mortimer turned it this way and that to see how much of it had been injured.

"An ear infection, eh?" Bricker said, and Sam noticed that his gaze was firmly on Mortimer as he said that. The man then glanced back to Sam and asked, "Can't they give you something for it?"

"They have," Jo answered for her. "They've given her every kind of antibiotic there is, I think, but it keeps coming back. Her doctor has finally made an appointment with a specialist."

"Yeah, but it takes forever to get in to see specialists. She'll be lucky if she doesn't kill herself before the appointment," Alex said with disgust. "I'm amazed she hasn't already. If she'd insisted her doctor send her to a specialist when I suggested it, she'd be infection-free by now. But no, not Miss I'm-Too-Busy-to-Be-Bothered. She let it drag on and on and—"

"Alex!" Sam snapped irritably. "I'm sitting right here, you know." She scowled at her sister and then paused when she noted the way Mortimer's lips were twitching. Apparently she'd amused him with her grumpiness. That just made her scowl harder.

"This is a nasty burn," Mortimer murmured. He bent over her arm to look closer, and Sam found herself staring at the top of his head. His hair was blond, cut short, and so thick she could barely see through it to the healthy pink scalp below. And he had a nice spicy sort of woodsy smell to him, Sam noted, and tried to inhale deeply without making it obvious she was sniffing the man.

Sam gave her head a shake, wondering if she'd hit it on the way down without realizing it. She was generally so wrapped up in her career that she took no notice of men. And this certainly wasn't a man she should find interesting. He was a stranger. She knew nothing more than his name and that he was staying at the cottage next door.

"Here, we'd best get you up."

Sam blinked in surprise as she was suddenly lifted off the floor and set on her feet by the man who had been examining her arm.

"Do you have any salve for the burn?" Mortimer asked, glancing to Alex as he urged Sam toward the old Formica-topped dining table a couple of feet away.

"In the bathroom," Alex answered. "I'll go get it."

"I'll start mopping up the floor," Jo said, turning to move off down the hall behind Alex.

"Here, sit down," Mortimer said, and Sam couldn't help but notice that his tone was less angry now and a touch gentler for some reason. Earlier he'd sounded like she'd deliberately thrown the potatoes around, burned herself, and tossed herself to the floor.

That thought reminded her of the potatoes, and Sam glanced toward the sink. Much to her relief, while water had splashed out and onto the counter and linoleum, none of the potatoes had. They remained mostly in the pot, with only a couple of stragglers lying in the sink. A quick rinse would fix them, she thought, grateful that was all that would be needed. It had taken her forever to peel and cut those damned things, and bringing them to a boil on the barbecue had seemed to take just as long. She'd have been mighty upset if all her efforts had been ruined.

"The potatoes are fine. Sit," Mortimer ordered, apparently noting where her concern had gone.

"I'll handle the potatoes," Bricker assured her, moving to the sink even as he spoke.

"There, see. Bricker will handle them. Now sit down and let me look at your arm."

"You already looked at it," she said with a scowl.

"Well, I want to look at it again in better light."

Sam opened her mouth and then closed it again. The table was by the window, and there *was* better light here. She hadn't noticed how dim it was getting as the day waned, but now glanced out the window to see that the sun was well down in the sky. It had taken them longer than expected to transfer the food they wouldn't be using to the refrigerator in the cottage next door and then to do all the prep work for the barbecue.

"Here. This should help." Alex reappeared with a tube of cream, which she handed to Mortimer rather than Sam. Her concerned gaze moved over the burn on

Sam's arm and then she said reluctantly, "I have to go out and check the stuff on the barbecue. Most of it was nearly done. I was just coming in to see if the potato salad would be much longer."

"I'll finish it up as soon as I put some cream on my arm," Sam assured her, and tried to take the salve from Mortimer, only to have him hold it out of her reach.

"Bricker will tend to the potato salad while I put cream on her arm," the irritating man corrected, brushing her still-reaching hand aside. "We'll be out in a minute."

Alex's eyebrows rose at the authoritative tone the man used, and then she turned away to head back out of the cottage, but not before Sam saw the slow grin beginning to pluck at her lips. Alex was obviously finding this amusing. Sam was not. She was a strong, independent, career woman and wasn't at all used to being treated like a naughty child.

"I can take care of my own arm," Sam growled, a bit rudely she supposed, since the man was just trying to help her.

"I'm sure you can, but I'm going to do it," Mortimer announced, and ignored her stony glare as he opened the tube of cream. Since it seemed obvious she wasn't going to be allowed to do anything else, Sam glanced around to see that Jo had finished mopping up the water and was now busy at the sink helping Bricker with the potatoes. Her gaze jerked back to her arm, however, when Mortimer took it in hand again. She saw with relief that it didn't appear to be blistering.

Her attention shifted to Mortimer's fingers as they gently spread the cool cream over her injured skin. He was being incredibly gentle, his touch feather-soft, and

Sam noted that he had very nice hands; smooth and unblemished by calluses or any roughness. Whatever he did for a living, it obviously wasn't hard labor.

"Why didn't you see a specialist when your sister suggested it?" Mortimer asked, distracting her.

Sam shrugged, embarrassed to admit she hadn't been taking proper care of herself. "The infections started about the same time I graduated and started my job. It's been crazy busy while I learned the ropes and . . ." She shrugged uncomfortably and admitted, "I just kept hoping my body would fight it off."

When he didn't comment, her gaze shifted from the injury he was tending to him, to find that he was looking at her face rather than her arm. His expression was rather odd. It seemed to her that the man had avoided looking at her when she'd first met the men at their cottage, and when he had looked at her, she'd seen traces of what had seemed almost to be resentment or anger. Now, however, he was eyeing her almost speculatively. That made her extremely uncomfortable.

"You take your job seriously," he said slowly.

Sam glanced away and shrugged. "Doesn't everyone?"

"No, I don't think they do," Mortimer said quietly.

The slap of the screen door made both of them glance that way as Alex rushed back in.

"The meat's done. How are we doing in here?" she asked, her anxious gaze moving from Sam and Mortimer to Bricker and Jo.

"All set," Jo said cheerfully as Bricker picked up the bowl of potato salad that they'd finished putting together.

"Done here too, I think," Mortimer murmured, releasing Sam's arm and straightening to stand beside her. "Has Decker shown up yet?"

"Yes, he's down at the lake getting drinks for everyone," Alex said, not bothering to hide her relief that there wouldn't be a holdup and everything was ready. "Shall we?"

Without waiting for an answer, she turned and hustled back out of the cottage, leaving them to follow.

Sam stood up, unable to keep from stiffening when Mortimer immediately took her arm as if to steady her.

"We don't want any more accidents," he said calmly when she glanced at him.

"I'm fine really," she assured him. "I can walk."

The assurance had absolutely no effect. If anything, his grip on her arm became a little firmer as he urged her to the door. Sighing, Sam didn't bother to protest further. It seemed obvious to her that he was used to getting his own way. Why fight him over something so small? She preferred to pick her battles.

Decker had returned from the dock by the time Sam and the others arrived at the patio set on the deck. He was busily putting several bottles of beer and a couple of cans of soda on the table as they arrived. Sam glanced over the table now, silently inventorying everything. She'd set the table while waiting for the potatoes to boil earlier, laying out plates and napkins, as well as forks and spoons and all the condiments that could be needed. There were also the vegetables Jo had cut up and the dip Alex had made for them; two large bowls of potato chips, one barbecue and one sour cream and onion; and now the large bowl of potato salad Bricker had carried out.

"Everyone grab a seat," Alex ordered cheerfully as she set a large platter stacked with cheeseburgers, sausages, and steaks on the table.

Sam began to shuffle forward, held back slightly by Mortimer, who seemed to be moving at a snail's pace. By the time they reached the table there were only two seats left, and those were side by side. She managed not to grimace at the fact that she'd have to sit next to the bossy man as he politely pulled the chair out for her to sit down, but she would rather have sat away from him, like at the opposite end of the table.

Deciding she'd just ignore him, Sam settled in her chair and proceeded to try to do just that as the food began to be passed around. Unfortunately, that was impossible. The man seemed to have decided to take care of her like she was some ailing bird with an injured wing.

The food was circulating clockwise, and since Mortimer was on her right, it meant he got each dish first. Every time a new item came around, he placed food on his own plate and then on hers before passing it across her to Bricker on her other side. He didn't even ask if she wanted what he was serving up either. When the potato salad came by, he served her two large scoops, leaving a small mountain of the snowy dish on her plate. It was soon joined by two large servings of first barbecued potato chips and then sour cream and onion. The vegetables came next, and Sam finally got over her shock at his presumptuous behavior.

"I don't really care for broccoli. I'll serve myself, thank you."

"Greens are good for you," Mortimer said, setting

another floret on her plate and following it with cauli-
flower, celery, and several baby carrots before handing
the dish of vegetables off to Bricker.

A burble of sound drew her gaze to Alex, to see that
her sister was desperately trying to stifle a burst of
laughter. Apparently she was finding his behavior entertaining. Sam was not.

"Which would you like?"

Sam blinked and glanced to the tray of meat Mortimer was now holding. At least he was going to take her
wishes into account with this, she thought on a sigh.

"I'd like a cheeseburger," she said stiffly.

Mortimer nodded and set a cheeseburger on her plate,
then hesitated and picked up the fork on the plate to
stab one of the strips of steak as well.

"I don't want that," Sam said quickly, raising her
hand to block him from putting it on her already over-
flowing dish.

"You're too pale; you need more red meat in your
diet," he said firmly.

"But I can't possibly eat all this," she protested as the
steak landed on her potato salad mountain.

"You're too skinny. Eat up." He passed the platter on
to Bricker without further comment and then turned
his attention to his own meal.

Sam stared with disbelief as he proceeded to eat. She
couldn't believe the sheer gall of the man. Bossing her
around, deciding what she should and shouldn't eat,
and then ignoring her when she'd intended to ignore
him to begin with. Somehow the evening had turned
topsy-turvy and she hadn't a clue how or why.

Shaking her head, she glanced toward Alex and then

Jo, frowning when she saw that rather than being offended for her, both of her sisters seemed amused. She could have smacked them. Neither one would enjoy being treated like a child.

"It's all right."

Sam glanced to Bricker in question.

"He's just trying to help you," Bricker said, though she didn't think she'd seen his mouth move. Sam was frowning as that realization tried to grab hold of her thoughts, but it was the oddest thing . . . the thought was as slippery as a fish, slipping out of her grasp before she could get a proper hold on it.

"Don't be angry with him."

Those words distracted her from the worry about his lips moving and Sam stared at him silently.

"Just relax and enjoy yourself."

Relax and enjoy herself, she thought slowly. Yes, that made sense. She was on vacation, after all. She *should* relax and enjoy herself, Sam thought. Feeling her tension slipping away, she smiled serenely and turned to the food on her plate.

They ate in silence at first, everyone concentrating on the meal.

"This is good," Bricker said suddenly as he took a second of the thin strips of steak from the platter. "What did you put on the steak?"

"It's Alex's special marinade," Jo announced with a proud grin. "She won't tell you what's in it so don't even bother to ask."

"It's really good," Bricker complimented again, making Alex flush with pleasure. "So is the dip. What's—?"

"That's Alex's recipe too," Sam informed him. "And

again, don't even bother to ask the ingredients. She guards her recipes like a miser hoards his money."

"She has to. It's her business," Jo said in Alex's defense and then announced proudly, "Alex is the owner and head chef at La Bonne Vie, one of Toronto's premier cordon bleu restaurants. Normally any meal she cooks would cost the earth, so enjoy."

A round of murmuring went up at that, and there were several compliments on her cooking, but Sam couldn't help but notice that only Bricker and Mortimer were actually eating the food. Decker Pimms was mostly pushing his food around his plate. There was no worry about leftovers, however; Justin Bricker and Garrett Mortimer were eating enough for four men. She saw Decker and Bricker exchange a meaningful smile as they watched Mortimer eat, but didn't understand what that was about since Bricker was matching the man.

"What do you do, Sam?" Decker asked suddenly. His tone sounded interested, but she couldn't help but notice that his gaze was on Mortimer as he asked.

"I'm a junior lawyer at a firm in Toronto," she admitted.

Apparently deciding that her explanation was too tame, Alex elaborated, "She works for Babcock, Hillier, and Bundy."

A moment of silence passed as the men exchanged questioning glances. It was obvious none of them had heard of the firm, but then why should they? Unless they'd had legal difficulties or were in law themselves, they wouldn't. Alex decided to enlighten them. "Babcock, Hillier, and Bundy are one of the most prestigious firms in Canada. Lawyers from all over the country would kill to work for them, and she was headhunted straight out of university. It was a major coup."

"It's not that big a deal," Sam said modestly when the men all turned interested glances her way. "Mostly I'm a glorified law clerk. I do a lot of research and information gathering and gofering—"

"For Babcock, the head guy," Alex interjected firmly, and then informed them, "She's being groomed for a senior partnership."

"We hope," Sam insisted with embarrassment.

"His last assistant was Bundy," Alex pointed out insistently. "And he's a full partner now."

"Yes, but—" Sam cut herself off, knowing there was no sense arguing the point. Alex was sure she was brilliant and heading places and was proud enough of her to brag about it. There was only one way to shut her up, and that was to change the subject.

Sam was trying to think of how to do that when Bricker helped her out by asking Jo, "And what do you do?"

"Oh." Jo smiled wryly. "I'm the underachiever in the family. I work in a bar."

Sam frowned at the self-deprecating claim and spoke up. "She's working her way through university getting a degree in marine biology. She's also just been promoted to manager of the bar, so she's no slouch either."

"It's no big deal," Jo insisted. "It's a small bar, a hole in the wall really. I only have a dozen or so people under me."

Sam wanted to argue the point with her, but could see she was embarrassed by the attention. Alex apparently wasn't as aware of it, however, and opened her mouth, no doubt to tell them that Jo was being self-deprecating, but Jo quickly asked the men, "What do you guys do?"

Her question was followed by a sudden silence that was almost electrifying as the men again exchanged glances. It was Bricker who blurted, "We're in a rock band."

Sam felt her jaw drop in surprise and then peered sharply at Mortimer as his fork slipped from his fingers and clanged on the side of his plate. If *her* mouth was hanging open, he was positively gaping at his friend. As was Decker, she noted, her eyebrows rising.

Bricker noted it as well, cleared his throat, and explained apologetically, "I wasn't supposed to tell. We were going to keep a low profile this week. You know. Avoid the whole fan, groupie thing and jus—awkk!" His words ended on a startled squawk as Mortimer suddenly stood, jerking him up out of his seat by the collar.

"Er . . ." Decker's gaze shifted from the women to Mortimer, who was marching Bricker across the deck. Setting his napkin on the table, he got up. "We'll just be a moment, ladies. Please go on with your meal."

"Well," Alex murmured as they watched the men form a huddle at the far end of the deck and begin to speak in hushed tones. "I think Bricker just tried to feed us a line of bull."

"I'm afraid I'd have to agree," Jo said on a disappointed little sigh. "I've heard a lot of guys spew bullshit lines at work trying to pick up girls and 'I'm in a rock-and-roll band' is definitely a bullshit line."

Sam bit her lip on a laugh as she took in Jo's despondent expression. She hadn't missed the way her little sister and Bricker had seemed to be doing a bit of bonding over the potatoes. Jo was obviously disappointed that he had turned out to be just another guy on the make.

"He could have at least come up with something a little more believable," Alex said with disgust, her gaze narrowing on the huddle of men. "I mean a rock-and-roll band? Like we'd believe that?"

"What the hell are you doing?" Mortimer growled the minute he'd dragged Bricker to the end of the deck.

"What?" Bricker asked, wide-eyed. "I was just—"

"A rock-and-roll band?" Mortimer snarled. "Dear God! Are you mad? Why not just tell them you're Santa Claus?"

"No, wait, listen," Bricker began, but Decker had joined them now and was no more impressed than Mortimer with the claim.

"I'm afraid I have to concur with Mortimer," Decker said dryly. "That was just asinine."

"No it's not," he argued quickly. "Chicks dig that sort of thing."

"Stupid ones who are gullible enough to believe it, maybe," Mortimer snapped. "But these women are neither stupid nor gullible. Haven't you been paying attention? Sam is a lawyer, for God's sake! And Alex is a restaurateur and Jo is working on a degree in marine biology. These are not stupid women likely to fall for some I'm-a-rock-star line."

"I'm afraid he's right," Decker concurred, glancing

back toward the table they'd just left. "Right now they think it was a line."

"They do?" Bricker glanced back to the table with a frown.

"Yes." Decker was concentrating on the women, obviously reading them. "They're debating whether it's just you who's the twit, or we're all bald-faced lying assholes hoping to get laid."

"Oh man," Bricker muttered and then said accusingly, "Well, they wouldn't be thinking that if you two hadn't reacted like I'd announced we were Jack the Ripper wannabes. For Christ's sake! You're both older than me. You've had to lie to mortals about countless things for centuries. I would have expected you to be better able to carry this off."

"*You claimed we were in a rock band,*" Mortimer pointed out, as if that explained their inability to follow up the lie believably.

"Girls *like* that stuff," Bricker insisted. "They find it exciting. And it's not like I said we were band members in Nickelback or something. We don't have to be *successful* rock stars. And," he added grimly, "it saves having to come up with an individual lie for each of us."

He let them consider that for a moment and then added, "It wasn't like either of you were speaking up and coming out with something."

Another moment of silence passed, and then Mortimer said reluctantly, "We really should have considered cover stories before we came over tonight."

"Yes," Decker muttered, running a hand through his hair with a sigh.

"Look," Bricker said eagerly, seeing that his argument

had a chance of winning. "I've had more experience with women. I know what they—" He stopped abruptly as the two older immortals turned cold-eyed scowls on him. Both of them were much older than Bricker.

"I mean, I have more *recent* experience with women," he corrected himself quickly. "You two stopped bothering with them a long time ago. I still . . . er . . . socialize."

Mortimer and Decker relaxed.

Releasing a sigh, Bricker went on, "We can tell them that we're a road band, an opening show for bigger bands. We've just got our first recording contract, spent months in the studio recording our first CD, and we're taking a break together up here before we go back on the road."

"Jesus," Mortimer breathed, staring at him with disbelief. "How often do you use this line?"

"All the time," he admitted airily. "And it never fails. Trust me."

Mortimer shook his head and glanced at Decker in question.

The immortal hesitated, but then grimaced and shrugged. "I suppose it might work."

"I suppose," Mortimer muttered reluctantly.

"And it would save us having to come up with alternate lies," Decker pointed out. "Besides, if we don't go with it and pull it off, we either have to erase the memory or they're going to keep thinking we're a bunch of lying losers."

"Losers?" Bricker echoed, glancing toward the women with dismay.

"If they're having trouble believing it, we can always

slip into their thoughts and help out a little," Decker pointed out, ignoring him, and then glanced at Mortimer and offered, "I'll take Sam since you can't."

Mortimer nodded, but he was scowling. He now really didn't want Decker touching Sam's mind. His attitude toward the woman had changed since he'd learned her clumsiness was due to an ear infection. The more time he spent with her, the more he realized she was an intelligent, sharp-witted woman and the less he noticed that she was overly slender, lacking in a proper bosom, and befreckled. She was clever and amusing, and he was starting to like her a little. Mortimer wasn't ready to announce that she was definitely his life mate, but she was showing possibility, and as long as there was a possibility she might do for him, he didn't like anyone else messing with her.

"I'll take Jo."

Something about the eagerness in Bricker's voice made Mortimer turn his narrowed gaze on the man. "Can you read her?"

"Yes."

"Then don't mess with her romantically," Mortimer snapped.

"Oh, come on, Mortimer. She's cute. And I think she likes me. She—"

"She's Sam's sister. I'm not going to have her upset because you acted like a horndog."

"A horndog?" he echoed with amusement, and then, grinning, asked, "So you're willing to admit Sam is your life mate?"

"I didn't say that," he snapped. "But if it turns out she is—"

"Okay, okay," Bricker interrupted. "I won't take advantage of the situation."

Mortimer narrowed his eyes on the younger immortal for a moment and then nodded. "Okay."

"So." Bricker glanced at each of them. "We're in a rock band?"

Decker glanced at Mortimer. When he shrugged, Decker shrugged himself and said, "It would seem so."

"God help us," Mortimer muttered, turning back toward the table.

Chapter 5

"So you're telling us that you really *are* in a band?" Sam asked dubiously, her gaze slipping away from Bricker to Mortimer. For some reason she was sure that he'd tell the truth here. Mortimer, however, was avoiding her gaze and concentrating studiously on his burger.

"Yes. We are," Decker assured her, drawing her gaze across the table to where he sat. Once she was looking at him, he added, "We're not that big a deal, though."

"Yet," Bricker inserted. "We just got our first recording contract and we—"

"What's the name?" Sam interrupted suspiciously.

"Name?" Bricker echoed, and she didn't miss the alarm that flashed across his face.

"Of your band," she explained dryly.

His gaze shot to each of the other men before he blurted, "The Rippers."

"The Rippers?" Decker echoed with what sounded like dismay.

Sam turned her narrowed gaze his way to find him

glaring at Bricker, but then he gave his head a little disgruntled shake and glanced back to her. Clearing his throat, he managed to say, "Yes. The Rippers."

"We've been arguing about the band name," Bricker explained smoothly. "We have to decide by the end of our stay here. We're debating between a couple of them, but I like the Rippers the best."

"The Rippers, huh?" Sam said dubiously, and glanced at Alex and Jo to find them both looking at her. Apparently, as she was the lawyer in the family, sorting out whether this was the truth was her jurisdiction. She turned her gaze back to the men, her expression considering, and then asked, "You've just got your first recording contract?"

The men each nodded in turn.

"Wouldn't you have to choose the name before signing the contract? It would have to be on the contract, wouldn't it?" The question shot out of her mouth like a bullet, aimed at Mortimer. His eyes widened, his mouth freezing mid-chew.

"The contract just listed our names and said 'henceforth to be called The Band,'" Bricker drawled, appearing to be enjoying himself as he threw the legalese around. "There was some kind of codicil about the name to be chosen by us, with the recording company's approval, of course. That's why we're here, really. We just spent three months in the studio making the first CD. We came up here for a break and to figure out what we want our new name to be before heading out on tour to promote the CD."

"*New* name?" she asked sharply. "So your band had a different name?"

"Oh yes," he assured her, and then said, "Before the contract we opened for other bigger name bands, touring as Morty and the Muppets."

This brought a choking cough from Mortimer, and Sam glanced his way to see him pounding his own chest as he coughed up the bit of burger that had apparently gone down wrong. She watched with concern until his coughing stopped and some of the redness left his face, and then turned back to Bricker and asked, "Who did you open for?"

"Oh, well, the . . . er . . ." He paused and smiled wryly. "I bet you're a good lawyer."

"Very good," she agreed calmly. "And compliments aren't going to help your case."

Bricker nodded and then said, "We've mostly toured Europe up until now, opening for bands like Oasis and the Darkness." He paused to sip at his beer and then announced out of the blue, "Mortimer's the lead singer."

Sam glanced to the man in question as he suddenly began to choke again.

"All right, that's enough," Decker snapped, leaning around to thump Mortimer on the back. "It's time to help convince them."

Seeing that Mortimer had gotten down the bit of food he'd been choking on, Sam turned her gaze expectantly to Decker.

"We're in a band. Not a very successful one," he added, making Bricker groan. "The band is called the Rippers." His lip curled as he said the name, and then he slid an amused glance Mortimer's way and made him groan by adding, "Mortimer is the lead singer."

Sam opened her mouth to shoot another sharp question at him, but the question died in her throat as Decker's gaze narrowed on her. For some reason, it suddenly all seemed perfectly plausible, and she found herself relaxing back in her seat with a nod, satisfied this time that it was true. They were having dinner with the members of the band the Rippers . . . formerly Morty and the Muppets. Wasn't that nice?

"Would anyone like some dessert?" Jo asked, and Sam glanced her way to see her smiling cheerfully, apparently equally satisfied. "Alex brought up a lovely flan with her and we thought we'd have that. I'm afraid there's no coffee without power, but . . ." She shrugged.

"Flan sounds good even without coffee," Bricker assured her, and she smiled and stood.

"I'll get those," Sam said, standing to help when Jo began to collect the dirty plates.

In the next moment, the subject of what the men did for a living was completely forgotten and everyone was getting up, collecting plates and condiments to carry inside. Without power to run the pump there was no water, which made washing dishes out of the question, so they simply scraped the plates clean and set them in the sink. With everyone helping, the table was cleared in no time and the flan and small plates replaced the earlier mess. Everyone took a piece of the sweet offering, but Sam noted again that Decker seemed only to mush up his dessert and push it around his plate.

"This is excellent, Alex. Thank you," Mortimer murmured as he finished his.

"Would you like more?" she asked, flushing with pleasure.

"Yes, please."

"I see you have your appetite back," Bricker said meaningfully, and Sam glanced curiously from one man to the other, noting with interest that the comment seemed to annoy Mortimer.

"So where is the nightlife here?" Decker asked abruptly, distracting her.

Sam smiled wryly at the question. "There isn't one, really."

When the men exchanged a glance at this news, frowns gracing each face, she added, "I mean nightlife in cottage country is vastly different from nightlife in the city. You *are* all from Toronto, aren't you?"

"What would make you think that?" Decker asked with interest.

Sam considered the question and then admitted, "I'm not sure. You just seem to be big-city types. You know, seen it all, been everywhere, bought the T-shirt and the movie-of-the-week DVD."

"I think we pretty much have," Decker said dryly, and the other men nodded solemnly.

"I suppose you see a lot while touring in a band," Alex commented.

A small silence went around the table, and then Bricker announced, "Mortimer and I are from the L.A. area."

"L.A.?" Sam asked with surprise. She wouldn't have pegged them as L.A. people. At least not Mortimer.

"Just outside L.A.," Mortimer corrected even as she had the thought. Apparently he didn't want to be associated with the city.

Bricker nodded agreement and then added, "Decker is from England."

"England?" Jo glanced at the man in question with surprise. "You don't have an accent."

"I moved over a long time ago. I make my home in Toronto now," he said, and then added under his breath, "Not that I'm home much."

"Oh yes." Jo nodded, her ponytail bobbing. "I suppose you're on the road a lot."

"Back to this nightlife business," Mortimer said, sounding a bit abrupt.

Reminded of their original question, Sam quickly explained, "There isn't much up here to begin with, but even less on Sunday night."

He frowned. "No bars or nightclubs?"

"There's a bar in the Lakeside," Jo reminded her.

"The Lakeside?" Bricker asked.

"A small hotel in town. Although calling it a hotel is rather ambitious," Sam said, thinking of the dingy little place. She knew there were rooms on the second floor but wouldn't have risked sleeping in them. "It has a bar on the main floor, but I don't know that the bar itself is actually open on Sunday nights."

"There's always the Andersons," Alex said.

"What is that?" Mortimer asked.

"Cottage party central," Sam said dryly. "There's always a party at the Anderson cottage, even on Sundays if they're up here."

"They're up here," Alex announced. "I saw Jack out in the boat earlier when I was sinking the beer and pop."

"Would they have a party even without power?" Bricker asked.

"Especially without power," Sam assured him, and then explained, "You can't read without power to keep

the lights on, or play cards, or even watch television."
She shrugged. "There's nothing to do but sit around the
fire and visit."

"Where is the Andersons' cottage?" Decker asked curiously.

"The far end of the lake."

Mortimer nodded slowly. "So we take the main road
and . . . ?"

"You can't go by car," Sam said at once.

"You can't?" Bricker asked with surprise.

"Well . . ." She paused and frowned uncertainly and
then said, "I suppose you can, of course, but I can't
direct you there that way. The only way I've been there
is by boat."

Sam glanced at her sisters in question, but both shook
their heads. No one could show them the way by road.

"But you know the way there by boat?" Bricker asked.

"Yes."

"I don't have a boat," Decker pointed out quietly.

"The girls do," Bricker said cheerfully. "They can
take us."

Sam was just stiffening at the presumptuous words
when Alex said, "We'd be happy to."

Sam stared at her with amazement. Of the three of
them, Alex was the most likely to get upset by such
presumptuousness, but she was smiling and . . . Sam
frowned as she took in her smile. It was rather empty
and vague, lacking any of the sharpness and intelligence
of the usual Alex. In fact, it appeared more like a mask
than anything. Concern claiming her, she glanced at Jo.
The two of them exchanged worried frowns, and then
Jo suddenly looked away toward Bricker and visibly re-

laxed. In the next moment, Sam herself was relaxing in her seat as her confusion melted away.

"It's all right," she heard Decker say. "Everything is fine. Just relax and go with it."

At least she thought he said that. Though the truth was, it sounded more like it was in her head than her ears. Despite that, his words seemed perfectly reasonable to her, and she felt her worry slipping away.

"Goddammit, Pimms! You too, Bricker. Both of you, cut it out," Sam heard Mortimer snap, but couldn't seem to work up any curiosity about his upset. It was as if she were cocooned inside a bubble of calm and unconcern. She wasn't even curious when the men all suddenly rose as one and moved away from the table again. She was completely happy to simply sit there staring at nothing.

Mortimer led the men to the end of the deck, then whirled to face them and snapped, "Stop doing that!"

"Relax, Mortimer, we aren't hurting them," Decker said soothingly.

"The hell you aren't," he growled. "How would you like to have your free will taken away?"

Decker arched an eyebrow at the question. "We've done this a thousand times with a thousand different mortals while working together. What makes this time different?"

Mortimer opened his mouth, and then abruptly snapped it closed, his teeth grinding together. He had no answer. They had indeed done this previously, and he'd never before had a problem with it. Reading and controlling the minds of mortals was just another tool they sometimes used in their hunt for rogues. It didn't normally bother him, but this time . . . Eyes narrowing on Decker's expression, he accused, "You've been taking control of them on purpose."

"I don't know what you're talking about," he claimed, expression innocent.

"The hell you don't." Mortimer sighed wearily and ran a hand through his hair. He was pretty sure the man was trying to provoke him into admitting that Sam was his life mate. Mortimer wasn't ready to do that yet, but he also didn't like the way Decker kept taking control of Sam. "Just stop doing it, okay?"

Decker considered him silently and then said, "If it's what you wish, I won't control Sam anymore."

Mortimer nodded stiffly.

"Does that mean we can't control Alex and Jo anymore either?" Bricker asked.

"No," Decker said at once. "It means that—if necessary—we will control Alex and Jo. However, we'll leave Sam for Mortimer to deal with."

"But he can't control Sam," Bricker pointed out. "What if she gets upset about something or asks too many questions again?"

"Then it will be interesting to see how he deals with her, won't it," Decker said with dry amusement, and turned to move back to the table.

Mortimer let his breath out on a slow sigh as he followed them back to the table. For some reason he felt like he might have just made matters worse.

"I guess we'll have to take both boats."

Alex's comment as they stepped onto the dock made Sam pause and glance over the two small boats on either side of the dock. One was a gold runabout and the other a small aluminum fishing boat. Neither would take six people.

"Surely we can all fit on one," Bricker said, moving up between them with the cooler he'd volunteered to carry. It was stuffed full of bottles of beer, cans of pop, and the last of their melting ice, yet he carried it as if it were weightless. The man was stronger than he appeared.

"There are six of us and the speedboat only sits four, the fishing boat five," Sam answered. "Each only has one life jacket per seat." It wouldn't be safe for the six of them to pile onto one boat even for this short journey. Safety first had been drummed into them from youth when it came to boating. Glancing at Alex, she shrugged and said, "So we'll split into two groups. You captain one boat and I'll take the other."

"I get the *Goldie*!" Alex blurted at once and scrambled into the speedboat. Once safely onboard she turned back, stuck her tongue out at Sam, and said, "Neener neener neener."

"Oh, very mature." Sam laughed, shaking her head as she moved to the other side of the dock and the waiting aluminum fishing boat.

"Here, I'll go first." Mortimer was suddenly there, clambering down into the boat before her. Once standing in the bottom, he turned back and offered his hand, a concerned expression on his face.

Sam had been clambering on and off boats all her life and almost shunned his help, but knew this was because of her proven clumsiness caused by the ear infection. Knowing it would be more than humiliating should she refuse his help and end up getting a dunk in the lake, Sam heaved an inner sigh and accepted the hand he offered.

"Thank you," she murmured as she stepped onto the bench and then the floor of the small metal boat, but he didn't release her until she'd stepped back to settle herself on the seat in front of the outboard engine.

Telling herself it was all her own fault for not taking care of the ear issue when she should have, Sam set about opening the tank vent on the outboard motor. Once she'd finished prepping the engine, she forced a smile to her lips that probably came out as more of a grimace, and glanced around to see who else was joining them.

The answer was no one. The dock was empty. Everyone else had followed Alex onto the speedboat, taking the cooler with them.

"Must be my deodorant," Sam muttered with disgust as she turned back to prime the engine, but knew it wasn't true. The *Goldie* was the cooler of the two boats. She'd have taken it herself had Alex not beaten her to the punch.

"Would you like me to do that?" Mortimer asked with concern when she grabbed at the starter cord and pulled it out with no effect.

"No, thank you, I . . ." Her voice died as he was suddenly there, urging her out of the way so that he could pull the cord for her. Of course, it started on the first tug for him. She'd warmed it up for him, Sam told herself, muttering a thank-you as she reduced the choke and throttle while he moved back to the center bench.

Hanging on to the tiller handle, she leaned to the side

and quickly untied the back rope fastening them to the dock. The boat tilted a little wildly in the water as Mortimer jumped up and moved to the bow to take care of that rope.

Sam closed her eyes against the dizziness that instantly swamped her, but then forced them open again and managed a somewhat sickly smile as Mortimer moved back to his seat, sending the boat bobbing about again. Apparently her smile wasn't very convincing, because his expression immediately became concerned again.

"Is everything all right? Do you want me to drive?"

"No," Sam said at once, and then asked curiously, "Do you have a pleasure craft operator's license?"

"A what?" He looked startled.

"I gather that means you don't," she said with amusement, and then informed him, "You have to have a license to captain a boat here in Canada."

"Dear God, they license everything nowadays," he muttered with a shake of the head.

Sam smiled faintly and then said, "If you want a life jacket, there are two under your bench there."

Mortimer glanced down to see the glowing orange life jackets they always kept on board. He shook his head, however. "No thank you; I trust your driving."

Sam shrugged. She didn't like wearing one herself.

"See you later guys! Much later," Alex taunted.

Sam glanced over just in time to see Alex throttle the *Goldie* and send her shooting away from the dock. Eyes narrowing, she took up the challenge and throttled the aluminum boat's engine, sending her own craft shooting forward.

"I'm sorry!" she cried, throttling back immediately when Mortimer, not expecting the action, slid off his seat and onto his butt on the bottom of the boat.

"Don't worry about me," he yelled back, dragging himself back onto the bench. "That was a challenge if I ever heard one."

Sam glanced after the speeding boat with longing, but shook her head. "This engine is powerful, but not as powerful as the *Goldie*'s."

"Maybe," he agreed. "But we don't have four people and a heavy cooler on board either."

Mouth widening into a smile, Sam nodded. "Hold on!" she warned, and sent them shooting forward again. She ran the engine full out and managed to catch up to the other boat about halfway along the lake to the Andersons. She and Mortimer both waved gaily at the occupants of the other boat as they pulled alongside. They couldn't hear the answering boos and disparaging shouts over the engine's roar, but their expressions and gestures were telling enough. Sam and Mortimer shared triumphant grins as they pulled out in front, widening the distance between the two boats. The fishing boat might not normally be as fast, and she certainly wasn't as pretty, but she'd won that race for them, Sam thought affectionately, and almost gave the old boat a pat.

"There's only room for one boat," Mortimer pointed out, his concerned gaze moving over the ninety-foot, L-shaped dock and the boats all bobbing alongside it as she throttled down.

"Alex can tie *Goldie* to us," Sam said with unconcern as she steered them toward the last open spot. It was a common enough occurrence. In another hour or so there would be several boats tied off others, and some with three or even four boats off them.

Mortimer reached out, preparing to keep them from bumping into the dock, and shook his head as he took in the scene. "This is one huge dock."

Sam chuckled at his amazement. It *was* a huge dock, five times bigger than the next largest dock on the lake, but it had grown slowly over time. Jack Anderson added another ten feet every couple of years as the size of his parties grew.

"How many people come to these parties?" Mortimer asked, his gaze moving with amazement over the mass of bodies milling around the huge glowing fire on shore as Sam shut off the engine and they coasted the last few feet up to the dock.

"Pretty much everyone on the lake and several from neighboring lakes have been here at one time or other," she said, leaning to the side to grab the dock even as he did. "Jack makes them open parties. That way no one complains about the noise."

"They don't seem that noisy to me."

"The power's out," she reminded him. "Normally we would have heard the music from our cottage. As it is, they're reduced to strumming guitars or battery-operated radios that won't play as loud."

Mortimer nodded, and they both fell silent as they tied up to the dock. Once done, he helped her onto the dock, and they both paused and turned back to watch as the *Goldie* approached.

"All right, all right, go ahead and rub it in! You beat

us," Alex called as the *Goldie* coasted up beside the fishing boat, and Decker and Bricker worked to secure the slightly larger boat to the smaller one.

"Would I do that?" Sam asked with a grin.

Alex snorted as she left the helm and moved to follow the others now scrambling from one boat to the other and then to the dock.

"Jesus. *This* is a Sunday night in cottage country?" Bricker asked, peering over the dancing and laughing people on shore with amazement as he stepped onto the deck with the cooler.

"If they're up here at their cottages they're on holiday," Sam pointed out with amusement. "Every night is Friday night when you're on vacation."

"And here I thought cottage country was all about peace and quiet and listening to crickets at night," Bricker said wryly.

"You've got a lot to learn, my boy," Alex teased as they all started up the dock.

Jack Anderson himself saw them approaching and met them at the foot of the dock. He had been a good friend and fishing buddy of their father's, and gave Sam and each of her sisters a bear hug in greeting before turning to the men for introductions. He'd barely finished assuring them they were all welcome before another boat arrived. Admonishing them all to have a good time, he then hurried off up the dock to direct the newcomers to tie themselves up to his own boat.

"Come on," Sam said, and led the group to a relatively open spot around a fallen log near the trees at this edge of the party. "This seems like a good spot. Bricker, set the cooler down there beside the log; someone can use it as a seat if they like."

She watched him set it down, frowning over the fact that he didn't look the least strained under the weight. A touch on her arm distracted her, drawing her around, and a smile of greeting claimed her lips as she recognized Margo and John Hemming, who had a cottage two doors down. They were only the first to approach. Everyone knew pretty much everyone else up here, and since this was the first time Sam and her sisters had been at the cottage this year, they were greeted like long-lost relatives. On top of that, everyone was curious about the three men they'd brought with them.

Sam suspected it was all a bit overwhelming for the men. Shortly after Bricker set down the cooler, the men had a powwow, and then Decker and Bricker slid away to mingle with the crowd. Mortimer remained behind, however. He stayed with Sam and her sisters, meeting everyone who came over, smiling and chatting and proving he could be extremely charming. The man had a sharp wit, could set everyone laughing with a mere comment, and handled it all beautifully. Still, even Sam was relieved when everyone eventually drifted away to meet and greet others, and they were left to relax and simply enjoy themselves.

"It's a pretty tight community up here, isn't it?" Mortimer said, sounding surprised as he followed her to the log by their cooler.

Sam nodded as she settled on the fallen tree trunk. She waited until he'd seated himself next to her before saying, "You kind of have to be. It's not like the city where police, fire, ambulance, and even grocery stores are near and handy. Everyone looks out for everyone else up here."

"You passed the test, by the way," Alex announced as she dropped onto the log on Sam's other side.

"What test is that?" Mortimer asked with surprise.

"The once-over by the other cottagers," Jo explained with a laugh as she laid claim to the cooler for a seat. "Why do you think we were so mobbed for such a long time?"

"Because you are three young women who are as charming as you are attractive, but you've all been so wrapped up in your careers that you haven't been up as much as you used to be and your presence has been missed," he said with a certainty that left all of them briefly silent.

It was Jo who finally broke the silence by saying, "Yeah, well, maybe, but they were still giving you the once-over."

"So you said," he murmured with amusement. "You also said I passed."

"Yes, you did," Sam assured him.

"How would you know that?"

"Because everyone was giving a thumbs-up behind your back," Alex announced in dry tones.

When he turned a questioning glance to Sam, she nodded solemnly. "Not very subtle maybe, but it works."

"Hmm," Mortimer muttered, but he was scowling as if the idea of being judged didn't sit well with him.

Jo laughed at his expression and pointed out, "This is

a good thing, Mortimer. The other cottagers can make life difficult for people they don't like."

"I'll have to warn Decker about that," he muttered.

"Later," Jo suggested with a laugh and then said, "In the meantime, if I were to go drag Bobby and his guitar over this way, would you sing us a song?"

Sam frowned with concern and began to pat Mortimer's back as he choked up the mouthful of beer he'd been in the process of swallowing.

They were all silent as he regained his breath, but the moment he seemed recovered Jo asked, "Was that a yes or a no?"

"Oh, leave him alone, Jo," Sam said. "It's what he does for a living. He'll hardly want to do it while on vacation."

"Right," Jo said unhappily, and then pursed her lips and asked him, "So what do you like to do on your downtime?"

Mortimer hesitated for a minute and then admitted, "I'm not sure. I don't get much downtime."

"Ah." She nodded knowingly. "A workaholic like our Sam."

Mortimer opened his mouth as if to protest the label, but paused as Bricker suddenly appeared before them.

"We found someone Decker thinks you should meet," he announced, a solemn expression on his face.

Mortimer raised his eyebrows, but excused himself and rose to follow the man through the milling people.

Distracted by watching the two men disappear into the crowd, Sam didn't notice the way Jo scooted over to take up the empty spot Mortimer had left until Jo bumped Sam's shoulder with her own, and said in a teasing, singsong voice, "I think he likes you."

Sam glanced at her with surprise. "Who?"

"Mortimer," Alex said dryly from her other side. "Who else? The man hasn't left your side since we got here."

Sam felt her face grow warm, but shrugged. "I'm not in the market for a boyfriend, thanks."

"Why not? You're free and single now."

Sam wrinkled her nose at the *now*. Up until six months ago she'd been engaged to her high school sweetheart, Tom Granger, but he'd broken it off at Christmas. She shouldn't have been surprised by the timing; he'd never been the most sensitive soul. Timing wasn't the only thing about him that had sucked. While he'd seemed sweet and considerate when they were dating in high school and at university, things had changed considerably once they'd graduated and moved in together.

Tom had worked a nine-to-five job as a law clerk with the city, while she'd worked much longer hours at the firm, yet she'd come home late in the evening to find him sitting with his feet up waiting for supper. When she asked why he hadn't started the meal, he'd always claim he wasn't hungry, but then he'd always been more than happy to eat her food when she cooked it. She'd soon realized that the truth was he was too damned lazy to cook and was leaving it for her to do.

He'd also offered little help with cleaning. There was no need to bother, he'd always insisted; the house looked fine. When she brought up the subject or complained, he'd claimed that her standards were just higher than his. But it had been hard for Sam to ignore that if his mom called and said she was coming over, those lax standards of his suddenly jumped upward to match her supposedly higher ones and there was a mad dash to clean the house.

Tom hadn't even been willing to do the manly-type stuff around the house. Sam was the one who'd spent her rare time off climbing a ladder to clean the eave troughs in the fall. When a pipe burst and their basement flooded, she was the one who'd had to call in the plumbers and the city to tend it, and when it came to insulating the attic of the older house they'd bought together—

Sam cut her thoughts off. Just thinking about these things upset her all over again. Every incident had left her feeling more and more on her own, as if they weren't a couple at all, but as if it was her house, her responsibility, and he was just visiting and needn't help out or take some of the burden. It had left her feeling unloved and taken advantage of.

Worse yet, while she'd been killing herself at work and doing everything around the house, he'd been running around whining that he wasn't happy, that she worked too many hours, that he hated their house with all its "time-consuming needs," and so on.

"It's been more than six months, Sam," Jo said gently, distracting her from the distressing memories.

"Yeah." Alex nudged her from the other side. "What are you planning to do? Swear off men and join a convent?"

"Maybe," Sam said, thinking the idea wasn't without merit. Honestly, men could be such a pain. The lawyers she worked with all seemed to be selfish, greedy, demanding bastards. Not unlike Tom.

"Tom was a jerk," Alex said abruptly. "Don't let him put you off men."

"I thought you liked him," she said with surprise.

Alex made a face. "He was all right at first, but by the end I was ready to strangle him myself."

Sam's jaw dropped. "Really? You never said anything."

"How could I?" she asked helplessly. "You were with him forever. Everyone thought the two of you would marry. I mean, you were talking marriage after graduation, but then you got that job and were so busy and put it off and the two of you just moved in together . . ." She shrugged and then shook her head. "I couldn't make you uncomfortable by telling you I thought you could do better. But I kept hoping and praying you'd see what an egotistical little jackass he was."

"Egotistical little jackass?" Sam echoed with a slow smile.

"Definitely," she said firmly. "He was envious as hell when you were approached by Babcock, Hillier, and Bundy. Everyone else was happy, and he claimed he was too, but you could see the resentment and bitterness on his face that it was you and not him. He was miserable about it and set out to make you miserable too."

"Really?" Sam asked, almost eagerly. She'd been obsessing over her broken relationship ever since it had ended. While she'd been angry and resentful of Tom's behavior, his insults to her attractiveness and womanliness at the end of their relationship had still hit home and left their mark. Her logical mind had reasoned that if he'd loved her enough and found her attractive enough and wanted to keep her, surely he would have tried a little harder? Surely he would have helped out. The logical answer to that question was that she had somehow been lacking and not worth his expending the effort to keep her. She truly hadn't been "woman enough," as he claimed.

"I don't think Mortimer is anything like Tom," Alex added suddenly.

Sam stiffened. She wasn't ready to get back into a relationship. She didn't want to be told, once again, that she wasn't good enough, or didn't give enough, or was insecure and needy when she tried to get her mate to help out. She needed time to lick her wounds and rebuild her self-esteem, because—sadly enough—she'd allowed Tom to take that from her. She, who had been top of her class in high school, and on the dean's list in university. She, who had worked her butt off and earned her law degree and got a much-sought-after job . . . She had achieved all that on her own, and yet eight months of living with Tom had taken away her sense of achievement, her belief in herself, and left her feeling like an unattractive, useless drudge.

Sam didn't know how that had come to pass. It wasn't like she could point to a day when he walked up and snatched it from her. It had been a gradual process; one incident after another, one letdown after another. Refrain after refrain, it had built up into an entire song—the "You Ain't Good Enough" blues.

"And Mortimer's cute," Jo said, drawing her out of her thoughts and making her mouth tighten.

"So was Tom," she pointed out dryly, and could feel both of her sisters staring at her, suddenly silent. After a moment, they both turned their attention to watching the people around them, and Sam let her breath out on a slow sigh as they let the subject drop. She was grateful for it. She was better on her own for now, Sam thought firmly. She would concentrate on her career, climb her way up the totem pole, and maybe go out dancing at the clubs once in a while with her sisters or friends to let off a little steam.

"Where are we going?" Mortimer asked when Bricker led him all the way across the sand and right out of the group of partiers onto a path through the trees.

"Decker found someone with bite marks," Bricker announced over his shoulder. "At least we think they're bite marks, but we needed a flashlight to see it better. I told him you have a penlight. You do have it, don't you?"

"Yes, of course." Mortimer reached into his pocket for the small penlight he always carried with him. It had come in handy countless times over the years, and he often wondered that none of the other enforcers bothered to get one. Maybe he'd get Bricker one for Christmas, he thought absently as he followed him into a small clearing where Decker waited with a young blond woman who looked no more than eighteen. Obviously presently being controlled, she stood docilely, her expression blank.

"We've read her thoughts, but he's blanked them, of course," Decker announced as Mortimer stopped in front of the blond, switched on his penlight, and ran it quickly over her neck until it landed on the bite marks.

"Of course," he murmured, peering at the marks for a moment before announcing, "They're fresh."

"How fresh?" Decker asked, crowding up next to him

to see the small marks under the penlight's beam for himself.

"Like minutes-old fresh," Mortimer said dryly. "Our rogue is at the party, or he was."

Decker frowned. "He might have fed and fled."

"Would one be enough?" Bricker asked, drawing their questioning glances. "I mean, she's the only one we've found with bite marks. Would that be enough to satisfy him?" His gaze shifted to the girl's face. "She doesn't look overly pale. Do you think he took enough from this one that he'll stop and leave now, or might we be able to catch him in the act?"

Mortimer shifted the small beam of the penlight to the girl's face, taking in her relatively healthy color, before shining it on her eyes to examine them. "It doesn't look like he took much at all. If he's not supplementing with bagged blood, then he'll definitely have to hit more than this one, if he hasn't already."

They all turned and glanced back toward the light and laughter.

"They're like sheep in the field with a wolf among them," Bricker murmured.

Chapter 6

"I wonder what they're looking for?"

Sam glanced at Jo with bewilderment when she murmured that comment. "Who?"

"Bricker and Decker," Jo explained. "They're checking out everyone, almost as if they're looking for someone."

"Yeah, the easy chick in the group," Sam said dryly.

Jo gave her a dirty look. "You are such a cynic. I don't think they're like that."

"Oh?" Sam said dubiously, and Jo turned back to survey the crowd, an irritated expression on her face.

"You could just use him," Alex blurted suddenly.

Sam turned a confused expression to her. "Who?"

"Mortimer," she explained.

"I should *use* him?" she asked with amazement.

"I don't mean *use* use him," Alex said quickly. "I mean just . . ."

"I think she means just have fun with him," Jo said helpfully. "You know, a little dancing, a little smooching, maybe some hot monkey sex to help you get over Tom."

"Hot monkey sex?" Sam choked out.

"Oh come on," Alex chided. "You're a liberated career woman. What's wrong with hot monkey sex with no strings attached? It's like riding a bike. You've fallen off, now you need to get back on and ride another one."

Sam gaped with horror. "I don't—He's not—I—"

Alex interrupted her stammerings to say, "Do not even try to tell me you don't like him. I've seen you looking at him, and you were sniffing him when he was fixing your arm. *And* the two of you were laughing up a storm while packing the cooler with beer and cola."

"And he's cute too," Jo inserted. "He makes me think of that soccer player from Britain."

Sam stared at her blankly, but she was thinking about what Alex had said about them laughing up a storm while packing the cooler. She and Mortimer had been assigned that task while Alex and Jo had rushed around inside the cottage gathering jackets and shoes for the girls, and Bricker and Decker had returned to their cottage to do the same. Mortimer had annoyed her by insisting on retrieving the fish baskets from the water to prevent her falling in, only to lose his balance as he leaned off the dock and nearly go in himself. Somehow the tension between them had been broken then and they'd teased and joked as they worked.

"You know who I mean," Jo said with a grimace of frustration. "He's married to that woman from that girl band."

"Oh yes! I do know who you mean!" Alex exclaimed, and then frowned. "Can't remember the name though."

Sam relaxed a little and laughed at the pair of them.

She knew exactly who they were talking about, the new player for Galaxy in America. He and his wife were making a big splash on the celebrity scene. But she had no intention of putting her sisters out of their misery. They were making her suffer enough.

Though, Sam admitted to herself slowly, Mortimer did actually look a bit like the Brit in question. Just a bit though. His features were more chiseled, and his eyes a beautiful green that appeared silvered when the light hit them. Mortimer definitely had gorgeous eyes, she admitted, and then realized what she was thinking and gave herself a mental shake.

"It doesn't matter," Jo decided. "The point is he's a hottie, a veritable McSteamy."

"Yes he is," Alex agreed. "You should use him to get over Tom. Tom couldn't hold a candle to this guy."

"I bet he's hot in bed too," Jo added.

Sam closed her eyes, shook her head, and then popped her eyes open again and said, "I cannot believe you're even suggesting this. How much beer have you had tonight?"

"Two," Jo answered promptly and held up her almost full bottle. "It'll be three after this one."

"You didn't use to be such a cheap drunk," Sam muttered.

"I've changed my mind," Alex announced suddenly. "I don't think you should have a fling with Mortimer."

Sam swiveled to peer at her in question and asked warily, "I shouldn't?"

"She shouldn't?" Jo echoed with disappointment.

"No, you definitely shouldn't," Alex said firmly.

"Why?" Jo asked.

"I don't think she can handle it. She's too much a virgin," Alex explained.

"A virgin!" Sam cried with outrage. "Tom and I had sex the first time way back in high school. God! I lived with him for eight months."

"Yes. Practically a virgin," Alex repeated and peered at her seriously. "Sam honey, you *are*. Tom was the first and only boy you went out with. You haven't ever dated anyone else. I don't even know if you *can* just have a fling. You might not have the right emotional makeup for it."

"I could fling," Sam assured her firmly and then realized what she was saying, and added, "If I wanted to." She didn't want to have a fling with Mortimer. Did she?

Before she could answer herself, the man in question returned. He paused at the cooler to collect a beer, and then moved to the log. Jo immediately scooted sideways to make room for him, and he reclaimed his position between them.

"Everything all right?" Alex leaned forward to ask around Sam.

"Oh yes, fine," he assured her, unscrewing the cap of the Alexander Keith's beer he'd selected from the cooler. "Pimms just wanted me to meet someone."

"Pimms," Sam echoed. It was the first time she could recall him calling Decker by his last name, but Mortimer and Bricker seemed to go exclusively by their own last names. She and her sisters had automatically followed the men's lead in doing so, but Sam was curious about it and asked, "Why do you and Bricker go by your last names?"

Mortimer appeared surprised by the question, and

then considered it briefly before shrugging. "I'm not sure. We just always have."

"It's a guy thing," Jo announced knowledgeably. "The guys at the bar tend to do that too, either using each other's last names or a nickname like Moose." She wrinkled her nose as she said the name.

"So, how did you guys get together?" Alex now leaned forward to ask Mortimer.

He hesitated and then said, "We met on a job."

"A job?" Sam asked with interest.

Mortimer shrugged. "We weren't always in a band."

"What did you do before you were in a band?" Jo asked, never shy about being nosy. When Mortimer hesitated, she grinned and said, "Come on, it can't be that bad."

When he merely shifted uncomfortably, she added, "Shall I guess?"

That made his eyebrows rise and amusement tug at his lips. "Be my guest."

"You'll tell us if I guess right?" Jo bargained.

A definite smile claiming his lips now, he nodded. "If you get it right. But you won't."

"That was a mistake," Sam told him as he raised his beer to his lips and took a swallow. "Jo loves a challenge."

"Yes I do," she agreed with a grin and then gained a more serious expression and said thoughtfully, "Hmm. Let me see. A job you were all on and that would bring together two men from California, and one from Toronto . . . I've got it! You were all Chippendale dancers!"

The golden liquid he'd just taken into his mouth suddenly shot out again at the very suggestion. Wiping his lips, Mortimer turned horrified eyes to Jo. "Chippendale dancers?"

"Sure. You're all good-looking guys, well-built, and each handsome enough in his own way." She shrugged, still grinning widely. "Am I right?"

"God, no!" he assured her. "I wouldn't even think of doing such a job."

"That's a shame," Alex murmured on Sam's other side, and despite how softly she said the words, Mortimer apparently heard because he actually blushed.

Sam bit her lip and quickly turned her head away to try to keep her composure. He was just so darned adorable when he blushed.

"Well," Jo said, "I was thinking that only something else in the entertainment industry could bring together three men who lived so far away from each other . . . Where exactly did you meet? L.A. or Toronto?"

Mortimer shook his head. "No hints."

"Oh, bother," Jo muttered, and then fell silent, her face screwed up with concentration. After a moment, she glanced to Sam. "Help."

Sam hesitated, her gaze slipping to Mortimer as he turned curious eyes her way. It was obvious he was interested in what she might guess. She let her gaze run over him, taking in eyes that spoke of having seen too much, and a mouth that seemed far too used to appearing solemn, and then running swiftly down over his body, which spoke of lean strength. Any one of the men could have been described thusly. While Mortimer was a blond, and Bricker and Decker both brunette, they all had the same time-weary eyes and most of the time wore grim expressions that couldn't completely be abolished by the charming smiles they occasionally flashed, or even the laughter they occasionally, almost grudgingly, gave up.

She considered that and then added the fact that each of them was a take-charge kind of guy. Mortimer had definitely taken charge when she'd burned herself, and again at the table. Since meeting the men, she'd seen hints of that character in each of them. Sam was quite sure these men were used to situations that called for action, and to being the ones who decided what that action should be. They each walked tall, with the confidence of men who could handle themselves as well as others when necessary.

"I'd have said police officers or some type of law enforcement," she said finally, and something like admiration flickered briefly in Mortimer's eyes.

"*Were* you police officers?" Alex asked, and it seemed obvious from her tone of voice that she was sure Sam was right.

"We were not police officers," Decker announced, drawing their attention to the fact that he and Bricker had rejoined them, but Mortimer stared at Sam another moment before turning to glance up at the other man. She noted the way his eyebrows rose in question, and that Decker gave a silent shake of the head, and then the silence died as Bricker commented on how friendly everyone was here and moved to drag the cooler around in front of the log. He retrieved a beer for each of the men, and then settled himself on the sand a few feet in front of Jo, leaving the wide cooler for Decker to use as a seat.

That was when the evening turned somewhat surreal for Sam. What followed was quite a long space of time when Bricker and Decker alternated with Jo and Alex in asking questions. The men were asking Sam questions, drawing her out about her past, her job, and her life. At the same time, her sisters were asking Mortimer the same sorts of questions. It was a rather bizarre situation and made her think of meeting Tom's family for the first time. What made it worse was that while she knew her sisters were grilling Mortimer because they were considering him as a prospective "fling" for her, she had no idea why the men were grilling her. That was just weird as far as she was concerned, and it made her incredibly uncomfortable. She felt like she was at a very long, very stressful job interview. So much so that she was actually relieved when she noticed Jo trying to smother a yawn and suggested they call it a night.

"Should we go let our host know we're leaving?" Mortimer asked as everyone stood and Bricker picked up the cooler.

Sam glanced around until she spotted Jack Anderson feeding more logs to the fire. She took half a dozen steps toward him, but paused when he suddenly glanced up, his eyes meeting hers. Smiling, she pointed toward the dock and then waved.

Getting the message, the older gentleman smiled and nodded back and then put his hand to his ear with thumb and pinky extended, indicating he'd give them a call. Sam nodded and then turned toward the dock.

"That's it?" Mortimer asked with amusement as he fell into step beside her.

"No. We'll have Jack and his wife, Gladys, over for

dinner before we head back home. We always do," she explained. "They hold the parties and get stuck with cleanup and then everyone feeds them most of the summer."

"Not a bad deal," Mortimer said wryly.

"No." She laughed. "Especially since everyone is pretty good about taking their empties and garbage away with them."

Alex and the others were already on the speedboat by the time Sam and Mortimer reached their boat. The men were just finishing untying the ropes they'd used to bind the two boats together, and Alex was starting the engine.

"You may have beat us here, but I bet we beat you back," Alex called over the roar of the engine as Mortimer climbed down into the aluminum boat they'd ridden over in and turned to offer Sam his hand.

Tired after the late night the evening before and the long day and evening tonight, Sam just shook her head as she stepped down into the boat. Once on board, she moved to the back bench to prep the motor as the speedboat eased away from their side. By the time Sam had the engine going, the other boat was shooting away across the lake.

"Let me." Mortimer was there beside her, taking the starter cord the moment she'd finished prepping the engine.

Distracted by his scent and the way his arm unintentionally brushed across her breast as he pulled the cord, Sam didn't protest. Instead she found herself inhaling his scent as she had in their cottage earlier. He really smelled lovely. She was actually disappointed when the engine roared to life with the first pull and he moved away to take care of the rope at the bow.

Shaking her head, Sam reached out to untie the rope next to her. She then checked to be sure Mortimer was safely back on his bench and holding on before sending them shooting away from the dock.

She didn't make the outboard go all out on the return trip, but the weight of the extra passengers in the run-about slowed the *Goldie* down enough that they still caught up to her long before reaching their own dock. Sam throttled back to keep pace with the other boat, her eyes moving over the beautiful night sky and calm lake surface as they crossed the last little distance to the dock. They didn't have the huge bonfire as a beacon to direct them home, but Sam had grown up on the lake and had no trouble recognizing their own dock in the darkness.

Alex and Jo were talking quietly with the men as Mortimer helped Sam onto the dock. It sounded as if they were giving directions to an all-night coffee shop in the next town over. Mortimer stopped beside them to listen, but Sam was tired and merely murmured a good-night and headed up to the cottage.

She'd taken several steps before she realized that Mortimer had followed. Sam paused at once and glanced at him uncomfortably.

"I thought it might be best if I walked you up," he said quietly. "It's dark and the ground is uneven, and your balance . . ." He let the words trail away, not saying what they both knew, that her balance was undepend-able at the moment.

Sam nodded and turned back toward the cottage, not

protesting when he took her arm to steer her around the half-submerged boulders and tree roots in her path.

"Do you need help finding a candle or something in the cottage?" he offered as they mounted the steps.

Sam was tempted to say yes to invite him inside, and see if he might try to kiss her, or . . . She caught herself and quickly shook her head. She wasn't ready for that. "No. That's okay. We keep the flashlights on a shelf just inside the door. But thank you," she added, pausing by the door. Turning back, she opened her mouth to say something. What it would have been, she didn't know, because it slipped from her mind the moment she saw the way his eyes were shining in the darkness. It was as if they were soaking up the moonlight and reflecting it back at her.

Like a night predator, Sam thought, and felt a shiver run up her back under her T-shirt. They stared at each other silently, and then Mortimer's face grew larger as he leaned toward her . . . or perhaps she was leaning toward him, but a burst of laughter from the dock made them both straighten abruptly.

"Well," Mortimer said, and his voice was husky. He paused to clear his throat, then turned away. "Good night."

"Good night," Sam whispered as he moved down the steps and headed toward the path through the trees bordering the two cottages. She watched until his dark shape merged with the shadows under the trees and then released a little sigh, pulled the cottage door open, and slid inside.

Sam had brushed her teeth, washed her face, and followed her flashlight beam to her room. She was changing into the overlarge T-shirt she liked to sleep in when she heard the screen door of the cottage slam. The soft murmur of her sisters' voices followed, and then faded to a silence disturbed only by the soft clicks of two closing doors.

Switching off the flashlight, Sam moved blindly toward the bed, but paused as the growl of an engine reached her through the open window. She glanced toward the neighboring cottage as headlights came to life and moved up the driveway toward the road. It seemed the men weren't ready to call it a night.

Turning away from the dark cottage next door, Sam felt for the bed, slid under the sheets, and tried to go to sleep. Unfortunately, tired as she'd been on the ride back, Sam now tossed and turned in the overwarm double bed, alternately cursing the power outage that meant she couldn't turn on the ceiling fan to cool the room, and wondering what the men were doing.

The first faint fingers of dawn were creeping up in the sky before the men returned. It was only then she was able to drift off to sleep, but it was fitful, disturbed by strange dreams.

Sam was walking along the lakeshore in front of the cottage, hand in hand with Tom as he'd looked when they first started dating. But he was saying all the things he said when he broke up with her. She was too needy, too demanding, expected too much from him. He started to tug his hand away and she tightened her hold, but his skin was as slippery as a greased pig and she couldn't hold on.

As he tugged his hand free, her other hand was suddenly taken in a warm, strong grip. Turning in confusion, she found herself peering up at Mortimer. Suddenly Tom was gone and Mortimer too was releasing her hand, but only to clasp her face in his hands and tip it up so that he could meet her gaze.

"You are the one," he said solemnly.

"The one?" she whispered, not understanding.

Mortimer nodded; the silver in his eyes almost seemed to glow as he lowered his face until their lips met. Sam held her breath, almost afraid to move. He was the first man to kiss her since Tom. Only the second man to kiss her in her life, and despite knowing it was a dream, she felt uncertain and ill-equipped for the task as his lips moved gently over hers.

Tom had never been big on kissing. He'd give her pecks, brushing his lips over hers in an almost disinterested fashion as his hands reached for other parts, and then his lips would drift away to find what he apparently considered more interesting territory. She'd always regretted that he never seemed to kiss her properly, like they did in the romance novels she read as a secret pleasure. Between the covers of those books she'd read about open mouths, wrestling tongues, and exploding passion, and had always yearned to experience that. In this dream she did.

Mortimer's mouth moved over hers once, twice, and then a third time, the pressure growing with each pass until she felt his tongue slip out to nudge her lips apart. She opened at once under the bidding and his tongue invaded, filling her with his taste.

Sam's eyes immediately blinked open, and then drifted closed as a soft "oh" of realization sounded in her throat. This then was what she'd missed out on all those years, she thought dazedly as his tongue rasped over her own and a surge of excitement rose up through her. This was . . . It was . . .

"Oh," she breathed into his mouth again, and allowed her hands to creep up around the dream Mortimer's back as he tilted her head slightly and kissed her more thoroughly than she'd ever thought possible. Where Tom's kisses had always been tepid at best, this was hot, this was wet, this was sex with your clothes on . . . and she never wanted it to end. Until it did and his mouth trailed across her cheek to her neck, where it followed the line of her throat down toward her collarbone, finding all sorts of delicious spots along the way. Her skin felt as if it were trying to leap from her bones where he touched it, as if eager to throw itself into his mouth.

It was overwhelmingly exciting, and Sam soon found herself catching the fingers of one hand in his hair in an effort to drag his mouth back to hers, in the hopes of soothing some of the excitement screaming through her. He answered the call, raising his head to find her lips once more, but if she'd thought the first kiss was the passion storm she'd read about, it was nothing compared to this one. Now he seemed to be trying to devour her, his mouth almost rough and his tongue filling her in a way that made her breasts ache and heat pool between her suddenly shaky legs.

Moaning into the caress, Sam clutched at him and gave him back some of that passion, uncertainly and even clumsily at first, but then with growing confidence and need. Wrapped up in the sensations he was bringing to bear with just a kiss, she didn't notice he was lowering her to the ground until she felt cool sand against the backs of her bare legs and through the thin cloth of her T-shirt. The cool lick of the breeze on her upper thighs and then her stomach was her first notification that he was pushing her T-shirt upward, but she didn't protest. Had her hands not been busy trying to pull him tighter, she might have helped him with the chore. Fortunately her dream lover didn't need the help. He managed to lift her enough to raise the T-shirt up to pool above her breasts without ever disrupting their kiss, and then the hand that wasn't under her back, supporting her, covered one sensitive breast.

Sam groaned into his mouth and immediately arched to press the small mound into his caressing hand and then groaned again as he squeezed it almost painfully. In the next moment, his mouth broke away from hers again. This time she didn't stop his downward journey as his mouth trailed kisses along her neck. He paused briefly at her collarbone to offer it special attention, making her shudder in his arms, and then his hand shifted down to splay itself over her flat stomach and his mouth dropped down to replace it. Sam went a little crazy as he latched on to one very excited nipple and drew it between his lips so that he could flick at it with his tongue.

Her eyes opened with disappointment when his mouth left her, but that soon turned to alarm when she realized he'd raised his head to peer at her in the moonlight. Embarrassed, she tried to catch him by the hair and draw him down to kiss her again so that he would stop his looking, but he ignored her.

When he breathed the word *beautiful* under his breath, she squirmed under his gaze, more than aware that he was lying. Tom had always said she was too scrawny and suggested she get breast implants.

"Too skinny," Sam gasped apologetically and tried to draw him down again, but he shook his head and met her gaze, eyes glowing silver-green in the dark.

"I thought so," he admitted solemnly, and then spread balm on her soul by adding, "Until now. Seeing you like this . . ." He let the words die away, and she saw the hunger alive in his eyes. He finally lowered his head to kiss her again and let her taste the excitement she was raising in him . . . and there was no doubt the man was excited. Sam could feel that excitement pressing against her hip as his chest angled over her, the cloth of his own T-shirt feeling almost abrasive against her fevered flesh.

Reminded that he was still dressed while she lay splayed beneath him, Sam found some of her usual gumption and began to rectify that. Dropping her hands to his lower back, she curled her fingers in the cotton shirt and tugged it free of the jeans it had been tucked into. The moment she had it halfway up his back, she released it to touch his bare flesh, sighing as her fingertips glided over smooth, hot skin.

Feeling bold, especially since this was a dream, she then slid her hands around between them so that she could run them over his chest. Finding his nipples, she paused to pay them special attention, smiling around his tongue when he groaned into her mouth and thrust his hips against her in response. That drew her attention lower, and she immediately slid one hand down to the front of his jeans and wormed it between them until she could run it firmly over the bulge there.

Mortimer's response this time was to growl into her mouth, the sound vibrating along his lips and tongue and then transmitting to hers, and she squeezed him again. The second caress garnered a more passionate response, and he suddenly shifted between her legs so that he could grind himself against her in an imitation of what she sincerely hoped was coming. He already had her more excited than she'd ever dreamed possible.

Alex was right, Sam realized. She was a veritable virgin . . . and she'd been missing out on a hell of a lot. Tom's breaking it off with her seemed like the best damned thing he'd ever done for her.

Who knew? The thought brought a small giggle from her lips that died abruptly, replaced by a deep, throaty groan as Mortimer ground against her again, this time thrusting his tongue into her mouth at the same time.

Alex was wrong, Sam realized suddenly. She could definitely have a fling with Mortimer. In fact, if this was just the opening act, there was no damned way she was missing the main event.

Reaching between them, she undid his jeans with hands that were trembling and clumsy, but also determined. Mortimer raised his hips slightly to aid her, and then a pillow hit her in the face.

"That must have been one hell of a dream you were having. We could hear you moaning and groaning from the kitchen."

Sam blinked her eyes open and stared, first at Alex's wry expression and then at Jo's grinning face. The pair were kneeling on the bed, one on either side of her. Jo was the one holding the pillow that had accosted her, she realized, her mind howling with disappointment at the interruption.

"Come on, sleepyhead. It's past noon." Alex slid off the bed and headed for the door. "The power's on and coffee's brewing. It's the second pot," she added dryly.

Pausing in the door, she turned sideways to let Jo slip past her and then announced, "We're starving, but can't start breakfast until you go next door and get the sausage."

"Me? Why me?" Sam asked. "What if they aren't up yet?"

Alex shrugged. "It's noon. They're probably up, at least one of them probably is. Now hurry up and get ready; we're starved."

"Well, why don't you go get it then?" she asked irritably.

"Because before we came in to wake you we voted about who should go, and you were the winner," she said with a grin and then added, "By the way, I've changed my mind again. I think you *should* have a fling with Mortimer after all."

"You have?" Sam asked with confusion. "Why?"

"Because if he makes you moan his name while awake half as much as you were doing while dreaming, it would be worth any heartache it might cause," she said dryly, and waited just long enough to see the flush of embarrassment rise up to cover Sam's face before stepping out of the room and closing the door.

Sam let her head drop back with a groan. Whether it

was for the interruption to the dream, or humiliation at learning she'd been moaning and groaning and calling Mortimer's name in her sleep, even she couldn't say at that point.

"Don't fall back to sleep," Alex warned through the closed door. "If you aren't out here in five minutes we're coming back."

Sighing, Sam tossed her sheet aside and stood up, her gaze sliding to the window. Her eyes moved over the trees that acted as a curtain between the two properties. It was still early summer up here, the foliage not fully formed, so there were little gaps here and there causing a peekaboo effect that wouldn't be there in another couple of weeks. She could see enough to tell that there wasn't a sign of movement from the other cottage.

Biting her lip, she turned her attention to finding clothes to wear, spending more time than usual over the chore. She was torn over the task her sisters had "voted" she should complete. Part of her was embarrassed by her dream and wanted to avoid seeing Mortimer. The other part was eager to see him again and wanted to look her best when she did.

Sam flushed as she acknowledged that. Even looking her best, she would never be considered pretty, but in her dream Mortimer had looked at her as if she were the most beautiful woman he'd ever seen, and some small part of her heart was hoping he might look at her like that in real life someday too.

"Fool," Sam muttered under her breath as she grabbed up the clothes she'd chosen and headed out of the room. It seemed pretty obvious that Alex had been right last night. She was too inexperienced to handle a fling. She'd get her heart broken or humiliate herself for sure if she even tried. The best thing she could do for herself was give the man a wide berth. And she would . . . right after she went over and collected the sausage.

Chapter 7

Mortimer sat up in bed with a growl of frustration. He'd been having an incredibly erotic dream and Sam had been the star. He could still feel her slender body writhing in his arms, and it just increased the ache in his groin.

He peered down at himself, not at all surprised to see the erection he sported. He scrubbed his palms over his face, half in frustration, and half in an effort to force away the memories tormenting him. He could still taste Sam on his tongue, and feel her delicious body on his skin. There was no use denying it—it was most definitely starting to look like Sam was his life mate.

The funny thing was, Mortimer was starting to think that wasn't such a bad thing now that he was getting to know her. Sam still wasn't stacked like his fantasy Jessica Rabbit, but that hadn't hindered his attraction to her in their shared dream. He'd found her sleek, muscled body rather sexy then. It had reminded him of a cat. He felt little Mortimer twitch at the memory and shook his head.

Truly he was proving himself to be fickle and contrary. One moment he was moaning about her being a gangly Olive Oyl and not at all what he wanted, and now he was eager to see her again and perhaps find an opportunity to repeat the performance they'd experienced in the dream. But for real this time.

The woman had proven to be as passionate as she was intelligent in their shared dream. Her little moans of pleasure and the feel and taste of her had driven him wild and made him desperate to plunge his hardness into her moist heat . . . which he'd be doing now if she hadn't suddenly disappeared from the dream like a whiff of smoke.

It had been a connection dream, of course. His mind had reached out while they both slept, drawing her into the erotic conflagration. That, of course, was just another sign that she was his life mate. Unfortunately she'd obviously been woken, breaking their connection. She was probably just as frustrated as he was at that moment, he realized, and wondered if there was any possibility she'd go back to sleep. If she did, they could continue the dream.

The thought made Mortimer stiffen. It wasn't very likely. She was probably up and about, but the possibility that she might was enough to make him lie back on the bed and close his eyes. He was determined to return to sleep to find out, but now that he was awake, his hunger for her wasn't the only one Mortimer was suffering.

He should have had a bag of blood before retiring that

morning, Mortimer acknowledged with irritation. He'd
fed well before heading next door the night before, but
he'd also consumed a couple of beers over the course of
the evening, and the blood he'd binged on would have
been used up countering the effects of the alcohol and
removing it from his system. He was obviously in need
of replenishing. The hunger was enough that he was
actually suffering pangs, which meant he wasn't likely
to sleep.

Muttering under his breath, he got up, tugged on his
jeans, and quickly headed out of the room.

He'd have a quick bag and then try to sleep again,
Mortimer told himself as he crossed the nearly pitch-
black rec room to the refrigerator. They'd emptied out
the tainted blood and refilled it with the blood from
the cooler the day before. He now retrieved a bag, considered a second, decided against it for now, and then
popped the bag he'd taken to his teeth as he moved to
the blinds covering the wall of glass.

At the window, he used a finger to cautiously tug one
vertical slat aside and then winced at the bright light
that greeted him. It was still god-awful bright out there.
Mortimer wasn't used to being up at midday.

After giving himself a moment to adjust to the glare,
he shifted his gaze to the cottage next door. There was
no one outside, but he thought he caught a glimpse of
movement by the kitchen window and hoped it wasn't
Sam up and about for the day. He hadn't given up hope
of returning to bed to enjoy the completion of their
shared dream. Neither had his erection. It was still
flying at full mast.

A floorboard creaked overhead, and Mortimer let the vertical blind slat fall back into place. It was past noon, but early for them. On leaving the women after the party they had spent several hours fruitlessly searching the nearby coffee shop and other places they'd hoped their rogue might frequent in his hunt for a quick bite. It had been dawn by the time they'd returned to the cottage. No one should be up yet.

Frowning, he drew the now-empty blood bag off his fangs and crumpled it in his hand as he silently crossed to mount the stairs. Mortimer stepped off the top step a moment later to see someone's butt and legs sticking out of the open refrigerator door.

It was Bricker, he realized, recognizing him despite the fact that his upper body was bent over and appeared to be crammed into the appliance. It looked to him like the younger immortal was trying to climb into the refrigerator to be with the food.

"What are you doing?" he asked.

Startled, Bricker jerked upward and cursed loudly as he smashed his head into the bottom of the freezer. He backed out of the appliance and turned, a scowl claiming his lips when he spotted Mortimer.

"Eating," he answered, and then added accusingly, "We should have stopped for something to eat on the way back like I asked. Hunger pangs woke me up."

"It was too late. The sun was rising by the time we got back," Mortimer reminded him, and then frowned at the sight of the Polish sausage Bricker held in one hand and the hunk of cheese in the other. "Those aren't our groceries."

"I know, but we'll replace them as soon as the stores open." When that didn't make Mortimer's tight-lipped expression soften, he added, "I'm hungry."

Mortimer's frown did ease at that plaintive claim. Despite having fed, his own hunger pangs were still attacking him. The bag of blood hadn't touched his hunger. It seemed it wasn't what he hungered for. His stomach wanted more food to follow up on what it had enjoyed the night before. All his appetites had been reawakened. Certainly his sex drive seemed in full swing, something he hadn't been bothered by for centuries. Mortimer couldn't even recall the woman he'd last been with, but he was still flying at half mast at that moment for Sam.

"Do you hear the generator?" Bricker asked suddenly, and Mortimer frowned as he realized the loud roar of the engine that had propelled the lights and run the refrigerator since Decker had turned it on was silent. Now that he was thinking about it, he didn't recall hearing it on returning from the party last night either.

Bricker frowned down at the Polish sausage in his hand and said, "Everything in the refrigerator feels cold. The power must be back on . . . But . . ."

"But?" Mortimer asked sharply.

"I don't remember the generator being on when we returned from the Anderson party last night," he admitted reluctantly, and then added, "And the Polish sausage tastes a little off."

Mortimer peered down at the bag in his hand with sudden concern. It had felt cold to the touch when he'd taken it out of the refrigerator downstairs, but just because it was cold now didn't mean it had been all night.

And that was just bad. Blood had to be kept at a temperature between one and six degrees centigrade; otherwise cell lysis could occur. He might have just downed tainted blood without knowing it.

That was the one downside of their method of feeding. Had he poured some in a glass to drink, he would have tasted if it was off and simply spat it out. Puncturing the bag with his fangs, however, prevented his tasting the blood.

A shuffling sound drew him from his worried thoughts to see that Decker was stepping off the stairs into the kitchen and scowling at Bricker and Mortimer as he moved to toss an empty blood bag into the garbage can. Obviously he'd stopped to grab a bag on the way up.

"What's going on? What are you two doing up? Besides waking me up, that is," he added dryly.

"The generator's not running," Mortimer said, ignoring his bad temper. "We think it might have died last night."

Immediately realizing the implications, Decker cursed and turned to head out the door. Mortimer tossed his own empty blood bag into the garbage and followed, aware that Bricker was close on his heels.

The generator was housed in a small shed behind the cottage. When Decker dragged the door open, the three men crowded inside to stare at the metal mystery that was the generator.

"It's definitely not running," Bricker pointed out.

There was a general nod of agreement and then silence as they all continued to stare at the machine. Mortimer didn't think any of them knew a thing about generators. They were hunters, chasing down rogue immortals and serving them up to the Council to punish. None of them was mechanically minded . . . except when it came to weapons, of course. Now if this was a flamethrower or something of that ilk, they'd have had it taken apart and put back together again and had it working in a trice.

His gaze shifted over the large engine before them. It didn't in any way resemble a flamethrower.

Decker moved closer to the machine, bent slightly, and cocked his head one way and then the other, appearing to examine the various gauges and buttons. After a moment of doing that, he straightened, paused, and then gave the generator a healthy kick. Nothing happened.

"I guess I'll have to call someone to take a look at it," Decker said finally, scowling at the recalcitrant machine.

Bricker groaned. "I ate tainted sausage."

"And I had some of the tainted blood," Decker muttered with disgust.

Mortimer sighed. "So did I."

While the tainted food and blood alone wouldn't hurt them, it would force their bodies to work harder to remove it . . . which meant they would need more blood, and all they had was a refrigerator full of tainted supplies.

"I'll call ABB and have them send out a fresh cooler," Mortimer muttered, turning toward the door, only to freeze when he saw Sam stumbling along the path between the cottage and the shed. The sight of her in the flesh after the dream he'd had was unsettling enough that he took a startled step back, stomping on someone's toes. Bricker's, he realized as he glanced back to mutter an apology.

"Good morning, or afternoon I guess," Sam said cheerfully, drawing his gaze as she reached them. A blush of color rose in her cheeks as their eyes met, and she looked away with an alacrity that made Mortimer smile. He suspected she was recalling their shared dream. He heard the way her heartbeat suddenly sped up as well, and that just reaffirmed his belief, as did the sudden difference in her breathing. It became shallow and fast as excitement coursed through her, an excitement he could actually smell.

"I thought I saw you guys heading back here." She sounded nervous, and while she was avoiding looking directly at him, was keeping him in her peripheral vision like prey trying to avoid drawing a predator's attention by looking straight on.

It made all of Mortimer's predatory instincts fire to life, urging him to move closer. Instead he backed farther away, forcing the other men back into the corner behind him as he fought the urges claiming him. The wash of desire in her scent made him want to smell her, to press his nose to her throat and inhale the scent gushing off her. It was nervous excitement, but more excitement than nerves.

"Is there something wrong with it? The generator, I mean?" Sam asked, shifting nervously away as if sensing what he wanted to do.

The question made him suddenly worry that she'd overheard their conversation on approaching, and he asked sharply, "Why? What makes you think that?"

"Because you're in the shed and the only thing in here is the generator," she said, as if that should be obvious.

"She didn't hear anything," Decker muttered quietly behind him, and Mortimer took a moment to scowl over his shoulder at him for obviously reading her thoughts.

"Would you like me to take a look at it?" Sam offered, sounding uncertain. When they all just stared at her blankly, she moved toward the generator, saying, "The power's back on by the way, so you don't need it anymore, but I could see if I can't fix the generator for next time."

"That's okay. I'll call someone in," Decker said, but she was already looking it over.

"I thought you were a lawyer not a mechanic?" Bricker teased.

"I am, but my dad was a mechanic with his own business. My sisters and I all worked in his shop as teenagers. He insisted on teaching us a few things so we wouldn't be helpless," Sam said and bent slightly, her attention on examining the gauges more closely.

As she did, Mortimer found himself examining her rear end. It was really quite nice. He generally went for women with a little more meat on such places; hips, butt, breasts, but there was something about her sleek lines that appealed to him. And the more he saw her smile, the more attractive he found every aspect of her.

"It's not her smile you're looking at," Decker said dryly under his breath, and Mortimer swiveled to scowl at him again, wishing he'd stop taking advantage of the situation and reading his thoughts.

"Hmm, I think I see the problem," Sam announced, and Mortimer turned back in time to see her straighten

and turn to face them. She now wore a happy, satisfied smile and Mortimer found himself focusing on her
lips as she explained what was wrong with Decker's
generator. Mortimer didn't hear a word of it, he simply
watched her lips move as he considered how clever she
was turning out to be, and damn he wished he could
kiss her right now as he had in his dream. He wished he
could kiss her and touch her, scoop her up in his arms
and carry her down to the beach where he would strip
away the cream shorts and burgundy T-shirt she was
wearing and—

"God, Mortimer, get a room for those thoughts,
huh?" Decker muttered.

"What?" Sam asked with confusion, obviously not
having caught what he'd said.

"Nothing," Mortimer said quickly before Decker
could respond. "Ignore him; you were saying something
about the . . . er . . . something or other."

Sam's lips quirked with amusement at his vague
words. "You've been standing there with this glazed
look on your face the whole time I've been talking. All
of you have. Not one of you understood what I was
trying to explain, did you?"

Mortimer glanced behind him to the men who were
each shrugging helplessly. Turning back, he said, "No."

Sam nodded and then turned her gaze onto Decker.
"Basically, your generator is old and you should probably replace it. You could have it repaired, but it would
probably be cheaper just to get a new one."

"Right." Decker pushed Mortimer out of the way,
forcing him up against Sam so he could slip through the
door. "A new generator it is. Right after I call ABB."

"Sorry," Mortimer muttered, and tried to back up and give her some space, but Bricker just pushed him up against her again as he too escaped the small building. "Sorry," he muttered again, and then reached out to catch her arms to steady her as he nearly backed her over the generator.

Eyes wide, Sam grabbed at his shirtfront to stay upright, and then bit her lip and glanced away until they were finally alone and Mortimer was able to, reluctantly, back away. She released her hold on his T-shirt at once and quickly scooted past him to follow the men.

It was full-on daylight, the sun pouring down its damaging rays. They hadn't paid much attention to that in their rush to check on the generator, but now it made the other two men hasten to get to the shelter offered by the cottage. They moved swiftly, and in response, Sam hurried too, though Mortimer suspected that was because she was trying to avoid being left alone with him.

He could have rushed ahead with the others as his survival instincts were urging him to do, but found he couldn't be that rude. Besides, the path around the house was uneven, just a dirt path beaten into the ground by years of trampling feet, and he was concerned about the balance issue her ear infection caused her. So Mortimer followed Sam, staying close enough to steady her if her balance proved shaky.

"I was sent over to grab some sausage and eggs for breakfast," she announced a little breathlessly as they reached the stairs. "I was also told to tell you that you're welcome to join us for breakfast if you like."

"Ah." Mortimer glanced up, his eyes landing directly on her bottom and staying focused there, watching the way it shifted and moved as she mounted the steps.

"Ah?"

When she paused at the top and glanced back, he jerked his eyes up with a combination of confusion and guilt—the guilt for getting caught ogling her ass, and the confusion because he wasn't sure what she was asking.

"You said 'ah' as if that might be a problem," Sam explained, her face flaming pink.

"Well, it rather is," Mortimer admitted, taking her arm to urge her across the deck and inside. The more time he spent outside, the more he was going to suffer for it. It would be hours before a fresh supply of blood could be delivered. It wasn't going to be comfortable for any of them, and Mortimer wasn't willing to add to his suffering any more than necessary and wanted to get inside. But Sam was now digging in her heels.

"What is the problem with getting our food back?" she asked suspiciously.

"The generator's dead," he pointed out.

"Yes, I know. I just— Oh," she said with realization and allowed him to propel her into the cottage. Frowning, she asked, "How long has it been off?"

"We aren't sure. We don't remember hearing it last night when we got back," he admitted.

"You're right," Sam said thoughtfully. "I could hear the murmur of your voices from my room when you got back this morning. I wouldn't have been able to had the generator been going. It's quite loud."

Mortimer nodded, but his gaze had shifted to Decker who was standing on the other side of the counter, talking on the phone. He had no doubt the man was ordering fresh blood from ABB, the Argeneau Blood Bank. As for Bricker, he'd sprawled on the couch, a tragic expression on his face and a hand on his stomach as he contemplated the tainted sausage he'd eaten. Bricker could be a bit dramatic. It was his youth. At under a hundred he was still a baby.

"Have you checked the food, though? It might still be all right," Sam suggested drawing his gaze back to her.

"The sausage was tainted," Bricker said mournfully from the couch, drawing Sam's surprised expression.

"Bricker got into the sausage and cheese when he woke up," Mortimer explained. "We'll replace it, of course. In fact, we'll replace all of the food since it was ruined because of our generator."

Sam waved the offer away. "Don't be silly. It would have been just as ruined had we left it in our cooler. But I'd best get back and let the girls know. They're hungry. I suppose we'll have to go into town for breakfast and then pick up supplies."

"Breakfast in town?" Bricker asked with interest and sat up abruptly on the couch.

Mortimer glanced at him with disbelief. A moment ago he'd looked like he was ready to write his own memorial.

"Do you want to come?" Sam asked, and Bricker was off the couch at once.

"Oh yeah. I'm starved," the younger man said, hurrying to join them.

"Bricker," Mortimer said grimly, and then nodded his head toward the windows. Treated as they were against UV rays, there was no need to close the blinds. The bright sunlight outside was plainly visible.

Bricker followed the gesture, peered outside, and then shrugged. "We can take our SUV. The windows are treated."

"Treated?" Sam asked as Mortimer glared at his partner for the slip.

"Mortimer has a sensitivity to the sun. The windows on the truck are specially coated to help with that."

"Oh." Sam turned a concerned gaze his way. "What happens? Do you break out in hives or something?"

"Or something," he muttered, and then said to Bricker, "Even if we took the SUV we'd still have to walk back and forth to the store, and we don't have any . . . er . . . medicine here," he ended lamely, unable to say *blood*.

"It will be hours before the *medicine* can be delivered," Bricker responded. "Better not to be suffering from hunger too."

Mortimer opened his mouth to argue, but Bricker forestalled him. "You probably don't remember, Mortimer, but trust me, being hungry isn't going to help."

"Bricker's probably right," Decker said. He had hung up the phone and was now moving around the kitchen counter to join them. "It's going to be dinnertime before the medicine gets here, and a nice rare steak and eggs might help. If things get too bad you can always take emergency measures."

Decker meant that if things got too bad he and Bricker could bite a mortal in town for the blood they needed. They were allowed to do so in emergency situations, and this situation could quickly turn into an emergency. Still, Mortimer was more concerned by the effect the words might be having on Sam and wasn't surprised when he

saw the confusion on her face as she listened to their conversation. Between the talk of "medicine" and "emergency measures," she was probably wondering what the
hell was going on.

Sighing, Mortimer ran a hand through his hair as he
considered what to do. In the end, his decision was made
based not on either Bricker's pleading look or Decker's
argument, but on the simple fact that he'd rather go to
town with Sam than stay here without her.

"Okay," he said, bringing a grin to Bricker's face.
Mortimer ignored that and said to Sam, "We'll take
our SUV though. You and your sisters are welcome to
ride with us."

"I'll go tell them." Sam was through the door almost
before the last word was spoken.

"While you're on your outing with the girls, I'm going
to go buy a new generator," Decker announced. "And
before you ask, no, I'm not interested in coming with
you to do so. I like to get in, get what I need, and get
out. Women like to lollygag when they shop. I'm not in
the mood for lollygagging."

Bricker smiled with amusement, but merely said,
"Why not leave that until after dark? The power's back
on now so there's no urgency about it."

"I somehow don't think the Canadian Tire stays open
until ten o'clock," Decker said dryly. "Besides, I won't
have the blood arrive, the power go out, and this batch
be ruined as well."

"Right." Bricker nodded. "Makes sense."

"Thank you, I have been known to make sense once
in a while," he said dryly and then glanced from Bricker
to Mortimer, his eyes narrowing. "You're already start-

ing to look pale. I suspect you're both going to have to bite someone in town."

Mortimer turned a firm gaze on Bricker. "Not Sam or her sisters."

"Scout's honor," the younger immortal said, holding up a hand as if giving an oath. He then moved to the window to peer out toward the cottage next door. "I hope they don't take too long, I'm—"

"—hungry," Mortimer and Decker finished for him at the same time.

Chapter 8

"I love food."

Sam chuckled at Bricker's words as she peered at the cart he was pushing across the parking lot toward their vehicles. It was stacked full of bagged groceries, as was the cart Mortimer was pushing. The men had acted like they hadn't eaten in days when they reached here, throwing everything and anything into their carts. She now saw why they'd insisted they'd need two large coolers of their own on top of the one Sam and her sisters had planned to bring, to store the perishable food for the ride back to the cottage. The men apparently had hearty appetites.

"I can't believe you bought all this," Alex said. "How long are you guys staying anyway?"

They exchanged a glance, and then Mortimer shrugged. "Awhile. How long are you staying?"

"Two weeks," Jo answered, and then added, "So you'd better not drag your feet."

Sam narrowed her eyes, scowling at her sister's teasing grin. Slowing a bit, she dropped back to walk beside her and muttered, "I'm not riding back with Mortimer and Bricker. I rode here with them. You get to take a turn for the ride back."

"Oh, but—" Jo began in protest, but Sam held up a hand to silence her. She was not going to lose this argument. While the wet dream featuring Mortimer had been extremely exciting and made part of her want desperately to engage in a real affair with the man, the other part of her was realistic enough to know she didn't have a chance with him. He was simply out of her league. Of course, he was kind and concerned when he was around her, sticking close and constantly taking her arm to steady her, but Sam wasn't foolish enough to think that was a sign of attraction. The man was just a nice guy, a protective type who appreciated their inviting him and his friends to share their meal last night, and obviously was determined to look out for her like a kid sister as a thank-you.

At least that's what she feared. Sam just couldn't believe that a man as drop-dead gorgeous as he would find her attractive. She'd decided to preserve her heart, not to mention her pride. The easiest way to do that was to avoid him as much as possible. That was why she'd suggested she and her sisters should take their own vehicle as well. Of course she'd used the excuse of needing the extra vehicle for space to accommodate the groceries and coolers. Much to her relief, Jo and Alex had agreed at once, and she thought she'd succeeded at neatly avoiding having to make the longer journey in the SUV with the men.

At this point, Sam still wasn't sure how she'd ended

up riding with Bricker and Mortimer. Well, she did, but couldn't believe it had turned out so wrong. The problem came when they'd decided to do their shopping in Huntsville. It was a forty-five-minute drive away, but also a larger town with several grocery outlets, restaurants, and fun little tourist-type shops for them to wander through.

That had been fine until Bricker had asked where Huntsville was and Alex had decided the easiest thing was for one of them to ride with the men and show them the way. Her sisters had voted Sam should be the one to ride with them, and here she was. She'd spent the majority of the ride desperately wishing herself anywhere else in the world but in that vehicle. Not that the men weren't perfectly charming and nice about it. In fact, they'd both made an effort to include her in all conversation during the journey.

With Bricker driving, Mortimer had even turned sideways in his seat to include her. They'd been entertaining and funny and made her laugh several times on the way, and if it weren't for the fact that she'd found herself inhaling Mortimer's scent with every breath, unable to look away from him, her eyes traveling again and again from his beautiful silver-green eyes, to his soft but firm lips, to his hands, which in her dreams had given her so much pleasure, and then to the chest that had looked so strong and beautiful in moonlight . . . Well, the ride had been hell, and one she wasn't repeating for the forty-five minutes back.

Nope, one of her sisters could do the return journey to Magnetawan with the men. She'd done her bit.

"I am not riding back with them," she said now, firmly.

The glare she was gracing her little sister with was brought to an abrupt end when a ringing started in her purse.

"What's that?" Jo asked suspiciously. "You didn't bring your cell phone, did you? You were supposed to leave that at home."

Sam ignored her and reached into her purse to find her cell phone. Pulling it out, she read the name, mouth flattening when she saw it read Clarence Babcock, the senior of the senior partners and her boss. Sam briefly debated not answering. She was on vacation after all.

The phone rang again, sounding strident to her sensitive ears. It might be important, Sam chastised herself. She should answer.

"It's work, isn't it? Don't you dare answer that," Jo said grimly. "You deserve a holiday as much as the next person. Sam!" she snapped, and marched off after the others as Sam flipped her phone open and put it to her ear. She simply couldn't *not* answer.

"Hello?" she said warily.

"Oh, Samantha! Good, good, you took your phone with you. Listen, I hate to bother you on vacation, but we need a quick favor of you. It shouldn't take long. Just a few moments, I'm sure. It's the Latimers, you see."

Sam's eyes widened. The Latimers were the firm's biggest clients. They were also old friends of her boss, who happened to be their daughter's godfather. But they were in Europe at the moment, and she couldn't imagine what favor they would need of her.

"Martin and Trisha Latimer are in Europe right now, but Cathy, their daughter, is up at their cottage in Minden and they can't seem to get ahold of her. They're a bit frantic so called me, and I said you were up that way and that I was sure it wouldn't be a problem for you to drop in on the girl and see she's all right and maybe tell her to give her parents a call so they stop worrying. It isn't, is it? A problem, I mean?"

Sam stood completely still. She even held her breath. Minden was more than an hour away from where they were now, and more than two hours from the cabin, which meant more than four hours round trip plus whatever amount of time it took to talk to Cathy Latimer.

Part of Sam wanted to tell him to go to hell, that this was her vacation, that she worked eighty-hour weeks for the firm, that this was some very precious time off she dearly needed and she had no intention of haring off to check on some spoiled brat who couldn't be bothered to call her parents or even answer their calls. But then her more sensible side kicked in, reminding her that her hard work had taken her from an internship to junior partner in less than a year, something previously unheard of. If she just bit the bullet and kept her nose to the grindstone, in a couple of years she would make senior partner and then she wouldn't have to work so hard, and her life wouldn't be ruled by constant running and bowing and scraping and . . .

"Of course it won't be a problem, sir. I'm afraid I'm in Huntsville right now, but we should be heading back to Magnetawan soon. Once we get there I can rent a car and drive to Minden. I should be there in . . ." She paused as if she hadn't already worked it out in her head and then said, "Let's see, it's almost an hour back to Magnetawan and then more than two hours to Minden from there . . . I should arrive there in a little more than three hours and will call you right after I talk to Cathy Latimer. Will that do?"

There was a pause on the opposite end of the phone, and she knew the man was taking note of the length of the drive and the trouble involved to handle this "small favor." Sam wasn't stupid. There was little use letting yourself be roped into these kinds of things if they didn't have a clue what they were asking of you. Her boss now knew exactly how much effort she would be expending on his behalf—on her vacation.

"Thank you, Samantha," he said finally, sounding very solemn. "I appreciate this, and I'm sure the Latimers will too. I'll let them know how far out of your way you are having to go to help ease their minds. It will mean a lot to them."

"Not a problem, sir," Sam said simply, but wondered if making senior partner was really worth all this hassle. Did she even want to be senior partner? Pushing such doubts and uncertainties away, she said good-bye to her boss and signed off.

"I didn't just hear you agree to do business on your vacation."

Sam grimaced at Alex's irritated tone and turned with a forced smile. "Actually, it's not business. It's a favor for the Latimers. Their daughter's up at their cottage and they can't reach her. I'm just going to drive by and check on her."

"You're just going to drive to *Minden* to check on her?" she asked dryly, and Sam grimaced. She'd rather hoped Alex hadn't heard that part.

"She's Mr. Babcock's goddaughter," Sam said, hoping that would ease some of her obvious anger. "And he's worried about her."

"Is Minden far?" Mortimer asked with a frown, drawing her attention to the fact that he, Bricker, and Jo had all returned with their carts to find out what was going on.

"It's about an hour and twenty minutes from here," Alex informed him and then added, "But it's more than two hours from the cottage. She won't get back from doing this little *favor* until after nine-thirty, ten o'clock, if then."

Sam frowned at this prediction and glanced at her wristwatch, startled to see that it was already four-thirty. Where had the day gone, she wondered, and then realized that it had been after noon when she'd woken up and headed over to get the sausage and eggs for breakfast. Then they'd stopped for brunch, followed by another stop at Canadian Tire for Bricker to buy the two huge coolers he was sure he and Mortimer would need to transport their food back to the cottage. Only then had they finally come here to the grocery store.

"We should get the groceries in the car," she said, trying to distract Alex from the subject. Her sisters were worried about her, about the hours she worked and the pressure she was under. It was part of the reason they'd planned this two-week trip with her to open the cottage. It was supposed to force her to take a vacation. They'd talked her into booking the time off months ago, when she'd been delusional enough to think she'd be out from under by now.

Sam grimaced at the thought. She'd been as deeply buried in work by the time the vacation had come around as she had been before and had actually considered canceling the vacation in favor of work. The very suggestion had spurred such upset and anger in her sisters that she'd quickly changed her mind.

"I can take her."

Sam glanced at Mortimer with confusion. Had she heard him right? She wasn't sure. He wasn't looking at her. He was talking to her sisters.

"We can load the groceries and ice into the coolers and—if you don't mind taking Bricker and the coolers back with you—I can take Sam to Minden in the SUV. It'll be faster this way. It'll cut at least two hours out of the trip."

Like magic, all the stiffness and anger in Alex and Jo seemed to evaporate.

"Okay," they both agreed cheerfully, and then Alex said, "We'd best get these groceries in the coolers then."

Sam watched the quartet head for the cars and shook her head with bewilderment, wondering when she'd lost control of her life. Everyone seemed to be making decisions for her. She briefly considered refusing Mortimer's kind offer, but then realized she'd be cutting off her nose to spite her face. Accepting his offer *would* cut two hours off the journey. It also soothed Alex's temper.

Mind you, it meant she'd have to spend three and a half hours or more trapped in a car with Mortimer . . . That was rather dismaying, Sam thought, and almost called out to them to decline the offer after all, but then Bricker turned and smiled at her and said, "Everything's fine. It will be all right. Relax and enjoy his company."

Sam nodded slowly. Bricker was right, everything would be fine, but she had to wonder how he kept talking to her without his mouth moving. Perhaps she needed to get her eyes checked, she thought a little fuzzily, and crossed to help move the men's two coolers to Alex's Matrix and then unload the groceries into them. It was done amazingly quickly, and then she found herself in the front passenger seat of the SUV doing up her seat belt.

"Your sisters are worried about you," Mortimer commented as he started the engine.

"Yes," Sam agreed on an unhappy little sigh. The truth was, sometimes she worried herself. Everyone she worked with worked hard and kept long hours, but she had no idea how they coped. The stress was starting to get to her.

"They think you're ruining your health for this job," he added, sounding a tad unhappy himself.

"It's a career, not a job. And I only have to work this way until I get a senior partnership. Then I can slow down and let junior people do the grunt work."

Mortimer nodded solemnly, but then asked, "Is it worth it?"

Sam frowned. That was a question she often asked herself. She enjoyed the law, and for the most part, loved her job. Except for the long hours. And while she told herself that once she'd gotten a senior partnership, she could slow down and let juniors and interns do the work for her as her own boss did, she didn't know that she'd actually be able to. She'd be afraid they'd miss something and would simply double-check everything herself anyway. Sam had issues with control and knew it. Besides, having been there, she'd feel bad piling work on underlings like her own bosses did to her. Everyone deserved a life.

Releasing her breath on a small sigh, Sam shook her head. "Let's talk about something else."

Mortimer was silent for a moment as he negotiated traffic, but then nodded. "All right. For now."

She blinked in surprise at the proviso, but he was already asking, "What do you want to talk about?"

Sam hesitated, her mind seeking a safe subject to discuss, but none of them seemed safe, at least not to her. Every possible subject her mind was tossing up had to do with the man next to her, his life and his likes and dislikes. The worst was the recurring question, Did he like her? Did he find her at all attractive? Could he see himself having a fling with her? Would he please kiss her? Touch her? Make her body weep for him as it had in her dream?

Definitely not safe subjects, Sam decided. Aware that Mortimer was glancing at her curiously, she cleared her throat and said, "I don't know. How do you like it up here so far?"

"I like it," he said easily. "It's quiet and peaceful and surprisingly relaxing."

"I suppose it makes a big change from what you're used to in L.A."

"I don't spend much time in L.A. anymore," he said quietly.

"Do you have a house there?" Sam asked curiously.

"Bricker and I share an apartment, but considering how little time we spend there, we really shouldn't bother," he said wryly. "We stop in L.A. occasionally to visit family on holidays and so on, but mostly we're on the road."

"Oh yes, touring with the band and such," she murmured, considering what he'd said. Mortimer often referred to he and Bricker doing this, or he and Bricker doing that. She wouldn't have thought it odd since they were in a band together and therefore probably worked and played together . . . except that it was always he and Bricker and not he, Bricker, and Decker. The way he spoke made it sound almost like they were partners, she thought with a frown, and then her eyes widened with horror as she wondered if they *were* partners. A gay couple.

Dear God, it would be just like her to be interested in a gay man. And it was more than possible, she realized with dismay. Sam already knew she was completely lacking in gaydar. One of the lawyers at the firm was apparently gay, but she hadn't had a clue until her secretary had commented on how handsome and nice he was and it being such a shame he was gay. Sam had spent the last year just thinking his life partner was a roommate and friend until that point.

Now that the thought was in her head, Sam couldn't shake it. It hung there at the back of her mind like a bat waiting to unfurl itself and fly madly about inside her skull. Mortimer tried to start several conversations, but Sam had difficulty responding in more than one-word answers. He eventually gave up and left her to her thoughts.

Sam was sorry he did because now she found herself examining every little thing he'd said and every moment she'd seen the men together. She was also feeling horrible about the hot dream she'd had. Despite the fact that he couldn't know about it, she felt as if she'd molested him in some way. Mental rape of her poor gay neighbor. Dear God!

"Do you think they have a restaurant or coffee shop around here?" Mortimer asked suddenly, drawing her from her unpleasant thoughts. "I could do with something to eat."

Sam glanced around to see that they had arrived in Minden. They were driving past a large Independent grocers. Frowning, she admitted, "I'm not sure. I've only been here once and that was with my parents when we were kids. I'm sure they must have something."

A restaurant stop was probably a good idea. She was a bit hungry herself and could use a washroom break. Sam glanced along the businesses spread out on the street and then gestured ahead on their right as she spotted a plaza on the corner with several shops in it.

"There might be someplace there where we can stop."

"Good," Mortimer said with relief. "We can stretch our legs, grab a bite to eat, and look at the map to see where we have to go to find these Latimer people. Do you have the address?"

Sam nodded. Her boss hadn't thought to give it to her, but she knew it. She'd spent the first three months of her internship on a case for the Latimers and was constantly couriering papers to them at the cottage. She had written the address down so often, she didn't think she'd ever forget it. "I'll find it on the map while we're eating."

Nodding, Mortimer turned into the plaza.

They had their choice of a pizza joint or a small restaurant that served fish and chips and other simple foods. They chose the restaurant. Mortimer and Sam placed their orders at the counter and then each headed for the washrooms. Mortimer had already returned and found them a table by the time Sam reentered the dining area. He was peering down at the map book and didn't notice her arrival, so she took the opportunity to look him over as she approached, desperately seeking some sign of his sexual preference. Unfortunately, she didn't see anything that she recognized as either gay or nongay. The man wore the standard attire of jeans and a T-shirt; had short, kempt dirty-blond hair; and was clean-shaven. That didn't tell her anything, Sam thought, and then frowned as she noted that he was also very pale.

Mortimer glanced up as she scooted into the opposite side of the booth, his eyebrows rising in question as he noted her frown. "What's up?"

"You look pale," she said with worry. "Are you not feeling well?"

Mortimer hesitated and then looked away with a shrug. "I'm fine. Food will help."

His answer made her wonder if he wasn't diabetic or suffering some other ailment that affected his system, but before she could ask, they were interrupted by the arrival of their food, and she decided to let the question go for now. It wasn't like Mortimer could answer with his mouth full, and the man kept his mouth full until every last scrap of food on his plate was gone. He and Bricker certainly had good appetites, Sam thought, and then frowned as she realized they were now paired in her head. She couldn't seem to think of one anymore without the other coming up in her thoughts. In her mind, she was already convinced she was lusting after a gay man.

"Are you gay?" Sam hadn't meant to ask that, at least she wouldn't have done it so bluntly, but the words popped out before she could stop them. She then closed her eyes in dismay at her own behavior before opening them slowly to see Mortimer gaping at her with some dismay of his own. Whether it was because he wasn't gay or because she'd asked the question at all, she couldn't tell, and said apologetically, "I'm sorry. Really, terribly sorry. It's none of my business if you are, and I don't have any issue with homosexuality. I'm happy to be friends with you and Bricker. I—" Sam's apology ended on a gasp as he suddenly stood up, caught her hand, and used it to drag her from the booth.

"Really, I didn't mean to offend you," Sam babbled as he tugged her across the restaurant and out the door. "It's all right if you are. I would just like to know, because . . ." She brought her words to a halt before she could blurt that she liked him, and then quickly said, "Because Jo seems to be a little interested in Bricker and I wouldn't want her to be hurt because—" Her words died abruptly on another gasp, this time because she'd stumbled on something in the parking lot and tripped.

Mortimer immediately slowed, dropped her hand, and grabbed her around the waist, pulling her against his side for the last few feet to the SUV. He opened the passenger door and tried to hustle her into the vehicle, but Sam prevented it by putting a hand on the door and whirling to face him. "Please don't be angry, I just wanted to know."

She was silenced this time when his mouth came down on hers. Sam froze. As in her dream, this was no mere pecking or brushing of lips, this was a *kiss*; hungry, demanding, and all-consuming. Mortimer cupped the back of her head with one hand, holding her in place as he proved that he was definitely not gay. Well, unless her boyish figure misled him into thinking she was really a Sam and not a Samantha, she thought fuzzily, and then gave up that thought as his free hand moved to cover her breast through the cotton of her burgundy T-shirt.

Sam moaned into his mouth and pressed closer against him as he kissed her. It was just like her dream, and her body responded accordingly, her nipples immediately coming to attention and her thighs squeezing together as heat began to throb between them. She felt the frame of the SUV door press into her back as he urged her backward, and then the hand at her head dropped away to clasp one cheek of her behind and urge her forward to grind against him. Sam found herself clutching at his shoulders as she desperately fought the urge to wrap her legs around his hips and urge him on. She hadn't completely lost her mind, however, and some part of her mind was telling her that he was just trying to prove the point that he was not gay. Sam tore her mouth away and turned her head to prevent his kissing her again as she gasped, "Okay. You aren't gay. You don't have to—"

"I want to," he growled, urging himself against her so that she could feel just how much he wanted to as his mouth settled on her throat for want of her lips.

"Oh," Sam breathed as his hardness pressed into her. He definitely wanted to, she acknowledged as his mouth burned a trail along the vein in her throat. And she wanted to too, desperately, but they were standing outside, for crying out loud, and it was still daylight out, and they were in plain view of anyone who cared to look.

A point that was driven home when wolf whistles and catcalls reached her ears. Sam wasn't the only one to hear. Suddenly Mortimer was thrusting her away and turning her toward the SUV. "Get in."

Sam climbed dutifully inside, her eyes shooting out the windshield to find a trio of young men grinning and still calling out lewd suggestions as they moved to the door of the restaurant.

"I forgot the map book inside; I'll be right back," Mortimer said, and then closed the door behind her and followed the men into the restaurant.

Sam stared after him, marveling that he looked so calm and composed after that passionate embrace when she felt completely flummoxed. For several moments, she simply sat there enjoying the tingling radiating through her body, but then she began to worry. First she worried that there might be trouble in the restaurant with their trio of hecklers. She no sooner convinced herself that he was an intelligent, seemingly even-tempered guy and it would be fine, when she began to worry about his return. How was she supposed to act after the passionate embrace they'd just shared? Were they a couple now?

That question made her groan inwardly. That she could even ask herself that after one kiss just proved that Alex's worries were founded. Despite Tom, she was definitely a virgin when it came to affairs, Sam acknowledged. A kiss did not mean they were a couple nowadays. Heck, even having sex didn't mean that anymore. People had one-night stands all the time, never for a minute imagining they were a couple. She really wasn't ready for this fling business. What was she doing? And what was taking Mortimer so long?

Mortimer was relieved to see the map on the table where he'd left it. He retrieved the item, but didn't immediately head back out to the SUV. It wasn't the main reason he'd returned—it was just a handy excuse. The fact was, Mortimer had been seconds away from sinking his teeth into Sam's neck and feeding the hunger that was presently twisting his stomach when the catcalls and whistles had reminded him of where he was and what he was doing.

He hadn't kissed Sam with the intention of biting her. He'd kissed her because of her question as to his sexual orientation. It had first shocked him, and then he'd found himself a tad outraged that the woman he was lusting after was doubting his sexual preference. Then he worried that if she thought he was gay, she wouldn't be interested in him as he wanted her to be, and hoped she was.

Somehow all of that had culminated in the he-man tactic of "showing" her where his interests lay. The kiss. He'd only meant it to be a quick, demonstrative caress, but the moment he'd tasted her on his lips, it had turned into more. And when she'd responded, his good intentions had flown out the window altogether. The woman was as much a powder keg out of their dreams as she was in. Her response had been eager and passionate, making him lose his head entirely. Mortimer had let his hands begin to wander, his mind filling with images of ripping her clothes off and making love to her against the SUV. But then she'd broken the kiss and turned her head away.

When Mortimer had trailed his mouth down her neck and felt the vein pulsing with excitement there, his passion had briefly been waylaid by another hunger—his desperate need for blood. And he *was* feeling pretty desperate at the moment.

Despite their best efforts, he and Bricker hadn't been able to completely avoid exposing themselves to sunlight today. While he'd worn jeans rather than the more comfortable shorts to help avoid as much exposure as possible, a long-sleeved shirt would have seemed odd on what was a hot summer day, so his arms, hands, and face had been exposed. And while they'd been safe enough from the damage of UV rays in the SUV, every stop they'd made that day had meant at least a short walk under the sun's punishing glare.

All that, combined with his body's need to deal with the alcohol the night before and the tainted blood he'd consumed when he woke up at noon, had left him dehydrated and in serious need of blood. This was one of those emergencies when his people were allowed to feed "off the hoof" and bite mortals. But Mortimer wouldn't feed on Sam. He couldn't control her, so he couldn't erase the memory of his biting her afterward, and it was much too soon to reveal what he was to her and hope she could accept it without running screaming into the night.

No, he couldn't bite Sam. He needed another donor. Mortimer's gaze slid around the restaurant, noting and discounting various customers before his gaze landed on the trio of laughing young men who had so rudely interrupted them outside. Mortimer considered each briefly, then chose the one who looked healthiest and slipped into his thoughts. Within seconds the lad was excusing himself and making his way to the men's room.

Mortimer followed.

Chapter 9

Sam was sufficiently worried at the length of time Mortimer was taking to retrieve the book that she seriously feared he'd gotten into a mix-up with their hecklers after all. She was actually reaching for the door handle to get out of the car when he finally appeared.

Releasing the door handle with relief, she watched him walk to the car. There was no sign that he'd been in any kind of a confrontation; he looked perfectly fine. In fact, he looked better than he had before he'd gone in. Certainly he had more color than he'd had when he left her.

"Here you go," Mortimer said, opening his door and handing her the map book as he got behind the wheel. "You can be the navigator."

Sam accepted the book and quickly began to leaf through the pages, relieved to have something to do besides thinking about their kiss. She buried her head in the atlas and concentrated on finding the Latimer cottage.

"It looks like we have to go back the way we came

in," she announced once he'd started the engine and she felt him looking at her.

Only when he turned his attention to shifting the SUV into drive and began to back out of the parking space did Sam risk a quick glance in his direction. However, she immediately returned her gaze to the map when he glanced her way.

"Are you all right?" Mortimer asked quietly as he steered them onto the road.

Sam looked up sharply to find his eyes fixed on her mouth. She supposed he was asking whether she was all right about their having kissed, and felt at a loss as to how to answer.

"I— Yes, of course," she muttered finally, flushing with embarrassment as she met his gaze briefly and then reluctantly asked, "Are you?"

"Oh yeah," he murmured with what almost sounded like glee.

Between that and the satisfied smile on his face, Sam found a reluctant smile curving her own lips. It froze there briefly when he suddenly took one hand from the steering wheel and reached out to clasp her hand in his. Sam didn't pull away, but simply stared at their entwined fingers, confusion rife within her. *Were* they a couple now? Dear Lord, this was all so new and confusing. She hadn't had to face modern dating with all its uncertainties and rules since her teens. If there even were rules anymore.

"How long do we stay on this road?"

Sam gave a start and then forced herself to look around. They'd passed the Independent grocers again and were now traveling away from town. She turned her attention back to the map to trace their route. "You'll turn right in just a few minutes, I think."

Sam glanced up to read the sign of the next road they came to, her eyes widening as she read the name. "Here. Turn right here. We take this to the end and then take a left," she told him, considering the map, a bit more comfortable now that he wasn't holding her hand. Sam didn't think she'd be wholly comfortable again, however, until she was safely back at the cottage with her sisters. And without Mortimer around. She wished she was there now. She wanted time to process what was happening and figure out what she wanted. But if life had taught her nothing else, it was that you didn't always get what you want.

Several moments later they were turning onto the long driveway of the Latimer cottage. It was paved rather than the bumpy dirt lane most cottages up here had. Sam wasn't surprised to hear Mortimer blow through his teeth in an almost silent whistle as the last line of trees finally cleared away.

"Nice," he said dryly.

Sam merely stared. It wasn't a cottage, it was a bloody mansion, but then she hadn't expected any less of the Latimers. They were wealthy and liked to spend that wealth. And why not? They couldn't take it with them when they died.

"Is that the daughter's car?"

Sam followed Mortimer's gesture and saw the little red sports car sticking out around the side of the house.

"Yes," she said with relief and reached for the door

handle. This would be quick and easy. She just had to tell Cathy to call her parents and they could leave. Easy, she thought as she opened the car door.

"You can wait here if you like. I should only be a minute," Sam said as she got out.

Mortimer's answer was simply to get out on his own side and move around the car to join her in the walk to the front door of the house. Back door, really, she supposed. Up here the part of the house facing the lake was considered the front of the house.

Shrugging that absent thought away as they arrived at the double doors, Sam reached for the doorknob, only to stiffen when the brush of her fingertips sent it swinging open. It hadn't been closed all the way.

Before she could quite wrap her mind around that realization and what it might mean, Mortimer was catching her by the waist. He pulled her quickly back and to the side, setting her out of the way so that he could move forward.

"Wait here," he hissed, and then slid through the opening and disappeared.

Sam stared wide-eyed after him for one stunned moment. Tom never would have manned-up like that and taken control. He would have let her lead the way. It was kind of nice to have someone looking out for her.

And frustrating, she decided in the next breath. She wanted to know what was going on inside and couldn't tell from her safe spot on the stoop. Sam shifted impatiently, but simply couldn't be a good girl and wait outside while the big he-man investigated. This was her job anyway. She was the one who'd been asked to check on

Cathy Latimer, Sam reminded herself as she followed the path Mortimer had taken and slid through the open door.

Sam heard the soft strums of music the moment she stepped inside. A radio was playing, she realized, her eyes sliding over the luxurious space before her, taking in the gleaming marble floors and double curving staircases on either side of the large white foyer.

Dear God, the Latimers didn't have a clue what cottaging was, Sam thought, her mouth hanging open as she moved as silently as possible across the entry.

The foyer gave way to a huge open room with a wall of glass facing out over the lake. The view was breathtaking and made her stop and stare before she reminded herself why she was here. Dragging her eyes away from the incredible view, she cast them over the living area, noting the open television guide on the coffee table in front of the couch, a jacket tossed over the back of the couch, and a large beach towel strewn over a bar stool along the breakfast bar separating the living area from the large kitchen.

Sam moved instinctively to the bar stool and felt the towel to find it dry but with bits of grit and sand on it. It had been used, either to sunbathe or to dry off with, but had since dried.

Releasing it, she moved around the bar to peer over the kitchen. A full glass of what appeared to be cola sat on the counter, the liquid at the top of the glass a bit clearer, as if it had been poured over ice and that ice had melted. She often let drinks sit untouched until the ice melted in the glass, so recognized the signs. Her gaze slid to a plate with an uneaten sandwich on it. Cheese was sticking out beyond the crust, and Sam frowned as she noted it was dried out and a bit hard-looking.

It looked as if Cathy had come in from the beach, poured herself a drink, and just finished making a snack when something or someone had interrupted her.

Sam moved reluctantly forward, peered at the cheese, and then poked at it gently. It was turning a darker shade and growing hard.

"I thought I told you to wait outside."

Sam nearly leaped out of her skin when that sharp comment broke the silence. Turning, she shot a scowl at Mortimer. "*I* am the one who was supposed to come check on her, not you," she reminded him, and then forced her scowl away. "Is she here?"

A combination of worry and relief coursed through her when he shook his head. The relief was because, as silent as the house was and with the uneaten snack in the kitchen, she feared that had Cathy been there, she wouldn't have been in good shape. The worry was because it meant Cathy Latimer was missing, and the open door and uneaten snack suggested unusual circumstances. Probably not good unusual circumstances either, but movie-of-the-week-type stuff.

Sighing, she moved out of the kitchen and crossed the living area to a hallway leading to the rest of the house on this floor.

"I checked every room," Mortimer assured her, following as she toured the main floor, moving quickly along the hall to peer into a library, a media room, a dining room . . . "There's no one here."

"I know. I'm not looking for anyone," Sam replied,

turning back the way she'd come and then he
to the second level.

"What are you looking for?" Mortimer asked, jog
ging up the stairs behind her.

"Her . . ." Sam paused as she swung open the first
door and found herself looking at a room that appeared
to have been hit by a cyclone. Letting her breath out,
she finished, ". . . bedroom."

Mortimer followed her into the room, his gaze moving
over the chaos as he proved he had looked up here too
by admitting, "I figure she was attacked in here."

"Attacked?" Sam turned on him with surprise.

"Well, she's missing and—" He gestured around the
room as if that said it all.

Sam shook her head. "This isn't because of an attack;
this is just barely-twenty-and-still-as-lazy-as-a-teen
living."

When he raised his eyebrows, she confessed, "My
room used to look like this."

"Used to?" he asked, eyes suddenly narrowing.

"Hmm." Sam nodded and wryly admitted, "I had a
habit of just throwing my clothes on the floor. Then one
year—in the midst of final exams—I discovered how
handy it was to use a clothes hamper and not be stumbling over clothes when I got home from the library in
the wee hours, exhausted from cramming."

"Ah." He smiled faintly, but remained silent as she
crossed the room back toward him.

"I suppose I should report this."

Mortimer nodded and straightened away from the
doorjamb to allow her to pass. "I saw an O.P.P. building on the way into town."

"O.P.P.?" Sam paused and glanced back at him with surprise at the mention of the Ontario Provincial Police.

"Yes." He frowned and considered her expression and then asked, "Isn't that who you meant to report to?"

"No, I was thinking of my boss," she admitted, biting her lip now. She'd intended to go downstairs and use the phone she'd seen in the living room. Now, however, Sam realized that perhaps reporting to the O.P.P. might be better. They might actually know what had happened to the girl. It might be that she'd simply been in a car accident, or . . . Well, all right, the car accident bit was out with her car here, but maybe an ATV or even a Sea-Doo accident. The emergency response team may have been called in and in their rush left the door open . . .

It didn't seem likely, but, on the other hand, it did seem better to check in with the O.P.P. and make sure Cathy Latimer hadn't been in an accident or something before calling her boss and starting some sort of panic. Besides, he'd probably send her to the O.P.P. anyway.

Letting out the breath she'd unconsciously been holding, Sam nodded. "Yes, we'd better report to the O.P.P. first."

Mortimer ushered her from the room and followed her back downstairs. They were walking to the door when she spotted the purse on the table in the entry. Sam stopped but didn't touch it. She'd seen enough crime shows to know you weren't supposed to touch anything at a crime scene, and this might very well be one. She did try to look inside though. Unfortunately, it had folded over on itself, and she couldn't see inside. Her gaze slid to the keys next to it, and after a hesitation, Sam did pick those up. She simply couldn't see walking out and leaving the house unlocked. Crime was low up here but it wasn't unheard of, and leaving the door unlocked was just inviting trouble.

The third key she tried locked the front door. Sighing with relief, Sam smiled a little stiffly at Mortimer and then dropped the keys in her purse as he walked her to the SUV.

Mortimer didn't like Sergeant Belmont from the moment the tall, gray-haired man came strutting out of a door at the back of the reception room at the O.P.P. headquarters and sauntered to the front toward them. He liked him even less after five minutes of watching him treat Sam like a panicky female fretting over nothing.

"I'm sure your friend is fine," the man repeated for the third time, interrupting Sam's attempts to explain for the third time as well. He added, "We'll fill out and file a report, but there's no sense doing anything beyond that. She'll probably turn up in a day or two, hung over and full of tales of some new guy she met."

"Are you even listening to me?" Sam asked with disbelief. "The front door of the house was unlocked and ajar. Her purse was on the table, the radio was on, and there was an uneaten sandwich—"

"So she changed her mind about eating a sandwich and headed out to a friend's instead," the man interrupted condescendingly. "That's no call to get everyone in an uproar,"

"Her parents haven't been able to contact her for several days," Sam said grimly.

"Well then maybe she's run away," he said with unconcern. "That happens in these parts. Little local gals see the cottagers coming up here year after year with their fancy cars and ATVs and Sea-Doos and Ski-Doos and the money they flash around, and suddenly their poky little hometown starts to looking boring and they start yearning to head to the big city with dreams of making it big as a singer or actress or model or some nonsense and living the big life they see all these cottagers live. That's probably what your friend has up and done too. Run off to find the big-city lights."

Mortimer was about to take control of the man's mind and convince him he needed to do more than file a report when he noticed the way Sam's eyes had narrowed. She was mad, and he suspected Sergeant Belmont was about to meet his match.

"Are you new up here, Belmont?" she asked sharply, eyes narrowed on the man.

The sergeant's expression became somewhat suspicious, as if he thought this might be a trick question, but after a moment he hitched his pants up and nodded slowly, "As it happens, I was transferred here last month."

"Right," Sam said grimly. "That explains a lot."

"What does it explain?" Belmont asked with a frown.

"Why you've no idea who I'm talking about," she snapped. "Let me rectify the situation. Cathy Latimer is a cottager, not a local running away to escape her small-town life. She also isn't a teenager, but is the twenty-year-old daughter of a very wealthy businessman *whom my law firm represents*," she added pointedly. "She drives a sports car, lives in her parents' mansions, and has all the money she could want. She has not run away to the big city. She *lives* in the big city and came here to get away from it for a bit. Now she's missing."

A moment of silence passed as Belmont blinked repeatedly, digesting the change in her attitude from respectful complainant to cold, hard lawyer. But Sam wasn't finished. "Her parents have important friends, Belmont. They include the Ontario Provincial Police commissioner. You do not want me reporting to Martin Latimer that you aren't using due diligence in looking into this matter. I can guarantee you the first thing he'll do is give the commissioner a call . . . and then you'll find your ass in a sling." She paused a moment more to let that sink in and then added, "I suggest you do all you can to find Cathy Latimer."

Mortimer wasn't at all surprised to see the dismay on Belmont's face. He was a little surprised, however, at how quick the sergeant could move when he wanted. The way he'd leaned on the counter since they'd arrived hadn't suggested he was much of a mover. The man who now tugged his gun belt up higher on his hips, and turned for the door bellowing orders to officers who suddenly appeared in the open doorways, was definitely moving, however.

"Get all the information you can from the lady, Constable Mack," Sergeant Belmont barked to the first man who stepped into the room. "I'm heading out to the Latimer house to look the situation over."

"Sergeant Belmont," Sam said, sweet as pie now that she'd gotten the man going. When the officer stopped and glanced warily back, she held up the keys she'd taken from the Latimer house. "You'll need these to get into the house. I took them off the table by the door so we could lock it."

Mouth tightening, he walked back to collect the keys and then hurried out of the building.

"I knew the sergeant had met his match when I saw the two of you pull up and get out of the SUV. Thing is, I thought you'd be the one to put him in his place."

Mortimer glanced to the speaker—the Constable Mack that Belmont had barked at before leaving—and smiled faintly in response to the grin on the young officer's face. Shrugging, he said, "She didn't need my help in the end."

"No, she sure didn't," he agreed with a soft laugh. "That's one lady who can take care of herself. I bet she's killer in the courtroom."

Mortimer's eyebrows rose at this proof that the men in the back had been listening as he'd suspected, and then lowered at the admiration in Mack's eyes as the officer peered at Sam. He suspected the man wasn't imagining her in the courtroom as he watched her walk back toward them, and the possibility of what Mack might be imagining rankled. Mortimer slid into the man's thoughts at once and immediately stiffened at the lascivious thoughts he found there. It seemed while Mortimer had been slow to see her attractiveness, this man liked his women lean and commanding. Mack was imagining being cuffed and helpless in front of Sam in an outfit made up of thigh-high leather boots, a leather cap, and a riding crop.

Fortunately, the image evaporated before Mortimer

had to pop the man for the fantasy. Releasing a little sigh as the image slipped away, Constable Mack turned to Mortimer to say, "Sergeant Belmont's a throwback. Old school. None of us like his methods or attitudes much, but he's the sergeant."

"Hmm," Mortimer grunted, still irritated by the man's imaginings. Good Christ, now he had the image stuck in his own head. Only he was taking the crop away, pulling Sam into his arms and—

"Someone like this Latimer fellow she mentioned could change that," the man added hopefully.

Mortimer cleared his throat and forced the image from his mind to say, "No doubt."

He then turned to glance to the fully dressed Sam as her phone rang and she slipped it out of her purse.

Sam peered at the readout on her phone. The sight of her boss's number made her frown and glance to her watch. She'd told him three hours, and it was a little past that now. He was obviously looking for a progress report. Sucking in a deep breath, she flipped her phone open and paced to the door of the building as she pressed it to her ear. "Hello?"

"Samantha? You said you'd call in three hours." The tone was definitely reprimanding.

Nice greeting, she thought on a sigh and agreed pleasantly, "Yes, I did. But I thought you'd prefer I call after I had something to tell you."

"Something to tell me? Haven't you gone to Minden yet?" Clarence Babcock asked, and she could hear the irritation in his voice.

"Yes. I'm in Minden right now. Cathy wasn't at the

cottage. Her car was there, the lights were on, the doors unlocked and open, and a radio was playing, but there was no sign of her."

His only response to that was a long, heavy sigh. This wasn't good news.

"I'm at the O.P.P. office right now making a report."

"I see. Yes, a report, that's good," he muttered, sounding old and tired. It was the first time she'd ever heard the vital senior partner sound his age, but Cathy was his goddaughter.

"Is there any way to tell how long she's been . . . not there," he finished unhappily.

Sam turned to glance toward Mortimer and the officer he was talking to while she considered his question. There hadn't been any delivered newspapers lying on the deck, no calendar with the days conveniently ticked off. Other than the dried-out cheese, there was nothing to indicate how long the house had been empty.

"I'm sorry, no," Sam said finally, and then asked, "How long has it been since her parents spoke to her?"

Clarence Babcock's breath hissed over the phone. "I'm not sure. I'll call them and ask." There was a clicking sound as if he were clucking his tongue and then an impatient sigh. "I didn't think to ask anything like this. In truth I expected you to find her there and all to be well."

"Yes, of course," Sam murmured. No one expected tragedy when it struck, she thought, and then frowned at herself as she realized she was already writing off Cathy Latimer when she should really try to remain positive. Cathy might be all right. Maybe. Doubtful, but— Hell, she thought on a sigh and then asked, "What do you want me to do, sir?"

"I realize you're on vacation, Samantha, but . . ."

Sam closed her eyes, suspecting what was coming.

"Could you stay there to keep an eye on the progress the police make? I realize the house might be a crime scene and you probably can't stay there, but there are several guest cottages on the property, and you could stay in one of those."

Bingo, Sam thought on a sigh. And she couldn't refuse under the circumstances. Alex and Jo were going to be *so* pissed at her.

"I'll call Martin and his wife at once," Clarence Babcock continued. "I'm sure they'll want to fly back and head up there to be in on the search. I'll come up as soon as I can, but I'd really appreciate it if you could stay there and make sure the local law enforcement are doing everything they can until we arrive."

There was no way she could say no. Not because Babcock was her boss, but because a young woman was missing and her family was frantic. She'd just have to find a way to work it.

"Of course, sir," Sam said quietly, and was glad she had when she heard the relief and gratitude in his voice.

"Thank you, Samantha. I won't forget this," he assured her. "Now I'd best call Martin and Trisha. I'll call you back after I know when they're returning and when I can get up there, but if anything happens in the meantime . . ."

"I'll keep you informed," Samantha assured him.

"Very good. Thank you," he said gruffly, and hung up.

Sam closed the phone with a sigh and then grimaced as her gaze slid to Mortimer. While she might be stuck there, he wasn't. In fact, he could leave at once if he wished. She was sure the police could take her out to the house after she'd finished the report. Still, she felt bad about his having to drive back to Magnetawan on his own at this hour after kindly volunteering to drive her here. And part of her was disappointed that work, or at least a work-related issue, had stomped on the first chance she'd had of a social life in a long time.

At least that's what Sam told herself, but she wasn't fooling herself. She knew she was secretly relieved to have the matter taken out of her hands. Now she didn't have to agonize over whether she was ready for her first fling or not. She also wouldn't have to fear having her heart broken. Cathy Latimer's disappearing had seen to that nicely.

Shaking her head, Sam slipped her phone back into her purse and walked over to Mortimer.

Chapter 10

"That was my boss, Mr. Babcock, on the phone."
Mortimer nodded at this announcement from Sam as she reached him. He'd suspected as much. "Is he contacting the girl's parents?"

"Yes. He's probably calling them right now," she answered, and then blurted, "But he asked me to stay here and keep an eye on"—Sam hesitated, her gaze sliding to Constable Mack, before she simply said—"things until he or the Latimers can get here. And I agreed."

"Of course," Mortimer murmured, not at all surprised.

"If you're staying," Constable Mack piped up, "I could call the Dominion for you and see if they can find you a room for the night. It's the hotel here in Minden. It's on Main Street."

"Oh, thank you," Sam said, offering him a wide, surprised smile for his helpfulness. Apparently it was the last thing she'd expected after the completely unhelpful behavior of his sergeant. Mortimer doubted she'd be so surprised if she knew the role she'd played in the fantasy the man had enjoyed moments ago. He was just bending a scowl on the officer for his "helpfulness" when Sam said, "But Mr. Babcock asked me to stay at the Latimers', in one of the guest cottages."

Mortimer was just relaxing over the fact that there was no need for the man's helpfulness when she added, "But I'll probably need a ride out to the Latimers' after we get this report business done, if you wouldn't mind."

That brought the scowl right back to Mortimer's mouth. "You don't need a ride. I'm here. I'll drive you."

"Oh." Sam glanced at him uncertainly. "I thought you'd want to head back to the cottage right away rather than wait around. That way you wouldn't be on the road too late."

Mortimer was silent for a minute as he considered the matter. The fact was, under different circumstances he might very well have felt he had to leave her and return to Decker and Bricker and their hunt. But this disappearance bothered him. While the abandoned state of the house with the uneaten sandwich, the still-playing music, and the open door convinced Sam that foul play was involved, the fact that there was no sign at all of struggle was what bothered him. It might seem unusual to Sam and other mortals, but it was something he'd seen many times while working cases involving rogue immortals. His kind could slip into a mortal's mind and walk them out the door with no muss, no fuss, and little effort at all.

The problem was that up to this point they'd thought their rogue was just running around biting locals. A no-no, but as long as he or she wasn't doing lasting harm, they would have merely found out the who, what, and why of it all and then passed the individual over to the Council to deal with. Nobody had really thought they had a mad dog on their hands or someone dangerous.

This was not something they liked to admit to their mortal friends or even the younger of their kind, but the fact was, sometimes older immortals grew weary of cold, bagged blood and longed for the "good old days" of the hunt. In such cases they had been known to sneak about and eat "off the hoof." Once caught, they usually agreed to stop and went back to bagged blood, or they were invited to move to Europe, where the practice of eating "off the hoof" was more acceptable. That was what Mortimer had expected to find here; a lonely old immortal, bored with eating bagged blood, and seeking out the intimacy of biting mortals.

But Cathy Latimer's disappearance changed all that. The lack of any sign of a struggle suggested an immortal was involved, and if their rogue was behind this, the girl wouldn't have been taken away for a good purpose. Mortimer feared Cathy's bloodless body probably now lay somewhere in the woods awaiting discovery by mortals, and that would not be a good thing for his kind. Most of Mortimer's family had been wiped out by vampire hunters during the hysteria after the release of Stoker's damned book. Finding a young girl drained of her lifeblood, but with no wounds but fang marks, might lead to the same hysteria and see more of his kind hunted down and killed. It was the kind of thing he'd become a hunter to prevent. Cathy Latimer had to be found. If she was alive and he had misread all this, then good, but if she was dead at the hands of an immortal as he feared, then her body would have to be burned or otherwise destroyed.

He needed to talk to Decker and Bricker about this, but Mortimer suspected he was going to be staying in the area and helping Sam with her search. Or hindering it if necessary.

"Can you find your way back to Magnetawan on your own?" Sam asked, dragging him from his thoughts.

"Of course I can find my way back," he said with irritation.

"I'm sure there'll be no problem with my driving you out to the Latimers' after we finish with the report," Constable Mack said helpfully. "If worse came to worst and Belmont had a problem with it, my shift is done in an hour and I could take you on my own time."

Mortimer found himself glaring at the young man again. He'd just bet the fellow wouldn't mind taking her on his own time, but he wasn't going to get the chance.

"I'll take her out," he said firmly. "Now let's get to those reports."

It took much longer than Mortimer had expected to fill out the reports, mostly, he suspected, because young Mack was taking as much time about it as he could just to keep Sam there as long as possible. He probably hoped Mortimer would get tired of the long delay and head back to Magnetawan, leaving him free to drive Sam out to the Latimers'. Mortimer knew his suspicions were right when, halfway through the process, Constable Mack apologized for the time it was taking and again assured him he'd be happy to drive Sam out to the Latimers' if Mortimer wished to leave.

Mortimer's response was a snort that brought confusion to Sam's face and understanding to Constable Mack's. Apparently realizing that he wasn't going to be left alone with her, the constable stopped dragging his feet and hurried the process along.

While Sam was busy signing papers, Mortimer excused himself and stepped outside to call Decker. It was nearly nine o'clock and still light out, but it was the gray light of dusk. He wasn't surprised, however, when the phone was answered. The men were probably waiting to hear back from him, he thought as he recognized Decker's voice.

"Is Bricker nearby?" Mortimer asked at once, not bothering with a hello.

"Yes, do you want to talk to him?" Decker asked, sounding surprised.

"No. Yes, but to both of you at once," Mortimer explained. "Call Bricker into the room if he isn't there and then put me on speakerphone."

"He's here," Decker said, and then a click sounded and he asked, "Can you hear me?"

"Yeah," Mortimer assured him.

"Hey Mort. How's it hangin'? Are you getting any or is Sam playing hard to get?" Bricker teased, letting him know he was there.

"Bricker?" he said grimly.

"Yeah?" the younger man asked, his smile evident in his tone of voice.

"I will remember this and repay you accordingly when you finally meet your life mate," he said silkily.

"I think you've pissed him off, Bricker," Decker said with amusement.

Mortimer just shook his head and launched into a quick rundown of what he and Sam had found at the Latimer cottage.

A prolonged silence followed when he finished, and then Decker said, "You're thinking it's our rogue and that he's gone beyond just biting now."

"What?" Bricker said, sounding surprised over the phone. "How do you figure that? I mean, yeah, the cottage being in tip-top condition and the food left out and door open might suggest an immortal's involvement, but the Latimer cottage is in Minden, a good two hours from us here in Magnetawan. Are you two thinking we have more than one rogue, or what?"

Mortimer frowned. This issue hadn't occurred to him. Two hours *was* quite a distance for the rogue to go. It made for a large feeding ground. Perhaps he'd been influenced by a wish to stay with Sam and built a whole scenario that was—

"The bite marks weren't just spotted here in Magnetawan," Decker said, interrupting his thoughts. "There were reports in Huntsville, Bracebridge, and Gravenhurst. Minden isn't that far away."

Mortimer's eyebrows rose at this news. "I didn't know the bites had been spotted anywhere but Magnetawan."

Decker gave a dry laugh. "Then Uncle Lucian's slipping. But then he's a little distracted by wedding plans and Leigh at the moment and not as efficient as usual."

A smile curved Mortimer's lips at the mention of the head of the Council and Leigh, his life mate. Mortimer and Bricker had been there when Lucian had first encountered the woman. Neither of them had any idea then that the two would end up life mates. Of course, she'd been unconscious at the time. On the second occasion that they'd seen them together, however . . . Mortimer's smile widened at the memory. He'd never seen Lucian act as he had around Leigh. It had been easy to tell they were meant for each other.

"Uncle Lucian couriered the full report when he realized he hadn't given it to you and Bricker. It arrived today," Decker added.

"I see," Mortimer murmured slowly. "Are they still thinking one rogue or a group of them now?"

"One," Decker responded. "The reports of bite sightings are far enough apart in both time and distance that they think it's one. And whoever it is obviously isn't surviving off biting immortals alone unless there are a hell of a lot that aren't noticed or reported."

"Or that just go missing and aren't recognized as one of his victims," Mortimer said quietly.

"Yeah," Decker muttered, sounding unhappy.

Mortimer considered what he'd just learned and then said, "It might help us out to contact Bastien and have him make the boys at the Argeneau Blood Bank send us a list of anyone they deliver blood to up here. It will give us a short list of immortals in the area that we can question. Our rogue may be one of them."

"Good thinking," Decker said. "I'll call Bastien about ABB as soon as I get off here. Do you want Bricker and me to come down there to help with the search for this Latimer girl?"

Mortimer frowned as he considered the situation, and then said, "No. This looks like a rogue's involved, but may not be. Until I have a little more evidence one way or the other I'd rather not pull you two off our original grid search of the area. You two keep on with that, and Sam and I will look for Cathy."

"Okay," Decker agreed.

"Yo, hey Mort?" Bricker said just as Mortimer opened his mouth to say good-bye.

"Yeah?" he asked warily.

"What about clothes and blood and stuff? You want us to bring you supplies?"

Mortimer hesitated; he hadn't considered that. But it was a two-hour drive and he'd be dragging the two men away from their own search . . .

"We're kind of headed down that way anyway," Decker announced suddenly, and then explained, "We marked all the reported bite sightings on a map of the area and then found the center. For some reason Bricker thinks that's most likely where the rogue's home base is."

"I saw it on a cop show on television," Bricker said defensively. "Or maybe it was a movie. Anyway, if you work out the center, that's usually where the bad guy lives."

"And where's the center?" Mortimer asked, half amused and half curious. While the idea sounded nuts, it just might work.

"The middle of Cardwell Lake," Decker answered.

"You think he has a home or cottage there?" Mortimer asked.

"Maybe," Decker admitted. "Stranger things have happened. We're going to check that out tonight. We were going to wait for your return, but now we'll probably head right out after I call ABB for that list you suggested. Bricker could throw some clothes and blood together for you while I make the call, and you could meet us at Cardwell Lake. It would cut your trip in half."

"And I could jog next door and see if Sam's sisters can throw some clothes together for her too," Bricker put in.

"Good thinking," he agreed, and then added, "All right, I'll take Sam back to the Latimers' and then meet you two at Cardwell Lake. I'll call your cell when I get there so you can let me know exactly where you are."

"Sounds good," Decker said.

"To me too," Bricker agreed, and then asked, "Is there anything special you want me to pack for you? Something Sam will think is sexy?"

"Bricker," Mortimer growled in warning.

"Oh, you don't have anything sexy, do you," the younger man went on, ignoring him. "I could loan you something."

"Justin," he snapped.

"You'd look good in my black leather pants," Bricker continued blithely, and Mortimer could hear Decker chuckling in the background. "They might be a little tight, but they look best that way anyway, and—Oh hey! I just got this new zebra-striped thong before the trip. It's never been worn; you could—"

Mortimer snapped his cell phone closed, cutting off his annoying partner, but a smile was also tugging on his lips. A zebra-striped thong? Dear God! Although the leather pants might not have gone amiss . . . he *had* noticed the way women looked at Bricker when he was wearing his leather pants, and wouldn't have minded Sam looking at him that way.

* * *

Sam paced the small front room of the Latimers' guest cottage, and then paused at the window to peer out over the dark landscape. All there was to see was inky blackness. Anything could have been standing cloaked in darkness on the other side of the window and she wouldn't know it. She should have been used to that from her own family's cottage, but this wasn't her family's cottage. This was one of the Latimers' guest cabins, and Sam wasn't terribly comfortable in it. She was very aware that Cathy Latimer had gone missing from the main house not a hundred feet behind the cabin she was in. That knowledge was creeping her out. What if Cathy had been kidnapped? What if whoever had taken her was still around? What if—?

She stopped that train of thought at once, knowing it couldn't lead anywhere good. It didn't stop her wishing that Mortimer would hurry and get back so she was no longer alone. He'd brought her directly here after leaving the O.P.P. station. They'd arrived to find Sergeant Belmont standing around with a couple of his constables, looking officious but not actually doing anything useful.

The man had admitted that the situation appeared fishy and promised that he'd look into the matter. He'd then been reluctant to hand over the keys to the property. Sam had been forced to call her boss, and have him call the Latimers in Europe, to have *them* call Belmont on his own cell phone, to tell him they wanted her to stay there and he had their permission to give her the keys.

Martin Latimer had then apparently asked to speak

to her. Tight-lipped, Belmont had handed over his phone and stomped off to kick at rocks and branches a little distance away. Mr. Latimer had thanked Sam for what she was doing and assured her she was welcome to use anything at the estate while there. In the meantime, he was working on arranging a flight back. He hoped he and his wife, Trisha, would be able to return to Canada the next day and be up at the cottage by evening.

Sam had assured him she'd do what she could until they arrived, but couldn't offer much reassurance to the man. He wouldn't be reassured until his daughter was found safe and sound. The moment the phone call had ended, Sam had approached Belmont and traded the mobile phone for Cathy's keys. At least most of them. He'd kept the key to the house, claiming it was a crime scene and she couldn't enter. The man and his officers had left shortly after.

Once they were gone, Mortimer had joined her on a tour of the three guest cottages on the property, holding her arm to steady her as they traveled the paths in the darkening evening. He'd stayed until she'd decided which cabin to use and then had headed back to Magnetawan. But he was returning. Mortimer was only heading back to get them both a change of clothes and some groceries to last them a day or so, and then he was making the long drive back. Sam had assured him that wasn't necessary and that she'd manage okay without his going to so much trouble, but he'd waved her words away, assured her he'd be back as quickly as he could, and driven off.

Sam had been pacing ever since. She turned now and

walked the length of the small room again, her gaze moving absently over the furniture and accessories. It was very nice as guest cottages went, she supposed. At least everything was expensive-looking, but it was also tiny, with two well-appointed but small bedrooms taking up the back of the cottage and this room in front with a kitchenette on one side and a sitting area just big enough to hold a couch and chair on the other. It was also the cottage closest to the lake. By then she'd known Mortimer intended to return, however, and the two bedrooms were really why she'd chosen it.

Not that her sisters expected them to use both rooms, Sam thought dryly as she recalled the phone call she'd made as soon as Garrett Mortimer left. Bricker hadn't yet arrived at the cottage in search of clothes for her, so she'd gotten to break the news of what was happening to them. Both Jo and Alex had been up in arms about her staying until they'd heard the part about Mortimer staying with her. Suddenly they hadn't minded at all. That was when the sly suggestions and innuendo had started. She'd been relieved to end that conversation as well.

Sam paced the room once more, again pausing to peer out into the darkness. There was still nothing for her to see. There was also nothing to eat, and nothing to do in the cottage, and this endless waiting was driving her crazy. The heat wasn't helping. The cottage had been tightly closed up and was terribly warm inside despite the overhead fans being on for the last . . . Her gaze slid to her watch to see that it had been almost four hours since Garrett Mortimer had left her.

Four hours. She bit her lip and glanced outside again,

but there was no sudden flash of headlights on the trees announcing his return. Sam knew she was expecting too much to even hope for that. She probably had another hour wait before she could expect him back, Sam realized and grimaced, unsure she could bear another minute there, let alone sixty.

The sound of a boat engine drew her gaze to the lake, and Sam saw the bow light of a boat cruise slowly into view. She stood still, watching it move by. The light was nearly out of sight before she heard the sound of the water washing up on the beach.

The sound made her think of how cool the lake must be and how lovely it would feel on her overheated skin. She then wondered if Jo and Alex were taking a night swim that very moment. When the sound of the boat engine died in the distance, Sam turned to grab the flashlight, one of the first things she'd looked for after Mortimer had left. She went into the tiny bathroom that ate up a corner of the sitting area and grabbed a beach towel from the rack before flicking on the flashlight and moving back across the room.

Sam paused at the screen door, suddenly nervous about stepping out into the darkness, but then remonstrated with herself over being a coward and shone the light on the ground before stepping outside.

She'd just go for a quick swim. Just a dunk, really, Sam assured herself, enough to cool off, and then she'd return to the cabin to wait for Mortimer. It was better than pacing a rut in the hardwood floor of the cottage.

Sam shone her flashlight over the sloping land between where she stood and the beach. She then shifted the beam to her left and then her right, telling herself as she did that she wasn't *really* looking for kidnappers or even serial killers lurking behind trees.

It was hard to fool oneself, however, and Sam rolled her eyes at her newly developed yellow streak as she turned the light forward once more and started cautiously off the porch. The fifty feet to the Latimer dock were the longest Sam had ever traversed. Between her repeated stops to shine the flashlight over the surrounding trees, her own inability to maintain her balance as she glanced nervously around at every tiny rustle of sound, and then the need to pick herself back up off the ground each time she lost that balance and fell, the walk probably took five times as long as it should have.

By the time Sam reached the beach, she was sorely regretting the urge that had brought her out. She was also swearing to herself that she would never again delay heading to the doctor's to have any complaint taken care of. Thanks to her ear infection, she was sure she'd bruised herself in at least three different places and scraped her palms something fierce.

Relief slithered through Sam as she stepped off the path and felt sand underfoot. Some of the lakes were all rock and leeches were a problem, but either this lake was naturally sandy or the Latimers had shipped sand in. Either way, as long as she stayed away from the rocks she could see off to the side and protruding from the water, she should be fine.

After dropping her towel on the ground, Sam took a moment to run her flashlight over the trees behind her one more time. When nothing seemed out of place and no one leaped out at her, she turned out the light. For a moment Sam couldn't see a bloody thing and nearly turned it back on, but then her eyes began to pick up the moonlight reflecting off the lake and she was slowly able to make out more.

Letting out the breath she hadn't realized she'd been holding, Sam set the flashlight on the dark shape that was her towel, and then moved forward to dip one foot into the water. Lovely, she thought, and quickly stripped, removing her shorts and panties first and dropping them onto the towel before reaching for the hem of her T-shirt. That soon joined her shorts, as did the bra that she didn't really need, and Sam turned back to the lake. The water was cool against her heated skin as she walked into it, but not unpleasantly so, and she closed her eyes and sighed as it began to draw the heat from her body. The liquid lapped higher as she continued forward, caressing her calves, her knees, her thighs, her—

A small gasp slid from her lips as the cold water reached her groin and a slight frisson of shock ran through her, but she knew it would pass quickly, and kept going until the water covered her breasts. Leaning back in the water then, Sam let it soak into her hair as she peered up at the stars overhead. She was just noting that there didn't seem to be as many of the twinkling lights here as there were visible in Magnetawan, and wondering why that would be, when the snap of a branch caught her ear.

Stiffening in the water, Sam lifted her head to peer toward shore, eyes widening when she saw a dark figure standing onshore beside her towel. Panic was just starting to course through her when she recognized Mortimer's shape.

"You're back sooner than I expected," she called, relief thick in her voice.

"Decker and Bricker met me halfway to save me some driving," he explained.

Sam's eyebrows rose. In that case, he'd taken much longer than he should have. She supposed he'd stopped to have a coffee with Decker and Bricker, though, before returning. Considering the trouble they'd gone to and the driving they'd saved him, it seemed only right. She didn't comment, however. Her mind was on other matters as it suddenly occurred to her that she was stark naked in the water. A quick glance down assured her that all the important bits were under water. She glanced back to Mortimer and said, "It's hot in the cottage. I thought I'd cool off. I'm glad you're back though; I was getting hungry."

"So am I," Mortimer said, and Sam stilled. The words were husky and carried a suggestive tone that made her eyes sharpen.

Surely he hadn't meant what it sounded like, she thought, and simply gaped as he suddenly tugged his T-shirt off and dropped it on her own pile of clothes. His jeans quickly followed, and then Mortimer walked forward into the water.

Sam's eyes were wide open, but all she could see of his body in the darkness was shadow and more shadow. She couldn't help but think it was a damned shame she'd left her flashlight on shore. In the next moment, these thoughts fled and her heart rate sped up as she realized he was wading straight toward her. Sam had the brief urge to flee for shore, but it was very brief and easily overwhelmed by an even stronger urge to wait and see what would happen. She was distinctly recalling the passion and fervor of those moments outside the restaurant in town, and her body was growing heavy and tingly with anticipation.

Mortimer continued steadily forward until he was a bare few inches away and then stopped abruptly. He then stood silently, perhaps allowing her the time to protest or flee, but when a moment passed and she did neither, he reached out, slid a hand into her wet hair, and drew her forward.

Sam went willingly, sucking in a little gasp of air as their bodies brushed together in the water, and then his mouth was on hers. The kiss started out gentle, almost questing. He was obviously making an effort to go slow, but Sam didn't need *slow*. Either just the memory of what had happened earlier had wound her up for this, or that earlier passion had never really died, merely been buried under other concerns. The need and yearning and aching want he'd stirred then came roaring back to life almost the moment his lips covered hers. Sam barely managed to remain quiescent in his arms for the first moments of his gentle kisses before her body acted of its own accord. It wrapped itself around him like a wet blanket, legs closing around his hips and arms around his shoulders even as her mouth opened under his.

Mortimer immediately gave up any semblance of questing or gentleness. His tongue slid out to invade, his kiss becoming demanding, and his hands began to move over her, cupping, fondling, and squeezing even as they urged her tighter still against him so that she rubbed against his hardness where it was trapped between them.

Sam groaned into his mouth with pleading. She was sure every last drop of water had been squeezed out from between them and still it wasn't enough. The lake suddenly didn't seem so delightfully cool. It almost seemed they were heating the water with their passion, and then Mortimer tore his mouth away and began to trail kisses downward as the hand at her bottom lifted her up slightly.

Sam let her head fall backward with a groan, offering her throat to him, and he paid it due homage, but it was just a passing pleasure; his mouth soon continued down and he lifted her higher out of the water until he could latch on to one erect nipple. That brought another gasp from her, and she shifted her hands to his head to hold on as he drew the bud into his mouth and laved it lovingly. Her hips were now shifting against his stomach, her legs now caught around him above his hips, and she missed the hardness of his erection between them. Sam had no sooner had the thought than Mortimer's hand dipped down and brushed lightly over the open center of her.

Despite her thoughts of a moment ago, that was too much for Sam. She'd never experienced pleasure this intense. It was as if she were experiencing it in some sort of strange echo chamber. The pleasure seemed to redouble with each touch and caress until it filled her head and body. Crying out, she kicked her legs free

and tugged on his head, forcing it away from her breast
and upward so that she could reclaim his lips as she
slid down his body. Sam kissed him almost desperately
then, little mewls of pleading sounding in her throat.

Mortimer kissed her back as she demanded. She was
vaguely aware of his moving them toward shore, and
when sand brushed against the bottoms of her feet, she
instinctively jerked them upward and then wrapped
them around his hips again. That was when she felt
the shift of muscles under her legs and realized he was
walking, but the movement was rubbing his hardness
against her core again with each step, and all she could
do was moan and arch into the caress as she was bombarded with wave after wave of increasing pleasure.

Apparently Mortimer was affected too because halfway back to shore he changed direction, and after a
couple more steps, she felt cold stone against her bottom.
Letting her feet drop so that she was standing, Sam
glanced around as he again broke their kiss. She saw that
he'd taken her only as far as the nearest half-submerged
boulder, and something niggled at her mind, but then
Mortimer urged her to lean back against the rock and
began to lick and suckle at her breasts again.

Moaning, Sam allowed herself to be distracted and
slid her hands into his hair to hold on as he leaned her
back over the boulder. Her hips and legs were trapped
against the front of it by his as he concentrated on first
one breast and then the other. Each shift of his body
made his erection rub against her enticingly, and Sam
was gasping and almost whimpering, the fingers of one
hand tangled in his hair and the nails of the other no

doubt scoring his shoulder as wave after mounting wave of pleasure accosted her.

When he lifted his head and caught her mouth with his, she opened for him and gasped as his tongue thrust in, rasping her own. But she wanted more. She wanted him inside her, thrusting into her like that. Her body was actually aching and weeping for him.

Much to Sam's relief, Mortimer seemed to want it too because he suddenly caught her at the waist and lifted her to sit on the edge of the boulder. She immediately spread her knees for him to step between them and then when he did, kissed him without reservation, thrusting her own tongue inside to wrestle with his. At the same time, her hand moved to his behind to squeeze and urge him forward as her feet rose to push against the submerged front of the rock and shift her lower body forward until his hips were cradled between her open knees.

Mortimer urged her back to lie on the boulder as he kissed her, but then, much to her dismay, he paused. She blinked her eyes open, staring up at the dark shape of his head and—though she couldn't see his face in the darkness—she heard the strain in his voice as he asked, "Are you sure?"

"Are you kidding me?" The words slid out on a disbelieving laugh before she could catch them back, and then she bit her lip. Most men wouldn't have had the strength to give her the option to back out at this stage. She owed it to him to at least consider it seriously, Sam thought, and did just that. The facts were they'd known each other only a couple of days. There had been no promises. This could be a one-time deal, a wham-bam-thank-you-ma'am-and-he-disappears thing. She'd never had a fling in her life and had, in fact, only had one lover prior to this. Oh yeah, and they had no protection. She could get a venereal disease, or pregnant, or—

Dear God, what the hell was she thinking? Sam screamed silently as all her excitement of a moment ago began to rapidly wane. She was just trying to figure out a way to tell him that she wasn't so sure after all when she became aware that his hand was moving over her hip in a probing manner that had nothing to do with the heat and passion of a moment ago.

"What?" she asked with bewilderment when he suddenly moved back a bit and bent to look at her hip.

"I'm not sure," Mortimer muttered. "Just a minute. Stay here."

Much to her amazement, he was suddenly gone, splashing through the shallow water to shore. Sitting up on the boulder, Sam stared after him with incredulity as he bent to pick up something.

"What is it?" Sam asked with confusion. She didn't realize he'd grabbed the flashlight until he turned it on and the beam hit her square in the eyes.

"Sorry." Mortimer turned it down along her body and then around to her hip where his attention had been captured. "I just—Oh . . . That's not good."

Sam blinked rapidly to try to recover her vision and twisted to look where he was shining the flashlight beam. She found herself staring at some sort of dark spot on her hip. She stared at it blankly and then realized there were more than one. She could see at least three fuzzy, dark spots that slowly came into focus.

Sam stared with dawning horror as she realized what they were . . . and that there were more than three.

"Leeches!" That horrified shriek tore from her throat as she threw herself wildly off the boulder. She hardly even noticed that she'd toppled Mortimer into the water; she was too busy scrambling out of the leech-filled lake and running for the cottage.

Chapter 11

"Leeches."

Mortimer had to fight to hide his amusement as Sam muttered that word with a loathing that went bone-deep. His gaze traveled over her back where she lay before him on a towel on the table in the cottage, and he shook his head at the sheer number of the little bloodsuckers. There must have been a whole nest of them living on that boulder, he thought, and silently berated himself once again for setting her on the boulder rather than carrying her the few feet to her towel on the beach. If he had, he'd probably be buried inside her warm heat, shouting out his release. Instead he stood, frustrated and bare-chested, in the now damp, uncomfortable jeans he'd dragged on, removing leeches from Sam's back. Well, her back, her buttocks, her legs . . . He still had to do her front too.

Grimacing, he bent to slide one finger next to where a leech was feeding and used his nail to push the sucker away from the wound until he broke the seal. At the same time, he used another finger to detach the posterior sucker and then quickly plucked it from her back before it could fasten itself to her again. It was a time-consuming process.

"Can't you just burn the little bastards off," Sam snarled, shifting uncomfortably on the table.

Surprised by the first curse he'd heard from her, Mortimer glanced up to find her glaring back over her shoulder with resentment.

"I already told you that it's best not to," he said patiently, knowing she was embarrassed. On top of that, every spot where he removed a leech was probably itching like crazy . . . and being covered with leeches was just gross, really. Well, it would be for her. Not that it was exactly a joy to see her so, but he wasn't shuddering with horror every couple of minutes as she was.

Mortimer's gaze slid over the spots where he'd removed leeches, noting the free-flowing blood coming from the wounds. He was glad he'd fed—and fed well—on the fresh supply of blood that had waited in Decker's truck when he'd met them.

"Yeah, yeah, yeah," Sam muttered, drawing his attention again. "If you burn them off, they regurgitate their meal, spitting up their stomach contents back into the open wound, and that could cause infection because of the bacteria in their bellies and blah blah blah."

It seemed obvious to Mortimer that Sam was angry at him. He supposed she held him responsible for this mess. He couldn't blame her. If he'd just chosen the towel over the boulder, or, hell, even the sand—

"This could only happen to me," she said suddenly. "It is *so* me to be . . . er . . . relaxing in the water and end up covered in leeches."

"Relaxing, huh?" he asked dryly. If she'd found what they were doing relaxing, he'd been doing something wrong. When Sam blushed, she apparently blushed everywhere. Mortimer could see the color rising under the pale, naked skin splayed before him. Feeling bad for adding to her discomfort, he tried to distract her and said the first thing he thought of. "Actually, I'm sort of relieved that leeches are all it was. When I first felt it, I feared you had some kind of strange growth."

Sam was not impressed, he realized as she rose up slightly on her arms to swivel her upper body and look at him. The glare she turned his way could have singed the hair off a cow. Mortimer soon understood the true source of her resentment and anger, however, when she snapped, "Why did they all attack me? You haven't got a single one on you, but they're on my back, my front, my sides. What kind of karma is that? *You* picked the damned boulder."

Mortimer bit his lip as she flopped back on the table. He really had no idea why not him. The only thing he could think was that an immortal's blood was somehow unattractive to leeches. He couldn't say that to her, however. Clearing his throat, he bent to remove another one and said apologetically, "Perhaps my blood is bitter."

Sam released her breath on a gusty sigh, dropped her head on her folded arms, and moaned. After a moment, she raised her head and said quietly, "I'm sorry. I don't mean to be so snappy. It's just that my back itches like crazy, and my skin feels like it's crawling with the horrid little things, and this is just plain humiliating. I'd rather be dunked in boiling oil than suffer this, and all I really want to do is get into the hottest bath I can manage, scrub every inch of my skin off, and go to sleep and forget this night ever happened."

Mortimer said quietly, "Not all of it, I hope."

After a brief silence, she admitted into her arms, "No. Not all of it."

His lips curving with relief, Mortimer turned his attention back to the leeches. As he worked, he got quicker at removing them. Still, it was a relief to drop the last one into the pot where he'd been placing them.

"I'm done with your back," he announced. "If you'd like to roll over, I'll get the few off your front too."

Mortimer braced himself, expecting a protest and having to convince her, but it appeared she'd rather have the leeches off than preserve what was left of her dignity. After the briefest hesitation, Sam sighed with resignation and began to shift on the table. Mortimer schooled his face into a neutral expression as she turned over. His gaze ran over her clinically once she settled on her back. Much to his relief, there were only a couple of leeches here. There had been ten times that on her back and sides.

Mortimer was quick to remove the ones from her front. At least the ones he could see. His gaze slid to her groin as he removed the last visible one from her thigh. He turned away to drop the last leech in the pot and set the plate back over it before saying carefully, "I think I have them all, but you might want to check the spots I can't see."

Sam peered at him with bewilderment as she quickly sat up and pulled up the towel she'd been lying on to cover herself. "You've seen everything. And in glaring light," she added unhappily.

"Not everything," he pointed out, gesturing vaguely toward her groin as she slid off the table.

Sam froze.

"No," she breathed, paling. In the next moment, she'd disappeared into the bathroom.

It was a tiny bathroom. Mortimer had noticed as much when they'd toured this cottage. It had a toilet, sink, and shower all crowded in so tightly, one would have difficulty turning around in the room. He bit his lip as he heard her banging about inside, presumably performing acrobatics in an effort to get a look between her legs, and then remonstrated with himself about finding any of this amusing. This was a terrible situation. One that had put a halt to any possibility of their finishing what had started in the water. Perhaps ever. Sam might think of leeches every time he kissed her from now on and shrink from him with disgust.

That wiped the smile off Mortimer's face.

Aware of the silence now from the bathroom, he moved to the door and listened briefly before asking, "Sam? Are you all right? Do you need a mirror? I have one in my shaving kit I could fetch for you."

"No, there's a hand mirror in here," she said, sounding strained. "It's just hard— It's so tiny in here— Just a minute," she ended finally, not bothering to explain.

"Okay." Mortimer said, managing to bite back the words *shout if you need help*. He didn't think she'd appreciate the offer.

Another moment passed, and then he heard her relieved sigh through the door. "No more leeches. I'm going to take a shower."

The hiss of the water turned on immediately, so Mortimer didn't bother to answer. Moving away from the door, he peered around the room, his gaze landing on the plate-covered pot. Deciding it might be best to get rid of that before she came out, Mortimer quickly scooped up the pot and headed out of the cottage. It was on the edge of the small front porch that he paused, unsure what to do with the little critters. His first instinct was to somehow kill them, but they had only been doing what they needed to do to survive. Just like his people did.

Mortimer's gaze dropped to the pot in his hand, and he grimaced. He didn't fancy pulling them out one by one and stomping on them for that. He also couldn't think of another kinder way to kill them. He'd heard salt might do the trick, but if so, he suspected it would be a long, painful death. Rather like being staked out in the sun was for his kind.

Nope. He just couldn't do it. It was back to the water for them, Mortimer decided, and immediately started down the path, eager to get the chore done before Sam came out of the shower. He was pretty sure she wouldn't appreciate his solution to the situation. She'd probably like to roast them all slowly in the oven at this point.

Dark as it was, Mortimer had no more trouble now negotiating the path than he had when he'd gone in search of Sam on returning from meeting the boys. He released the leeches in the lake and was leaning off the dock, waving the pot in the water, rinsing it out, when he heard the growl of engines. At first he thought it must be boats, but after a moment a group of riders on Sea-Doos came into view around the point.

Lifting the pot out of the water, Mortimer gave it a shake and then sat back on his haunches to watch the four Sea-Doos. It looked like two men and two women, and they appeared to be having a good time. Too good a time. The group were obviously drunk and likely to get themselves killed mucking about on the lake at this hour, Mortimer thought as he watched them turn, narrowly missing one another, and then roar back around the point and out of sight again.

Shaking his head, he stood and headed back toward the cottage, but wondered if there was somewhere to rent Sea-Doos up here. They did look like fun, and he wouldn't mind trying them out. He did have a rogue to find, and now the missing Cathy Latimer too, but surely they could find a free moment at some point to enjoy themselves.

Sam was still in the shower when Mortimer reached the cottage. Steam was wafting from the cracks above and below the door of the bathroom, suggesting she was trying to boil herself alive. He wouldn't doubt she was probably scrubbing herself raw as well. Sam had really been upset by having the leeches on her. He could have told her tales of them being used for medicinal purposes when he was younger, but she would have thought him nuts if he announced that he was eight hundred years old and had seen pretty much everything there was to see in this world.

Mortimer set the pot and plate in the sink and then headed back out of the cottage again. He'd left the cooler in the SUV when he'd first returned. He hadn't wanted to carry it inside while Sam might be up and about, so had brought in only their clothes and groceries earlier. The bathroom door had been closed when he'd entered, and he'd at first assumed she was in there, so had quickly unpacked the groceries and stowed them away. It was only after he'd finished that he'd found she wasn't in the bathroom after all and rushed outside in search of her. He'd been relieved when he'd heard the faint splashing of water from the lake and followed the sound to the shore to see her there.

He should have headed back up to the SUV to retrieve the cooler then and plug it in, in his room. However, the blood had been the last thing on Mortimer's mind when he'd seen the pale glow of moonlight reflecting off her skin.

Now he was thinking of the blood, however, and hurried out to the car to retrieve it, grateful to find her still in the shower when he returned. Once he had it plugged in, in his room, Mortimer moved back out to the kitchen and glanced around. When his gaze landed on the pot and plate he'd set in the sink, he decided to wash and put them away so there was no evidence to remind Sam of her unfortunate adventure when she came out of her extremely long shower.

Grabbing up the bottle of dish soap on the sink, he poured a healthy amount into the pot and then turned on the hot water. A sudden shriek from the bathroom made him whirl and rush toward the door, but he found it locked.

"Sam? What's happening?" Mortimer shouted.

"Nothing! I'm fine," she gasped at once, probably

afraid he was about to break down the door. She had a right to that worry, as he'd been about to do just that. "The water just went cold. I guess I used up all the hot."

Mortimer's eyes widened, and he hurried back to turn off the tap as he realized he'd probably diverted all the hot water by turning on the sink tap.

"I'll be out in a minute."

Mortimer grimaced at her words and set about frantically cleaning the pot and plate and then rinsing and drying them both to remove the evidence that it was he who'd ruined her shower. He'd just finished putting the two items back where he'd found them and was laying the dish towel on the counter to dry when the bathroom door opened and Sam stepped out.

Mortimer turned to offer her a smile, his eyes widening when he saw that she was red as a lobster from head to toe. A result of the combination of hot water and scrubbing, he suspected. Her hair was slicked back and damp, and she had wrapped her towel around herself toga style. She was also sidling toward the hall to the bedrooms.

"I'm going to bed. Thanks for . . . everything. G'night," she mumbled, flushing even redder.

"Good," Mortimer began, but she was already whirling away and rushing off up the hall as he finished, "night."

So much for their first night alone together.

The insistent, not to mention irritating, ring of her phone woke Sam in the morning. Rolling over in bed, she reached down to feel around on the floor for her purse and then dragged it up onto the bed with her as she sat up. She didn't bother digging through the contents, but simply upended the purse and then snatched up her phone when it tumbled out with everything else.

"Hello?" Sam said groggily into the phone.

"Good morning, Samantha. I'm sorry. Obviously I've woken you up."

Straightening at the disapproval in Clarence Babcock's voice, Sam cleared her throat. "Yes. I stayed in one of the cottages here at the Latimers', but I hadn't realized I'd be staying when I headed here and had no clothes or groceries, which meant a bit of a drive to collect them. It was quite late by the time that was accomplished," she explained, framing her words carefully so that she wasn't lying. There was no need to mention that it was actually someone else who had made the drive and that she had merely stayed up to wait for him. She'd rather leave Mortimer out of it for now.

"I am sorry about intruding on your vacation this way, and I sincerely appreciate your aiding us, Samantha," Mr. Babcock said solemnly.

"That's all right, sir," Sam said at once, feeling guilty. She hadn't meant to make him feel bad. She just hadn't wanted him to think she was a layabout. Clearing her throat, she changed the subject. "I haven't heard from Sergeant Belmont, so I'm guessing there's no news yet, but I'll call and check with him and then get right back to you."

"Good, good. That will be fine. In the meantime, I'm afraid Martin and Trisha are stuck in Europe for the moment. It seems a rather severe weather system has all flights canceled. Martin's hoping to catch one of the first flights out, but I've been checking with the airline, and they don't seem to think they'll be able to start moving planes until tomorrow morning."

"Oh." Sam bit her lip and waited to see what else he had to say.

"I intended to drive up there with them when I talked to you yesterday, but I'm afraid in all the worry, I quite forgot about the Manning case starting today."

Sam stiffened at the mention of the Manning case. It was a big deal for the firm, and she wasn't surprised when he said, "I have to be there. I might even have to have my son collect Martin and Trisha from the airport and drive them up tomorrow, though I'm hoping I can arrange something so that I can get away."

She shifted on the bed and almost sighed aloud at the expectant silence that followed, but finally offered, "Did you want me to stay here then and keep an eye on things until tomorrow?"

"That would be very kind of you, Samantha. Thank you. I appreciate it."

"Right," she sighed. "Well, I'll call Belmont now and see if he has any news."

"Thank you. Be sure to call me back right after."

Sam assured him she would and then said good-bye and snapped her phone closed, ending the connection. Grimacing at it, she then set it on the bedside table and quickly scooped everything back into her purse before tossing the sheets aside and getting up. She wasn't calling Belmont until she was dressed. Sam just didn't have the heart to talk to the odious man in her nightie, especially not the one she was presently wearing. The short, see-through black lace camisole belonged to either Alex or Jo. Sam was very surprised when she'd found it among the things they sent, but then she'd realized that she shouldn't be. Her sisters were trying to get her laid. How humiliating was that?

Shaking her head, she quickly stripped off the delicate nightie, pulled on clothes, and then grabbed her phone and left her room.

Sam wasn't at all surprised to find the kitchenette/living area empty when she entered. It was early yet, and she had no doubt Mortimer was sleeping. She set her phone on the counter and moved to make coffee. Once that was done, she grabbed her phone and moved out onto the front porch to make her call so that she wouldn't wake Mortimer.

What followed was the most frustrating ten minutes of conversation she'd ever suffered. When the phone was answered with the O.P.P. spiel, she asked for Belmont and was told to hold. She held . . . for several minutes, and then the very professional-sounding woman who had answered explained that he was out investigating an "incident." Since Sam had been asked to hold at first as if he were in, she didn't believe that for a minute, but could hardly call the woman a liar.

Instead she asked, "May I speak to Constable Mack then, please?"

"He's off today," came the reply.

Sam began to tap her nails impatiently against her thigh as she considered what to do next. Finally she asked, "Well, then, is there *anyone* there who might be able to update me on the progress in the search for Cathy Latimer?"

There was a hesitation and then the woman asked her to hold again. Sighing, Sam waited impatiently for the woman to return, stiffening when she heard the click of the call being reengaged.

"I'm afraid there's no one here who can help you at the moment," she was told. "I'll have Sergeant Belmont call you when he returns. Have a good day."

"Oh, but—" Sam began and then growled with frustration as a click sounded, followed by the dial tone. Snapping the phone closed, she forced herself to take a deep breath and calm down. She'd just have to wait for his call. Unfortunately, while she did, she'd have to report back to her boss that she'd learned absolutely nothing. So much for her riding herd on the police, Sam thought dryly as she punched in the number for the office.

Much to her relief, she found herself talking to Mr. Babcock's secretary, Madge. Mr. Babcock had already left for court and wouldn't be available for the rest of the day unless it was an emergency.

"Is it an emergency?" Madge asked carefully.

"No," Sam said at once. "If he calls in looking for a message from me, just tell him that the police have no news yet and I'll get back to him as soon as they do."

"All right," the woman answered easily, and then added, "I hope you're at least getting to have a little fun up there, Samantha. You *are* supposed to be on a well-earned vacation."

"Yes, well . . . such is life," Sam muttered.

"No, such is how you're allowing life to treat you, dear. Don't sit up there in the Latimers' cottage waiting to hear from people all day. You have your cell phone. Go have a little fun while you wait for calls."

"But Cathy—"

"I've known Cathy Latimer since she was a child," the woman interrupted, reminding her that she'd been Mr. Babcock's secretary for nearly thirty years. "That girl is constantly running off and doing this or that and scaring everyone silly. Don't let her antics upset your vacation; you need to take some time for yourself today and have fun."

"She may have been troublesome in the past, Madge, but I think she might really be in trouble this time," Sam said quietly. She'd dealt a lot with the woman while working for Mr. Babcock and always liked and respected her opinion, but this time she was sure Madge was wrong. "The door to the house was unlocked and ajar, and there was an uneaten sandwich and drink there and—"

"I know, I heard all of that from Clarence," Madge interrupted. "I still think it's just Cathy being irresponsible again. But whether it is or not, you're not expected to hunt for her yourself. That's a job for the police. From what I understand, Clarence just wants you to keep calling and harassing the police in the area so that they don't forget to look for the girl. You can have fun between phone calls, can't you?"

"Yes, I suppose," Sam said reluctantly.

"Well then, do it," Madge said firmly. "Life's too short to work as hard as you do."

"Yes, Madge," she murmured, wondering if the woman wasn't right. She *could* have fun between phone calls to Belmont. And if he didn't call by noon, she'd call again. And if she still couldn't reach him, she'd go down to the O.P.P. office in person and hunt him down.

Finding her mood lifting immediately, Sam smiled and said into the phone, "Thank you, Madge."

"You're welcome. Now hang up and go have fun."

"I will. Have a good day." Sam closed her phone more gently this time. Feeling much better than she had after the call to the O.P.P. station, she slid it into her front pocket and then headed back into the cottage.

There was no sign of Mortimer yet, but the coffee was done. Sam poured herself a cup and then started checking out what groceries he'd brought back with him. She would have settled for a piece of toast or a bowl of cereal. What she found was a box of pancake mix, some maple syrup, and sausage links. Her sisters had always bugged her about needing to put on weight, and she supposed this was their attempt to try to help in that area. However, Sam had always had difficulty putting on weight. She ate like a horse and never gained an ounce. It was depressing. She had met several women who claimed they could gain a pound just looking at food and didn't doubt them for a minute, but she'd give a lot to trade her metabolism for theirs for a couple of months just so she'd look less like a half-starved war camp victim.

Sam set to work making pancakes and sausages. It was nearly done and she was just wondering whether she should wake Mortimer up or just set his aside to be warmed later when his door opened and he stumbled up the hall into the kitchen. He wore just his jeans and carried a stack of clothes that only half hid his gorgeous chest. He also looked half asleep, his hair standing up in all directions in a manner she found adorable.

Mumbling something about a shower, he ducked into the bathroom.

Sam let her breath out on a slow hiss as the door

closed, hiding all that male beauty. Had she nearly had sex by the lake last night with that specimen of male perfection? It must have been a fantasy. No one that pretty would be interested in someone as bony and flat as her.

Shaking her head, Sam turned back to her cooking and pondered why he'd bothered with her. A drive downtown could have garnered him at least half a dozen willing beauties. And every one would probably have had a better figure than she. Sam was very aware that she had not exactly been blessed in that area. She had been teased and called names like Twiggy, Olive Oyl, and "the boobless wonder" as a teenager. And then her figure had been one of the things Tom had complained loudest about in the months before leaving.

It wasn't just her lack of figure that made her wonder why he'd bother with her. Added to that was the fact that it seemed she hadn't been much blessed with grace or luck lately either; first there was this ear infection and the way it made her constantly trip over her own feet, and then there was last night. Sam doubted there were many people, men or women, who could have gotten themselves nearly eaten alive by leeches in the middle of an intimate moment.

Aware as she was that she was presently lacking in anything resembling a figure, grace, or even luck, Sam found it hard to imagine Mortimer might be interested in her in that way. She wasn't completely without self-esteem. Sam knew she was smart, and she did have a rather successful career, but it wasn't a woman's career or her brains a man was interested in taking to his bed, so—all in all—it was pretty hard for her to believe Mortimer could really be interested. It made more sense that last night had been some sort of an aberration: He'd been there and horny, and she'd been available, naked, and easy . . . at least until the leeches latched on and ruined things. She supposed Mortimer had just settled for her because she was on the spot. It was a depressing thought and one she tortured herself with while she waited for him to reappear from the bathroom.

Sam had just flipped the last pancake when the bathroom door opened and a waft of male cologne floated out to intoxicate her.

"Mmm, food," Mortimer murmured.

"Yes, I—" Sam nearly bit her tongue off in surprise as one of Mortimer's hands slid around her waist from behind and he gave her a quick kiss on the ear. He then reached around and above her to retrieve plates from the cupboard.

"I'll set the table, shall I?"

"Thank you," Sam mumbled, feeling her face flush as he gave her waist a little squeeze and moved off with the plates. She stared down at the pancakes for a second, and then glanced over her shoulder at the man.

Okay, Sam told herself as she watched him hum under his breath and set the table, so they were going to play house while they were here, but she shouldn't take it to heart and start imagining that it meant they were in a relationship. He was just taking advantage of the situation, settling for what or who was available. And so was she, Sam assured herself, but was surprised her nose didn't grow.

Rolling her eyes at herself, she asked, "How many pancakes do you want, Mor— Garrett?"

Mortimer paused beside the table and turned a surprised face her way, and Sam grimaced, but said, "I think of you as Mortimer because the guys call you that all the time, but I thought I should probably call you by your first name since we—" She stopped abruptly, not saying the *nearly had sex* part. Flushing over the words she hadn't said, Sam tried, "I mean if we're going to—" Her words stuttered to a halt once more. *If we're going to what? Sleep together? Be boyfriend and girlfriend? Sheesh.*

"Most people call me Mortimer, but you can call me Garrett if you like," Mortimer said gently.

Sam immediately wrinkled her nose, and then realizing what she'd done and that he—of course—had noticed, sighed and explained, "I don't really like the name Garrett. It reminds me of a rather annoying relative we had growing up and—" She fell silent as he crossed the room and took her face in his hands, amusement clear in his expression.

He kissed her gently and then confessed, "I don't really like Garrett either. It's not even really a first name. It was my mother's maiden name. And the only time anyone calls me Garrett is when I'm in trouble, then it's 'Garrett Gordon Mortimer,'" he said in deep accusing tones.

She smiled faintly, but then asked dubiously, "Gordon, huh?"

"No better than Garrett, is it?" he asked dryly and laughed at her expression. Releasing her, he said, "You can call me whatever you want, Sam. Mortimer, Mort, Mo." He shrugged and moved to the table, adding, "Or make up a pet name for me."

"A pet name," Sam murmured thoughtfully, turning back to rescue the last pancake from being burned. Retrieving the plate of pancakes she'd been keeping warm in the oven, she slid the last one on it and then turned off the stove and moved to the table. "Any suggestions of what this pet name could be?"

Mortimer tilted his head thoughtfully as she set the pancakes down, then began to lift some onto his plate when she gestured that he should.

Sam settled in her seat and waited curiously, but the man was taking his time. Before he answered she'd taken two pancakes onto her own plate, buttered them, poured syrup over top, cut off a piece, and popped it in her mouth.

"Sweet Toes?" Mortimer suggested finally and then jumped quickly to his feet to rush around and thump her back as she began to choke on her pancake. "God, I'm sorry. Are you all right?"

"Sweet Toes?" Sam gasped with disbelief as he continued to thump her.

Mortimer grimaced. "It was something my mother called my father."

Her eyes widened incredulously at this news and she unthinkingly said, "I can't wait to meet them."

"You can't."

Sam stiffened and then felt herself flush. "No, of course not. I didn't mean to suggest that there would be any reason for you to take me to meet your parents someday, I just—"

"I'd love to be able to take you to meet my parents, Sam," he interrupted solemnly, and then added, "But I can't because they're dead."

"Oh, I'm sorry," she offered quietly.

Mortimer's lips twisted into what she suspected was supposed to be a smile, then he kissed her cheek, straightened, and moved back to his own chair. Sam watched him, her mind in something of an uproar. He'd said he'd love to be able to take her to meet his parents, and she was now wondering if that was because he liked her, or if he'd meant that he'd just love to be able to take anyone to meet his parents, that he wished they were still alive?

Sam pondered the question briefly and then realized what she was doing and nearly smacked herself in the head. In high school a teacher had once told her she thought too much, and she seemed to be proving his point right there that moment. For God's sake! Was she going to analyze every little thing the man said? She had to stop this. Now. She needed to just sit back and enjoy the experience for what it was. Whatever that was. Or she'd drive herself crazy.

"Okay, so Sweet Toes is obviously no good," Mortimer said suddenly, reclaiming her attention.

"Well, I . . ." She paused to clear her throat and then admitted, "I just don't see myself calling you that."

"How about something more standard then like *dear,* or *honey?*" he suggested, and then added huskily, "I'd like to be your honey."

Sam gaped, hardly believing he'd just said that. Surely there was no way to misinterpret those words? Surely he meant—

The ringing of her phone interrupted her excited thoughts, and Sam scowled and even considered ignoring it until she recalled where she was and why. Cursing under her breath, she snatched up her cell phone and stood to walk toward the cottage door as she snapped it open.

"Yes?" she barked as she stepped out onto the small porch on the front of the cottage.

"Ms. Willan?"

Sam managed not to grind her teeth together as she recognized Belmont's voice. The man's timing was incredible. Pushing that worry aside, she said, "Yes, Sergeant. Thank you for returning my call. I was ringing you for an update on Cathy's case."

A snort sounded, and the man growled, "The update is that she's still not at home. I still think she's off having fun somewhere, but I'm driving around looking for her instead of dealing with other things that need tending because your boss is gonna make trouble if I don't. So why don't you and all his other little assistants and junior this and executive that stop calling and wasting my time making me talk to you all and let me get on with my job?"

Sam frowned at the news that Mr. Babcock apparently had others from the firm calling. She supposed she shouldn't be surprised. It was the way he worked, putting as many people on a job as possible and basically driving the other side crazy until they either gave up the case or lost their temper and made a mistake. This wasn't a court case though, and she didn't think it was a smart thing to be driving the sergeant crazy while he was trying to work. She would have actually apologized to the man for it, but apparently Belmont had done all the talking he felt he needed to. A sharp click was followed by the dial tone in her ear.

Sam made a face and closed her phone as most of her sympathy slid away. Truly the man had something of an attitude problem, and she had to wonder how he'd made it to sergeant.

"Judging by your irritated expression, I'd say that was Belmont," Mortimer commented as she stepped back into the cottage. "I take it the man didn't have any news for you?"

"No," Sam admitted unhappily.

"What are you going to do?" Mortimer asked.

She shook her head and then shrugged unhappily. "What can I do? As Madge said, I'm not a police officer."

"Madge?" Mortimer asked curiously.

"Mr. Babcock's secretary," she explained. "She pointed out this morning that Mr. Babcock only wanted me to keep calling the police and making sure they're on the case. She seemed to think that I should be having fun and enjoying my vacation in between calls."

He was silent for a moment and then said, "You don't look happy with the suggestion."

Sam shrugged. "I feel like I should be doing more to help find Cathy, but I haven't got a clue what that *more* could be. I mean, I have no idea where she's been taken, or by whom. And for all I know Belmont's right and she wasn't taken at all. Madge seems positive that's the case."

"Really?" Mortimer asked with interest.

"Yes. She reminded me that Cathy is a bit . . . er . . . well, her parents are kind of indulgent," she finished uncomfortably.

"You meant she's spoiled," he suggested with amusement.

Sam grimaced apologetically. "They're big clients at the firm. I would never say spoiled . . . but she is," she added heavily. "Very very spoiled. The kind of spoiled that has all the juniors and assistants at the firm fleeing the room when there's even a hint something has to be done involving interaction with her."

Mortimer smiled faintly, but then said, "Perhaps we could do both."

"Both what?" she asked with confusion.

"Perhaps we can satisfy both Madge's suggestion that you enjoy your vacation, as well as your desire to do more to help search for the girl."

Sam raised her eyebrows. "How?"

Chapter 12

"You were right. I see three of them in there," Mortimer said as he framed his hands around his eyes and peered through the window of the boathouse at the runabout, aluminum fishing boat, and three Sea-Doos inside. Glancing her way, he suggested, "Come look," and made room for her to squeeze up beside him at the window.

Sam hesitated, but then moved into the space allotted and peered through the window.

Mortimer watched her, smiling faintly as he inhaled her scent. Her natural smell was mixed with an outdoorsy scent from their excursion that morning. They'd spent the time since breakfast searching the grounds and some of the trails for the missing Cathy Latimer. The search had turned up exactly nothing. There was no bloodless body waiting on one of the trails, not even any sign of recent activity on the paths that he could tell; at least nothing other than animal droppings and such.

Now they were going to check around the lake a bit,

not just the water itself, but the shoreline too. If Cathy Latimer's lifeless body was about somewhere, Mortimer wanted to be the one to find it in case his people needed to be called in to do some serious evidence tampering. He'd rather do so without Sam along, but since he was unable to control her thoughts or behavior, Mortimer saw no way to manage that. As far as she knew, he was just helping her and shouldn't even have any desire to find the girl. She thought he was in a band, for God's sake.

"The boathouse key must be one of these," Sam said suddenly, retrieving Cathy's key ring from her pocket. She started to sort through them and then suddenly paused and tried the doorknob. A frown flickered over her face when the door proved unlocked and opened for them. Mortimer was a little surprised himself. He'd come to realize that security could be pretty lax up here, but the door really should have been locked. These were expensive items to leave lying around for someone to steal.

He followed Sam inside and around the walkway to where the Sea-Doos rested, his eyes caressing one gleaming machine after another.

"I wonder why three?" he commented. "It seems an odd number."

Sam shrugged. "There are only three of them; Martin; his wife, Trisha; and their daughter, Cathy."

Nodding, Mortimer dropped to his haunches to examine one of the machines more closely. While they would be using the Sea-Doos to search the lake and shoreline, he was excited at the prospect of riding one of the vehicles. To him it was definitely a case of mixing business and pleasure. "Do you really know how to ride one of these?"

"Yes. We have two of them ourselves," she answered, and when he glanced at her with a raised eyebrow, explained, "We take turns on them, but we're thinking of buying a third this summer."

"I didn't see any at the cottage," he said with a small frown as he thought of the yard and dock at the cottage next door to Decker's.

"They aren't in yet. Well, actually, they probably are now," she added wryly. "Grant usually puts the boat and Sea-Doos in for us the first time we come up. He launched the boats last week and was going to put the Sea-Doos in when we got there."

"Grant?" Mortimer asked curiously.

"Our neighbor on the other side from Decker's," Sam explained. "He's a year-round resident. A writer or something. The starving-artist type. He's lived there for the last five years or so, and we pay him to do certain things."

"Things like what?" Mortimer asked, hackles rising at the idea of the "things" this Grant might do.

Sam shrugged. "At the beginning of summer he puts the boats and Sea-Doos in, lays fresh gravel on the drive, and brings in sand for the beach to keep the leeches away." She grimaced as she said that, and then rushed on, "Then through the summer he cuts the lawn if we don't come up for a couple of weeks and keeps an eye on the place. Once October rolls around, he pulls the boat and Sea-Doos out, winter proofs them, and stores them in the garage and then does any maintenance to the cottage that needs doing, and cuts down trees that start looking like they might not last the winter." She shrugged. "We had another fellow that did all of this before him, but he was getting older and decided it was getting too much for him."

Mortimer nodded. It sounded like this Grant was a glorified handyman for the girls, and he immediately lost interest in him and turned his gaze back to the Sea-Doos. "Do you think the keys to these will be on that set?"

Sam glanced down at the keys in her hand, but shook her head. "They usually have little floaty things attached to the keys to keep them afloat should you lose them in the water."

"Floaty things?" Mortimer asked with amusement.

"I don't know what they're called," she admitted, and turned to peer around the boathouse.

When a little "aha," slipped from her lips, he followed her gaze to see a panel of keys on the wall. The sight made him think it was even odder that the boathouse door had been unlocked. Anyone could have come in and stolen one or all of the watercraft. But Mortimer shrugged the thought away in favor of teasing her.

"Ah, the floaty things," he murmured, and straightened to follow as she led the way to the panel. There were six hooks, but only five sets of keys, and he wondered if there had been another Sea-Doo or boat at one time as his gaze slid over the row of offerings. Each key had a bright colored "floaty thing" on it, which turned out to be a long, skinny, oblong shape of Styrofoam. Each was a neon color of yellow, orange, pink, purple, or green, and was marked with permanent black Magic Marker, stating which vehicle each belonged to.

"So?" Sam turned to glance at him. "Are you ready for a lesson? Shall we change into our swimsuits and give it a go?"

Mortimer grinned and nodded, and she headed for the door. He paused just long enough to cast one last glance at the Sea-Doos before following.

The sunlight seemed quite glaring after the cool interior of the boathouse, and Mortimer did take a moment to wonder if he'd lost his mind. He'd spent eight hundred years shunning daylight to avoid having to consume more blood, and yet here he was planning to tear about under its punishing rays, half naked on a Sea-Doo. It wasn't the brightest thing he'd done, but felt sure he'd brought enough blood to manage the feat as long as he didn't spend too long out there.

When Mortimer had first brought up the subject of searching the lake, he'd been thinking along the lines of a nice ride around dusk. Of course, Sam had assumed he meant during the day. By the time he'd realized that, she was up and headed for the boathouse. He could have reminded her about his sensitivity to the sun and suggested they wait until dusk, but she would have just said that they wouldn't be able to see as well. He couldn't argue that point without revealing his special abilities and feared she would suggest he stay at the cottage while she searched alone, and he supposed he could have done that. Certainly Sam should be safe enough during the day and he could have watched from the shade offered by the boathouse, but this was his job. Besides, he'd enjoyed their hike through the woods that morning. He enjoyed Sam's company; just being with her was soothing . . . and he'd be damned if he was missing out on trying the Sea-Doos.

So Mortimer was going to change into his swimsuit, ingest several bags of blood from the cooler in his room, and then tear around the lake half naked on the back of a Sea-Doo in search of a dead Cathy Latimer. Should be fun.

Sam was laughing at Mortimer's antics as he raced around her in the middle of the lake when something caught his attention, and he tore off away from her with a shout she couldn't hear over the roar of her own engine.

They'd been riding around on the lake for the last hour or more. The first part of that had been spent scouring the shoreline for any sign of Cathy Latimer, but they'd finished that task quickly. The Latimers' cottage was on a smaller lake than Magnetawan. Once they had finished their circuit and reached the boathouse again, Mortimer had suggested they take the Sea-Doos out and see what they could do before putting them away. They'd been having a really good time racing each other about since then, but as she glanced over curiously to see what had caught his eye, Sam felt the laughter die on her lips and concern clutch briefly at her heart. Mortimer was heading for a pair of buoys bobbing on the water, and she suddenly realized she hadn't warned him what those were for.

They usually signified something under the surface, often a rock formation or something of that ilk that could damage a boat. The spot between the two buoys was a spot boats should stay away from. She doubted they would do a Sea-Doo any good either.

Speeding up to try to catch up to him, Sam shouted out a warning, but Mortimer couldn't hear her any more than she had him. Fortunately he wasn't a fool, and did slow down as he approached the buoys, and that was probably what saved his life, she thought as the Sea-Doo jolted as it hit whatever was below the surface and he took a header off the machine.

Sam felt panic clutch her as she watched him go under. He was wearing a life jacket, but that wouldn't save his head from hitting whatever was under the surface, she thought as she sped up and raced toward the now bobbing Sea-Doo. The breath she hadn't realized she'd been holding slid from her lips when Mortimer surfaced as she drew near and slowed. Sam sent a silent prayer of thanks upward as she urged her own machine as close as she dared. She was preparing to dive off and swim over to see if he was all right when he grabbed at his Sea-Doo and climbed back onboard. At first he seemed just fine, but then she saw the blood flowing down the side of his head and felt panic clutch her again.

"Back!" Mortimer growled before she could try either to swim to him or to get closer. He immediately pushed backward off whatever had stopped the Sea-Doo and shot away across the lake in the direction of the Latimers' boathouse.

Sam followed, grateful the Sea-Doo seemed fine, but more worried about Mortimer. She knew head wounds bled a lot, but the amount of blood she'd seen had been frightening, and he'd looked extremely pale too. She tried to catch up to get a better look at him as they rode, but he was riding all out. He was already off the Sea-Doo and straightening from tying it up when she steered her own inside the boathouse.

Sam quickly lashed her Sea-Doo to the dock and then—afraid they might need to call an ambulance for

him—paused to retrieve her phone from the waterproof
storage compartment on the Sea-Doo. She then clam-
bered onto the walkway and hurried after Mortimer as
he stumbled toward the door.

"Let me see," she said worriedly.

"I'm fine," he growled, rushing ahead and leaving her
to chase after him the best she could. Mortimer could
move when he wished to, and it seemed he was running away as if she were the Devil himself as he hurried
toward the cottage.

Cursing, Sam moved as quickly as she could, but
didn't have the agility or speed he did. Mortimer was
inside the cottage before she was halfway up the trail.

She should have thought to explain to him what the
buoys were for before they'd set out, Sam berated herself furiously. What kind of teacher forgot something
like that? This was all her fault.

Sam was nearly to the cottage when her phone began
to ring. She glanced at the readout, scowling when she
saw that it was Mr. Babcock, but didn't answer. She had
an emergency situation here and he would just have to
wait. It wasn't like she had any news for him anyway.
While she'd taken the time to call the O.P.P. station again
before they'd set out for their ride, Sam hadn't been able
to get ahold of Belmont. The man seemed to be avoiding
her. Much as Mortimer was now, she thought grimly as
she entered the cottage and saw that the bathroom door
was closed.

"Mortimer?" she called, hurrying to the bathroom
door. "You have to let me see. We might have to take
you to the hospital."

When she got no answer, Sam cautiously opened

the door, afraid he'd passed out and lay in a huddled mass on the floor of the tiny room beyond. Instead, she found it empty. Frowning, she pulled it closed again and turned to the hall.

"Mortimer?" Sam stopped at his door and tried to open it, surprised when she found it locked. She hadn't realized there even *were* locks on the doors. Concern creasing her forehead, she called, "Mortimer, open the door."

A moment of silence passed and then he answered, "I'm fine, Sam. I just nicked my forehead on a rock. I'm just drying off and changing and then I'll come out."

Sam stared at the door with disbelief. She'd seen him plummet into the water. And she'd seen the blood when he'd climbed back on his machine. He'd more than nicked it.

"Mortimer—" she began grimly.

"How about we head into town for lunch?" he suggested, and then added in teasing tones, "We can stop at the O.P.P. station afterward so you can beat up Belmont for taking so long to return your calls. I'll help."

Sam stared at the wooden surface of the door with bewilderment. His voice really did sound perfectly fine.

"Why don't you go change so we can go into town for lunch?" he added. "I'll be out in a minute. I promise I'm all right."

Sam let her breath out on a sigh. Maybe he really hadn't been as hurt as she'd first thought. Still, she asked, "Are you sure you're all right?"

"I'd open the door and show you, but I'm naked at the moment and can't be responsible for what happens if I do."

Sam's eyes widened incredulously at the threat, but she found herself backing away from the door. If he was healthy enough to say something like that, he was probably all right. Then she cursed as her phone began to ring again.

"I'm going to take this and then get dressed. But shout if you start feeling woozy or anything," she ordered, and then moved into her room to answer her phone.

It was Mr. Babcock, calling during the court lunch break to check on things. Sam explained that there was no news yet and promised to call Mr. Babcock back as soon as there was any, then tried to rush him off the phone so that she could change and check on Mortimer again. If he wasn't out of his room by the time she'd changed, Sam thought, she might very well try to jimmy the lock or something to get in to see for herself that he was all right.

Unfortunately, Mr. Babcock insisted on updating her on the status of the Latimers' flight, which was that they were still grounded at the airport. He then felt it necessary to fill her in on what was happening in court since she'd been involved with research and interviews on the case. He must have spent his entire lunch break talking to her because it was more than half an hour before she could get him off the phone. Any other time, Sam would have been jubilant. It probably meant good things for her career that he was bothering to talk to her, but at that moment, she didn't much care about anything but seeing that Mortimer was all right.

Hanging up with relief, Sam tossed the phone on the bed and quickly dragged off her life jacket and swimsuit, and then pulled on clothes. When she rushed out into the hall, however, it was only to find Mortimer's door open and his room empty.

Frowning, Sam moved out into the kitchenette/living area, but he wasn't there either, so she hurried out of the cottage. The first place she looked was the SUV. When he wasn't there, Sam followed her instincts down to the boathouse and rushed in to find Mortimer on his knees on the walkway, leaning down to peer at the bottom of the front of the Sea-Doo.

Breath leaving her on a relieved whoosh, Sam hurried to his side. "What are you doing?"

"Just checking to be sure I didn't damage the Sea-Doo. Much to my amazement it appears I didn't," Mortimer added, his head remaining down.

Sam shifted impatiently beside him, eager to see his head.

"Are you ready to go to lunch?" he asked, finally straightening, and she immediately moved closer, eyes narrowing as she noted that there was no injury on his forehead.

"It's about here," he said dryly, pointing to a spot an inch or so beyond his hairline.

"Let me take a look at it," Sam said, stepping forward and reaching for his head, but Mortimer caught her hands in his as he got to his feet.

"I'm fine," he insisted firmly. "I don't even have a headache. I must have just grazed my head in passing as I fell."

Sam really wanted to see the wound for herself, but she could see that he *appeared* fine. He had good color and his eyes were clear. Sighing, she gave in with a nod.

It seemed obvious he was one of those men who couldn't abide fussing. Letting her hands drop to her sides when he released them, she said apologetically, "I'm really sorry. I should have warned you about the buoys and what they're for."

"There's nothing to be sorry for," Mortimer assured her, urging her out of the boathouse. "I had some idea that the buoys must warn about something being there, but I thought it would be a fishing net and the Sea-Doo would skim over it. It didn't occur to me that it might be something else and not safe until just before I hit it. That's why I slowed down. My original intention was just to glance down as I rode over it."

Sam grimaced, still blaming herself.

"How the hell did a huge boulder get out there anyway?" he asked as they started up the trail toward the cottage.

Sam shrugged. "All these lakes were carved out when the glaciers passed through. I guess some of them left little bits of rock uncarved."

"Hmm," Mortimer muttered, and then fell silent.

They stopped long enough in the cottage for Sam to retrieve her purse, but then headed straight out to the SUV.

Minden was a small town, but they found a little bistro on the river. It was busy, and they had to make do with a table inside instead of enjoying being outside on the terrace. Mortimer didn't say anything, but was secretly relieved.

"How are you feeling?" Sam suddenly asked, drawing his attention to the fact that she was eyeing him with concern.

Mortimer grimaced and rolled his eyes. "I told you I'm fine. I don't even have a headache from the—"

"I didn't mean that," she interrupted, and then explained, "You looked a bit relieved rather than disappointed that we couldn't sit outside, and I just recalled that Bricker said you have a sensitivity to the sun. We've been outside most of the day so far and—"

"Oh, that," Mortimer waved her concern away. "It was shady under the trees while we were searching the woods."

"It wasn't shady on the lake though," she pointed out.

No, it certainly hadn't been shady on the lake, he acknowledged to himself. And he'd been just starting to notice the effects of the sun and thinking he should suggest heading back so that he could down a bag or two of blood when he'd spotted the buoys. After his little accident, the sun had been the least of his worries. He could hardly say all that to Sam, though, so merely shrugged and said, "I'm fine."

She frowned and opened her mouth to ask something else, but he forestalled her by asking, "What made you want to be a lawyer?"

Sam blinked, startled by the abrupt change of topic, but then sat back and considered the question seriously before saying, "*Twelve Angry Men.*"

Mortimer blinked in surprise.

"It's a movie," Sam added.

"I know," he said.

"Oh." She seemed surprised, but then shrugged and said, "Well, the jurors held that boy's life in their hands. And the way Henry Fonda's character affected and swayed the other jurors mesmerized me. I wanted

to be like him. I wanted to fight for truth and justice."
She gave an embarrassed smile and added, "Of course,
there's no such thing as a professional juror. Lawyer
was the next best thing." Shrugging, she glanced away
and then back and asked, "What about you? What
made you choose your career?"

"I wanted to fight for truth and justice too," he admitted wryly.

Sam frowned and tilted her head. "So you joined a
band?"

Mortimer blinked and then sat up abruptly, recalling
the lies they'd told as a cover story. "Oh, no. Well, that
was just— I mean I wanted that, but . . ."

"But music was where your heart was?" she suggested
when he fell silent and just stared helplessly at her.

"Yes." He almost gasped the word, relieved beyond
measure that she'd helped him off the hook like that.
The waitress chose that moment to arrive at their table.
Mortimer took the menu she offered, and assumed a
rapt expression as she rattled off the day's specials to
them, but didn't hear a word she said. He was busy berating himself for the stupid slip he'd made. Mortimer
had been an enforcer for more than a hundred years
and should be beyond such mistakes.

The waitress finished speaking and left them to consider the menu, and Mortimer turned his attention to
the food listed there. The names were meaningless to
him. He had no idea what a club sandwich was, or a
BLT, but the short descriptions beneath were more helpful. Almost too helpful. Several sounded delicious, and
he was now struggling to pick one. Mortimer finally
managed to narrow it down to two, but that was as

far as he could go. Rather than continue the struggle, he decided he'd order both of them and set the menu aside.

A glance to Sam showed her still considering the restaurant's offerings. She had laid the menu open on the table before her and was poring over it as if searching a map for the X that marked where the buried treasure would be. Mortimer found himself smiling faintly at her concentration and wanting to kiss her. He'd actually like more than that. He'd like to move around the table, lift her out of her chair, lay her back on the table as he had on the rock last night, and kiss and lick his way from her mouth, down her throat, to each breast, across her belly, and then kiss his way between her legs and—

"Are you ready to order?"

Mortimer blinked as his imaginings shattered and he found Sam had finished with her menu and set it aside and the waitress had returned to get their orders. Letting his breath out on a slow sigh, he waited as Sam placed her order. He then placed his own and handed over his menu. The moment the smiling server was gone, Mortimer glanced back to Sam. Unfortunately, he found his mind immediately flooded with images of the meal he'd like to make of her—it was a biting optional meal.

"Is something wrong?" Sam asked with a frown.

"No, of course not," he said quickly.

"Oh." She managed a smile. "You were looking at me a little strangely. I thought maybe I had something on my face or something."

"No," he assured her, and then sought his mind for something to say to distract him from the rather lascivious images trying to reclaim his thoughts. He needed something unsexy to talk about, and the most unsexy thing he could think of was parents, so he said, "Decker said he'd been told that your parents died in some sort of accident?"

"Yes," she said quietly, her expression turning sad. "A car accident on the way home from the movies on their anniversary."

Mortimer winced, thinking maybe this hadn't been such a good topic. He did want to know this stuff. He wanted to know everything about Sam, but it was a beautiful sunny day, they were out at a restaurant, and this seemed to him to be rainy-afternoon, cuddled-up-in-the-blankets, his-holding-her-close-after-amazing-mind-blowing-sex-type talk.

"You said your parents are dead?" Sam asked suddenly, managing to nudge his mind off the idea of amazing, mind-blowing sex with her, which was where it had seemed to stop a moment ago.

Clearing his throat, he nodded. "Yes."

"Was it an accident too?" she asked.

Mortimer stiffened and asked warily, "What makes you think it wasn't natural causes?"

Sam appeared surprised and then pointed out, "Well, you can't be much more than twenty-eight or twenty-nine, Mortimer. So unless your parents were extremely old when they had you, the chances of their both being dead from natural causes seems unlikely."

"Oh yes, of course," he muttered, giving himself a mental kick. "They died together. In a house fire."

Sam reached out to clasp his hand where it rested on the tabletop. She gave it a brief squeeze of sympathy and then started to release him, but Mortimer turned his hand over and caught her fingers with his own, holding on to her. Her eyes jerked to his with surprise, and he had the mad urge to tell her the truth about his parents. About everything, but of course he couldn't.

"How old were you when they died?" Sam asked, leaving her hand in his.

Mortimer had been six hundred and eighty-eight years old in 1898 when his parents died. He said, "Eighteen."

"Oh, I'm sorry," Sam squeezed his hand again. "That's how old Jo was when our parents died."

The waitress chose that moment to appear with their food, and Sam retrieved her hand and sat back out of the way as the girl set down their plates and drinks.

"Thank you," Sam murmured as the girl finished and turned away. She then raised an eyebrow at Mortimer's two plates with two sandwiches and two heaps of fries and asked, "Are you related to Bricker?"

The question surprised a laugh out of Mortimer, but he shook his head. "No relation at all, though I don't blame you for thinking so at the moment."

"Hmm," Sam said dubiously.

"Perhaps I'm sublimating my other hunger for a hunger for food," he suggested with a wicked grin, and chuckled when she got what he was hinting at and flushed a dark red. He regretted his teasing, though, when she then turned her attention to her food and gave up talking for eating. He suspected his teasing had upset her a bit, though he wasn't sure why. Sorry about that, he let her eat in peace.

Neither of them spoke again until they'd finished eating, but the moment he pushed his plate away, Sam asked a bit abruptly, "So, other than sex, drugs, and rock and roll, what do you like best about being in a band?"

"I don't like sex, drugs, and rock and roll," he assured her with a frown, and then realized what he'd said and added, "I mean I do. The sex, that is, not the drugs and rock and roll." When that just made her tilt her head and eye him with further confusion, he added, "I mean, I like sex but not with groupies or anything like that."

"But not the drugs or rock and roll?" she asked.

"Right." He nodded and then stopped and shook his head as his brain picked apart the words. "No, not right. I like rock and roll too, obviously. I'm in a band, but I— It's just the drugs I don't like . . . and the groupies," he added, and then stopped and tried to sort out her expression. Her lips were twitching, but he couldn't tell if it was with amusement or disgust. Deciding moving the conversation along might be good, he blurted, "Travel. I like that part of my job."

And it was true. Mortimer had always enjoyed seeing new places and people.

"Where all have you played?" she asked curiously.

"California, Kansas City, New York. We've pretty much been to every state, as well as every province in Canada," he said honestly.

"Your band has played in Canada?" Sam asked with surprise.

Mortimer grimaced, but managed to avoid lying by saying, "We've worked in lots of places in Canada."

"Not Toronto," Sam said with certainty. "I'd remember a band named Morty and the Muppets playing in Toronto."

Mortimer groaned inwardly at the horrible name, and then turned to the waitress with relief as she brought the bill.

"I think we've done about all we can looking for your boss's goddaughter today," Mortimer announced as they walked out to the SUV. "Why don't we take Madge's advice and do something fun?"

"Like what?" Sam asked curiously.

He was silent for a minute, his thoughts working. The truth was, Mortimer felt like he should be working, but he'd really rather spend time with Sam. It was a new situation for him to find himself in. His job as an enforcer had been the focus of his life for a long time. It had ruled where and how he lived, whom he interacted with, and . . . well, basically every aspect of his life. Until now. Now he found his sense of duty battling with his desire to be with Sam, and he was struggling. Part of him felt honor-bound to concentrate on the job at hand, while the other part was arguing that he'd given a lot of years to the Council working as an enforcer and deserved some time off.

Mortimer was hoping to settle the issue by doing both at once as they had this morning. Since the hunt for Cathy Latimer wasn't turning up anything, he'd decided he should maybe poke around one of the other bite-sightings spots and see what he could find. The closest one was at a bakery in a town called Haliburton. One of the workers had apparently sported a bite mark on her neck about a month ago, so in answer to Sam's question, he suggested, "We could drive to Haliburton and see what it has to offer."

"Haliburton?" she asked with surprise.

"I saw it on the map. It looks a little bigger than Minden and isn't far away." When she hesitated, Mortimer added, "You have your cell if Belmont calls with any news."

Recalling Madge's words of wisdom, Sam managed a smile. "Haliburton it is then."

Haliburton turned out to be just what Sam needed. She found herself relaxing as they enjoyed a leisurely stroll along the few short blocks downtown. When Mortimer stopped to peer over the listings in the window of a Realtor's office, Sam raised her eyebrows.

"Thinking about buying down here?" she teased.

"More likely up in Magnetawan," Mortimer answered seriously, and when her eyes went round, added, "It's relaxing up here. Nice. I like it. And the company is good."

Sam's heart fluttered briefly and she blushed as he met her gaze, but then his eyes slipped past her and brightened.

"A bakery!" He urged her through a small courtyard beside the Realtor's toward a building that stood back farther from the road. "I haven't had fresh-baked bread in centuries."

"Centuries, huh?" Sam laughed at what she knew must be an exaggeration and allowed him to usher her inside.

Mortimer liked his baked goods. Sam came to that conclusion as she watched him nearly clean out the bakery. The man spent a good deal of time talking to both women who worked in the bakery, but also bought six different loaves of bread, every last bit of apple strudel, plus several other items. They were both weighed down with packages when they finally left. It made it rather shocking to her when he said, "We should stop at the grocery store on the way back."

"The grocery store?" she asked with disbelief.

"We don't have anything for breakfast tomorrow morning," he pointed out. "I think I'll make you bacon and eggs. Those were really good when I had them in Huntsville."

Sam chuckled and shook her head. If there was one thing she'd come to learn about Mortimer, it was that he really liked his food.

They stopped at the Independent grocery store in Minden on the way back. Mortimer once again proved his love for food by buying way too much. He was in good shape, without a bit of fat on him, so the only thing she could think was that he either had a metabolism like her own, or he really worked his food off while on stage. Having seen the way some singers bounced around under the hot lights during a performance, she suspected it was the latter.

"How does barbecued steak sound for dinner?" Mortimer asked as he parked the SUV beside the cottage.

"Sounds good," Sam decided as she slid out and moved around to the back to help him with their purchases. "I'm going to try to call Belmont again, but then I'll get started on it."

"I'll cook," Mortimer offered, and Sam sucked in a breath, not so much surprised as almost afraid to believe she'd heard right. Seeing her expression, he raised an eyebrow and asked with amusement, "What? You've never seen a man cook before?"

"Not for a while," she admitted wryly. While her

father had made the occasional Sunday breakfast and barbecued with the best of them, her ex— Sam pushed that thought away. Garrett Mortimer wasn't Tom, and she had to stop comparing them. Besides, Mortimer had already won that race hands down.

"Well, this is the twenty-first century," Mortimer announced as if she might not have noticed. "I have it on good authority that men cook now."

"What authority would that be?" she asked with amusement.

"Some magazine I read last year in Tallahassee," he answered promptly.

"Tallahassee?" she said with a laugh.

"What's wrong with Tallahassee?" he asked at once.

"Nothing," she assured him quickly, and then admitted, "It's just that the way you say it suggests you've never actually cooked yourself."

"I haven't," he admitted, lifting most of the bags out of the truck, leaving her only two. "But it's not brain surgery. It can't be that hard."

"Don't say that around Alex," Sam suggested dryly as she gathered the two remaining bags and closed the hatchback to follow him to the cottage.

"I'll get this stuff put away. You call Belmont," Mortimer said as they stepped inside.

Sam hesitated, but then took her phone outside to make the call. She wasn't terribly surprised to be told he was out of the office, but this time she didn't allow herself to get irritated. She merely left a message that she'd called and then called Mr. Babcock, relieved when she reached his voice mail and didn't have to speak to him personally. She was leaving a message when Mortimer came outside with the steaks and began to fiddle with the barbecue that sat on the porch to the side of the door. Concentrating on what she was saying, Sam wasn't really paying attention to what Mortimer was doing until a sudden whoosh and his curse drew her attention to where he appeared to be trying to barbecue his hand.

Ending her message much more abruptly than she'd intended, Sam snapped her phone shut and rushed to his side as he snatched his hand and the barbecue lighter out of the base of the barbecue. "What did you do?"

"Nothing," he said soothingly. "I was just trying to get the barbecue started."

"From the top?" she asked with dismay.

"Is there another way?" he asked with surprise.

"The hole!" Sam exclaimed with horror as she realized he'd turned the gas on and reached in to light the thing. "Underneath. See the holes. Those are—You stick the lighter up through those. You don't light it from the top."

"Oh." He glanced at the barbecue and shrugged. "Well, no harm done."

"No—You could have—" Sam stopped and took a deep breath. He could have really hurt himself and was damned lucky he hadn't. Letting her breath out slowly, she said, "You've never barbecued before either?"

"No, but there's a first time for everything. I'm fine," he assured her. "And it's lit now. I can cook. Why don't you go on inside and get the wine?"

"Maybe I should do this for y—"

"No, I'm cooking. If you want to be helpful, you can bring me my wine. I poured us both a glass."

"But—"

"No," he insisted, pushing her toward the door. "In you go. I'm the man. I get to barbecue while you stand around and look cute."

Sam blushed at the suggestion, but allowed him to urge her to the door. Inside she found that—aside from having opened and poured the wine—Mortimer had already thrown together the Caesar salad mix and cut up bread and set both on the table along with plates and silverware. Shaking her head, Sam turned to pick up the wine and hurried back outside to be sure he didn't blow up the barbecue.

Chapter 13

"Strudel and wine?"

Mortimer glanced up from the table on which he'd just set strudel, a freshly opened bottle of wine, and a deck of cards, and considered Sam's expression as she stepped back inside. Her voice had been amused and she was trying to smile, but he could tell by the set of her jaw and the tension in her shoulders that the phone calls hadn't gone well. He wished she hadn't insisted on trying Belmont again once they'd finished their meal, but she was a woman who took her responsibilities seriously, and the man hadn't bothered to return her calls since that morning. The least he could have done was check in with her, if only to tell her there was nothing new to report and he was still looking.

"No Belmont?" he asked instead of responding to her comment.

"No," she admitted with disgust, irritation flaring up in her eyes. Shaking her head, she added, "Mr. Babcock was angry enough at the man evading my calls that he's calling some 'friends.'"

"Friends?" Mortimer asked as he pulled out her chair for her.

"Hmm." Sam grimaced as she sat down. "I suspect he'll call the commissioner of the Provincial Police. The commissioner is friends with Mr. Babcock and the Latimers."

"Ah." Mortimer nodded as he moved around to his own seat. "I suspect the elusive Sergeant Belmont is about to find himself in a world of trouble."

"Maybe." Sam sighed. "If so, he brought it on himself, the turkey. Still, I'm sorry I failed Mr. Babcock like this."

"You didn't fail him," Mortimer said firmly. "You've done everything you could, including looking for her yourself. And on your vacation. Sergeant Belmont is the problem here. He really should be keeping in touch with you and letting you know what's going on."

Sam relaxed a little at his words, and then glanced at the goodies on the table and raised her eyebrows as she asked again, "Strudel and wine?"

"I was hungry for dessert, but thought you might need a drink after your phone calls," he explained.

"And the cards?" she asked, glancing at the deck in the center of the table.

"Your sisters sent those. I thought you might like to play something."

"I like cards," Sam admitted, brightening visibly. "What shall we play?"

Mortimer hesitated and then suggested, "Poker?"

"What would we use for chips?" she asked.

Mortimer considered the situation and then suggested, "We could play truth poker."

"What's that?"

"If you win a hand, you ask me a question that I have to answer truthfully, and vice versa."

Sam's eyes widened, but after the briefest hesitation, she nodded.

Smiling, Mortimer collected the deck of cards and began shuffling.

She watched for a moment and then commented, "I've never heard of this version of poker."

"Neither have I, I just made it up," he admitted with a laugh.

"Really?"

Mortimer shrugged. "Your sisters suggested strip poker, but I didn't think you'd go for that."

Sam groaned. "You'll have to forgive them. They weren't raised right."

He grinned at her apology. "Don't they have the same parents as you?"

"Yes, but they didn't listen to them and I did," she responded at once.

Mortimer chuckled and began to deal. When he'd come up with the idea of truth poker, it hadn't occurred to him that he might be causing himself some problems should Sam ask the wrong question. Fortunately, he'd dealt himself a good hand.

"Go ahead, ask your question," Sam said grimly as she scooped up the cards.

He almost teased her, but she was obviously as nervous about what he might ask as he was, so he merely said, "What's your favorite flower?"

"Gladiolas," she answered promptly and offered him a bright smile. Sam was unquestionably relieved that he'd asked such an easy question and was much more relaxed as she dealt the next hand. She began to tense up again, however, when she picked up her cards, and Mortimer soon understood why. She'd dealt herself a horrid hand. He won the round with a pair of threes.

"Go on." She sighed as he began to collect the cards. Despite his first question, it seemed obvious she was expecting a more personal, possibly embarrassing question this time.

"What's your favorite candy?"

Her shoulders slumped and she peered at him with a touch of confusion, as if suspecting he was up to something with these easy questions, but not sure what. Still, she answered, "Hazelnut chocolates."

Mortimer was on a roll and won the next hand too, this time asking what her favorite food was. Sam just shook her head and answered, "Chinese" as she dealt the next round.

This time she was the one to win the round and it was Mortimer's turn to wait anxiously for her question as he gathered the cards and began to shuffle them.

"Do you have any brothers or sisters?" Sam asked after a pause.

Mortimer stilled and then nodded. "Two brothers."

"Really?" she asked with surprise and then bit her lip and muttered, "That's kind of weird, isn't it?"

"It is?" Mortimer asked with confusion.

"Well . . ." She grimaced and said, "It's just you have two brothers, I have two sisters. Your parents died in a house fire, and mine in a car accident where the car exploded."

"Their car exploded?" Mortimer asked. She hadn't mentioned that earlier, and if she hadn't it was probably because thinking about it upset her, he thought with a frown as Sam nodded in answer to his question. He hesitated briefly, but had to ask, "Were they killed by the accident or—"

Sam shook her head and he didn't bother finishing the question. Her parents had burned to death like his own. And that was about enough serious conversation for one night, Mortimer decided, and reached for the bottle of wine to top up their glasses as he said, "There's a DVD player hooked up to that TV and a shelf full of DVDs in my room, most of them comedies. Do you like comedies?"

"I love comedies," she said, brightening visibly.

"Good. Let's watch a comedy."

"Okay," she said, standing up. "You pick it, and I'll move the wine and strudel over to the table."

Nodding, Mortimer stood and moved up the hall to his room. He picked three or four comedies from the shelf and took them out to Sam. He found her just settling on the small couch with their wine and goodies spread out on the coffee table before her. She considered the movies he held out and, apparently unable to decide, did a quick "Eenie, meenie, minie mo."

Chuckling at her sophisticated selection process, Mortimer turned on the television and DVD player, slid the movie in, then grabbed the remotes and moved to join her on the couch. She was seated primly on one side of the couch, leaving him plenty of room on his own. Mortimer didn't intend to use it, however. He had an urge to cuddle up with her on the little love seat while they watched the show . . . or maybe didn't watch the show, he thought hopefully, and then caught a whiff of her as he reached the couch. Mortimer froze.

"Mortimer? Is something wrong?" Sam asked when he continued to just stand there, and he felt his mouth twist at the question.

"No," he growled, and abruptly settled on his side of the love seat, as far from her as he could get without actually choosing another seat. The movie had been his idea, he could hardly back out of it now, but the moment it was over he needed to find an excuse to go out. In the meantime, he needed to keep as much distance as he could between them . . . and maybe try not to breathe in her scent.

Mortimer rolled his eyes at the thought, and then forced himself to turn his attention to the movie as it started, hoping it would be distracting enough to help him ignore the smell presently tantalizing his nostrils. It was a useless hope. Sam seemed to enjoy the movie and laughed several times, but he didn't have a clue what was happening on the screen. His mind was completely and utterly wrapped up in the fragrant aroma wafting off Sam and rolling across the love seat to surround him. Eau de Sam was a heady mix that was making his mouth water to the point that Mortimer feared drooling all over himself.

It was a great relief when the movie ended. He was off the couch and ejecting the DVD almost before the first credit began to roll down the screen. Mortimer popped the disc into its case and turned back toward the couch, his mouth opening, but then paused. Sam was yawning. Beaming at her as if she'd done something clever, he said, "You're all in. I guess we should call it a night."

"Oh." Sam looked startled at the suggestion, but hesitated, and he knew from the uncertainty that crossed her face that she wasn't sure if she should assure him she was fine to continue, or if he wished to end the evening. Mortimer held his tongue, silently praying she'd simply go to bed.

He was in dire need of blood and desperate to get her off to bed so that he could slip out and find some. Between his time in the sun and his head wound, Mortimer had run through the supply he'd brought back with him. The head wound had been much more serious than he'd led Sam to believe. He'd hit the rock under the surface of the water at whiplash speed and suspected he'd fractured his skull. It was why he'd rushed back ahead of her and locked himself in his room. There was no way she would have taken no for an answer about going to the hospital had she seen it.

Mortimer had binged on the blood left in the cooler in an effort to speed along his healing and then managed—with a little help from her boss's phone call—to avoid her just long enough for the bleeding to stop and his head to begin to heal. Unfortunately, that binge had used up the last of the blood.

Mortimer might have been all right and lasted until their return to Magnetawan the next day had he not then burned his hand while trying to light the barbecue. He'd managed to hide that from her as well, and it was nearly completely healed now where he rested it against his leg, but he was in desperate need of blood again.

"I— Yes, I guess I should go to bed," Sam said finally. She paused then, her gaze flickering to him and away.

Mortimer knew she was hoping that he'd give her an excuse to stay up, but he remained silent. Waiting.

"Well." She stood and moved slowly away from the love seat, her tone brisk. "This was fun. Thank you. And thank you for cooking too. I guess I'll see you in the morning."

"Good night," Mortimer murmured as she headed up the hall toward the room she was using. He watched her silently until she disappeared into her room and closed the door behind her, only then allowing himself to breathe out a sigh of mingled relief and regret.

Mortimer hadn't missed the disappointment in her eyes. She was definitely getting mixed signals from him and probably hadn't a clue what to make of his behavior. Last night he'd been an eager, demanding lover, only stopped in his attempt to bed her—or boulder her—by the incident with the leeches. And then tonight . . . nothing. Not even a kiss good night. But Mortimer didn't dare let himself get that close to her. His hunger could too easily overpower his desire and he might bite her.

Mortimer was sure Sam wasn't ready to hear what he had to tell her. He'd rather wait a couple more days and give her the chance to start thinking of them as a couple. To that end, he was attempting to woo her as she deserved, but wasn't even able to do that properly at the moment.

Grimacing, Mortimer turned and began to pace the kitchen, counting off the passing minutes. He'd wait half an hour to give her a chance to fall asleep, and then he had to go out in search of blood. He was back to feeding "off the hoof."

Sam lay in bed a long time, staring into the darkness with bewilderment as she listened to Mortimer pacing the kitchen. She had no idea what to make of the man. He was driving her crazy with the way he blew hot and cold. The first night he was all over her, and then today she'd received a morning kiss, but then nothing. He hadn't even tried for a good-night kiss, let alone take advantage of the love seat for some serious action. All that just convinced her that she'd been right and that the night before had been an anomaly, something unlikely to be repeated.

She was sighing miserably at the realization when the sound of the cottage door opening and closing reached her. Sam stiffened and sat up. Her first thought was that he might be going for a swim, but then she heard the SUV start up and the crunch of gravel as it drove away.

Sam slowly lay back down, sure Mortimer was going to find the nightlife that he and the others had kept asking about the first night after they'd met. The idea wasn't a pleasant one, but was followed by even more unpleasant ones. She found herself lying there, imagining him walking into some poky little local bar, and dancing with shapely locals and cottagers, then stumbling back to his SUV with his arm around one of them and doing all those lovely things he'd done with her . . . before she'd been attacked by leeches and made to look like a diseased hooker.

Groaning, Sam turned on her side and punched her pillow, then closed her eyes and tried to will herself to sleep. However, with thoughts like that plaguing her, she was still wide awake when the crunch of tires on gravel announced the SUV's return and Mortimer slipped quietly back inside. She listened to him move around until the cottage fell silent, and then she listened to that silence for a while before finally drifting off.

Sam had no idea what time it was when she finally fell asleep, but she was awake by nine A.M. Even so, Mortimer was already up and around. She heard him moving about as she collected clean clothes and her sandals. When she then slipped out of her room, it was to find the air redolent with the scent of coffee and cooking bacon.

Inhaling the lovely scents, Sam snuck up the hall in her nightie, her clothes held before her like a shield. At the end of the hall, she peeked around the corner to see him frying up potato wedges at the stove with his back to her, and quickly ducked into the bathroom to take a shower.

Ten minutes later, she presented herself in the kitchen, dressed, damp hair brushed back off her face, and completely makeup-free. Mortimer did not run screaming from the cottage.

"Good morning," he greeted, smiling at her widely.

"Morning," Sam mumbled, and started to move past him, only to gasp in surprise when he caught her arm and pulled her close for a quick, but very hard and thorough kiss. When he released her and turned back to his cooking, Sam was left panting and at a complete loss as to what to make of that.

Honestly, she had no idea what the man was about. One minute he was hot and passionate, the next just friendly and treating her like a buddy or kid sister. Then he landed a good-morning kiss on her that was definitely not what one gave to either a buddy or a kid sister. He had her thoroughly confused now.

Sam stood there fretting about that until he announced that breakfast was ready and she should grab a plate. Shaking her head, she grabbed them both a plate and moved to his side so he could serve up the food. Once he was finished, she carried them to the table. Sam sat down before she really glanced at her breakfast. The bacon was burned to a cinder, the eggs not quite cooked, and the potatoes were blackened . . . and she knew it would still be quite the most delicious breakfast she'd ever been treated to just because he'd gone to the trouble to make it.

Smiling wryly at herself, Sam picked up her fork and dug in. They ate in silence at first, and then Mortimer began to chatter cheerfully away about things they should do that day. He carried the conversation alone at first and didn't seem to mind. It wasn't until she joined in with suggestions of her own and noticed the way he relaxed that she realized her silence had bothered him. They chatted easily after that, sticking to topics like the weather, foreign politics, the sorts of books they each liked to read, what types of movies and music they enjoyed, and so on.

Once the meal was finished, they did the dishes together, she washing and he drying until her cell phone rang. Mortimer continued on as she stepped outside to take the call, finishing the dishes and then washing down the counters and stove too while he waited. He had it all done by the time she snapped her phone closed and stepped back inside.

"The Latimers are supposed to land at four-thirty this afternoon," she announced, passing on the information Clarence Babcock had given her. "Mr. Babcock's son is picking them up from the airport and the three of them are driving straight up here."

"That gives us the day to play, then," Mortimer said lightly as he turned back to set the washcloth on the sink. He then leaned against the counter, incredibly sexy in his jeans and black T-shirt, looking good enough to eat.

Flushing as that thought crossed her mind, Sam turned away. "I'd better call Belmont and see what he's doing about finding Cathy so I can report to her parents when they arrive."

"Good idea," Mortimer murmured. "I'm just going to take a quick shower while you do."

Sam watched him walk up the hall and disappear into his room, a small sigh slipping from her lips, but then forced herself to turn her attention back to her phone. She punched in the number and leaned against the counter as she pressed it to her ear, her eyes shifting to Mortimer as he stepped out of the room. Her eyes widened to drink him in as he came back up the hall. He'd stripped off the T-shirt he'd been wearing and was now bare-chested and barefoot in jeans, fresh clothes held in his hand.

Sam stared, automatically responding to his smile as she watched him duck into the bathroom and close the door. The phone continued to ring in her ear, but she hardly noticed. The walls in the cottage were incredibly thin. Sam could actually hear the ratcheting sound of Mortimer's zipper going down and then the rustle of cloth from behind the door as he stripped. Her mouth went dry as her mind produced a picture of what was happening, and then the hiss of the shower sounded and she imagined him stepping naked under the warm spray.

Suddenly hot, Sam began to fan herself, but then realized it was her phone she was fanning herself with and that it was speaking to her. She quickly shifted it back to her ear. She had a job to do and shouldn't allow herself to be distracted. Not a work-type job, per se, but she'd promised to ride herd on the police until her boss got there, and that was exactly what she was going to do.

Mortimer took one look at Sam's furious face when he stepped out of the bathroom and knew the call hadn't gone well. After a pause, he moved to snatch up his sandals and carried them to one of the chairs at the small kitchen table. He sat down and began to pull them on as he asked, "What did Belmont have to say?"

"Oh," Sam said with obvious exasperation. "He avoided my call again. He's supposedly out 'investigating another incident.' I'm sure he's there though and avoiding me."

Mortimer raised his eyebrows. "Who did you speak to then?"

"No one," she said dryly. "Apparently there was no one available to give me an accounting of what's being done, again. I guess Babcock's call to 'friends' didn't help at all."

"It's early yet," Mortimer pointed out. "It may still work."

"Hmm," Sam murmured.

Finished donning his sandals, Mortimer stood, caught her hand in his, and led her to the door.

"Where are we going?" she asked with surprise.

"To walk off some of that worry and anger I see bubbling under your skin," he said dryly.

Sam opened her mouth, probably to protest that she should stay at the cottage as she had promised to do, but he forestalled her by adding, "You have your cell if someone calls, and it's better than pacing this tiny cottage waiting to hear something."

She glanced down at the phone in her hand with surprise. Apparently she hadn't realized she was still clutching it in her white-knuckled fingers. Sam stared at it briefly and then gave in with a little sigh and slid the phone into the pocket of her shorts.

Mortimer felt himself relax at her easy compliance. He'd expected a bit more of a battle, but he would have won it anyway. He could be stubborn when he had to be, and it seemed to him, Sam needed someone to be stubborn with her. From what her sisters had said and what he'd learned from her in their conversations, it seemed obvious that she worked too hard and played too little. She could do with a little fun and relaxation, and he was just the man to give her that.

Well, at least he wanted to be, Mortimer thought wryly. He wasn't exactly a party animal himself. In fact, both those comments could have been applied to him as well. But he didn't like seeing it in Sam. He wanted to ease her burden a bit and see her happy, Mortimer thought as he led her along a trail near the cottage.

"You went out last night," Sam commented several minutes later.

Mortimer glanced at her, happy to see that she was beginning to let go of her anger and looked a little more relaxed. The walking strategy was working, though it had taken a bit of time to do so. They were a good distance along the trail he'd chosen, one of many they'd found wended through the property. The cottage was out of sight now, and all he could see were trees and more trees. Those trees were the only reason he was out here. They were like a canopy overhead, protecting him from the sun. He could safely be out in daylight here, which was a nice experience.

"Mortimer?" Sam said, reminding him that he hadn't replied to her comment.

Mortimer hesitated about how to respond, and then finally said, "I was restless. I thought a drive might relax me and help me get to sleep."

"It was a long drive," she muttered, and he didn't deny it. It had taken forever for him to find the four donors who supplied him with enough blood to make him feel safe to be around Sam again. He couldn't tell her that, though.

"If you heard me return, you must have still been awake too," he said instead.

Sam flushed. "I had trouble getting to sleep."

"So did I, despite the drive," he admitted wryly, and then unthinkingly added, "I'm not used to going to bed so early."

Sam's eyebrows flew up. "Early? It must have been

after two or maybe even three o'clock in the morning by the time you returned."

Mortimer was grimacing over his slip when she added, "Although I guess being in a band must be a wild life-style. You're probably all hyped up after a show, too wound up to sleep. You guys probably party until dawn when you're on tour."

Sam was looking troubled as she said that, probably comparing their very different lifestyles, he realized, and then acknowledged to himself that their lifestyles *were* very different. But not for the reasons she thought. He was constantly on the road, chasing after rogues or performing some other task for the Council, while she lived in Toronto and worked at the same place every day. He fed on the blood of mortals, and she was one of those mortals he fed on. In fact, if she'd ever donated blood, he might very well have ingested it at some point. That wasn't likely, but it wasn't impossible either.

"You must find it very boring up here," she commented suddenly, sounding worried.

"Boring?" Mortimer came to a startled halt and pulled her in front of him. Releasing her hand then, he clasped her face between his palms and assured her, "I haven't had a boring moment since meeting you."

Sam's mouth parted in pleased surprise at the words, and Mortimer immediately took advantage. He covered her mouth with his, his tongue immediately slipping out to move between her parted lips. Much to his satisfaction, she didn't resist, but breathed a little sigh of pleasure and slipped hands around his shoulders as he shifted his own arms around her waist to draw her closer.

Mortimer deepened the kiss, thrusting his tongue into her mouth until she moaned and tightened her arms eagerly around his neck. When she shifted, her pelvis rubbing against him, Mortimer couldn't resist letting his hands drop to her behind to clasp her there. He pulled her up tight against himself until he was holding all her negligible weight and her feet dangled just above the ground. He then eased slowly forward off the trail, aiming for the tree he knew was just a few feet behind her.

When he felt the bark of the tree brush against the backs of his hands, he shifted his hold and pinned her up against the tree with his lower body so that she had no doubt of his complete lack of boredom and his hands were free to explore.

Mortimer had done a good deal of exploring their first night here, and he was eager to strip her naked and look her over in daylight. He didn't want to rush and scare her off, however, so started by shifting his hands between their upper bodies to cover her breasts through her T-shirt.

Sam immediately groaned into his mouth and arched, pushing the tiny buds into his touch. When he concentrated on the nipples, tugging at them lightly through the cotton, she gasped and then began to suck almost frantically at his tongue, pulling on his hair at the same time. Mortimer chuckled, enjoying how responsive she was, and then slid one knee between both of hers and urged it upward until his upper thigh rubbed against her core through her shorts. That made her go a little crazy. He could feel it, her exploding desire flowing into him and exciting him as well.

Little mewls of pleasure were slipping from her mouth

to his as she moved her hands down to clasp his ass and urge him on until the scent of her excitement permeated the air around them. Mortimer inhaled that scent and then broke their kiss and reached for the button of her shorts, asking in a growl, "Have you ever made love in the woods?"

Sam shook her head breathlessly.

"Do you want to?" he growled as the button slid free.

She started to nod, but then paused, eyes widening, and shook her head frantically.

"No?" Mortimer asked with surprise, his hand freezing on her zipper.

"Bare," came her answer in a squeak.

"Yes, we'd both have to be bare," he said with a laugh.

"Not bare naked," she gasped. "*Bear* bear. Furry bear. Bear!"

Mortimer turned to look where she was pointing. For one moment, he couldn't believe what he was seeing. It *was* a bear. The damned thing wasn't ten feet away. How the hell had it gotten so close without his hearing?

"Mortimer," Sam hissed, bringing his attention to the fact that he was just standing there, staring at the creature who—while much larger than a leech and much less slimy—was ruining yet another attempt to make love to Sam. Would he never have her?

"Hell," he muttered, and briefly considered doing something to scare the animal off. Something like punching it in the nose would be good, he thought viciously. Frustrated and mad as he was, Mortimer was sure he could take the bear. He was so pissed at that moment that he thought he could take a pair of them, but doing so would reveal more to Sam than he was ready for, and the moment was ruined anyway. She wasn't likely to want to continue out here in the woods whether this bear was gone or not. Another might come along, or the sky would open up and dump dead frogs on them, he thought dryly. He just wasn't having any luck at all with the outdoors.

"Mort—" Sam began, but he brought an end to this latest hiss by whirling back to face her. Catching her by the waist, he hefted her over his shoulder and then headed back the way they'd come at a dead run, hoping that Sam was too distracted by her worries of being bear brunch to notice that he was moving much faster than a mortal should.

"You . . . can't . . . out . . . run . . . bears," Sam managed to get out as she bounced along over his shoulder and Mortimer took a moment to hope that he wasn't doing her any damage jarring her repeatedly in the stomach like this, but then decided if she could talk, he probably wasn't hurting her.

"Do you see the bear?" he asked in response to her question.

There was a pause, and he felt her nails dig into his back as she tried to lever herself up to look back up the trail behind them.

"No," she admitted, managing to sound surprised despite her position.

"Good," Mortimer muttered, and wondered if he'd outrun the bear, or it just hadn't bothered to give chase. He suspected it was the latter. The bear hadn't looked terribly aggressive, just kind of hungry and maybe a little curious as it had ambled toward them. In truth, he didn't care either way how it had been left behind.

The damned animal had already done the damage and wrecked what had looked to be a very promising moment.

Sighing, he adjusted his pace, slowing to a jog, then a walk before stopping and easing Sam off his shoulder and back to her feet.

Eyeing her flushed face with worry, Mortimer steadied her as she swayed before him, and asked, "Are you all right?"

Sam clutched at his arms for balance as she oriented herself, but nodded. "Yes. Fine," she breathed, and then added wryly, "I'm alive and uneaten, at any rate."

Mortimer smiled at her quick recovery, but gave her another moment to regain herself before slowly urging her to start walking. They had taken several steps when a groan from her drew his attention. Glancing down, he noted her miserable expression. "What is it?"

"Nothing," she assured him, and then admitted, "But Mother Nature seems to hate me. Perhaps we should avoid doing this sort of thing out of doors from now on."

"Amen to that," Mortimer muttered, and then laughed at himself and the situation and pulled her into his side for a hug, before urging her to move again. They had walked another few feet before he teased huskily, "In that case, I'd really like to get back to the cottage."

Chapter 14

Sam frowned as they left the cover of the trees moments later and stepped out—not by the cottage where they were staying—but near the main house instead. It appeared Mortimer had somehow taken a wrong turn during that wild dash back. She sighed as she spotted the O.P.P. cruiser parked in the driveway and the open door of the house. It looked like the cottage would have to wait.

"I suppose I should find out what's happening," she said reluctantly. She really didn't want to deal with Belmont just then, but knew she had to.

"Yes," Mortimer agreed and then gave her hand a squeeze, drawing her gaze up to his gentle smile. "It's all right. We have plenty of time."

Sam relaxed a little and even managed a small smile as she walked with him to the house, but her smile soon slipped when they entered to find Belmont sitting on one of the bar stools at the kitchen counter, laughing at something another officer was saying. It seemed obvious that Mr. Babcock's call to "friends" either hadn't achieved anything, or its effects hadn't yet reached Belmont. This didn't look like investigating to her.

"Oh." Sergeant Belmont's smile died and he stood up as she and Mortimer crossed the room to stand before him. Looking grim now, he nodded and announced, "I came by to give you an update, but you weren't around."

"We were taking a walk," she said calmly. "You should have called the number I gave you, Sergeant. I took my cell phone."

"Hmm," Belmont grunted and then announced, "I've put out a missing person's report across Canada."

Sam nodded and waited to hear what else he'd done . . . and waited. When he just stood there, she peered at him with disbelief and asked, "And that's it?"

Belmont immediately stiffened up like a bantam rooster about to crow and then snapped belligerently, "Well what the hell do you expect me to do? We've examined the scene. Our crime scene guy took fingerprints and we're running those." He paused and scowled before adding, "Which reminds me, did you two touch anything?"

Sam and Mortimer shook their heads. She'd barely brushed the door and it had slid open. She hadn't touched anything inside except when she'd poked the cheese, and Sam didn't think they'd probably printed that.

"Nothing but the keys," she assured him and then asked, "Did you speak to the Latimers' neighbors?"

"What about?" he asked with surprise. "They wouldn't have seen anything. All these properties are big wooded lots, built for privacy. There's no use talking to them."

"Maybe, but you could *try*," Sam said, so exasperated she didn't realize she was yelling. "It only takes a minute and they may have seen an unusual person in the area or noticed a car that didn't belong as they were arriving or leaving."

Belmont blew out an irritated breath. "Fine. I'll go talk to the damned neighbors, but it will be a waste of time."

He started stomping toward the door and then paused and turned back to return and slap a key into her hand. "That Babcock fellow left a message saying the Latimers were returning today. Give them the house key. And lock up as you leave," he snapped, and then whirled away and strode out of the house. The other officer paused long enough to give them an apologetic look, but then hurried after him.

"What an irritating, bloated, self-important twit," Sam growled as the door closed behind the departing men.

"I'd have to agree with that assessment," Mortimer said lightly, and Sam glanced at him, surprised to see he was smiling.

"How can you be so amused?" she asked with amazement. "That man makes me furious."

"I know, and you're scary in a kind of adorable way when your dander's up," he explained, moving closer. "I've never seen a man pale like he did when you started bellowing."

"I didn't bellow," Sam denied as his hands slipped around her waist, and then frowned. "Did I?"

Mortimer nodded, a smile still tugging at his mouth. "But he deserved it. He *is* an irritating, bloated, self-important twit."

Sam let her breath out on a small laugh as he bent to nuzzle her ear, but her gaze was on the door and her mind on the self-important twit and his complete uselessness so far.

"Sam," Mortimer murmured by her ear.

"Hmm?" she asked, clasping her hands absently around his waist.

He lifted his head and brushed his mouth across hers, then caught her lower lip between his teeth and tugged at it gently before releasing it to lean back and point out, "We're inside."

Sam shifted her gaze and attention back to him, her eyes widening as he began to tug her T-shirt out of her shorts.

"Oh," she breathed as his hands slid up her stomach, but then giving herself a mental shake, said, "No. We shouldn't. Not here."

"Yes we should," he breathed, catching her by the waist and turning to set her on the counter. "There are no leeches, no bears, and no Mother Nature to interrupt us here."

Mortimer pushed her T-shirt up farther, baring her breasts, and then leaned forward to lick his way from the middle of her stomach to one nipple, which he immediately drew into his mouth.

"We really shouldn't here," Sam moaned, her fingers curling into the hair at the back of his head and tugging him closer. "The Latimers are returning today."

"*Later* today," he breathed against her flesh as his fingers worked at the waist of her shorts, undoing buttons and zipper. "Hours from now. Plenty of time."

"What if Belmont returns?" she asked on a groan

as he nipped at her nipple and his hand found its way inside her shorts.

"I'll kill him," Mortimer said, surprising a laugh from Sam.

Apparently her comment made him reconsider, though, because while he claimed her mouth with his, Mortimer also lifted her off the counter and carried her into the kitchen.

"Now we're safe from discovery," he whispered as he lowered them both to the floor.

Sam knew they weren't really safe, but it was good enough. She began to kiss him back as his body came down on hers.

The moment Sam started participating, Mortimer apparently realized he'd won the argument and stepped up the game. Within moments her T-shirt and his were pillowing the back of her head, and while they were both still dressed from the waist down, Mortimer was cradled between her thighs, grinding himself against her as his mouth explored hers and his hands traveled what he'd revealed of her body.

Sam had never made love on a kitchen floor before, and quickly realized that wasn't a bad thing. The ceramic tile was cold beneath her naked back and hard against her shoulder blades. When Mortimer began to push at her shorts, trying to remove them, and she got her first taste of the cold on the top of her behind, she decided she didn't want to be on the bottom and that she'd been passive with him long enough.

Catching him by surprise, Sam shifted her leg, knocking his out from under him, and pushed at his chest at the same time, so that he rolled off and onto his back with a soft "oomph" of surprise. She immediately rolled on top of him, smiling at his startled expression at the change in position.

"Got ya," she whispered, and then bent to kiss him before straightening to reach for the button of his jeans. Her hand froze, however, and she sat up when she heard the front door of the house open and slam shut.

She raised herself slightly to peer into the living area, a gasp slipping from her lips as she spotted the woman entering from the foyer.

"Cathy!"

Mortimer blinked his eyes open as that name burst from Sam's lips with a horror usually reserved only for the sudden appearance of monsters in movies. Then she suddenly dropped back down and began to scrabble around to reach her T-shirt. An "oomph" of shock slid from his lips as her knee came down on his groin.

"Sorry," Sam hissed, but wasn't even looking his way. Her head was buried in the shirt she was desperately yanking over her head.

"Hello? Is someone here?"

Mortimer cursed and quickly redid the button Sam had undone on his jeans. By the time he was done, Sam had her T-shirt in place and her shorts done up and was wildly trying to finger-brush her hair into order as she bounced to her feet.

"Cathy! Hi!"

The smile she offered looked pretty panicked and plastic to him, but Mortimer didn't hear any suspicion or concern in the other woman's voice as she said, "You look familiar. Who are you? One of Daddy's lackeys?"

"I work for your father's lawyer, Clarence Babcock,"

Sam said a bit stiffly. "We've met a time or two when you accompanied your parents to the office."

The supposedly missing girl must have been moving nearer. At least her voice sounded nearer, Mortimer thought as he snatched up his T-shirt and began to pull it on. Aside from that, Sam was scooting around the counter in what looked to him like a defensive maneuver to keep her from coming back there and spotting him.

"I was sent here because you were missing," Mortimer heard Sam say as she moved out of sight. "Your parents have been worried sick; they're flying back from Europe as we speak,"

Grimacing, he finished pulling his shirt into place, tucked it awkwardly into his jeans, ran his hands through his hair, and then shifted to his knees to peer cautiously over the counter.

"Oh, it's just like them to panic," Cathy Latimer said with exasperation, waving the matter away with one uncaring hand as she flounced onto the couch. Mortimer couldn't help but notice that she was a buxom blond and looked rather like the human embodiment of his Jessica Rabbit . . . er . . . his long-imagined life mate, he corrected himself at once.

"It wasn't just your parents," Sam assured her. "Mr. Babcock's been worried too, and the police put out a missing person's alert."

"Well, they shouldn't have. I was just at a friend's," the girl said petulantly, sounding more annoyed at the fuss than upset or embarrassed that she'd caused it.

Sam obviously wasn't impressed. Mouth tightening, she said grimly, "The door was left open, not just unlocked, but *open*. The radio was playing, there was an untouched sandwich and drink on the counter, and your purse, car, and keys were still here . . . It looked like foul play."

"Oh." Cathy snorted at the idea. "So I forgot to lock the door."

Mortimer saw Sam close her eyes briefly and just knew she was having to rein in her temper. She was reasonably good at it; her voice sounded almost calm as she asked, "What happened?"

"I was about to have a sandwich when Mattie next door called and said her cousins were up from the States. They're twins, and gorgeous," she explained, and then shrugged. "So I rushed out, jumped on the Sea-Doo, and headed right over. I guess I forgot to lock the door."

Mortimer nodded to himself. He'd wondered why there were only three when there had been four spots in the boathouse for the vehicles.

"I see," Sam said stiffly. "How long ago was this?"

"Umm, three days ago, I think. Maybe four," Cathy shrugged indifferently and gave a pleased little sigh. "Those two really know how to party, which is what we've been doing the last few days. Then that asshole Belmont showed up to spoil the fun. He went on and on about the trouble I'd caused until Mattie's dad said maybe I'd better come home and let everyone know I'm all right. Idiot," she added bitterly, and then glanced hopefully at Sam. "Are you everyone? The plebe Uncle Clarence sent up here to cause all this fuss? If so, I can go back now and tell Mattie's dad I did as he asked, can't I?"

Mortimer's gaze switched to Sam. She wasn't at all

impressed with being called a plebe, or with Ms. Rabbit herself, for that matter. Mortimer wasn't that impressed either, but it looked to him like Sam was about to blast the girl and give her a good dressing-down she wouldn't soon forget. Unfortunately, satisfying as that would be, it might put her job in jeopardy.

Mortimer couldn't control Sam, and he couldn't think of a thing to make Cathy Latimer say or do that might prevent the rage about to spew forth from Sam, so he did the only thing he could think of. He got to his feet and walked calmly around the counter and into view, distracting both women.

Sam's reaction was to hesitate and bite her lip, which relieved him. Cathy's reaction was a sudden widening of the eyes and a brief parting of the lips before she stood and sashayed toward him, drawling, "Hello gorgeous."

She even had the Jessica Rabbit sashay, Mortimer thought with amazement as he watched her hips roll with each step. And the "Hello gorgeous" line was even something Ms. Rabbit might say. Oddly enough, however, while her stacked figure, rolling walk, and the way she was eating him alive with her eyes as she approached all could have been plucked out of one of his fantasies of his life mate . . . in reality, it left him cold. He actually felt his erection shrivel inside his jeans. Mortimer preferred his Olive Oyl.

Not that Sam was an Olive Oyl, he thought quickly. She was beautiful and intelligent and had lovely eyes, and really, he was sure she'd be much more graceful when he turned her. Her stubborn ear infection would be a thing of the past then.

Realizing what he was thinking, Mortimer glanced to Sam and found himself smiling. He had decided—despite her clumsiness, the leeches, and the bear—he did want her for his life mate. He couldn't think of a finer woman to have at his side.

A finger running suggestively down his chest drew his attention back to Cathy-Jessica-Rabbit-Latimer. Mortimer caught that hand in a hard grip just as it crested over the button of his jeans. "No thank you, honey. I like my women all grown-up."

An ugly scowl immediately replaced the seductive look of a moment ago. Cathy Latimer wasn't used to rejection. With a figure and moves like hers, Mortimer wasn't surprised. Few would refuse what she offered so freely, and no doubt frequently. But while another man might have taken her up on the offer, Mortimer was sure that man would have then tossed her aside like a used tissue when he was done. At least he would if he thought like Mortimer. In his opinion, there was little value in something everyone could—and probably had—had.

Moving around the girl, he caught Sam's arm and ushered her toward the door, saying over his shoulder, "You should probably call your parents and let them know you're alive and just selfish, thoughtless, and uncaring. Despite your not deserving it, they appear to love you."

Ignoring her outraged gasp, Mortimer pulled the door of the house closed behind them and then hustled Sam along the path to the cottage. She was stiff in her movements and oddly silent as they walked, but he didn't try to make her talk. She was still struggling with her anger and a strange jumble of other emotions if he was to judge from the expressions flitting across her face. Amusement, resentment, bitterness, and determination were just a few of the emotions that flashed by.

Once at the cottage, they packed up their things in silence, locked the cottage, and then carried their stuff to the car. The moment everything was stowed away, Sam paused and peered at the keys in her hand.

Mortimer plucked them from her fingers and strode quickly back to the house.

"Uncle Clarence! Finally! I've been trying to reach you forever!" he heard Cathy shriek as he entered. He quickly moved into the living room to see that she was on the phone. Mortimer immediately slipped into her thoughts and read the venom there. She had no idea who he was and couldn't get him in trouble, but she did know he was somehow connected to Sam, and therefore intended on getting back at him for his rejection by trashing Sam to her "Uncle Clarence" and insisting he fire her. Cathy-Jessica-Rabbit-Latimer was about as ugly inside as she was lovely on the outside.

Mortimer quickly did a little rearranging of her memories and threw in some remorse and then slipped out of her thoughts. He then waited long enough to be sure his work had taken before setting her keys on the table by the door and slipping back outside.

"What happened?" Sam asked worriedly as he rejoined her by the SUV.

"Nothing," he said easily. "She was talking to your boss, so I just set the keys on the table and came back."

"There goes my career," Sam muttered, climbing into the passenger seat of the SUV.

Mortimer pushed her door closed for her and hurried

around to the driver's side. He started the engine as he said, "I'm sure your career is fine. She wasn't saying anything nasty about you from what I heard."

"You were in there awhile," she commented.

Mortimer peered at her sharply, but she was looking away out the side window; he couldn't see her expression. He thought he'd heard something like jealousy in her voice when she'd spoken, though. He must have imagined it. Surely Sam was too smart to be jealous?

"I waited a minute to give her back her keys, but she sounded like she was going to take a while, so I just set them on the table," he said, steering the SUV up the drive.

"Hmm." Sam continued to look out the window and then suddenly commented, "She's a pretty girl, isn't she?"

Mortimer swiveled his head sharply and nearly sent the SUV into the trees on the side of the lane before he turned his attention back to the road and straightened the wheel. She *was* jealous, he realized. Sam didn't have a clue how special she was if she was jealous of that little bit of fluff.

Spotting a patch of treeless grass just ahead, Mortimer steered the car off the road.

"What are you doing?" she asked with surprise as he shifted into park.

Mortimer's response was to swivel in his seat, lean across the gearshift, and kiss her. He kissed her until she responded and then continued to kiss her, this time keeping his hands to himself. When he'd kissed her so thoroughly he thought he could make a mold of her teeth from memory, he finally broke the kiss.

They were both breathing heavily as he pulled back to peer at her. Staring Sam in the eyes, Mortimer then said, "She's stacked, she's pretty, and she's as loose as a goose and mean as a rattlesnake. I like my women lean, dark-haired, and . . . you." He let that sink in and then added, "And in case you didn't notice, when she touched me, I completely lost the erection that was still straining my pants from our kiss in the kitchen."

Sam stared at him wide-eyed for the longest time and then suddenly threw herself at him. Her mouth was on his, her hands on his shoulders, her chest pressed tight against him. Realizing that she had to be sitting on the gearshift, and that it must be uncomfortable, Mortimer promptly pulled her across it and arranged them both so that he was facing front and she straddled his lap in the driver's seat.

The honk of the horn was what told him her butt was pressed against it. Mortimer immediately grasped her hips and pulled her tight against him to bring an end to the strident sound. Finding he liked it, he pulled her tighter still as he kissed her back, letting his tongue slip out to wrestle with hers as he rubbed her against himself.

Mortimer had completely lost his mind, of course. Clearly, he hadn't yet learned his lesson about picking his spot or moment. It was bright daylight out and they were in an SUV on the side of the road. He'd obviously learned nothing from the leeches, the bear, and Cathy Latimer, he realized moments later when a knock on the window brought them both to a breathless halt and made them turn to peer out the window.

Sam's response when they saw Belmont leering at

them was to roll off his lap and back into her seat with a moan of humiliation. Mortimer understood completely. Really, getting caught by Sergeant Belmont was the living end.

"I thought it was you two," the man said dryly as Mortimer hit the button to roll down the window. "This here's a public road, and up here we don't take kindly to public displays of affection." He sneered the word. "You two go find a room if you want to carry on like that."

Mortimer scowled at the man, knowing he was enjoying himself.

Belmont merely grinned at his silent fury and then said smugly, "I take it Cathy made it home all right? Seems she was just off visiting friends like I thought and all this fuss was for nothing."

Mortimer was winding up to take control of the man's mind and make him piss himself or something else equally humiliating when Sam said sweetly, "Yes. Isn't it good that you listened to me and did your job and went to talk to the neighbors so we could find that out? Such a shame you didn't think to do it earlier on your own *as one would expect* so that all this needless worry could have been avoided."

A small smile of admiration curved Mortimer's lips.

Belmont was less appreciative. Flushing furiously, he straightened away from the vehicle and snapped, "Get out of here before I fine you both for indecent exposure."

"Nothing was exposed, Officer. We were just kissing," Sam said in hard tones. "And while that's illegal in Malaysia, it isn't in Canada. I learned that in law school."

Belmont started back to his waiting patrol car, snarling, "Just get on out of here."

Sam released a little puff of air and glared after the man until Mortimer reached out and took her hand. When she turned a startled glance his way, he smiled. "This round goes to Ms. Willan."

She smiled faintly at his teasing and then shook her head. "I think the universe is trying to tell us something. We just aren't meant to—"

Mortimer silenced her by quickly placing a finger over her lips. "That's speculation, Ms. Willan. We only deal with the facts here."

"Oh?" she asked wryly. "And what are the facts telling *you*?"

"The facts are that we were put into cottages next door to each other. So maybe that's where we're supposed to be together." He smiled gently and suggested, "Let's get back home. Hmm?"

"Home," Sam said as he shifted into drive and steered the SUV back onto the road. "Our cottage is like a second home to me, but Decker's cottage isn't your home."

"It's more a home to me than any of the hotels I usually stay in," he said dryly.

Sam was silent as she digested that and then said, "I suppose you spend a lot of time on the road with the band."

Mortimer frowned, not comfortable with lying, but unable to tell the truth. Instead he said carefully, "I spend a lot of time on the road."

"I'll bet you have a lot of groupies."

Mortimer glanced at her sharply, but she didn't look angry or jealous, just curious. Clearing his throat, he said, "I wouldn't bother with groupies. In fact, I haven't been with a woman in a long time."

"Really?" She didn't hide her surprise.

"Really," he assured her.

"I'd think groupies were part of the attraction of being in a band for a guy."

"I'm not your average guy," he said dryly.

"I'm beginning to see that," Sam admitted.

Mortimer smiled and reached for her hand. It felt right in his. Like that was where it belonged. It just re-affirmed what he'd already decided. It seemed whoever made it so immortals couldn't read certain people didn't make mistakes when they assigned life mates after all. They'd picked the perfect woman for him.

Now he just had to convince her of that.

Chapter 15

"We're heading into town to pick up more beer and stuff. Want to come with?"

Sam glanced up from the book she'd been pretending to read and smiled at Jo as she dropped beside her on the blanket she'd laid out in the sun. "No thanks. I'm enjoying this book."

Jo snorted. "Sure you are. And here I thought you were watching the cottage next door for a sign of Mortimer."

Sam flushed guiltily, but didn't deny it. She had indeed been watching the cottage next door. She'd hardly seen Mortimer in the three days since they'd returned. Once back, his time had been taken up by his friends. He went out with them as soon as it was dark, didn't return until dawn, and then slept until at least noon, appearing in the early afternoon to spend a little time with her until Bricker and Decker got up. Then he'd apologize, explain he had to work, and disappear with the men again.

Sam supposed they'd rented a place in town to practice their new songs or something before they had to tour. She couldn't be sure, however, because Mortimer was being pretty closemouthed about it. Sam would have given up on him by now but for the fact that he was obviously cutting his sleep short to be with her. He hadn't gotten more than five or six hours a night since returning from Minden.

Unfortunately, none of that time had been spent alone. Alex and Jo were always around, cajoling them into trips here and there or simply hanging out with them, so that all she and Mortimer had managed in the way of intimacy were a few stolen kisses.

"Don't let her tease you," Alex said, dropping onto the blanket on her other side. "It's come to our attention that Mortimer only seems to be able to get away from his friends in the afternoon, so we decided to cut you a break and leave the two of you alone today."

"Really?" Sam asked with pleased surprise.

"Really," Alex drawled. "But I hope we don't regret it. If he breaks your heart I'm going to hog-tie him and roast him over a spit."

"He won't break my heart," Sam said quickly.

"Honey, you're already half in love with that man," Alex said dryly. "The only way he won't break your heart is if this ends with the two of you walking down the aisle."

"I'm not half in love—" Sam began indignantly, but paused, unable to finish the lie. The truth was, she feared she might very well be half in love with Garrett Mortimer. She was certainly in lust with him. Sam also found herself jonesing for his presence when he wasn't around and wishing she could spend every minute with him. She thought about him constantly, even while sleeping. The dreams she'd had since returning to Magnetawan were full of him, and usually very, very hot. Was that love?

"I think Sam's right," Jo said suddenly. "She's not half in love, she's fully there. And she's got it bad."

Sam flushed and gave her younger sister a push. "Stop harassing me and go if you're going."

"Oh, we're going," Alex assured her, getting to her feet even as Jo did. "And we're not coming back until dark. That's usually when our friendly neighborhood vampires head out."

"Vampires?" Sam asked.

"They sleep all day and stay out all night. What else could they be?" Alex teased.

Knowing Alex was just saying that to bug her because of her phobia about bats and such, Sam simply shook her head and said, "Have fun."

"You too," Jo called with a grin as they moved to Alex's Matrix.

Sam watched them go, glanced toward the lifeless cottage next door, and then turned her eyes back to the book in her hand before closing it and setting it down. She was just debating whether to go inside and get herself something to drink when the snap of a branch drew her gaze to the path, and she saw Bricker moving across the yard toward her.

"Hi," he said as he reached the edge of her blanket.

"Hi," she responded, raising a hand to shade her eyes as she peered up at him.

"Decker and I are sneaking off to work on our own," he announced.

"Sneaking?" she asked.

Bricker nodded. "If we don't sneak out while he's sleeping, Mortimer will insist he has to come with us."

When she arched an eyebrow, he grimaced and explained, "Mortimer has this whole responsibility-issue thing."

"He does, does he?" she asked with a laugh.

"Yeah, and normally that's a good thing, but . . ." Bricker shrugged. "He's got more important things to do here."

"Does he?" she asked curiously.

"Yes, he does," Bricker assured her. "Much more important, lifelong-type things."

Sam was puzzling over that when he said, "So we're sneaking off, but I thought I'd best come let you know so you can tell him when he gets up."

"I see," she murmured, and then tilted her head and asked, "Don't you need him with you to work?"

"Nah." Bricker waved that away. "Decker and I can handle this."

"But he's the lead singer," she pointed out. "How can you practice without him there?"

"Oh yeah," he muttered, and then shrugged. "He knows all his lines. It's just Decker and I who need to practice."

"Oh," Sam said uncertainly.

"Anyway, you're welcome to go inside the cottage and wait for him if you like," he suggested, and when her eyebrows rose, he added, "Decker said so. You could even sneak down to Mortimer's room and wake him with the good news that he has the evening off if you like." He grinned and then added helpfully, "His room is the one farthest from the stairs."

Sam pursed her lips as she considered him, and then shook her head and said, "It's funny."

Bricker paused, his head tilting. "What is?"

"You don't look like I imagined," Sam said, and then teased, "For some reason I always assumed Cupid would be taller."

Bricker laughed, but merely turned and headed back along the path through the trees. Decker came out as he reached the other cottage, and the two men immediately moved to the vehicles in front of the cottage. Much to her surprise, Bricker got in the SUV and Decker in his pickup. While she sat wondering why they were taking both vehicles to get to the same place, the trucks growled to life and started up the driveway.

Sam waited until they had disappeared from view before getting up. Her movements then were slow and almost reluctant as she gathered her book, drink, and blanket and headed into the cottage. She put her things away, brushed her hair, and then briefly toyed with the idea of changing her clothes, or even showering, but then gave her head a shake. She'd showered when she'd gotten up that morning, her clothes were fine, and she was just stalling about going next door because she suddenly found herself feeling nervous.

Shaking her head, Sam made herself turn and march out of the cottage and straight across the yard to Decker's cottage. She automatically stopped at the door, her hand rising to knock, but then caught herself before her knuckles actually rapped wood. Muttering under her breath, she opened the screen door and slid inside. She was standing just inside the door, trying to decide if she had the nerve to go downstairs and wake Mortimer up in his bed, when he suddenly appeared at the bottom of the stairs.

"Sam!" he exclaimed, freezing when he saw her. He crumpled something that looked like a plastic bag with a reddish tinge in his hand, and then continued up the stairs asking, "What are you doing here?"

"Bricker said it would be okay if I came over and waited for you to get up," she said awkwardly as he reached the top of the stairs and slid past her into the kitchen.

"He did, did he?" Mortimer moved to drop the bag she'd glimpsed in the garbage bin, and then turned back to ask. "Where is Bricker?"

"He and Decker left to go to work. He asked me to tell you that too, and that you have the day off."

"They've left?" he asked with amazement. "This early in the day?"

Sam wasn't surprised at the frown that flickered over his face. The other two men usually didn't stir until the sun was out of sight and the waning light of day was all that remained. "Bricker said if they didn't go while you were sleeping, you'd insist on going with them and that you had more important lifelong-type things to do here, so they decided to sneak off."

The frown on Mortimer's face eased and he smiled wryly. "He was right."

"What is it you have to do that's so important?" she asked curiously.

Mortimer's eyes focused on her, his expression becoming solemn, but instead of answering, he asked, "Where are your sisters?"

"They went to town. They said they wouldn't be back until dark," she added, managing not to blush as she recalled what else they'd said.

The rest of the tension remaining in his body slid out of Mortimer at this news. "That was very accommodating of them. Did Decker and Bricker talk to them first?"

"What?" she asked with surprise. "No. At least I don't think so."

"Hmm." Mortimer shrugged the concern away and slid one hand around her waist, drawing her nearer. "You're a nice sight to wake up to."

"Thank you," she whispered as he caught her chin with one finger and lifted her face so that he could press a kiss to the corner of her mouth.

"Is there anything you wanted to do today?" he asked softly, trailing kisses along her jawline toward her ear.

"No," Sam breathed as he nibbled at her lobe.

"There's something I'd like to do," he growled, sliding his arms around her and drawing her closer as his mouth moved back to her lips.

Sam sighed, her lips opening for his onslaught as he kissed her. She let her arms creep up around his neck then, but found her eyes blinking open and moving nervously to the door, half expecting the men to return, or someone else to suddenly knock at the door. Their track record to date was enough to make anyone leery.

Seeming to notice her distraction, Mortimer pulled

back and said quietly, "I think my room has a lock on it."

Sam swallowed, but whispered, "Perhaps we could go there, then."

A small, relieved smile curving his lips, Mortimer caught her hand in his and drew her toward the stairs he'd just ascended.

Sam allowed him to tug her down the steps and across the rec room to a door that presumably led to his room. She peered around curiously as he ushered her inside, noting the pale tan colors on the wall and the dark blue bedspread . . . on the bed.

"There."

Glancing toward the door, she saw Mortimer straighten from locking it. Turning with a satisfied grin, he announced, "Safe and sound."

Sam managed a smile. "Good," she murmured, her eyes drawn to his. She found herself unable to look away as she noted they seemed more silver than green. She'd noticed it before, mostly at night. They wore sunglasses a lot during the day, so it was really only at night or the early evening that Sam saw his eyes, and she'd put down that odd silver glow to the poor lighting at the time, but the light in this room was just fine. Artificial, but fine, she thought, and then cast a distracted glance down as he took her hand in his.

"I want you." The words were a sexy growl as he drew her closer, and Sam forgot about his silver eyes as warmth radiated from his body, and then his body itself pressed against her. Every nerve and fiber in her being immediately seemed to come alive inside Sam so that a frisson of excitement and awareness was suddenly vibrating through her from head to toe. She instinctively lifted her face to his, her eyes closing as her lips broke open, allowing a small sigh to slip through as his mouth covered hers. But this first caress was just a light brushing of his lips over hers, a sweet caress rather than the mad passion of some of their previous kisses.

"I want to take this slow," he whispered, his mouth moving across her cheek to her ear. "I want to savor it."

"Oh," Sam breathed, tilting her head as he found her earlobe again. She felt his hands slip under her T-shirt and brush lightly across her lower stomach, and bit her lip as her stomach muscles jumped excitedly under the caress. Then his hands were easing her top up, revealing her belly button, her midriff, her breasts. Mortimer lifted the shirt up over her head and dropped it to the floor. Despite having had her breasts bared, and even being fully naked in front of him before, Sam had to work hard to keep from raising her hands to cover herself as his eyes traveled lazily over her.

"I find you beautiful," he whispered, soothing her soul and washing away her discomfort. "Perfect."

And then he kissed her again; this time his tongue dipped out for a lazy sashay around her mouth before retracting again so that his mouth could move to the side of her chin, where he nipped lightly at her jawbone.

"I want to see all of you."

Sam swallowed, but didn't protest when his hands moved to her waist to work the button there and then the zipper. Her shorts dropped to pool around her ankles. She found herself standing in just her panties and not sure she liked it, despite the way his eyes glowed and his mouth curved in appreciation.

She stopped worrying about that and gasped in surprise, however, when he suddenly dropped to his haunches. Sam took a small step back and felt her behind bump against the dresser. She peered down with confusion, unsure what he was doing until Mortimer urged her to lift first one foot and then the other so that he could move her shorts out of the way. He didn't straighten again then as she'd expected, but shifted to his knees and reached for her hips as he pressed a kiss to her stomach.

Sam licked her lips and then did a little shimmy against the dresser. She giggled as his tongue briefly dipped teasingly into her belly button, but it died on a gasp as his tongue then traveled down to the waistband of her white lace bikini panties.

"Pretty," he whispered appreciatively against her skin, and she felt herself blush. Lingerie was her one great weakness. She had to look professional and busi-nesslike at work, but her lace bras and panties were her little rebellion underneath, her own private secret.

Her thoughts evaporated under a wave of surprise and pleasure as Mortimer's tongue slid along the line of lace. She sucked in an expectant breath as his fingers curled over the lace-covered elastic and began to draw it down over her hips. The panties dropped to pool at her ankles. This time he didn't pause to look, but imme-diately moved his hand to one foot and then the other so that she stepped out of the delicate lace. Mortimer tossed the item onto the small pile of her clothes, and only then turned to admire her.

Now Sam was really having to struggle not to cover herself. Then his hand ran lightly up the back of her calf in a soft caress that was almost soothing . . . and he bent his head to press a kiss to the inside of her knee, allowing his tongue to slip out and lick at her warm flesh.

Sam inhaled on a gasp and reached for the dresser behind her to help stay upright as she felt her legs tremble, and then clutched the edge of the dresser tighter still as his mouth began to follow a lazy trail up the inside of her thigh. She was panting when he stopped and turned to kiss the inside of her other knee, urging her legs a little farther apart. He then licked his way along another invisible trail there. This time he didn't stop halfway, but, shifting his hands to her thighs, clasped them lightly and urged them apart as he kissed his way up to the very core of her.

Sam cried out and threw her head back, one hand releasing the dresser and searching blindly for his head. Her fingers curled into his hair and she held on as his tongue lashed over her. When her legs gave out beneath her and her behind began to slide off the edge of the dresser, Mortimer simply used his hold to lift her to sit farther back on it and then caught her legs and drew them up over his shoulders as he continued what he was doing. And what he was doing was reducing her to a trembling mass of gasping, mindless need. Sam had never experienced pleasure the like of what he gave her. It didn't just feel good. It wasn't a wave of pleasure rolling over her at each caress. It was waves in the plural. The initial pleasure would crash down over her and then as a new wave crashed down, an echo of the first would be striking too so that Sam was doubly bombarded. It was as if each sensation was bouncing off to some place and then bouncing back doubled, and then trebled and so on until her mind and body were afire and filled with the echoing pleasure.

It was overwhelming, almost excruciating, and just when Sam thought she couldn't stand another moment of it, Mortimer released his hold on one thigh and brought his hand into play, slipping one finger inside her.

If there was anyone in the house, there was no way he could have missed the scream that action ripped from her throat. Truthfully, Sam wouldn't have been surprised to be told it was heard across the lake. It vibrated through her whole body, shredding her vocal cords and trumpeting from her lips. Her body convulsed and shook on the dresser top as unbearable pleasure exploded inside her. It was almost a relief when the darkness began to crowd in, and then took her away.

Sam woke up sometime later to find herself in a tangled heap with Mortimer on the bedroom's carpeted floor. She knew she had fainted, but he appeared to have lost consciousness as well.

Biting her lip, she untangled herself from his limp body and sat up to peer at him with concern, wondering what had happened. Surely she hadn't squeezed her thighs so hard in her excitement that she'd suffocated the man?

That seemed the only plausible explanation, and Sam was horrified by it. Dear God, she might have unintentionally killed him. Death by sex, she thought with dismay, and leaned down to press her ear to his chest to see if his heart was still beating.

Sam heard the first strong thump of his heart just as

she felt his hand in her hair. Sitting up abruptly, she saw he was awake and wailed, "I'm sorry!"

Confusion immediately filled Mortimer's features, and he sat up as she began to babble, "I didn't mean to smother you. I was just so excited. But I shouldn't have squeezed so tight," she said with self-reproach, and then added in her own defense, "I didn't know I was. I'd never have smothered you on purpose. I swear, I—"

It was hard to talk with a mouthful of tongue, at least not without biting the tongue in question. Sam was certainly not going to do that after nearly killing the man who had given her so much pleasure, so was forced to silence.

Mortimer kissed her until she moaned with reawakened passion, only then breaking it off to say, "You didn't smother me."

"I must have," she said at once.

"You didn't," he assured her, brushing his thumb tenderly over the corner of her mouth.

"But you were unconscious," she pointed out with bewilderment.

"Too much excitement," Mortimer said with a shrug.

Sam made a face. "I was the one enjoying all the excitement. You were giving it."

"Then maybe it's something I ate." He was suddenly getting to his feet, and she couldn't see his expression, but his voice sounded unconcerned.

Sam frowned, sure he was just trying to make her feel better. She'd have to be more careful in the future. The last place she wanted to find herself was standing in a courtroom with a charge of negligent homicide against her, trying to explain how she'd "accidentally" smothered her lover to death. If he ever dared do that again and risked such a dicey death, she thought. He might not ever want to—

Sam's thought died on a small gasp as Mortimer suddenly lifted her into his arms. Grabbing at his shoulders, she peered up into his face. He had good color and seemed perfectly fine now. She felt fine too, though she wouldn't bet on her legs holding her up at this moment.

"Thank you," Sam whispered, but didn't mean for carrying her. She'd never experienced pleasure like that before. Surely it deserved a thank-you. Actually, it deserved more than that, she thought, and when he reached the bed, she kissed him before he could set her down.

Mortimer's arms tightened around her as he kissed her back, his tongue eagerly meeting hers. That was all it took for Sam's earlier excitement to start pulsing through her again, and she soon moaned into his mouth and kicked her legs, urging him to let her go.

He released her legs at once, shifting both arms around her back as her feet hit the ground so that she was standing in the circle of his embrace. Sam was still a bit shaky, but merely leaned against him as they kissed. She allowed her hands to roam the vast expanse of his back and then slid them around to his front to urge him away.

When he broke the kiss and raised his head slightly to peer down at her, she smiled and whispered, "My turn."

As she eased to sit on the edge of the bed, Sam drew her hands down his body, dragging them over his chest and stomach until she reached the button of his jeans. She undid that and the zipper and then glanced up through her eyelashes as she curled her fingers over both his pants and boxers and began to pull them down over his hips. Mortimer was watching everything she did with an expectant fascination that made her smile before she dropped her eyes back to what she was doing.

Sam undressed him as he had her, urging him back from the bed so that she could help him step out of his clothes, and then she began to brush feather-light kisses along his inner thighs, intending to torment him as he had her, but she found the actions a bit tormenting herself. Every kiss she fluttered across his skin felt like one along her own so that Sam found herself squirming a bit as she ministered to him. She was incredibly excited herself by the time she turned her attention to his erection and took him into her mouth. Sam drew her lips along its length, drawing a moan from them both as her own excitement level shot through the roof.

Confused by the excitement and pleasure she was experiencing along with him, Sam hesitated and then did it again, her eyes widening and darting up toward him as pleasure pulsed through her as keen as if he were doing something similar to her.

Mortimer caught the way Sam's eyes widened in surprise as she ran her mouth over him and knew she was experiencing his pleasure as her own and was confused by it. It was another attribute of life mates; lovemaking was a much more shared event, each experiencing the other's pleasure so that it bound together, growing as it bounced between them until they both reached their explosive release at the same time. He'd experienced that while pleasuring her at the dresser, enjoying the pleasure he gave her, feeling when it sharpened or waned. It had spurred him on, telling him what felt best and how to drive them both wild until they found their release together before fainting. That was another attribute. Lovemaking between life mates was so powerful, mortals and immortals alike lost consciousness briefly afterward. It would continue for decades until their minds and bodies adjusted to the new sensations and could withstand the overwhelming pleasure.

Sam didn't know any of this, however, and he couldn't tell her. As much as Mortimer hated to stop her, he had to. There would be too many questions he couldn't answer if he allowed her to continue.

Reaching down, he caught her by the upper arms and drew her to her feet.

"Oh, but I wanted to—" Sam protested, trying to resist.

"Another time," Mortimer growled, pulling her up insistently. "After you're—" He caught himself before saying the word *turned*, and silently berated himself for nearly bringing on some of those questions he was trying to avoid.

"After I'm what?" she asked with bewilderment.

Mortimer kissed her with a passion meant to drive the question right out of her mind. His mouth was determined and demanding, and his hands grazed every inch of flesh he could reach. He ran them up her back, down her arms, and then up her stomach so that they rode right up to crest her breasts, and then closed them there, briefly squeezing the small buds and teasing her nipples. It sent pleasure rocketing through her that then pinged through him as well, sharp and exciting with building echoes.

Groaning, he dropped his hands to her behind next,

and cupped her there firmly to draw her up against him so that their groins met and they rubbed across each other, and then he moved forward, taking her with him. Mortimer urged her onto the bed, easing her back until she lay with her legs dangling off at the knees, her feet brushing the floor.

Sam gasped and clutched at his shoulders, sucking frantically at his tongue. She also opened for him, spreading her legs to offer him a cradle. Mortimer took advantage of their position to drive them both crazy by simply rubbing his hardness against her slick heat until the pleasure bouncing between them reached the point where he just couldn't stand it anymore.

When Sam dug her nails into his back and tore her mouth from his to gasp, "Please!" he finally gave them what they both wanted and allowed himself to slide inside her moist heat.

It was like coming home and the Fourth of July all at once. Pleasure shocked through him, tearing at his control, urging him on as he caught her by the hips and drove himself into her again and again until they both shouted out with victory as release exploded over them. It seemed to go on forever before the darkness washed up over him, making his eyes slip closed as he started to lose consciousness. In the last moment before the lights went out completely, Mortimer tried to shift himself to the side so that he wouldn't crush Sam, and then he knew no more.

Chapter 16

Mortimer woke slowly and reached for Sam, only to find the expanse of bed beside him empty. Immediately awake, he sat up and glanced toward the door to see that it was closed but unlocked. He launched himself quickly out of bed, concern for Sam uppermost in his mind. He hadn't meant to, but he'd bit her the last time they'd made love, and he was now a bit frantic to see that Sam was all right.

She'd probably gone in search of the bathroom, Mortimer told himself as he dragged on his jeans. Of course there was the slim possibility Sam was in search of food again and might look in the fridge downstairs, where she'd find the bagged blood. That would be a problem, but Mortimer was more concerned about how she was feeling. He was feeling pretty damned good himself, but . . .

Having finally consummated their desire, Sam and Mortimer had binged on each other. He'd awoken several times in the last twelve-plus hours since finding

Sam in the cottage and had reached for her first thing. He'd found her warm, willing, and even welcoming each time, and together they'd repeatedly sought and found their ecstasy again.

Only once had they troubled themselves to go in search of food to power their pleasure. However, they'd hardly touched the goodies they'd managed to retrieve from the refrigerator upstairs before he'd been unable to resist kissing her, and their attention had once more turned to each other. That time they'd started on the kitchen counter, and it had almost been too late by the time he'd had the common sense to carry her to his room so that they wouldn't be found unconscious on the kitchen floor.

Mortimer had been stupid. While he might be able to ignore his hunger for food in favor of devouring Sam, his need for blood wasn't so easily subverted. He'd had only one bag before finding her upstairs after awakening that day. It hadn't been nearly enough. The last time they'd made love, his hunger for blood had exerted itself, and he'd unthinkingly sunk his teeth into her neck as he'd taken her. Worse yet, he'd been so excited and overwhelmed by the combination of both needs being fulfilled that he'd taken more blood than he should have before realizing what he was doing and forcing his fangs from her throat. His last thought before unconsciousness had claimed him had been to worry that she was all right.

And it was that worry that was foremost on his mind as Mortimer rushed out of his room, and hurried upstairs to find that she wasn't there either . . . but Bricker and Decker were. His gaze slid over the two men enjoy-

ing a bag of blood at the table and then to the window
where dawn was threatening on the horizon.

"Sam left right after we got here," Decker announced,
pulling his empty bag from his mouth.

"She snuck out the screen door downstairs," Bricker
added as he removed his own empty bag and grinned.
"We heard her, but pretended not to."

"Oh." Mortimer ran a hand through his hair, glanced
at the food he and Sam had left out on the counter earlier,
but then turned to go back downstairs, his feet taking
him to the refrigerator where the blood was stored. He
was worrying about whether she was all right as he retrieved a bag of blood and slapped it to his teeth.

"She's all right," Decker said, bringing Mortimer's
attention to the fact that the two men had followed
him and that Decker was again reading his mind. "She
looked a bit weak and pale as she crossed the lawn, and
she'll probably sleep all day while her body recuperates,
but there was no lasting harm done."

Mortimer felt relief slip through him. Unable to speak
around the nearly empty bag in his mouth, he merely
nodded.

"I put the thought in her head that she'd been bitten
by blackflies," Decker added as Mortimer finally tore
the empty bag away.

"Thank you," he said gruffly, opening the refrigerator door again.

"So?" Bricker asked.

"So what?" Mortimer growled as he retrieved another bag of blood.

"When are you going to tell her?" Bricker asked.

Mortimer frowned with irritation. Dear God, he'd just finally consummated his feelings for the woman and they were already on him about telling her. "I'll tell her next Saturday or Sunday."

"Waiting as long as you can, huh?" Decker asked dryly as he leaned past him to grab a bag himself. "I don't blame you for wanting to enjoy her as long as possible in case you have to give her up."

Mortimer frowned at that possibility being spoken aloud. It was what he most feared.

"But," Decker added, "you might want to factor in that she'll need time to consider everything before she makes her decision."

Mortimer popped the second bag of blood to his teeth in response.

Decker left him to think about that as he popped his own bag to his teeth. Bricker immediately leaned in to grab one for himself, and the three of them were silent until these were empty. But the moment Decker ripped his from his teeth, he said, "Giving her a couple of days to consider it seems reasonable, don't you think?"

"Maybe," Mortimer allowed reluctantly. "But she doesn't have to think about it up here. I can tell her before they leave Sunday and then drive down to Toronto after we catch our rogue and . . ." His voice trailed off. Decker was shaking his head. Shifting unhappily, he asked, "No?"

"No," Decker said firmly. "It's too dangerous. She might tell someone. Sam has to decide before she and her sisters leave so that we can wipe their memories if she decides against being your life mate."

Mortimer winced at the suggestion, but knew he was

right. Their people's safety came first. If he wanted to give her time to think about it, which was only fair, he had to tell her soon.

"I'll tell her tonight," he said quietly, and then taking another bag of blood, headed to his room so that he could be alone and figure out just how he was going to do that.

"You're glowing," Jo said with glee and then called out, "Isn't she glowing, Alex?"

"Stuff it, Jo," Sam muttered, feeling her face heat with embarrassment as she opened the refrigerator and peered inside at the offerings. It was late. Nearly eight o'clock and she had just finally woken up after sneaking home at dawn from the cottage next door. Sam couldn't believe how long she'd slept . . . or perhaps she could. She'd certainly had a workout with Mortimer. They'd made love so many times she'd lost count. Her body wasn't used to it and had apparently decided she needed rest.

Now Sam was hungry and crazy thirsty. She felt like all the liquid in her body had been sucked out of her.

"Yes, she's glowing," Alex agreed, coming into the kitchen from the hall. "I can't believe you slept all day. What time did you get in?"

"Six A.M.," Jo answered for her, and then explained. "I woke up when you crept past my door."

Sam flushed with embarrassment, but didn't comment as she pulled orange juice from the refrigerator and poured herself a glass.

"Well, it must have been something," Alex said almost enviously, pulling a set of pies from the oven. "We heard you screaming from over here at one point."

"What?" Sam turned with dismay to find Jo grinning widely and nodding.

"We weren't sure if he was killing you or what," her younger sister admitted.

"And you didn't come see?" she asked, struggling between embarrassment that her cries of pleasure had been heard, and indignation that they hadn't checked on her.

"Well, we considered it, but jeez, I mean if he was killing you, you were dying happy," Alex said dryly as she set the pies on the stove and turned to consider her with hands on hips. "Girl, I didn't know you had such healthy lungs. You sure can howl."

Sam groaned and turned back to her orange juice, gulping it down with a thirst that wouldn't be denied.

"I thought those blackfly bites had healed," Jo said suddenly, moving closer to her side. "They look almost fresh again."

Sam shrugged and poured herself more juice. "They got me again last night."

"When?" she asked dryly. "I thought you were inside. Oh! Were you two doing the nature thing again? I thought you'd sworn off that."

Sam flushed. Fool that she was, she'd told them about the stay in Minden. Her sisters had been very sympathetic, once they'd finished laughing themselves silly.

"It must have been on the walk back," Sam muttered, though she'd seen the marks in the bathroom mirror at Decker's as she'd dressed. She hadn't wanted to wake Mortimer, so had checked that the rec room was empty and then had gathered her clothes and slipped out to dress in the bathroom. She'd heard the men return just as she'd finished and had hurried to slip out through the sliding doors downstairs before her presence could be discovered.

Sam had seen the marks on her neck while in the bathroom, so knew she hadn't gained them on the walk back. It must have been on the walk over, she thought, and then frowned as she peered at the pies Alex was fussing over. No wonder she felt so dried out. Alex had been baking and heated up the cottage with the oven.

"Who is that for?" she asked, moving to peer hungrily down at the pies.

"Us and Grant," Alex answered. "I thought I might as well get it done today rather than tomorrow. That way we'll be sure to get it to him and not have to leave it on the deck with a note like last year. I swear, that man is hardly ever home."

Sam nodded. They always gave him a pie with the check to cover the work he did for them over the year. It had started as something their mother had done for Mr. Warner before him. Alex had carried on the tradition after their parents' death and simply continued to do so with Grant.

"Alex made the second pie for us," Jo said happily.

"I didn't have a choice," Alex commented dryly. "You two picked at the crust so much last year that he probably thought mice had been at it."

Sam smiled at the memory. "So can I have a slice?"

"No," Alex said at once. "You aren't having pie for breakfast."

"It's eight o'clock at night," Sam pointed out in an almost whining tone. "You can't call this breakfast."

"I can when you're just waking up for the day," she

said firmly and then added, "We'll have it tomorrow after dinner. Make yourself an egg or something now."

"So?" Jo said, following her to the refrigerator. "Are you going to tell us about it?"

"No," Sam said at once, opening the door between them and scouring the refrigerator. Her eyes settled on some lunch meat and cheese and she decided on a sandwich.

"Well, at least we know this time it wasn't interrupted by bats or some other form of wildlife," Jo teased, and then frowned and moved closer again to better examine her neck. "These bites look even more like a vampire's kiss than the last two. Those were a little too close, but these are the perfect distance apart to be from a vampire bite."

"Eww! Stop saying stuff like that," Sam said with disgust, but suddenly had a flash of memory of a pinch at her neck as Mortimer nibbled on it while thrusting himself into her. In the next moment that pain had been rolled under by the wave of ecstasy that had claimed her as he drove them both toward a screaming climax.

Legs weakening under the onslaught of remembered passion, Sam shook her head and grabbed for the counter to steady herself. She really needed to eat.

"What if Mortimer was one," Jo teased. "I bet you wouldn't mind vampires so much then."

Pausing, Sam turned a glare on her. "That's so not funny. Don't even joke about it."

"Joke about what?"

Sam glanced around to see Mortimer at the screen door. Nothing could have stopped the welcoming smile that curved her lips as he pulled the door open and stepped inside to join them.

"About you being a vampire," Jo said with a laugh as he moved to Sam's side, slid his arm around her, and gave her a quick hello kiss. "Sam isn't keen on them. I think she'd toss you over if you were one."

"What?" Mortimer stiffened against her, and Sam smiled wryly when his gaze turned sharp on her face.

"She's probably right. Good thing you aren't a vampire, huh?" she teased, slipping her own arm around his waist and giving him a squeeze. When Mortimer simply stared at her, looking slightly stunned, she added, "Ignore Jo."

"Yeah, ignore her," Alex said lightly. "She's just teasing. Our Sam has a phobia about bats, you see."

"Bats," he murmured, sounding confused.

"Yeah. So she isn't keen on vampires and all that nonsense either. You know, they turn into bats and stuff." She shrugged.

"Right, bats and stuff," he said quietly and seemed relieved.

"Speaking of bats, Jo and I were thinking about going into town for bat night," Alex announced.

Mortimer looked bewildered. "What is bat night?"

"Oh, they're going to put up this huge wall of netting and catch bats and then everyone gets to look at them and learn what kind of bat they are and stuff before they set them free. You two should come with us. It'll be cool," Jo assured him.

"My sister is into bugs and bats and things," Sam said dryly. "She freaks if you dare swat a spider or some other disgusting creature. She likes them."

"Oh." Mortimer smiled faintly.

"Speaking of which, we'd best get going. It's nearly dark out," Alex said, turning to Jo.

"Yeah," Jo agreed, and then turned an impish smile on Sam and Mortimer. "Obviously you two would rather stay here and make out than go with us, so I guess we'll leave you to it."

"Thank you," Sam said dryly.

"Don't touch the pies," Alex ordered, picking up her purse and heading for the door. "See you later."

"See you later," Jo echoed as she followed and then glanced wickedly back and added, "Don't do anything I wouldn't do."

"Since there isn't much Jo wouldn't do, I'll honk three times to warn you when we return," Alex muttered as she pushed her way out the door.

Laughing at her promise, Sam slid out from under Mortimer's arm and moved to the window over the sink to watch her sisters get in the car, start it up, and head up the driveway. She was aware of Mortimer moving to stand behind her, could feel the heat of him against her back, but waited until the car was out of sight before turning to face him. The moment she did, she rose up on tiptoe, slipping her hand behind his head as she drew his face down so she could kiss him.

Mortimer responded, but in a distracted manner that carried none of the passion of the night before. Deciding that wouldn't do, she broke the kiss, caught his hand, and dragged him into the living area. Pausing beside the couch, she pushed him to sit on it, climbed on to straddle his lap, and started to kiss him again as she blindly began to undo the buttons of his short-sleeved shirt.

Much to her amazement, Mortimer caught her hands in his to stop her and then used them to urge her backward and break their kiss.

"What is it?" she asked with surprise. The last time she'd seen him he couldn't keep his hands off her. They'd both been insatiable. Now he apparently wasn't interested. Something must be wrong.

Mortimer hesitated. "About this vampire business."

Sam laughed with disbelief that such a silly thing seemed to be on his mind, and then her eyes widened as a thought came to her. "What is it? Did you want to play a game? You get to be the big scary vampire and I cower in fear as you ravish me?"

She smiled faintly at the idea and reached between them to find him semi-erect. He wasn't as unaffected as he appeared, Sam realized and gave a throaty laugh as she leaned closer again to kiss him, her hand stroking him through his jeans. She felt him twitch through the cloth under her hand, but he didn't open his mouth or try to kiss her back. Instead he turned his head away.

"Sam, we have to talk," he said solemnly when she paused and sat back with bewilderment.

Sam stilled at his serious tone of voice. They had to talk? she wondered worriedly. That always preceded a bad conversation. Things like "your parents were killed in a car accident," or "your dog Fluffy choked on a bone and died," or "I want to break up with you."

Since her parents were already dead and she didn't have a dog . . . Christ, Sam thought faintly. Was it over already?

"Sam, I like you. More than like you even."

Her breath slid out on a rush of relief, and she relaxed in his lap and leaned forward to press a kiss to the corner of his mouth. "I like you too."

"No," Mortimer said seriously. "I mean, I *really* like you. The ever-after kind of like."

Sam sat back and stared wide-eyed as she tried to think where this was going. Ever-after kind of like, he'd said. What was that? And what the hell was he trying to say? It was way too early in their relationship for anything really serious to even be considered. Sam liked him, she more than liked everything about him so far, but—

"I realize it seems fast and you're probably worried about making a mistake, but—" Mortimer caught her face between his hands and peered at her solemnly as he said, "It isn't a mistake, Sam. I can guarantee you that. You're my life mate."

She stared at him blankly. Life mate? That was a new term she'd never heard before. She'd heard mate, and life partner, but never life mate. And what the devil was he saying anyway? It sounded to her like he was looking for some kind of commitment, but she wasn't sure. And she wasn't sure how she should respond. In truth, Sam wouldn't really mind some sort of commitment between them, but she knew others would think they were rushing and—Well, there was really no reason to rush, was there? She knew it was more sensible to take things more slowly.

Releasing her hold on him, Sam settled more sedately in his lap and cleared her throat before speaking. "I like you too, Mortimer. But there's really no need to rush this. We could date awhile, maybe live together."

"That probably won't work," he said quietly, and

when she frowned, he grimaced and admitted, "I'd need a commitment from you before you leave this weekend."

Sam gaped with surprise. That was definitely rushing it in her book. "Why?"

"My work takes me away a lot," he said slowly, and then added, "And right now, I don't want to be away from you. Maybe I never will."

Sam melted at his words. They were so sweet. She found she didn't want to be away from him either . . . but she had her job at the law firm, and he was in his band.

"That's even more of a reason to take it slow, Mortimer," she said quietly. "To see if we can work out."

"We can," he assured her quickly.

"I hope so," she admitted. "But we have to work out how. I studied long and hard to be a lawyer; I'm not ready to just toss it over to follow your band around like some stalker groupie."

"I'm not in a band."

That blurted bit of information made her stare at him blankly. "What?"

"I—none of us—we aren't in a band. There is no Morty and the Muppets, or the Rippers."

Sam slid off his lap to sit on the couch. This was going to be terribly serious after all. "You lied to me?"

"No. Bricker did. I just didn't correct him," he said quickly.

"It's the same thing," she said with irritation.

"But there was a reason. I couldn't tell you the truth. You wouldn't have believed it."

"What is the truth?"

Mortimer hesitated and then said, "You know how that first night when Jo was guessing what we used to do and you said you would have guessed police of some description?" He waited for her to nod and then said, "Well, you were right."

Sam raised her eyebrows. "You're a police officer from L.A.?"

"Sort of," he said cautiously. "We're enforcers."

"Enforcers?" she echoed with bewilderment.

Mortimer nodded and then licked his lips and added, "For the Council."

"What Council?" she asked at once.

"Our Council, our governing body."

"You work for the government?" Sam asked with amazement, and then shook her head as she recalled that Bricker and Mortimer were from the U.S. and Decker from Canada. Mouth tightening, she asked, "Which government? The U.S. or Canada?"

"Our Council governs our people in both the U.S. and Canada," he said carefully.

Now Sam was getting angry. He was obviously stringing her another line of bull. "There is no such thing."

"Yes," he assured her. "There is."

"Oh, for God's sake, just tell her already."

Both of them swiveled to stare at Bricker as the other man tugged the screen door open and stepped inside. He moved to stand at the end of the couch, hands on hips and scowling.

"You're making her think you're a fruitcake with all this dancing around the subject," Bricker told him dryly, and then glanced to Sam. "I'm sorry I lied, but you and your sisters hardly would have believed it if I'd announced that we were rogue vampire hunters."

"Rogue vampire hunters!" Sam squawked and was suddenly off the couch. Backing up several feet, she glared at the pair of them. "If this is your idea of a joke—"

"We're not trying to be funny," Mortimer said quickly, getting to his feet. "Sam, he's telling the truth this time."

"Right. You're rogue vampire hunters," she said with disgust.

Mortimer winced at her disdain, but nodded. "Yes, we are."

Sam stared at him with disbelief. "You expect me to believe that vampires really exist and you guys—what? Hunt them down and stake them? Cut off their heads to give them rest? Puhleeze." She turned to storm out of the room, but Bricker was in the way. He also had his mouth open, and as she watched in sick fascination, his front canine teeth seemed to shift forward and drop like blinds sliding down a window.

"See," he said with his mouth still open so it sounded more like *thee*. His fangs retracted and then shot out again and then retracted once more. Shrugging, he said, "Vampires."

Sam stared. It had to be some trick, fake teeth controlled by battery-operated remote or something. But it was a good trick.

"Oh," she breathed finally. "You guys are good. I'll give you that. Now if you're done with your little joke, I'd like you both to leave."

"Get out of here Bricker," Mortimer said grimly and

waited for the other man to leave before turning to move toward her, saying quietly, "It isn't a joke, Sam."

"Don't touch me," she hissed, backing away. Her feelings were still confused, but anger was winning the battle. "Of course it's a joke. What is this? Your way of breaking up with me? Make me think you're crazy so I do the job for you?"

"I don't want to break up with you."

"Well, you don't want me with you or you wouldn't try spinning such a stupid story. And you must have planned this well ahead because I'm pretty sure there aren't any stores up here that carry specialty items like those teeth Bricker flashed. What did you guys do? Just head up here planning to sweet-talk some girl into bed and then play your little gag on her? Would any girl have done and I just happened to be handy?"

"No, I—"

"You didn't have to bother," Sam interrupted and then—hurt beyond words—added cruelly, "You were just supposed to be a fling for me anyway. You know, fall off a horse, get back on another. Did you really think someone like me could fall for a beatnik in a band? What did you imagine? That I was fantasizing about following you from gig to gig and flashing you my tits from the audience?"

"Sam." He tried to catch her hands again, but she backed quickly away.

"Don't. Don't try and play the nice guy now. You had your fun last night, wanted to break it off today and succeeded. Now you can go back to your buddies and laugh about how easy it was to get me into bed, and how upset

I was when you pulled this stunt. This will probably be as funny to them as the leech incident must have been. That should have given them a good laugh. I know my sisters laughed themselves silly," she added bitterly.

"Nobody will think this is funny," Mortimer said, reaching for her hand again.

Sam tugged it away, her mouth hardening. "Just get out."

"Sam," he pleaded quietly.

"Now," she growled, too furious to have any desire to listen. She was hurting and angry and just wanted to break something. That or cry. Either way, she wanted him out of there before she did either.

Much to her relief, Mortimer didn't try to argue further, but released his breath on a slow sigh and simply turned and left.

Sam watched through the window until he disappeared into the cottage next door before turning abruptly away to survey the room. She needed something to do, something to distract her, she thought wildly, and then suddenly found herself snatching up a book sitting on the corner of the table and wheeling it furiously at the wall. It crashed into a family portrait taken years ago, knocked it from the wall, and sent it crashing to the floor with a tinkle of shattering glass. And then Sam was crying.

Turning away from the accusing stares of her family in the photo, she moved over to the couch, climbed on it to sit with her legs gathered beneath her, caught up one of the cushions next to her, and pulled it to her chest to bury her face in it as she began to sob. It felt as if her heart was breaking, and she feared it just might be.

* * *

"You just left?" Bricker asked with disbelief.

"What was I supposed to do?" Mortimer snarled, pacing the kitchen floor. "She was too hurt and angry to listen."

Bricker exchanged a glance with Decker and then said, "You should have talked to her. Convinced her it wasn't a joke. Claimed her as your mate."

The younger man still thought you could win anything if you fought hard enough. But after eight hundred years, Mortimer had learned that there were some things that fighting would not get you, and that sometimes you just had to back off and give a person space. Shaking his head wearily, he said, "God, Bricker, sometimes you're so young."

"Yeah, well sometimes you're old and stubb—"

"He's right, Bricker. Fighting and forcing her to listen won't help here," Decker interrupted.

"What?" the young man turned on him with amazement. "Well, what else can you do? She—"

"—isn't going to listen to anything anyone says unless we can get her attention," Decker said, and then added, "And from what I can tell, right now she thinks she's been played and is too hurt and furious with Mortimer to listen to anything he has to say."

Bricker frowned over this and then turned to Mortimer and offered, "I could try to intervene for you."

His anger with the man softened at the offer, but he shook his head. "She thinks we're both dirtbags at the moment."

"Then I can," Decker said, and Mortimer closed his eyes. He had good friends.

"Thank you," he assented, trying not to let his hopes rise. Decker might not be able to get Sam to listen either. She probably thought him a dirtbag too now. "When will you—?"

"Now," Decker interrupted, and promptly walked out of the cottage.

Mortimer moved to the door and watched silently as the other immortal took the trail through the trees, very aware that the man held Mortimer's future in his hands.

Chapter 17

Sam had stopped crying when a knock at the door made her glance up from where she'd curled up on the couch with her pillow. The sight of Decker through the screen door made resentment rise up within her. It seemed the joke wasn't over yet, she thought, and asked bitterly, "What do you want?"

"To talk." He stepped inside without being invited and then paused to look her over.

Sam raised her chin in challenge, knowing he was seeing the evidence of her tears. After several moments of silence, she became aware of the oddest ruffling in her mind. It was something she'd experienced a time or two this last week, each time while with Mortimer and his friends, but it had been much quicker those times, and the men had distracted her from it. In the prolonged, silent standoff now occurring, there was nothing to distract her, and this time it seemed to last much longer than the others. Sam began to worry that she was growing a brain tumor or something.

"You aren't growing a brain tumor," Decker said abruptly, and then added, "It's in your best interests to listen to me."

Sam stared. How had he known she was worrying about a brain tumor? she wondered briefly, but then forgot that issue as her mind processed his comment about it being in her best interests to listen. The way he'd said it had almost sounded threatening.

First Bricker and Mortimer try to humiliate her, and now Decker was going to threaten her. Great, she thought, and asked grimly, "And if I don't listen to you?"

"You won't like what I do then."

"Is that a threat, Decker?"

He shrugged and explained, "If you won't listen, I'll be forced to erase the last several days from your memory. It will be as if you never met Mortimer."

That brought a burst of disbelieving laughter from Sam. "Sure. Right. Well, at the moment that's sounding attractive, so go ahead."

"You don't believe I can, of course."

"No, ya think?" Sam said dryly, and then gasped in surprise as she found herself suddenly setting the pillow aside and standing up. She hadn't intended or planned to do it. She just did. As she struggled with her confusion, Decker reached to the radio sitting on the counter beside the stove and flicked it on. Soft music poured into the room.

"Dance with me?" he asked.

"I—" Sam's words died as her body suddenly started across the room. It was as if her brain had disengaged or somehow been bypassed and she was being controlled by an outside source. Sam tried to stop herself, tried to make her legs stop moving, but her brain didn't appear to be getting the message. When she reached Decker, her body paused and her hands rose. One moved to his shoulder, the other to his waiting hand, and then they began to dance.

"How are you doing this?" Sam asked shakily as he swept her across the kitchen floor. "What are you doing to me?"

"Controlling you," he answered simply, seeming unconcerned by her upset. "Making you dance with me seemed kinder than some of the alternatives I could have chosen, but I had to pick something you wouldn't even conceive of doing to ensure you didn't manage to convince yourself that whatever I made you do was something you made yourself do. Mortals are very good at self-delusion."

"Mortals," Sam echoed faintly, not understanding any of this. There was no way her brain was willing to accept that he was controlling her, even if he was, which he appeared to be doing, Sam realized dizzily. She certainly wasn't controlling herself at the moment.

"Yes . . . mortal. You are . . . and I am not." He spun her away in time to the music, and Sam's body did a little twirl and then danced its way back into his arms. It was the last place she wanted to be, but her body didn't seem to care what her mind wanted.

"You're not mortal?" she asked in a dazed voice.

"Most decidedly not," Decker assured her, and then stopped dancing, but continued to hold her close as he opened his mouth. Sam stared in disbelief as fangs suddenly sprouted and dropped from behind his canines just as Bricker's had done earlier. He left his mouth open for her to peer over for a moment, and then let the fangs slide away and arched one eyebrow. "Shall I bite you now, or are you ready to believe?"

Her eyes jerked to his, but Sam couldn't speak. She couldn't even think.

Decker's other eyebrow arched to join the first. "Shall it be a bite then?"

"No," Sam gasped, and tried to struggle, but while she was sending the message out from her brain, her body remained in his arms, quiescent and unconcerned. Her heartbeat hadn't even sped up, Sam realized, though she was terrified and it should have been beating a rapid tattoo. That odd ruffling happened again inside her head, and then Decker said, "I'm controlling your heartbeat and keeping you calm. Mortimer would never forgive me if I let you drop dead from a heart attack."

"You can read my thoughts?" Sam asked with dismay.

"Oh yes," he said with a wry smile.

"And Mortimer?" she asked, the thought turning her dismay to horror. Had he heard every lustful thought she'd had about him? Dear Lord!

"No," Decker answered solemnly. "If he could, you wouldn't be his life mate."

"Life mate?" Sam echoed. She recalled Mortimer using the word.

Decker hesitated and then released her and stepped back. He didn't just release his hold on her, however, but her body was suddenly her own again too. Sam knew that when she started to sink to the ground, her knees unwilling to hold her up. Decker swiftly caught her arm to keep her upright.

"I apologize for my behavior," he said stiffly as he

half carried her to one of the chairs around the dining room table. "You were too hurt and angry at what you thought was a cruel joke to listen. I had to do something shocking to get your attention. I think you're ready to hear what Mortimer has to say now."

He didn't wait for her to agree or disagree, but turned to move to the door of the cottage.

Sam watched him go, her expression and mind blank.

"She's ready to listen."

Mortimer jumped up from the table as Decker entered on that announcement.

"Listen?" he asked uncertainly.

"I got her calmed down and convinced her you two weren't lying. You can explain things now. She'll listen," he assured him, and then added, "Whether she'll be your life mate, though . . ." He shrugged. "That's up to her."

Mortimer nodded and moved to the door.

"Garrett."

Pausing, he glanced back warily. Decker never called him Garrett; his doing so now was not good.

"She'll believe what you tell her now, but if she's unwilling to mate to you . . ." He let the sentence die, but Mortimer knew exactly what the man wasn't saying. If he couldn't convince Sam to be his life mate, her memory would have to be wiped completely, as would her sisters'. They wouldn't recall ever having met them.

The idea terrified Mortimer, but he knew it would have to be done to protect their people from discovery. That was always their main concern. One brokenhearted immortal meant nothing next to having them all hunted down and extinguished.

Nodding abruptly, he turned and headed out the door. Somehow he had to convince Sam to be with him, to be his life mate. It was that or lose her forever, because he'd never be able to go near her again after they wiped her memory. There was too much chance her memories might return were she to see him again. This was going to be the most important talk of his life. He only wished he felt confident about his success with it.

Mortimer spotted Sam the moment he mounted the deck and stepped up to the door. She was seated at the table, her head and shoulders bowed. She looked defeated, and it made him wonder what Decker had said. Or done, he worried suddenly. Decker had said she was ready to listen, which suggested he hadn't said much himself. So he must have done something to convince her this wasn't a joke.

Mortimer reached for the door handle to pull it open, but hesitated and then knocked instead. He saw Sam stiffen and then straighten, but she didn't look toward the door.

"Come in."

His nerves tightened at her grim voice, but Mortimer opened the door and stepped inside.

"Decker said you were ready to talk to me," he murmured, moving around the table to claim the chair opposite her.

"You mean listen, don't you?" Sam asked quietly, as he sank into the seat. They peered at each other silently, and then her gaze dropped to his mouth. "Show me your teeth."

It wasn't a request, Mortimer noted, but he wasn't angered by the demand in her voice. She was upset.

What mortal in her right mind wouldn't be? Up until now, vampires had always been mythical monsters to her. Besides, he'd rather mismanaged their talk earlier and knew it. While it was probably never easy to have this talk, surely there were better ways to handle it than he had? Still, Mortimer hesitated to reveal his teeth. She had a phobia about bats, or vampires, or both, and he didn't want to have to watch her turn away in disgust.

"Please." This time her tone was much less sharp, almost conciliatory. It gave him hope.

Surely Sam wouldn't care if she was rude if she didn't still care for him, he told himself as he opened his mouth and allowed his fangs to slide into place. He then quickly retracted them and closed his mouth, swallowing the liquid that had gathered at the back of his throat.

"Does it hurt when they drop down?" she asked, seeming more curious than anything.

"No."

"Do you feel it?"

Mortimer considered the question; he'd never really thought about how it felt when his teeth slid out. Finally he said, "Not really. It's more like the sensation of bending your knee. You don't really feel it per se, but you know it's happening."

Sam nodded slowly and then shifted her gaze from his mouth to his eyes. "Decker said you would explain things."

Mortimer nodded and then paused to gather his thoughts, unsure where to start. "Well," he said finally, "I'm an immortal."

"You mean vampire, don't you?" she asked dryly.

Mortimer grimaced. "Some call us that."

"But you don't like it?"

He shook his head. "Vampires are monsters. They attack unsuspecting prey . . . er . . . people, and feed off them."

"But you don't?"

"No," Mortimer said at once. "I ingest bags of blood that we get from a blood bank. Like a hemophiliac," he added on inspiration. "The only difference is they get transfusions and we ingest it through our teeth."

"You bite a *bag*?" Sam asked with a strange combination of disgust and disappointment.

"We don't bite it. Not really. We pop it to our teeth." Wishing he'd brought a bag with him to demonstrate, Mortimer opened his mouth, let his fangs drop, and then made the motion with his empty hand that he would if he were about to feed.

"Huh." Sam suddenly sat back in her seat, her body much more relaxed. It seemed a bag-sucking vampire was just not that frightening.

Mortimer briefly toyed with the idea of admitting that they did occasionally—in emergency situations—feed "off the hoof," as they liked to call it. That he himself had done it just days ago in Minden, but then decided it was probably best to leave that confession for later. Much later.

"You don't look dead."

Mortimer grimaced as he realized he had a lot to clarify here.

"I'm not dead," he said patiently. "Dracula is fiction, though he was based on one of us and is similar to us in some ways."

"If you aren't dead, how did you become—?" Sam gestured toward his mouth.

"Nanos," Mortimer blurted.

Sam raised her eyebrows. "Nanos? You mean science. Your vampirism is scientific in nature?"

"Exactly," he said happily. "You see, our scientists found a way to combine nano technology and microbiology to create microscopic little nanos that when shot into the bloodstream, live there and replicate. They were designed to repair injuries and fight infections or ailments like cancer and then to disintegrate and be shed from the body as waste."

Relieved that she was listening with a considering expression, Mortimer pointed out, "It was really quite a breakthrough scientifically when you think about it."

"Yes," she agreed faintly, and then asked, "So they gave you these nanos because you were injured or sick?"

"No. I was born an immortal. My parents were both immortals and passed it on in their blood."

"But . . . That would mean this technology's been around . . . what? Thirty years or something?" Sam asked incredulously.

Mortimer hesitated. This next was going to be hard for her to accept. "It isn't mortal doctors who came up with these nanos, Sam."

She sat back abruptly, a horrified expression on her face. "You're an alien? I slept with an *alien*?"

"No, no," he assured her, catching her hand as she started to leap up from the table.

Sam paused, her expression uncertain, but didn't sit back down.

"I'm not an alien," Mortimer assured her, relieved

when she sank slowly back into her seat, and then added, "I'm an Atlantean."

Seeing that this didn't appear much more palatable to her, he took a deep breath and began to explain.

"All right," Sam said slowly several minutes later. "So you're telling me there really was an Atlantis way back when. They were incredibly advanced technologically, and one of their scientists had a brain wave with this nano business and created little tiny nanos that could repair and regenerate the human body." She paused, and when he nodded, asked, "Atlanteans *are* human, aren't they?"

Mortimer nodded again and then added, "Actually, the nanos do much more than repair and regenerate. They keep their hosts at their peak condition. Better than peak even. We're stronger and faster than mortals."

Sam recalled the way he'd scooped her up and raced away from the bear in the woods. Nodding, she continued listing off what she'd learned, "Your scientists tried these nanos out on several of your people before they realized that because the human body is in constant need of repair, the nanos would never die off and disintegrate, but would continue their busy work keeping your people healthy and fit for . . ." She paused and asked, "How long?"

"How long?"

"How long does it last?" she explained. "For how long will you stay fit and healthy? Till you grow old and die of old age in your sleep?"

"Erm . . ." Mortimer pursed his lips. "Well, we don't really grow old."

"You don't grow old," she echoed faintly.

Mortimer shook his head. "Aging is seen as an injury, so the nanos repair cells and keep the body young and healthy."

Her eyes widened incredulously and she asked again, "For how long?"

"Well, that differs for everyone, of course. Nanos can't prevent against accidents. If one of us is beheaded, or burned to death in a fire . . ." He shrugged. "We die."

"Right, but barring an accident or being burned to death . . . how long will you stay fit and healthy and *young*?" Sam asked grimly.

"No one knows the answer to that," Mortimer admitted.

"No one knows," she said slowly, her mouth pursing with displeasure. "Then how old is the oldest immortal?"

"The oldest?" He shifted and glanced away, looking uncomfortable. "I guess the oldest one I know of is my boss, Lucian."

"And how old is he?"

"I'm not sure. He was born in Atlantis before the fall, but I don't know the exact year. He's—"

"Born in *Atlantis*?" Sam squawked. "And Atlantis fell—what? A couple *thousand* years ago?"

"Close enough," Mortimer muttered.

"And he looks as young as you are?" she asked with horror.

"Pretty much. We all look about twenty-five to thirty."

Sam sat back in her chair as she tried to accept that, and then glanced at him sharply as a question suddenly occurred to her. "How old are you?"

"Me?" he asked with a grimace.

"Yes. You aren't a couple thousand years old, are you?"

"No, no," he assured her quickly, and Sam was just starting to relax when he added, "I was only born in 1210."

The air washed out of her with a whoosh and then she sucked it back in to gasp, "You're, like, eight hundred years old!"

"Thereabouts," he admitted apologetically.

"But that—I—You could have dated my grandmother. My great-grandmother even."

"Highly unlikely," Mortimer assured her, and then added wryly, "I lost interest in women centuries ago."

Her eyebrows rose and she snapped, "You could have fooled me by last night's events. If that was disinterest, I'd hate to see what interest is for your people. You'd probably cripple me if you were interested."

"Oh, well, I meant I had no interest in other women; I *am* interested in you," he explained, and then added, "That's because you're my life mate."

When she stared at him blankly, Mortimer explained, "I can read the minds of most women, and control them too. It takes all the fun out of it. You don't have to guess what they like, you just pluck it from their minds. You don't have to have conversations; it's easier just to read their thoughts. As for sex . . ." He paused and made a face and then said, "Well, frankly, you might as well just masturbate because without meaning to, you'll have them doing everything you want. Sex, like feeding, is intimate enough that our mind instinctively takes control."

Mortimer reached for her hand and looked her in the

eye as he said, "But you're different. None of that is a worry with you. I can't read or control your mind."

Sam sighed. He looked and sounded earnest, and part of her wanted to throw her arms around him and hug him, but she still had so many questions. Grimacing, she retrieved her hand and said, "I still don't understand everything. Like, where does the whole fangs and blood issue come in?"

"Oh." Mortimer grimaced. "Well, the nanos use blood to fuel themselves as well as to make the repairs and regenerate and so on, but they use too much blood for our bodies to supply. It forces us to find more blood for them," he explained. "That wouldn't have been a problem if the nanos had deactivated and broken down as they were expected to do once they'd finished their repairs. But the scientists hadn't taken into account that the body is constantly in need of repair."

"It is?" she asked with surprise.

"Sure. Sunlight damages the body, as do environmental factors, and things we eat or drink. Even the simple passage of time damages the body. As we sit here your cells are aging, breaking down and dying, slowly, one by one. The body is never without something that needs repair."

"So the nanos never shut down and disintegrate," she realized.

He shook his head.

"And the fangs?"

"When the nanos were first created, the people who had been injected with them were given daily blood transfusions to keep the nanos from attacking the host's organs in search of blood. But when Atlantis fell, those who survived found themselves stranded in a world that was nowhere near as advanced as Atlantis. There were no doctors or blood banks and donors."

Sam nodded, imagining how horrible that must have been. It would be like her suddenly finding herself transported to the Dark Ages, only with a health issue. She couldn't imagine it. "What did they do?"

"Some died a horrible, painful death as the nanos attacked their body, eating away at their organs in search of blood. Others—"

"Others what?" she asked when he hesitated, knowing she wasn't going to like what was coming.

"Some became butchers, killing mortals, draining their blood into bowls or pails and then drinking it to survive. It's a time our people aren't proud of," he admitted unhappily, but then rushed on to say, "But in others, the nanos evolved. They'd been programmed to keep their host alive and so brought about physical changes to aid them in the new circumstances. For instance, our people—realizing that sunlight damaged the skin—avoided it as much as possible and moved about mostly at night so that they would have to take in as little blood as possible. In response, the nanos altered our eyes to allow for better night vision." He paused then and hesitated before admitting, "They also brought on the teeth as a medium to use to gain blood."

Sam closed her eyes. He'd said they didn't bite people but fed off blood from blood banks. Of course, that may very well be true, but the first blood bank had only been established in the 1930s. They'd had to get blood before that an alternate way . . . by feeding off mortals.

Dracula did exist, Sam realized. It was just that in reality, he was the result of science not a curse, and he wasn't undead, but still had his soul. Jesus, she thought suddenly, the man she loved was eight hundred years old.

Sam stiffened. She loved him? Of course she did. That was so her. Fall in love with a cute, lead singer of a not-too-successful band and he turned out to be a vampire. Perfect, she thought, and then frowned as she recalled that he wasn't in a band.

"So you hunt rogue vampires for the council of vampires," she recalled.

"Well, they're just called the Council, not the council of vampires," he said, looking pained.

"Whatever." Sam waved that away. "And you're up here looking for one now?"

"Yes."

"And what did this vampire do to become a rogue?"

"He or she has been biting mortals up here," he admitted reluctantly.

"I thought you said your people didn't bite my people but used bagged blood," she said accusingly.

"I did. We do," Mortimer said quickly. "That's what makes this guy a rogue. Biting mortals is against our laws. It's the reason we're here. To stop him, catch him, and present him or her to the Council for judgment."

Sam sat back in her seat with a small sigh. She supposed she couldn't blame them all for one bad apple. Mortals had criminals who broke their laws too. That thought made her ask with interest, "So your people have their own set of laws?"

"Oh yes. We can't really be bound by yours. I mean, mortals couldn't make immortals follow their laws. It's too easy for us to slip into your minds and convince you we haven't done something, or we weren't there, and so on."

Sam nodded slowly. She supposed it would be a nightmare for mortals to try to police immortals and that having their own laws and enforcers would be necessary. It made her curious though. "What are your laws?"

"We aren't allowed to bite mortals unless it's an absolute emergency, and we aren't allowed to turn more than one mortal in a lifetime."

Sam waited, but when he didn't add anything else, she asked with disbelief, "That's it? That's all there is? A couple thousand years to come up with your own laws, and that's the extent of it?" She snorted with disgust. "Jeez, even Moses had *ten* commandments."

"Well, we have a few more," he said defensively. "We aren't supposed to draw attention to our people or let mortals find out about us."

"Well, you've blown that one," Sam pointed out. "You just told me all about it."

"That's different, you're my life mate."

"Life mate?" She clucked impatiently. "That's the third time you've mentioned my being your life mate and Decker said something about it too. What is a life mate?"

Mortimer hesitated and then said, "It's the one person we can't read or control. That's the first sign of a life mate."

"The first sign?" Sam asked with interest. "There are others?"

He nodded. "When we first meet our life mate it becomes difficult to block our thoughts from being read by other immortals."

Sam's eyebrows rose. "You have to block your thoughts from other immortals?"

"We can read each other just like we read mortals if we don't block our thoughts. It's something we learn to do early. It's not difficult, but requires a certain amount of concentration that appears to be lacking when we first meet our life mate. We're suddenly open and vulnerable to being read by others," Mortimer admitted with a grimace, and then quickly added, "Another symptom is a sudden reawakening of appetites. For food . . . and sex," he added, and then quickly explained, "Most immortals lose interest in food shortly after they pass their first century. After that they will eat on occasion, special functions and such, but mostly they subsist on blood."

Since the man had eaten like a horse since she'd known him, Sam merely asked, "You lose interest in sex too after the first century?"

"That passes at different times depending on the individual," he said with a shrug. "For me, I lost interest about . . . I'm not sure, two or three hundred years ago."

"I notice that appetite survived longer than the one for food," she said dryly.

Mortimer grinned. "*C'est la vie.*"

His words surprised a short laugh out of Sam, and then she sighed. "What now?"

"Now," he said slowly, "you have to decide if you are willing to be my life mate."

"I thought I already was," she said with surprise. "You said you had all the symptoms."

"Yes, I do. And *you* are *my* life mate, but that doesn't mean that you will agree to *be* my life mate in return," he said quietly. "You might not wish to join your life to mine."

"What happens if I don't wish to?" she asked curiously.

Mortimer blanched at the suggestion, but said, "If you don't, your memory of me will be erased and your life will go on as if we'd never met."

Sam didn't care for that idea at all. "And if I *am* willing?"

"Then you have to decide if you are willing to be turned."

"Turned?" Sam frowned. "You mean I could be . . . ?"

"Immortal," Mortimer finished and nodded.

"Immortal," she whispered. Sam supposed that would mean some sort of transfusion of his nano-rich blood but was more concerned with the results of being turned. Being an immortal. The idea of staying young forever wasn't bad. And being stronger and faster sounded cool, but the biting-bags-of-blood bit was really kind of gross. She'd put up with the grossness, maybe, to be with Mortimer, but . . .

"What's the catch?" she asked suddenly.

"Catch?" Mortimer asked.

"The downside," she explained. "There's always a downside. You're offering me eternal youth, with you, a handsome, intelligent amusing mate . . . Biting bags of blood doesn't sound great, but there have to be more negatives than that."

"Well, you'd have to stay out of the sun as much as possible," he admitted.

"You went out in it the day we went shopping, and the day we went Sea-Dooing, and—"

"We can go out into sunlight, but it means consuming more blood."

"Oh." She considered that. "What about garlic and all that other stuff?"

"Garlic is delicious," Mortimer said simply. "You can eat garlic if you like. And go into churches. All those things in the vampire movies are myths . . ."

"But?" she queried sharply. "I hear a *but*."

Mortimer sighed and nodded slowly. "But we don't age. It can cause questions if you live anywhere near, or interact with, mortals for more than ten years or so and show no signs of aging. Most of us have to move every decade . . . and those who work among mortals have to change jobs that often as well."

"The catch," Sam breathed, and it was a doozy. She was working herself to death for a career she might have to give up in ten years, Sam realized, and then Mortimer told her the deal breaker.

"You'd have to leave your sisters in ten years too."

Chapter 18

Sam stared out the window, eyes fixed on Decker's cottage, searching for any sign of Mortimer. If the men were awake, she hadn't yet seen any sign of them, but wasn't surprised. Mortimer was avoiding her, trying to give her the chance to make her decision. He'd said that was what he intended to do when he'd left her last weekend after explaining the downside to what he offered her. Sam understood that he was giving her the space and time to think, and appreciated it, but she missed him.

A little frustrated sigh slipped from her lips, and she paced away from the window, only to whirl back and return to the spot she'd been haunting in the evenings since that night. Alex and Jo had taken to leaving the cottage after dinner, expecting that she and Mortimer would use that time to be together. Sam had allowed them to think that, knowing she needed the time alone to decide her future . . . and theirs, and Mortimer's too.

Whatever she decided affected everyone she loved, which was what made it such a hard decision to make. Did she grab that brass ring and choose Mortimer . . . and have to disappear from her sisters' lives in ten years? Or did she choose her sisters and have to give up Mortimer, even the memory of him?

The very thought made her mouth go dry and her muscles clench with anxiety. It was hard to believe that two weeks ago he hadn't even been on her radar. In that time he'd somehow made so much of a place in her heart that she now found it hard to continue on without him. Mortimer was always on her mind, her thoughts caught up in everything he'd said and done, her eyes constantly searching out the cottage next door in the hopes of just catching a glimpse of him walking to the SUV as the men left for their nightly hunt for their rogue. Only then would she give up her spot by the sink, and then it was only to pace the floor, her thoughts racing until she finally went to bed, where they continued to race until she heard the SUV return and could sit up to watch Mortimer make the short trek back inside the cottage again. Then Sam would finally drift off to sleep, only to be haunted by him in her dreams.

Despite her late hours, Sam usually woke around eleven. Exhausted and spent, she dragged herself through the day, her thoughts running around inside her mind like a rat trapped in a maze, searching for the right direction to take.

Sam's eyes narrowed on Decker's kitchen door. She'd thought she'd spotted movement beyond the window. For one moment, she allowed her heart to hope that

Mortimer might slip over to see her tonight before the men went on the hunt, but then she quashed that hope, knowing it wasn't going to happen. He would leave her to her decision until tomorrow morning as promised. Mortimer had said she had to give him her decision before leaving with her sisters to return to the city.

Sam still hadn't made up her mind. She turned away from the window with exasperation, her gaze sliding desperately around the cottage in search of a distraction. But it was silent and empty. Alex and Jo had gone to the Andersons'. The couple were having their usual Saturday night party, and since it was their last night, her sisters had decided to attend. They'd tried to convince her to go too, but not too hard because they were still under the mistaken belief that she was enjoying her evenings with Mortimer.

If they only knew, Sam thought bitterly, and wished that they did, and that she could explain things to them and—Alex and Jo would have understood, she was sure, and would have kept the secret, and then she wouldn't have had to choose between them or Mortimer, but he'd said that wasn't allowed. The more who knew the secret, the more risk there was of the knowledge getting out and his people being hunted down and slaughtered out of fear.

Sighing, Sam forced herself to calm down and think things through logically. There were a lot of pluses to choosing Mortimer. She would remain young, never get sick, etc. Of course the whole blood thing was a bit of an issue. She found the idea rather gross, but could get past that if she just thought of it as medicine like cod liver oil or something. Mortimer had said they didn't taste it when they "bit the bag" anyway. Mind you, she wasn't pleased with the idea of being stuck with her scrawny body for centuries, and suspected breast implants wouldn't be a possibility, but . . .

Sam made a cluck of disgust. None of that was important to her. She'd never dreamed of living forever, or feared losing her youth, and thinking about it was just a way to avoid the real issues. The true issue was the people involved. People she loved. Did she choose him and lose her sisters, as well as her career, one she'd worked long and hard for? Or did she choose her sisters, keep her career, and lose Mortimer? It was an impossible choice. She and her sisters only had one another. They weren't close with their one remaining aunt and uncle, but spent all their special occasions alone. Christmas, birthdays, Thanksgiving, and Easter all were spent with the three of them together. And they called one another all the time, and . . .

How could Sam remove herself from that equation and leave the two alone to fend for themselves? On the other hand, how could she give up Mortimer? She might not suffer so much, she reminded herself. He'd explained that they would erase her memories so at least she wouldn't remember what she was missing. But he would . . . And he'd explained that life mates were rare and special and sometimes once-in-a-lifetime occurrences, although he did know of a few who had been fortunate enough to find another after losing their first. She was the first Mortimer had encountered in eight hundred years. If she chose her sisters, while she might not recall what she had given up, he would, and it might be centuries before he found another to take her place, if ever. Sam loved Mortimer too much to do that to him. And despite the fact that she might not remember it, she didn't want to do that to herself either. He might be her only chance at love too. The idea of giving him up was unbearable, but so was the idea of having to leave her sisters.

She ran her hands into her hair and tugged viciously at the strands, frustration roiling through her. Sam didn't know what to do. She simply couldn't decide. She didn't want to leave any of them. The whole matter was making her hate the idea of not aging. If she just didn't stay young, but continued to age, she could have Mortimer and stay with her sisters too.

Sam paused abruptly as that thought claimed her. Mortimer had said she had to decide if she wished to be his life mate, and then whether she wished to be turned and become one of them. That meant she didn't *have* to turn to be with him, Sam realized, and if she didn't, she wouldn't have to abandon her sisters.

Not turning brought its own issues, of course. She would age while Mortimer wouldn't and so on, but at least she wouldn't have to leave her sisters after ten years. She could stay and see Alex and Jo settled and maybe allow him to turn her later or something.

Of course, Mortimer would have to bow out of their lives in ten years. Or maybe twenty, she thought. If they dyed his sideburns gray, and dressed him a little frumpy, they might be able to squeeze another ten years in before he had to stop seeing them. Maybe more; after all, there were breakthroughs every day in cosmetic advances. They might manage twenty-five or even thirty years before he had to stop seeing her sisters. But Sam could still see them if she did age, and could make up excuses for why Mortimer couldn't, or even claim to divorce him or something. She knew she'd eventually have to give them up, but hoped it would be easier if they were better settled with families of their own.

It was a risk, though, and Sam knew it. There was the chance she could have a heart attack or stroke, or be in an accident, but really even as an immortal there was the possibility of being in a car accident and getting decapitated, or trapped in the vehicle and burning alive. Life was full of risks.

She released a long, slow breath of relief at having come to a decision she could live with, and then frowned as the next issue then cropped up in her mind. That was that, while she knew she loved him, Mortimer—unfortunately—hadn't used the word *love* himself. Instead he'd said he liked her with the "ever-after kind of like."

What the heck was that, exactly? she wondered unhappily. And why hadn't he used the word *love*? Sam was a lawyer, and to her the fact that he hadn't said *I love you* was probably because he didn't. She feared he was merely settling for her because he couldn't read her mind or control her and those were considered signs of a life mate to his kind. Mortimer seemed to think that was the same thing as love, but Sam wasn't sure. She didn't want to be his I'll-settle-for-her girl. On the other hand, if there was a possibility that he did love her, or might even come to love her, she didn't want to give him up and have her mind wiped.

She paused by the window as the sound of an engine drew her gaze to the lake, and a boat cruised into view. It rode by, turning inland just as it passed their dock, and that's when she realized it was Grant returning home from an outing. Sam's eyes immediately shifted to the table and the pie waiting beside the check for his work.

The pie was the third one Alex had made this week. Unfortunately, their neighbor never seemed to be home to accept delivery, and rather than risk giving him a pie that had gone bad, Alex had made another on Tuesday and then another that morning. Of course, she, Jo, and Alex had been forced to eat the other pies rather than see them go to waste. It appeared that they wouldn't have to eat this one though. Alex had asked Sam to keep an eye out and deliver it should Grant make an appearance, and there he was.

She might as well do it now and get that chore out of her hair, Sam thought. The short walk and fresh air might help clear her thoughts.

Nodding, she picked up the pie and then headed out the door.

There was no path from their property to Grant's. His house was on something of a raised cliff. It was only about three and a half feet high, but it was lined with boulders and waist-high weeds. She had to walk up to the lane and along the gravel road to get to his driveway. Sam had to pay attention and go slow as she walked the rutted driveway to keep from stumbling or twisting an ankle, so it took a few moments for her to reach the little house on the small cliff.

Her gaze slid over the building as she moved to the small front deck. Grant was a year-round resident, and the house showed that, with a Ski-Doo parked next to a Sea-Doo under the wide awning beside the garage.

Sam turned her attention to the dock then, noting that the boat was tied up, and the dock empty. Her gaze then slid to the door of the house to see it was open. Sam walked up the steps to the yawning entrance and peered inside.

"Grant?" she called, and thought she heard him answer from somewhere inside. At least she heard him say something, and stepped cautiously over the threshold. Pausing in the unlit and shadowed kitchen inside the door, she called uncertainly, "Grant? Alex sent me with a pie and your check."

A loud crash sounded, followed by a curse, and Sam glanced toward an open door and then moved quickly to it and found herself at the top of a set of stairs leading down. Worried that the man had hurt himself, she hurried down and toward the only open door with a light on inside.

"Grant? Did you hurt yourself?" Sam asked, rushing to the door, and then froze at the entrance, her eyes widening at the sight before her. Grant stood in front of an open refrigerator, a cooler lying on its side at his feet. It had obviously fallen and crashed open, but its contents were what had brought her to an abrupt halt. Half a dozen blood bags had spilled out, at least one of them breaking in the fall. Blood was gushing from the punctured bag and running in rivulets across the white tiles.

"Oh," she breathed, her eyes lifting to Grant's stunned face as he glanced over to see her standing there. For a moment, both of them seemed frozen, and she stared at the man, noting the fact that he looked about twenty-five to thirty, was in peak condition, and there was a silver glint to his blue eyes that reminded her of Mortimer. If that and the blood hadn't convinced her he was an immortal, the fangs sliding out of his mouth made it obvious. Both her neighbors were immortals, it seemed . . . and unless there were scads of them running around up here, Grant was probably the rogue, she realized with horror.

Dropping the pie, Sam whirled and ran for the stairs, her heart sinking as a scuffling behind her warned that he was giving chase. Immortals were stronger and could run faster than mortals, she recalled Mortimer telling her, and knew she didn't have a chance.

"—love you."

Mortimer turned from pacing the floor in the rec room to glance at Bricker as the younger immortal stared at him impatiently. "What did you say?"

"I knew you weren't listening to me," Bricker said with exasperation.

Mortimer grimaced, acknowledging that he hadn't. He'd been distracted and lost in his own thoughts and worries since his talk with Sam. It had been the hardest thing in the world for him to stay away from her, but he knew he had to. She needed time to think without his distracting her. He was asking her to give up a lot. She was close to her sisters and had worked hard for her career.

"I said, when you talked to Sam the other night, did you say 'I love you,'" he repeated the words that had drawn Mortimer's attention back to him in the first place. "You do love her, right?"

Mortimer stared at him. Yes. He loved her. Dear God, why else would he be such a wreck? He'd been less than useless the last several nights while they were out hunting, mostly just a body following the other two without a single useful suggestion to make to find their rogue. While the other two had been planning and suggesting ways to lay a trap, Mortimer had sat wishing he'd stayed to somehow convince Sam to be his life mate. And berating himself for not simply taking her to bed and not letting her out until she agreed to be with him. She was his, dammit! There was no question of whether she should be his life mate. She simply was.

"You didn't tell her you love her," Bricker said, sounding disappointed as he made it obvious he'd read his mind. Shaking his head he said, "Girls like to hear that stuff, Mortimer."

"I told her I had the ever-after kind of like for her," Mortimer defended himself, but knew that just wasn't the same thing. He probably should have told her he loved her.

"Oh man." Bricker heaved out a sigh of mingled disgust and resignation. "This life mate business must really mess with your head. You used to be the smarter one."

Mortimer frowned. "I'm not smarter."

"Not anymore," Bricker agreed dryly. "Go back and tell the woman you love her. It's the least you can do if you hope she'll choose you over family."

Mortimer hesitated one moment, but then nodded and headed for the stairs. He'd go there right now, tell her he loved her, and then *show* her he loved her too. He'd worship every inch of her body until she couldn't bear the idea of never experiencing such pleasure again. He'd—

"I'll keep the girls busy if they return before you're done so you can do the job properly," Bricker offered, revealing once again that he was eavesdropping in his head. This time Mortimer didn't berate him; he'd appreciate his keeping Jo and Alex away, he decided as he stepped off the top step into the kitchen.

"No problem," Bricker assured him as if he'd spoken the thoughts aloud. He then slammed one hand onto his shoulder, opened the door to the deck with the other, and propelled him firmly through it. "Go get her, tiger."

Nodding, Mortimer strode out and crossed to the stairs at a quick clip. He continued that quick clip as he crossed the yard and traveled the trail through the trees, but his steps slowed as he crossed their yard and he contemplated how he should do this.

Did he just stride in like a conquering hero, sweep her into his arms, make mad passionate love to her, and then confess his love and beg her to be his life mate? Or did he make the confession of love first and then sweep her into his arms and make mad passionate love to her followed by groveling and pleas that she be his life mate? *Should* he plead at all? Maybe demanding or simply asking would be better.

Also, should he take her where she stood, or carry her off to the bedroom where he could take her in relative comfort? Both options had their good points. Comfort was definitely nice, but there was something to be said for the added excitement of a passion that wouldn't be denied and sex in strange places. Perhaps he should—

"Stop bloody thinking and get in there."

Mortimer whirled around to scowl as he saw that Bricker stood not three feet behind him. "What are you doing?"

"I knew you'd overthink it so I thought I'd follow to give you a push if you started to lag," he said dryly.

"I don't need—" Mortimer began, and then his eyes widened as he saw Decker approaching a few feet behind Bricker.

"What are you doing?" he asked.

"I was just coming to suggest that Bricker and I head out to look around for the rogue while you do this." When the younger man nodded agreement, Decker glanced back to Mortimer and added, "If you can't persuade Sam to be your life mate, just ring my cell and we'll head back so I can . . . do what needs doing." He shrugged. "There's no sense dragging it out until tomorrow morning."

"Nothing like burying me before I'm dead," Mortimer muttered.

"Don't listen to him," Bricker said quickly, grabbing his shoulders and turning him toward the steps to Sam's cottage. "You *will* convince her. It's meant to be."

"Is it?" Mortimer asked unhappily.

"Yes, it is," Bricker assured, propelling him up the stairs. "Just—"

His words died and both men froze as a scream sounded from next door.

"That sounded like Sam," Mortimer said anxiously, shoving his way past Bricker and lunging back down the steps. He was around the cottage in a heartbeat and leaping up the boulders that separated the two properties, aware that Bricker and Pimms were on his heels.

"What would she be doing over here?" Bricker asked as they hurried across the empty yard.

Mortimer didn't answer. He was too worried about Sam to take the time to sort it out. With her balance as iffy as it was, she could have fallen and broken something, and he was desperately hoping it wasn't her beautiful neck. If she died before he could turn her, he'd kill her, Mortimer thought illogically.

"If she's seriously injured you'd have an excuse to turn her without her permission," Bricker pointed out as Mortimer led the way to the house.

The idea was tempting, but he'd rather Sam chose him herself, not be forced into it by circumstances. Besides, she might resent being turned while injured and unconscious—even if it was to save her life—and never consent to be his life mate.

The door to the house was wide open. Mortimer led the way inside, his feet turning immediately toward a set of stairs as his ears caught the murmur of voices drifting up. The fact that those voices sounded completely calm now did not ease his anxiety, and he scrambled down the steps so fast he nearly flew. Mortimer then charged for the open door of a lit room and came to a screeching halt as he saw Sam kneeling in a pool of blood, helping to gather several unscathed bags of blood as she listened to the dark-haired man kneeling beside her.

Bricker and Pimms hadn't expected him to halt so abruptly and immediately careened into his back, nearly sending the three of them toppling to the floor.

Their less than graceful entrance hadn't gone unnoticed.

"Mortimer." Sam peered up at him with surprise, and then smiled uncertainly. "I think I may have solved your rogue case for you."

Relief coursed through him as he realized she was uninjured after all. His gaze slid from her to the stranger, who was indeed an immortal, he saw, and then he moved to Sam's side, caught her by the arm, and drew her to her feet and protectively to his side.

Sighing, the dark-haired immortal got to his feet and then held out one hand. "Grant Galloway," he introduced himself. "And I am *not* a rogue."

Mortimer tucked Sam safely behind him before turning to scowl at the man accusingly. "You are if you're the one who's been biting the mortals around here."

"As it happens I have, but as I was explaining to your life mate here, I only do it in cases of an emergency."

"How did you know I was his life mate?" Sam asked, scooting in front of Mortimer before he could stop her. "You were reading my mind, weren't you?"

"Yes. I apologize, Sam, but you sort of freaked out when you saw the blood and I had to take control of you to calm you down. I inadvertently read your thoughts," the man explained, craning his neck to keep eye contact with her as Mortimer shifted her behind him again. When he could no longer see her, he then turned his attention to Mortimer.

"I only bite mortals when the power goes out and my blood supply is tainted. And I stop the moment a fresh supply arrives," Grant said stiffly, kneeling once again to finish collecting the undamaged bags and put them in the refrigerator.

"There have been too many people spotted with bite marks for it only to have been in an emergency," Mortimer said with disbelief.

Grant shrugged as he put the last bag in the refrigerator and closed the door. "The power goes out a lot up here. It really isn't very reliable. It seems that every time there's a slight wind, or a heavy snow, some tree somewhere takes down a line and disrupts the power."

A moment of silence passed as Mortimer, Decker, and Bricker exchanged glances, and then Decker asked, "Why don't you have a generator? If you had a generator, it wouldn't be an issue."

"I can't afford a generator," Grant said dryly, and then scowled as he added, "Not all of us were fortunate enough to have ancestors clever enough to gain and maintain wealth over the centuries. Some of us are just regular folk."

The words made Sam snicker, and Mortimer noted the glare Grant turned on her as she peered around his arm. He scowled at him in response and stepped sideways to block her from view, but she simply rushed around his other side and in front of him so that she could say apologetically, "I'm sorry, Grant, but there's just nothing regular about any of you. You're vampires, for God's sake."

"We prefer the term *immortals*," Grant said, sounding somewhat mollified by her explanation.

"So you claim that you've only ever bitten mortals when the power went down and your blood was tainted?" Mortimer asked, forcing them back to the point. He also threw his arm around Sam's shoulders and dragged her to his side, thinking that if the damned woman wouldn't stay where he put her, he'd have to anchor her there to keep her safe.

"I'm not *claiming* it, it's true. Read my mind if you don't believe me," Grant added, and then stood patiently, waiting.

Mortimer reached out with his thoughts, finding the man's mind open. What he read there told him that it was indeed true. Grant Galloway only resorted to biting mortals when his blood was tainted and he was waiting for a delivery of fresh supplies.

"We got our emergency delivery of fresh blood the day after the power problem. Why did it take so long for you to receive your new supplies?" Mortimer asked, remaining in the man's head to read the answer as it popped to the forefront of his thoughts. He frowned as he read that answer. Grant Galloway had insulted the head of the order-taking department at the Argeneau Blood Bank some time ago and suspected she now watched for his orders to pass her desk and then temporarily lost them to make him wait for his deliveries. He suspected she was trying to make trouble for him, and—he thought—had succeeded in her efforts, or else he wouldn't have enforcers in his home gunning for his hide.

"Jesus," Decker muttered beside him, obviously reading the thoughts too. "Why the hell didn't you report her to someone higher up?"

"I wouldn't give her the satisfaction," Grant said stiffly. "I can make do on my own."

"Report who?" Sam asked with confusion, reminding them that she couldn't read Grant's thoughts.

Yet, Mortimer thought hopefully, and quickly explained the situation.

"Well, that just sounds petty," she said with disgust. "I would have thought your people were above that."

"We're immortal, but we're still human," he said quietly.

Her eyes widened slightly as he said this, as if she hadn't been thinking of them as human after learning about their somewhat unique status. It seemed obvious he had more explaining to do, and the sooner the better.

"Go on," Decker said suddenly. "We'll deal with the matter here."

Nodding, Mortimer turned Sam toward the door.

"What will they do with Grant?" she asked anxiously as he ushered her upstairs.

Mortimer waited until they'd left the cottage and were crossing the yard before answering, "They'll call our boss, Lucian, and tell him what's going on here."

"And what will this Lucian do?" Sam asked worriedly. Apparently she liked the guy enough to be concerned for him, but then he had been her neighbor for several years.

Mortimer paused and turned to scoop her up in his arms. He'd led her to the small cliff rather than walk all the way around, but wasn't risking her trying to climb down, losing her balance, and falling. Cradling her close, he leaped off the cliff, landing on her property with a grunt. Mortimer didn't set her down then, but continued to carry her as he crossed to the deck of her family cottage.

"Mortimer?" she asked as he mounted the steps to the deck. "What will he do?"

Mortimer blew out a small breath, but answered, "I'm not sure, but I suspect Lucian will let him off the hook this time. If so, he'll probably arrange for a generator to save further problems."

"He'd do that?" Sam asked with surprise.

"He might," Mortimer said with a shrug, unable to say one way or the other. Lucian could be a hard-ass, but he looked after their people the best he could.

"What about the woman who's holding up Grant's orders?" she asked with a small frown.

"Bastien will deal with her," he said. Catching the confusion on her face, he explained, "Bastien Argeneau. He's Lucian's nephew. He heads up Argeneau Enterprises, which runs our blood banks and various other things. Lucian will tell Bastien what she's been doing and he'll deal with her."

"*Deal* with her?" Sam echoed, eyes narrowing, and Mortimer paused in front of the door to the cottage to frown at her expression.

"He isn't going to stake her through the heart and set her on fire," he said dryly. "This isn't the Middle Ages and we aren't monsters. She'll probably get a strong warning and dressing-down along with the threat of losing her job if he hears of her doing any such thing again."

When she relaxed in his arms, he shook his head and then said, "Get the door, please, love."

Sam's eyes widened at the endearment, but she reached to open the door so that he could hook his foot around it, draw it all the way open, and carry her inside.

Mortimer considered setting her down in the living room and talking to her, but his original plan had been to make love to her until she agreed to be his life mate, and it still seemed like a good plan to him. Unfortunately, he was very aware that her sisters could come home at any time, so he carried her to the short hall leading to the bedrooms.

"What are we doing?" Sam asked with surprise. They'd reached her door by then, and she promptly followed the first question with "And how did you know this was my room?"

"I guessed," he muttered.

"You didn't answer my first question," she pointed out.

Mortimer paused beside the small double bed and kissed her before saying, "I love you, and I'm going to make love to you until you agree to be my life mate."

"I'll be your life mate," she said promptly as he lowered his head, intending to kiss her again.

Mortimer paused abruptly, unsure he'd heard her correctly. "You will?"

Sam nodded solemnly, but when he grinned and bent again to try to kiss her, she turned her head away and added, "But I don't want you turn me."

Mortimer stiffened at once, a lot of the joy that had just leaped in his chest dying at once. "What? Why not?"

Sam turned her head back and eyed him solemnly. "I can't abandon my sisters, Mortimer. I love you, but I also love them. We only have each other and I can't—"

"You have me now too," he interrupted.

"Yes." She smiled and placed her hand on his cheek. "Thank you for telling me you love me. It means a lot, and I do love you too. But Alex and Jo would be alone if I left them."

"They'll marry and have families of their own," he argued.

"And when they do I'll reconsider," she answered quietly.

Mortimer frowned, not satisfied with that. "But what if you have an accident or something, or—"

"You could turn me today and I could be in a car accident tomorrow, get trapped in the car and burn to death," she pointed out solemnly. "Isn't that true?"

Mortimer nodded reluctantly. Fire was one of the few ways one of their kind could die.

"Life is full of risks," she said softly. "I can only deal with what I know, and I know I don't want to lose you, but I don't want to lose Alex and Jo either. Besides," she added brightly. "I was thinking that Bricker and Jo really hit it off and if he were to turn her—"

"He can read her," Mortimer interrupted gently. "They aren't life mates."

"Oh." She frowned at this news, but then bounced back with "Well, you must know loads of immortals. We'll just have lots of dinner parties and introduce my sisters to your friends until—"

"Sam," he interrupted gently, "sweetheart, the chances of their also turning out to be life mates to an immortal are . . ." Mortimer paused as he saw the tears gathering in her eyes. Feeling his heart squeeze with pain for her, he said sadly, "I just don't want you to get your hopes up, honey."

"Hope is all I have," Sam said solemnly. "Let me hold on to it as long as I can. Please?"

Mortimer closed his eyes briefly, his mind whirling. She had chosen him, but couldn't yet let go of her family. With time he hoped that would change, but until then it meant a lot of worry and agony for them both. She would wear herself out trying to find life mates for her sisters, and when that failed, constantly fret about the day when she would have to make the final decision to give them up and allow herself to be turned. As for him, he would constantly fret about her health and well-being and not getting herself killed before he could turn her.

It seemed obvious that a lot of anxiety and heartache lay ahead for both of them, and for one brief moment Mortimer considered choosing the kinder path and having Decker wipe her mind to save her from it, but he couldn't. He was too selfish. Mortimer wanted her in his life any way he could get her. As his life mate, she could remain with him even if she wasn't turned, if—

"We'll have to go before the Council," he told her quietly.

"The Council?" Sam echoed, and he wasn't surprised by the worry on her face. "Why?"

"Because if you aren't turned, you have to be—" Mortimer hesitated and then admitted, "I'm not sure what they do. It might be a three-on-one or something, but they'll do something."

"A three-on-one?" she asked warily, and his mouth tipped at the suspicion in her eyes.

"It isn't a sexual thing," Mortimer said with a laugh, but the laugh died as he admitted, "Three Council members will slip into your mind at the same time and do stuff to ensure that you never accidentally tell anyone about us."

"They'll do stuff? What kind of stuff?" Sam asked dubiously.

"I don't know what it is exactly they do," Mortimer admitted wearily, suddenly sure she would balk at the procedure. "But they have a way of locking the knowledge away somewhere so that you know, but can't ever speak about it. It's the only way they'd allow us to be life mates without your turning."

"You mean like a hypnotic suggestion?" she asked slowly.

"I don't know," he admitted, unwilling to lie.

Sam worried her lip briefly, but then sighed and raised her eyes to his. "If that's what it takes, then I guess I'll have to let them do it. I don't want to lose you."

Mortimer let his breath out on a whoosh and hugged her close. "Thank God," he whispered into her hair.

"I do love you, Mortimer," Sam whispered into his chest. "I hope my not being willing to turn right away doesn't make you think I don't. I just—"

"I know." He let her feet slip to the floor. Once she was standing before him, he clasped her face in his hands and smiled down at her. "You love your sisters too. I noticed the closeness the three of you shared right away. I understand."

Sam smiled with relief, and then cleared her throat, and—eyes fixed on the front of his T-shirt—whispered, "Didn't you say something about making love to me earlier?" Raising her eyes to his, she added shyly, "I've missed you."

"I've missed you too," he admitted, brushing one thumb lightly across the corner of her mouth. "And I never want to be without you again."

"You won't," she promised on a whisper. "You have me now. Everything will work out in the end."

Mortimer smiled and bent to cover her mouth with his. He told himself that she was right. They'd found their rogue, and he had won his life mate. Perhaps the worries now floating through his thoughts were for naught. After all, it had turned out their rogue wasn't really a rogue at all. Maybe his worries weren't really worries. Perhaps everything would work out, he told himself, but a part of his mind stood firm and unconvinced. It saw trials ahead to overcome, and dangers that threatened Sam's life and his happiness. And it saw terrible heartache if he lost her to one of those threats.

His distraction was apparently noticeable in his kisses. Sam suddenly broke their kiss to whisper, "You're worrying. Let it go and come back to me."

Mortimer wished it were only that easy, and then Sam apparently decided to show him that it was. She kissed him, this time taking charge of the caress, her own tongue slipping out to urge his lips apart. He was so startled by the aggressive action that he didn't notice that her fingers were busily working on removing his shirt until the buttons were undone and she was pushing the material apart to run her fingers lightly over his bare chest. But in the next moment her attention shifted to his pants, and Mortimer found himself sucking in his breath on a surprised gasp as she merely unsnapped the button and then slid her hand inside to find him.

He almost bit down on her tongue in surprise when her fingers found and closed over him, then he groaned and quickly began undressing her. Mortimer managed to get her T-shirt off and unsnap her bra, but had to give up kissing her to manage it. The moment the bra hit the floor, though, he slid a hand into her hair and dragged her back to kiss again as his other hand moved down to begin tugging at her jogging shorts.

Sam hadn't been still while he worked. She'd left off caressing him to concentrate on finishing undoing his jeans and was pushing them down off his hips even as he tugged her shorts off her own. The moment their shorts dropped to tangle around their ankles, Mortimer tumbled Sam to the bed, but the shorts put him off balance and they landed on their sides, still kissing.

She laughed against his mouth as he rolled so that she was beneath him on the bed, and then groaned when he found and began to knead one breast even as he ground his hips forward so that his erection pressed eagerly against her. His own groan followed as her pleasure struck him, and—despite the fact that he'd experienced this with her the first time they'd made love—he marveled at it anew.

This shared pleasure was something Mortimer had heard about for centuries. Young immortals whispered about such things while growing up, wondering what it would be like, and just how good it might be. Neither he nor his young friends had had a clue, he thought now. There was simply no way to imagine the all-encompassing, overwhelming intensity of the experience. Between that and the safety one experienced being able to just be with someone without having to constantly guard one's thoughts, Mortimer thought he understood why immortals had killed for life mates, and even been known to destroy themselves at their loss. He already couldn't imagine a life without Sam in it.

"Oh God, Sweet Cheeks, please," Sam moaned by his ear, her nails digging into his behind and urging him closer still.

Mortimer stiffened slightly, and broke the kiss to rise up and peer at her blankly. "Sweet Cheeks?"

Sam blushed, but then gave a breathless laugh and admitted, "You suggested a pet name and I've been working on it. I don't know about your toes, but you have the nicest behind I've ever seen on a man, so . . ." When Mortimer just stared at her, she added seriously, "You have a very nice penis too, and it gives me a great deal of pleasure, but I somehow didn't think Sweet Penis would go over well in public. Although I guess I could shorten it to Sweet P."

Mortimer closed his eyes at the very suggestion. He could just imagine the men's reaction if she ever called him Sweet P in front of them. Hell, Sweet Cheeks wasn't much better. In reality, Sweet Penis would probably give him the most status with the guys. But he knew there was no way she would use it in public.

Seeming to sense his distress, she promised, "I'll keep working on it."

A soft chuckle slipped from his lips, and Mortimer opened his eyes and peered solemnly down at her. "I love you, Sam."

"I love you too, Garrett Gordon Mortimer," she said, sounding surprised at the solemn tone to his voice.

He nodded, and then said, "We can do this. I'm going to keep you safe and well until you're ready to turn. And I'm going to help you see your sisters settled and do whatever it takes for you to be willing to take that step."

Sam nodded solemnly and then said, "And I'll do whatever I have to to keep you safe and well too."

Mortimer blinked at the promise and then asked with amusement, "What makes you think I need keeping safe?"

"You're a cop, Mortimer," she pointed out quietly. "I deal with police officers all the time. I have friends who are cops. I know what I'm getting into here. The constant worry that you won't come home, the—"

"No, no, no," Mortimer interrupted, brushing a strand of hair back from her face. "No, Sam, sweetheart. You don't have to worry about that. I'm an immortal."

"You may be *an* immortal, but from what I understand that doesn't mean you *are* immortal," she pointed out. "And the rogues you hunt are also immortals, and they know how to kill you if they aren't wanting to be caught, don't they?"

His eyebrows rose at her words. He'd never thought about it like that.

"So," she said, raising her hands to frame his face now. "We'll keep each other safe and happy. We can do it, Mortimer . . . together."

"Together," he agreed, and felt his hope reawakening inside him.

As he bent to kiss her, Mortimer began to think that perhaps they could do it. Together. As long as they had each other, anything was possible.

Dear Reader,

I hope you enjoyed Sam and Mortimer's story. As you've probably guessed, you'll see more of this couple in the future. I'm happy to say you'll also see more of the Argeneau clan in coming stories.

However, between this vamp book and the next one comes something else.

As some of you may know I started out writing historical novels. They usually have some mystery and adventure to them like my vamps do, as well as the kinds of characters I like to write: smart, sassy females and strong, intelligent males. They also have my trademark humor. In fact, over the years, I've repeatedly heard them called "hysterical historicals." I fear that's because I find it difficult to write without humor, no matter what genre I am working in, and the historical time period (whether medieval or Regency) really makes it easy to write funny. I mean, if you thought Mortimer and Sam's difficulties getting together was the least bit amusing, you wouldn't believe the sorts of storylines I can come up with when you throw in arranged marriages, chastity belts, or ailing, flatulent horses. (Got you curious now, don't I? <grin>)

Anyway, my next historical novel will be published in February 2009. *Devil of the Highlands* is about Evelinde, an English gal forced to marry a Scottish laird, Cullen, the Devil of Donnachaidh. With a name like that you shouldn't be surprised to hear Cullen has a rather nasty reputation, but reputations aren't always earned, and he proves himself a sweetheart. Now if they could just figure out who's trying to kill her . . . well, things might just work out all right.

If you already read my historicals, then I hope you enjoy Evelinde and her devil as much as my previous stories. If you've never tried one of my historicals and have only read the vamps before this . . . well, why don't you give it a try? If nothing else it would give you a long backlist of stories to read while you're waiting for that next Argeneau book. (<grin>)

Lynsay

Turn the page for a sneak peek at

DEVIL OF THE HIGHLANDS

From Avon Books

Cullen was the first to see her. The sight made him rein in so sharply, his horse reared in response. He tightened his thighs around his mount to help keep his seat, moving automatically to calm the animal, but he didn't take his eyes off the woman in the glen.

"God's teeth. What is she doing?" Fergus asked as he halted beside him.

Cullen didn't even glance to the tall, burly redhead who was his first. He merely shook his head silently, transfixed by the sight. The woman was riding back and forth across the clearing, sending her horse charging first one way, then the other and back. That in itself was odd, but what had put the hush in Fergus's voice and completely captured Cullen's tongue was the fact she was doing so in nothing but a transparent chemise while holding the reins of her mount in her teeth. Her hands were otherwise occupied. They were upraised and holding what appeared to be a cape in the air so it billowed out behind her above her streams of golden hair as she rode back and forth . . . back and forth . . . back and forth.

"Who do you think she is?" Rory's question was the only way Cullen knew the other men had caught up as well.

"I doona ken, but I could watch the lass all day," Tavis said, his voice sounding hungry. "Though there are other things I'd rather be doing to her all day."

Cullen found himself irritated by that remark. Tavis was his cousin, and the charmer among his men; fair-haired, handsome, and with a winning smile, it took little effort for him to woo women to his bed of a night. And the man took full advantage of the ability, charming his way under women's skirts at every opportunity. Were titles awarded for such an ability, Tavis would have been the king of Scotland.

"I'd first be wanting to ken why she's doing what she is," Fergus said slowly. "I've no desire to bed a wench who isna right in the head."

"It isna her head I'd be taking to me bed." Tavis laughed.

"Aye." Gillie said, his voice sounding almost dreamy.

Cullen turned a hard glare on his men. "Ride on. I'll catch up to ye."

There was a moment of silence as eyebrows rose and glances were exchanged, then all five men took up their reins.

"Ride around the meadow," Cullen instructed, when they started to move forward.

There was another exchange of glances, but the men followed the tree line around the meadow.

Cullen waited until they had disappeared from sight, then turned back to the woman. His eyes followed her back and forth several times before he urged his mount forward.

It hadn't appeared so from the edge of the meadow, but the woman was actually moving at high speed on her beast, slowing only to make the turn before spurring her horse into a dead run toward the other side. The mare didn't seem to mind. If anything, the animal seemed to think it was some sort of game and threw herself into each run with an impressive burst of speed.

Cullen rode up beside the mare, but the woman didn't immediately notice him. Her attention was shifting between the path ahead and the cloth in her upraised hands. When she finally did glimpse him out of the corner of her eye, he wasn't at all prepared for her reaction.

The lass's eyes widened, and her head jerked back with a start, unintentionally yanking on the reins she clenched in her teeth. The mare suddenly jerked to a halt and reared. The lass immediately dropped her hands to grab for the reins and the cloth she'd been holding swung around and slapped—heavy and wet—across Cullen's face. It both stung and briefly blinded him, making him jerk on his own reins in surprise, and suddenly his own mount was turning away and rearing as well.

Cullen found himself tumbling to the ground, tangled

in a length of wet cloth that did nothing to cushion his landing. Pain slammed through his back, knocking the wind out of him, but it positively exploded through his head, a jagged blade of agony that actually made him briefly lose consciousness.

A tugging sensation woke him. Blinking his eyes open, he thought for one moment the blow to his head had blinded him, but then felt another tug and realized there was something over his face. The damp cloth, he recalled with relief. He wasn't blind. At least, he didn't think he was. He wouldn't know for sure until he got the cloth off.

Another tug came, but this was accompanied by a grunt and a good deal more strength. Enough that his head was actually jerked off the ground, bending his neck at an uncomfortable angle. Afraid that, at this rate, he'd end up with a broken neck *after* the fall, Cullen decided he'd best help with the effort to untangle himself from the cloth and lifted his hands toward his head, intending to grab for the clinging material. However, it seemed his tormentor was leaning over him, because he found himself grabbing at something else entirely. Two somethings . . . that were covered with a soft, damp cloth, were roundish in shape, soft yet firm at the same time, and had little pebble-like bumps in the center, he discovered, his fingers shifting about blindly. Absorbed as he was in sorting out all these details, he didn't at first hear the horrified gasps that were coming from beyond the cloth over his head.

"Sorry," Cullen muttered as he realized he was groping a woman's breasts. Forcing his hands away, he shifted them to the cloth on his head and immediately began tugging recklessly at the stuff, eager to get it off.

"Hold! Wait, sir, you will rip—" The warning ended on a groan as a rending sound cut through the air.

Cullen paused briefly, but then continued to tug at the material, this time without apologizing. He'd never been one to enjoy enclosed spaces and felt like he would surely smother to death if he did not get it off at once.

"Let me—I can—If you would just—"

The words barely registered with Cullen. They sounded like nothing more than witless chirping. He ignored them and continued battling the cloth, until— with another tearing sound—it fell away, and he could breathe again. Cullen closed his eyes and sucked in a deep breath with relief.

"Oh dear."

That soft, barely breathed moan made his eyes open and slip to the woman kneeling beside him. She was shifting the cloth through her hands, examining the damaged material with wide, dismayed eyes.

Cullen debated offering yet another apology, but he'd already given one, and it was more than he normally offered in a year. Before he'd made up his mind, the blonde from the horse stopped examining the cloth and turned alarmed eyes his way.

"You are bleeding!"

"What?" he asked with surprise.

"There is blood on my gown. You must have cut your head when you fell," she explained, leaning over him to examine his scalp. The position put her upper body inches above his face, and Cullen started getting that closed-in feeling again until he was distracted by the breasts jiggling before his eyes.

The chemise she wore was very thin and presently wet, he noted, which was no doubt what made it transparent. Cullen found himself staring at the beautiful, round orbs with fascination, shifting his eyes left and right and continuing to do so when she turned his head from side to side to search out the source of the blood.

Apparently finding no injury that could have bloodied her gown, she muttered, "It must be the back of your head," and suddenly lifted his head, pulling it up off the ground, presumably so she could examine the back of his skull. At least that was what he thought she must be doing when he found his face buried in those breasts he'd been watching with such interest.

"Aye, 'tis here. You must have hit your head on a rock or something when you fell," she announced with a combination of success and worry.

Cullen merely sighed and nuzzled into the breasts presently cuddling him. Really, damp though they were, they were quite lovely, and if a man had to be smothered to death, this was not a bad way to go. He felt something hard nudging his right cheek beside his mouth and realized her nipples had grown hard. She also suddenly stilled like prey sensing danger. Not wishing to send her running with fear, he opened his mouth and tried to turn his head to speak a word or two of reassurance to calm her.

"Calm yerself," was what he said. Cullen didn't believe in wasting words. However, it was doubtful if she understood what he said since his words came out muffled by the nipple suddenly filling his open mouth. Despite his intentions not to scare her, when he realized it was a nipple in his mouth, he couldn't resist closing his lips around it and flicking his tongue over the linen-covered bud.

In the next moment, he found pain shooting through his head once more as he was dropped back to the ground.